A CUT ABOVE

A CUT ABOVE

Lynda Page

headline

First published in 2002
by HEADLINE BOOK PUBLISHING

10 9 8 7 6 5 4 3 2 1

Cataloguing in Publication Data is available
from the British Library

ISBN 0 7472 7052 X

Typeset in Times New Roman by
Letterpart Limited, Reigate, Surrey

Printed and bound in Great Britain by
Mackays of Chatham plc, Chatham, Kent

HEADLINE BOOK PUBLISHING
A division of Hodder Headline
338 Euston Road
LONDON NW1 3BH

www.headline.co.uk
www.hodderheadline.com

For Edward Page
(Uncle Teddy)

I inherited you as my uncle through marriage and what a
wonderful inheritance it has proved to be.
You are just the best.
This one is for you and in memory of your beloved wife
and my much-loved Aunty Grace.

Acknowledgements

Charlotte and Kathryn Kozlowski – two beautiful girls who have entered my life and enriched it so much. I love you both dearly and I'm so proud you call me Grandma.

Mary Inchley – we all have days that we look back on and deem to be special. One of those days, for me, was when you knocked on my window, frightening me to death as I was immersed in my work. You introduced yourself to me as a neighbour and what a wonderful friend you have turned out to be.

Chapter One

'Ahhhhhh . . .'

The scream of sheer terror that exploded so unexpectedly made the occupants of Verna's Hairstylist jump, and fix their startled eyes accusingly on the culprit – all, that is, except for elderly Mrs Frimble, who snored on, oblivious of the mayhem, comfortable under the warmth of the domed dryer entombing her newly permed grey hair.

The sudden eruption caused Kathryn Cooper to upturn the container of pink and blue hair rollers she was holding, which were now scattered all over the grey and white speckled linoleum floor. She spun to face the person responsible.

'What on earth . . .?' Her voice trailed off, eyes widening in astonishment at the look of horror contorting the pretty face of Diane Morris, the apprentice who had caused the disruption. She watched in confusion as the seventeen-year-old then fled hysterically from the salon and up the stairs, which led to the stock-cum-staff room.

Aware all eyes were now expectantly upon her, Kacie faced the customers shrugging helplessly. 'Sorry, ladies. I've no idea what's got into her.'

'Well, 'adn't yer better go and find out?' demanded Mabel Shawditch, flicking her half-rollered head in the direction in which the wailing girl had just fled. 'I came in 'ere ter get me hair done, not watch a pantomime, and I've still shopping to do, and if my old man's dinner ain't on the table at six sharp then that young gel will definitely have summat to scream about.'

'Her behaviour don't shock me,' Cissie Doubleday piped up, her lined face screwed knowingly. ''Er mam's as daft as a brush, as you all well know. In fact it runs in the family 'cos the gran was a tanner short of a shilling. I've forgot the number of times they found 'er wandering the streets in the middle of the night with her nightie

1

tucked in her drawers, off to do her shopping. As I remember, she ended up in the nut house. As fer 'er dad . . . well, he's as thick as two short planks – yer've gotta be to do corporation lavy cleaning for a living and actually enjoy it, ain't yer? It's always bin a wonder to me how him and that wife of 'is ever found the intelligence between them to produce any kids, let alone raise 'em to adulthood. I don't know why Mrs Kozlopskiwapsi—'

'Mrs Kozpilopsi,' Hilda Biddles, sitting next to her, corrected, she now having composed herself enough to resume thumbing through a well-read copy of the *People's Friend*.

'That's warra said,' Cissie retorted indignantly. 'I don't know why she ever employed Diane.'

'I'll tell you why, Mrs Doubleday,' responded Kacie defensively. 'Because Diane is a lovely girl and a good little worker. She's worth two of some apprentices Mrs Kozlowski's taken on over the years. She might be a bit slow but she's certainly not thick. And, Mrs Doubleday, someone had to clean them stinking toilets in the marketplace and at least it's a job he's doing when there's many around here that's too lazy to do anything. Now, please excuse me for a minute while I go and see what the matter is.' Leaving the two women staring open-mouthed, she turned to address the customer whose matted locks Diane had been in the process of brushing out when she had had her outburst, in readiness for the woman's monthly shampoo and set. 'Won't keep you a minute, Mrs Simmons,' she said apologetically.

Beatrice Simmons gave a haughty sniff as she gave her scalp a vigorous scratch. 'See as you do. I've me kids coming from school soon and if I ain't there when they arrive home me pantry will resemble Old Mother Hubbard's and the kids'll 'ave 'alf killed each other.'

Kacie hid a wry smile as she hurried after Diane. Beattie's four villainous offspring, ages ranging from five to eleven, were constantly causing havoc, their favourite pastime not only beating hell out of each other but also terrorising all of the younger and smaller children of the area.

Beattie was not the type of customer Verna Kozlowski liked to encourage to use her salon. She felt Beattie's slovenliness gave her establishment a questionable reputation, but then Verna wasn't in a position to turn any paying customer away – even though how Beattie afforded the five shillings and sixpence for her treatment each month remained a total mystery. It was a well-known fact the

Simmons family lived on a knife edge and were always under threat of eviction through arrears of rent.

Kacie found Diane crouched underneath the ill-fitting window in the cluttered room above the salon. Face ashen, she was shaking violently. It was apparent her outburst hadn't been caused by something trivial.

Kacie kneeled down by the side of her and placed a hand on her arm. 'By God, gel, you look like you've seen a ghost. Whatever is it, Di?'

So consumed was she by what she had witnessed, Diane had not heard Kacie enter and she jumped. 'Oh, Kacie, yer gave me a turn.' Then, eyes filled with terror, she cried frenziedly, 'Oh, it's 'orrible, 'orrible. I ain't going back down there. I ain't, I ain't. Please don't make me,' she pleaded.

'Why ever not? Did that old witch say or do something to you?' Kacie demanded.

'No.'

'Well, what then? For God's sake, will you tell me before I lose me patience, Di? I've a salon full of women waiting to get their hair done. Mrs Koz will have a fit if she comes back from the wholesaler's and finds no one looking after them.'

Bottom lip trembling, Diane blurted, 'Wrigglin', they were. Hundreds of 'em, Kacie.'

'Wriggling? What on earth are you going on about?'

'Them things in Beattie's head. Maggots.'

Shocked ridged, Kacie nearly toppled backwards. 'Maggots? In Beattie's head? Are you sure you weren't seeing things, Di?'

'No, honest, Kacie. I was brushing out her hair. It was all matted and sticky like it always is. I 'ate doing Mrs Simmons' 'air. She stinks, so she does, and she makes me skin crawl. But like you've always told me, doin' things I don't like is part of me job in'it, Kacie, so I just close me eyes and get on with it. I'd took all the kirbys out of her French roll and wa' just untangling her beehive when I saw summat movin' and when I parted 'er 'air to 'ave a better look . . .' She gave a violent shudder. 'I couldn't believe me eyes, Kacie, but is wa' maggots I saw. They were just hatching out but I know maggots when I see 'em.'

Horrified, Kacie groaned, 'Oh God.' She had been a hairdresser, apprentice and qualified, for nine years, and during that time had had many difficult situations to handle, but never anything like this.

'What yer gonna do, Kacie?'

Kacie stared blankly at Diane for several long moments. She then inhaled deeply, slowly exhaled, then, steeling herself, stood up. 'The only thing I *can* do. If it is maggots you saw then I must get her out of the salon as quick as possible, hopefully without any of our other ladies getting wind or we'll have a mass evacuation on our hands and Mrs Koz won't be very pleased with that, will she? Now you take a couple of minutes to calm yourself, then get back down to the salon. Eh, and no mention of this to anyone. When they ask why you were screaming like that tell them . . . Oh, I don't know, I'm sure you can think of something as long as it's not the truth.'

Diane gave a great sigh of relief as she eyed the older women in adoration. Kathryn Cooper was her idol, all her favourite female vocalists rolled into one – Alma Cogan, Ruby Murray, Brenda Lee, to name but a few – and Diane imitated Kacie in every way possible. If Kacie herself was aware, she never commented. Despite Kacie's seven-year seniority over Diane, the girl sported a very similar grown-up hairstyle of bouffant at the front to flick out mid-neck length. Unfortunately the style didn't suit her youthful looks as much as Kacie's maturer attractiveness, nor did her fine mousy tresses hold the style quite as well as did Kacie's thick dark brown locks, regardless of how much hair lacquer Diane applied.

Neither did the latest fashions of circular and A-line skirts; fitted tops and little checked blouses, trews or Capri pants have quite the same eye-catching effects on her own girlish frame as they did on Kacie's womanly shape. The men didn't wolf-whistle at Diane in the street or stare openly in admiration as they did when Kacie walked by, her shapely backside swaying. But then Diane, who checked her developing figure every night in her age-mottled wardrobe mirror was delighted to see she was beginning to fill out in all the right places with the help of her mother's stodgy suet dumplings, and as time passed she hoped men would notice her as much as they did her mentor.

'I wish I wa' you, Kacie,' she uttered, awestruck.

Kacie gave her a withering look. 'Do you? I can't for the life of me think why. But if you're that desperate to be me then I'll gladly stand aside and let you deal with Beattie Simmons.'

Diane gasped, horrified. 'Oh, no, Kacie, I couldn't. I wouldn't know what to say to her.'

Kacie sighed. 'Neither do I, but I'd better think of something pretty quick.'

★ ★ ★

4

An hour or so later, shaking her head in utter disbelief, Verna Kozlowski leaned back in her worn black plastic-covered chair. 'Maggots! In all my born years I've never heard of the like. I've had nits, fleas, alopecia, women dyeing their hair with tea leaves and boot polish and whatever else too numerous to mention, but never *maggots*.' Her face was grim. 'I don't know why I'm so shocked to hear this, Kacie. Beattie never so much as puts a comb through her hair between shampoo-and-sets. It's that sugar spray she uses as a substitute hair lacquer. As she never washes it off, the sugar residue builds up on her hair and becomes a magnet for bluebottles and such like. Obviously a bluebottle got trapped in the matted mess and laid its eggs before it managed to escape.' She eyed Kacie incredulously. 'Was she serious when she said she didn't notice anything amiss?'

'She said her scalp itched no more than usual.'

Verna shuddered. 'Dirty cat. Well, as far as I'm concerned Beatrice Simmons never darkens my salon again.' Then her kindly face softened and she eyed her chief employee worriedly. 'I'll have a word with Diane later, but is she all right?'

'Yes, she's fine, Mrs Koz.' And Kacie added, her large eyes twinkling, 'As long as we don't mention anything that wriggles.'

Despite the situation that could have had catastrophic consequences on her business if it hadn't been handled right, Verna couldn't help but smile. 'I'll make a great effort to be sure I don't.' Then she asked anxiously, 'You are sure none of our other clients got wind? Because you know how fickle people are, Kacie. If any of our clients thought our standards were dropping and their health and safety were in jeopardy they'd be off like a shot to somewhere else.'

'Quite sure, Mrs Koz. They all knew something was going on but I managed to pass it off with a cock-and-bull that Beattie had got a bad rash on her scalp which I thought best she got seen to in case we put anything on it that made it worse, and I just said that Di had stabbed herself with the end of the comb and had over-reacted. I made her put a big plaster on her finger to add credibility to the story.' Kacie's attractive face split with a wide grin. 'Anyway, it gave the old ducks something to gossip over while they were getting their own hair done.'

'And don't we know how much they all love a good gossip.' Verna gave a sigh of relief. 'You handled that better than I could have, my dear. Thank you.' She eyed Kacie fondly. 'You are a blessing to me, Kacie. I don't know what I'd do if you ever left me.'

'You needn't worry on that score because I'm never going to leave you, Mrs Koz. I love working here, you know that.'

'And aren't I glad to hear that, because I'm not so daft I don't know that most of our clients come to my salon because you're such a good stylist. A natural, you are, Kacie. You've got that special extra that I was never blessed with.'

Kacie smiled warmly at the compliment.

A frown settled on Verna's face. 'I have heard some rumour that I don't quite know whether to be worried about or not.'

'Oh?'

'The vacant shop on Green Lane Road – I don't know whether you know the one, but it used to be the haberdasher's before the old lady who ran it died a few weeks ago – well, there is word going round in the trade that it's being turned into a hairdresser's.'

'Oh!' Kacie exclaimed. 'Oh, I see. But Green Lane Road is streets away from here so how do you think this will affect your business?'

Verna gave a shrug. 'Well, it's a grave possibility, isn't it? People like to try new places, see what they're missing, whether it's streets away or not. My worry is, if this shop does open and some of my clients defect, then how many could I afford to lose without going under myself?' She gave a wry laugh. 'I would most definitely be unable to sleep at night if it was you that was taking over the shop. I can only hope that if this salon does open then our reputation and long standing hold us in good stead. But I must admit I'm very concerned. Still, we'll wait and see how matters develop. It might just be a rumour, after all.'

'Business is OK, isn't it, Mrs Koz? I mean we seem to be busy enough most days.'

'Oh, yes, yes, we're doing all right. Enough to pay your and Diane's wages, so don't worry.' She eyed Kacie thoughtfully for a moment. 'You'll want your own place some day though, Kacie. A woman like you is bound to.'

Kacie nodded. 'Come time when the kids I hope to have are old enough I would, of course I would.' And she added wistfully, 'I do have a dream which I hope one day might come true.'

'Oh, and what's that, dear?' Verna asked.

'That Dennis and I have a combined shop. One side I can do my hairdressing and the other Dennis can sell records and maybe have a coffee bar or something in the middle. I know it sounds very ambitious but something like that is just what us young ones want

6

these days. Dennis says that when he makes his fortune it'll be the first thing we do – after, that is, he buys me my new Formica table and chairs.'

'A combined shop sounds a wonderful idea to me, Kacie,' Verna enthused. 'I also planned to have more than one salon but it hasn't worked out that way and I've had to content myself with just this.'

'And I'll have to content myself with working for you, Mrs Koz, because I might know my Dennis is the best, but it doesn't matter how much faith I have in him or he in himself, as far as I can see, unless they get some better venues to play in, like town or something, they're never going to be discovered. They try hard, but no one except the likes of Reg in the Star and Garter will give them a chance to even show how good they are, let alone given them a gig, and Dennis had to beg Reg to do that. So you see, I doubt very much he's ever going to achieve his ambition, God bless him. Still, all I can do is stand by him and back him all I can.'

'That's a wife's job, Kacie,' Verna said, 'and I happen to think you do it rather well. It's a shame someone in the know can't catch your Dennis's act. I switched on the television the other night and there was this group playing on some show or other, and I wouldn't call what they played music, more an unrhythmical din. I can't say that Dennis and his band play my type of thing but they did get my foot tapping when you persuaded us to come along and watch him that night, and I did enjoy myself and so did my husband. And the rest of the audience certainly did; they clapped loud enough.'

'That's because they were all drunk,' Kacie said, chuckling.

Verna Kozlowski missed the fact that Kacie had been joking. 'I certainly wasn't drunk, nor my Jan. Anyway, you can't fault your Dennis for having his ambition or for trying to achieve it.'

'Oh, he's trying all right,' Kacie responded, giggling. 'I just hope, though, that sooner rather than later the band either gets discovered or the lads decide to abandon it, and me and Dennis can then live a normal life like normal people.'

Clasping her hands, Verna leaned forward, resting her arms on her desk. 'It's my guess many of those normal people, as you put it, would give their eye-teeth to lead the exciting life you do, my dear.'

'Exciting! Is that how you see my life, Mrs Koz?'

'It could be deemed as that by some, yes. Well, it's certainly different, anyway.' Then, despite Kacie's assurance she was not in the position or ever would be to have her own business, another ever-present concern reared to the surface of Verna's mind. 'You still don't have any hankering to work in a salon in town, do you, Kacie?'

Kacie gawped, horrified at the very idea. 'Not on your life, Mrs Koz. I've told you many time before, I might get a bob or two a week less working for you but I'm happy, and some of those salons in town I've had on good authority are not so nice places to work in, or the owners don't treat their staff as well as you do me and Di.' She eyed her employer, deeply concerned. 'You're not trying to get rid of me, are you, Mrs Koz, by putting these ideas in my head?'

'Oh, my goodness no,' Verna gasped. 'Definitely not. Just the opposite, in fact.' She then noticed the mischievous grin spreading on Kacie's face. 'Oh, you little tinker, you're making fun of me, Kacie.'

Kacie laughed, a deep infectious chuckle. 'Sorry, Mrs Koz, I couldn't resist it. I know only too well getting rid of me is the last thing you want. How's Mr Koz, by the way? Did you have time to pop and check on him while you were out?'

'I did, dear, and thanks for asking. He's slightly better. Of course, you know, he'll never be right, not after what happened to him in the concentration camp. Dreadful, that was, oh, so terrible,' she said, her face filling with deep sadness. 'What all those poor Polish people must have suffered, and the other nations – we mustn't forget them – all through one madman's whims. Still, I've just got to be thankful that my dear husband managed to escape and get to England and that we met up.' Kacie had heard this story many times before, but listened politely. 'I knew when I married Jan that he'd never make old bones but whatever time we've got together is a blessing to me. People frown on me because I married a foreigner but, I tell you, my Jan is worth a thousand of the likes of my first husband who ran me ragged and bled me dry. Never a time when we weren't in debt through his wastrel ways. And people can call me what they like, Kacie, but I wasn't a distraught wife when he met his end when his ship got torpedoed, but a relieved one. Of course, I was sorry for his shipmates,' she added sincerely. 'I had no qualms, though, about using what was left of Wilfred's burial money to start up this place, considering how much I'd had to do without over the years we were married . . .

'The first month's rent on this place and having the alterations done was paid for by money I should have spent on a more expensive coffin and a headstone. Well, it wasn't as though he could sit back and admire it himself, was it? So I felt I was putting that money to much better use by financing my future. Anyway, back to the present. No other mishaps happened while I was out that I ought to know of?' she tentatively asked.

Kacie shook her head. 'No.'

Verna exhaled with relief. 'Thank God for that. One excitement like we've had today is enough to cope with.'

'I'd better get back, Mrs Koz,' Kacie said, rising up and pushing the chair she had been sitting on back into place. 'Di's washing a lady for me ready for a perm and I've one under the dryer who I suspect is well cooked by now.'

'Do you need a hand?' Verna asked.

'No, me and Di can manage fine, thanks. We've got back-to-back appointments but we've got a good system to cope with that, providing, that is, we don't get a last-minute rush.'

'I doubt that, dear, not on a Thursday, but the appointment book looks very healthy for tomorrow so I'd be prepared for a busy day. Right, I'll put the new supplies away, then I'd better tackle the accounts.'

'Oh, did you remember the pink rinse? Mrs Bates is coming in tomorrow for her usual and she wants to look extra special for her grandson's wedding in the afternoon.' Kacie pulled a worried face. 'I understand she's wearing a pink costume and wants her hair to match.'

'Oh, my goodness, it sounds delightful,' Verna said, shuddering at the vision her mind conjured up.

'Well, I did try and warn Mrs Bates she might resemble a stick of candyfloss but she still insists.'

'Well, if that's what the old duck wants, then who are we to refuse. Yes, I did get some more pink, and blue while I was at it, as we seem to be having a run of those colour rinses just lately. The wholesaler talked me into trying some new setting lotions Wella have brought out, and Clairol have added some lovely new colours to their range. I've picked up a new chart so we can order some when the rep comes in. It's here somewhere,' she said, flicking between copies of the *Hairdressing Journal* and other paperwork scattered on her desk. 'I was looking at it a minute ago. Oh, never mind, you can cast your eyes over it later.'

A smile twitched her lips at a distant memory. 'Talking of hair dyes brings to mind that when I was an apprentice and even well after I qualified we had to mix our own tints and perming

9

solutions, and it was hit and miss, believe me.' She gave a chuckle. 'Apart from several disasters, which I won't go into as I'm far too ashamed to admit to them, I will tell you about a customer of mine I was tinting coming out bright carrot red because I'd got the mixture slightly wrong after adding just a bit too much henna powder. She was most upset because she had wanted dark brown. Lavatory brown I called that particular colour, but I never let clients know that. Mind you, my disasters have never been as bad as some I know of, where clients' hair has turned a bright shade of green. Still, unless a customer is particularly difficult, we don't have that trouble of mixing our own tints now manufacturers have modernised methods for us. Thank God for the invention of plastic bottles and metal tubes, eh?' She suddenly stopped her flow. 'Oh dear, I am keeping you chatting, and your client under the dryer must be wondering if you've forgotten about her. Off you go, and next time Di mashes a cuppa ask her to bring me one through, will you, Kacie?'

'I will, Mrs Koz.'

Verna watched thoughtfully as Kacie left her office. It was a tiny room, right at the back of the premises and was very cramped, a desk, two chairs, bulging filing cabinet, shelving around the walls stacked high with all sorts of items to do with the business, practically filling the small area. She leaned back in her chair. She was a lucky woman. Not many women of fifty-five were as content with life as she was. Her establishment wasn't large, nor as equipped or up-to-date as bigger concerns in town, nor was it based in the most salubrious of areas, but its annual turnover – despite peaking and troughing throughout the year, depending on spare money in people's pockets, when short hairdos were the first luxury on the list to go – just managed to pay the wages of Kacie and Diane, settle bills and provide Verna and her beloved second husband with a reasonable standard of living.

It hadn't always been like that. When she had first started out on her own she had very quickly realised that her dream of running several shops was not very likely to happen as the huge demand for her services did not materialise as she had thought it would. Verna hadn't known when she'd ploughed every penny from her demised husband's estate into renting and refitting out these premises on St Saviours Road, the main shopping thoroughfare in Evington, an area on the outskirts of Leicester, that it would take much more than saving the time-consuming trek into town and the offer of cheaper-than-town salon rates to tempt in the affluent middle-class women in this highly populated vicinity.

Her regulars were the working-class locals, who, having a little more disposable income in their pockets in the good times at the start of 1950s, were treating themselves regularly at the hairdresser's instead of doing it themselves at home, and it was only due to that change in circumstance that Verna managed to scrape herself a living.

It was Kacie's arrival on the scene after a few years that eventually led to an improvement in her financial status.

Verna had spotted Kacie's special talents when, at the age of fourteen, she had taken her on as a Saturday help to replace a lazy girl who thought a sweeping brush was for propping herself up on whilst she watched everyone else working. Much to Verna's delight her new recruit proved very willing and able. Only weeks after she started work, fed up with the young girl's badgering, her employer had allowed Kacie to trim and style a couple of old wigs the girl had found abandoned in the stockroom. Much to Verna's surprise Kacie did an excellent restoration job, so much so she was able to sell them. Taking a gamble, she put Kacie in charge of the array of wigs she kept in the salon.

Again to her surprise, considering Kacie had had no training, Verna noted that, styled more fashionably and displayed more eye-catchingly under the young girl's charge, the sale of wigs started to escalate. Kacie possessed a special talent that needed nurturing and if Verna was lucky and treated her right then that gamble would be amply repaid by the clientele Kacie brought in when she qualified.

Despite a hard-fought battle with Kacie's parents, who expected their daughter to attend secretarial college on leaving school, Kacie enthusiastically accepted an apprenticeship under Verna's charge with a day release at the Charles Keene College.

Verna was delighted to see her instincts on Kacie's talents had been right. She excelled in her class, winning several awards and, despite several larger establishments trying to poach Kacie, seven years later the pair were still working happily together, a mutual respect and regard growing between them, and the salon was thriving, mostly due to Kacie's abilities to bring in the younger generation.

Now the imminent arrival of competition nearby could greatly upset the fine balance of Verna's business finances, which affected

11

the whole of her life, and the lives of those she employed, and that fact was most worrying. She supposed she could always sell the business, get out while the going was good, go back to working for someone else. Despite the fact she hated to be even considering it, it was something she'd have to think about should the rumours be true and this new salon did open and affect her livelihood.

She lifted her gaze as Diane came in carrying a cup of tea in Verna's own special china. 'Oh, bless you, dear,' she said, smiling. 'No worse for your ordeal, I hope?'

Diane grimaced. 'I should be used ter maggots, Mrs Koz, being's me dad keeps a tinful in the shed for his fishing, but in someone's head is not the place you expect to find 'em, is it? Still, it's like me mam always sez, it's usually a rum deal that brings good fortune.'

Verna stared, surprised. 'Does she? I've never heard it put exactly like that before.'

Diane frowned thoughtfully. 'Well, that's what she sez, and I tek it to mean we might have lost Mrs Simmons' custom but then I don't have to tackle her manky head no more.'

Verna could see the wisdom in that. 'Your mother's pearler does have its point,' she said kindly. 'Coping all right out the front, are you both?'

'All running like clockwork, Mrs Koz.'

Or things were running smoothly until five thirty-four, when the door burst open and a woman of Kacie's age charged through.

'Kacie, you've gotta help me!' she cried.

Holding a mirror at the back of a customer's head so she could witness her transformation from every angle, Kacie jerked round. Seeing who it was, she tutted loudly. 'I've no spare money to lend you, Brenda, if that's what you're after.'

'It ain't – well, not in quite the way you're thinking,' Brenda Cole said breathlessly, now at Kacie's side. 'Oh, yer 'air does look nice, Mrs Brown,' she enthused, addressing the woman Kacie was attending. 'A perm really suits your thick hair.'

Kacie hurriedly yanked Brenda aside. 'Brenda, how could you?' she scolded, keeping her voice hushed. 'Mrs Brown's as bald as a badger. Have you forgotten she lost all her hair in shock after that bomb blast during the war that killed her son and pregnant daughter-in-law? That's a new wig she's trying on. She's been saving for months for it.'

Brenda grimaced shamefully. 'Oh, sorry, Kacie.'

'You just thank God that the same blast partially deafened her and she never heard what you said. Look, what is it you want? I'm in a hurry to get finished up tonight and I've two other ladies to comb out, besides finishing off Mrs Brown.'

Brenda's face fell. 'Oh, Kacie, yer not in that much of a hurry to get home, are yer? I desperately need your help. I've got a hot date tonight with Jim from the cutting department and I've just gotta look me best.'

Kacie eyed her friend keenly. 'What, the Jim you've been trying to catch the eye of for the last six months?'

'Yeah. I thought he'd never bloody ask me out, and now he has I can't go looking like this, can I?' she wailed, running a hand through her hair, which looked perfectly all right to Kacie as she'd cut and styled it only a few days previously. 'Oh, please say you'll do it for me, please, Kacie? Look, if me and Jim get married I'll ask yer to be me bridesmaid,' she offered by way of a bribe.

Kacie tutted disdainfully. 'You can't be a bridesmaid when you're married, Brenda, and I am married, which you can't have forgotten because you got drunk at my reception and suffered for days afterwards.'

Mind racing frantically, Brenda blurted, 'Well, maybe not a bridesmaid, but you could be me *old married woman of honour*.'

Kacie couldn't help but laugh. 'Oh . . . just a quick spruce-up, but that's all, as I need to get home sharpish tonight.'

'Oh, ta, Kacie. I'll be forever in your debt,' Brenda said, throwing herself down in a vacant chair by a sink before Kacie changed her mind. 'Oh, talking of being in debt, can I square up with you tomorrow, only I ain't got quite enough on me to pay in full, being's it's Thursday.'

Before Kacie could respond the outside door burst open again and a tall, slim, ruggedly handsome man bounded in. Eyes lighting up in her obvious delight to see him, Kacie nevertheless gave a disdainful click of her tongue. Though looking work-worn in his factory boiler suit after his nine-hour shift as a skilled lathe operator for a firm producing machinery equipment, her Dennis still managed to keep every hair of his DA cut in place, but then she knew he would have preened himself in front of the mirror in the factory toilets before he had left for the night, and probably in several shop windows en route to Verna's.

'Evening, ladies, and how are you delightful creatures today? You're all looking lovely, I must say,' he addressed the gathering.

The three customers and Diane giggled girlishly at his flattering attentions. 'We're fine, thanks, Dennis,' they responded.

'And how's my Doll?' he said, sidling up to Kacie, giving her a tender look, and her backside a squeeze.

Kacie slapped his hand away with the back of a hairbrush.

'Ouch,' he cried out, nursing his hand. 'That hurt.'

'It was supposed to. Doll I am not, and I keep telling you not to call me that. Your wife is fine, though, thanks for asking. Did you get the spuds?'

'Eh?'

'Dennis, the spuds for dinner. I told you last night I had back-to-back appointments today, and I wouldn't have time to get to the shops. You forgot, didn't you?' she scolded.

He nodded sheepishly. 'We'll drop in the corner shop on the way home.'

'Not *we*, Dennis, *you*. I won't be finished for at least another hour, thanks to Brenda here,' she added, inclining her head in her friend's direction. 'You can have the spuds peeled, the chip pan heating up and the table set by the time I get in.'

His face fell. 'Ahh, Kacie, I've to be out by six thirty to help the lads set up for our gig.' He glared at her, annoyed. 'Had you forgot we were playing tonight?'

'Your Dennis and his lads are the star turn at the Star and Garter tonight, Kacie. Even *I* know that,' piped up Mrs Brown. She looked up at Dennis admiringly. 'Me and my old man are coming down to support you.' And added, a twinkle of amusement in her aged eyes, 'I'm even thinking of buying this new wig just for the occasion.'

Dennis bent down, threw his arms around the old lady's shoulders and gave her a friendly hug, plus a peck on her gnarled cheek. 'And ain't you just the tops, Mrs B. I'll make sure you and your wig get a ringside table.' He straightened up and looked Kacie in the eye. 'You can't have forgotten the band is playing tonight. You know how long it took me to get Reg to agree to giving us a spot,' he accused.

She looked at him sharply. 'How could anyone, especially me, forget you were playing tonight. It's all you've gone on about since you landed the gig two weeks ago. I only wanted to make sure you got some food inside you before you went, that's all.'

He looked at her, shame-faced. 'Ahh, I'm sorry, Doll . . . er, Kacie.' His face then filled with excitement as he rubbed his hands together. 'If the audience likes us, Reg has promised us a regular

14

weekly night and then it only needs a record company scout to come in and hear us and we could be on our way to the big time. I can just see us now on *6.5 Special*, Pete Murray introducing us.' He looked at Kacie so excitedly she thought he would burst. 'Wouldn't you be proud as punch, Kacie, seeing your old man singing on the telly?'

'I presume that if you're on the telly you'll be able to afford to buy me one to watch you on. I wish you wouldn't get your hopes up so high, Dennis,' she said, her face clouding in worry.

'Why not?'

Because she hated the thought of her beloved husband's huge disappointment if the band didn't get any further than they were right now, playing to inebriated audiences in backstreet pubs and working men's clubs. She clamped her lips tight, afraid she would say something to dampen his spirits. Dennis was convinced that it was only a matter of time before the band was discovered and propelled into the big time. Kacie didn't think it very likely herself that record company scouts looked for talent in the kind of places that Dennis and the lads played in, but then strange things did happen. Maybe a scout would somehow lose his way and end up in Reg's pub tonight. 'Yes, why not get your hopes up,' she answered, smiling at him winningly, 'because if you don't, Dennis, who will?'

'Just think, Kacie, your old man could be the next Perry Como,' said Brenda, knowing very well what reaction from Dennis this comparison would cause.

As expected, he spun round to her, face wreathed in indignation. 'Perry Como! Don't you swear at me, Brenda Cole. Perry Como indeed.' He turned back, leaning forward to scrutinise himself in the wall mirror. Taking a well-used comb out of his donkey jacket pocket, he gave a prospective straying strand a tweak back into place. 'Now Cliff Richard or Billy Fury I don't mind being likened to, but the likes of Perry Como is for the wrinklies. Present company excluded,' he hurriedly added, suddenly remembering the presence of older women.

Smiling to herself, Kacie appraised her childhood sweetheart, whom she had met at the local youth club, courted and, very much against her parents' wishes, had now been extremely happily married to for the last three years. He did have qualities of Cliff and Billy. He was certainly handsome enough, and could sing just as well, and in her opinion the band played their instruments as well as any other group in the charts. She, as much as Dennis, would be over the moon if the band did achieve their ambitions. Dennis dreamed of becoming a pop star, lived and breathed his ambition, and she loved him far too much ever to have a hand in dispelling those desires. So apart from the odd occasions when her tongue got the better of her, she kept her own counsel and displayed her support.

If she was honest, though, she enjoyed watching her husband singing on stage the few times they had managed to secure a gig; and the boys dropping into their flat unannounced at all times of the day or night to discuss band issues with Dennis, whom they looked on as their leader – and taking for granted they'd be watered and fed – meant lively company was always on their doorstep.

Kacie was an ardent lover of popular music and she and Dennis had built between them a large record collection which, money allowing, was continually being added to and which they played constantly on their Dansette player, the purchase of which had been top priority when they had married.

Her eyes tenderly scanned him. Most people had hopes and dreams that kept them going as they drudged day after day, year after year, scratching for their living. Maybe Dennis might be one of those lucky ones who achieved his. But whether he succeeded or not, she would love him just as much. He was annoying at times, had several male bad habits that would drive the most saintly of wives to pack her suitcase, but on the whole he was a good husband to her. He loved her completely, she had no doubt about that. As she had told Mrs Koz only a while ago, her Dennis was the best.

She suddenly realised he was talking to her. 'Sorry,' she said, giving him her full attention.

'Kacie,' he retorted, 'I was telling you my good news and you weren't listening.'

'Well, I'm listening now, so what good news?' she asked eagerly. 'Have you been promoted at work?' It was about time, considering what a conscientious worker he was.

'What? Oh, no. There'd have to be deaths and retirements before I get moved up the ladder, as you well know, Kacie. My good news is that I've finally come up with a proper name.'

'Proper name? For what?'

'The band. Jess Thunder and the Lightnings. Cliff's got his Shadows, Bill Haley's got his Comets and I'll have my Lightnings.

16

I think the lads will love it. Wadda yer think, Kacie?'

'Oh!' She shrugged. 'Not bad, I suppose, but you don't look like a Jess to me, Dennis.'

He looked hurt. 'Don't I?' he turned and scrutinised himself in the mirror. 'I think I do.' He turned back to face her. 'What do Jesses look like then, in your opinion? And what about you, Mrs Brown?' he asked, raising his voice so the deaf old lady could hear him. 'Do you think I could pass for a Jess?'

'Oh, don't ask me,' she answered, adjusting the wig she was trying on further down on to her forehead, which gave her the appearance of having no eyebrows. 'I never thought I looked like a Prudence, but me mother obviously did.'

'Me dad calls me brother a jessie 'cos he likes cricket better than football,' said Diane, who was sweeping up cut hair from the floor.

'I've never liked the name Brenda,' Brenda piped up. 'It's boring, is Brenda. If Dennis is thinking of changing his name, I might too,' she mused, then announced, 'Stephanie. Now that has a ring to it, don't yer think? And it makes you immediately think of someone tall and—'

'Well, as you're short that name would be no good for you, then, Bren, would it?' Kacie cut in exasperatedly, thinking if she didn't get a move on she'd never get home tonight.

'I've got an idea.'

They all turned and looked across at Diane.

'Let's hear it then?' Kacie asked.

Knowing they were all staring at her, the young girl's face turned scarlet with embarrassment. 'Well . . . er . . . I . . .'

'Oh, just spit it out, will yer, Di?' Brenda said irritatedly. 'We'll be here all night while we wait for you ter get yer brain in gear, and I've got a hot date.'

'And that's enough from you,' Kacie scolded her. 'It's OK, Di, take your time.'

Diane beamed at her idol in gratitude, then, puffing out her chest, announced proudly, 'Well, I wa' just thinking that why doesn't Dennis use his initials like you do, Kacie? I wa' thinking of using mine.'

'My nickname wasn't my choice,' Kacie said. 'I got lumbered with it when I was a tot at school because there were two Kathryn Carters – as I was then – in my class and we sat next to each other. So to stop confusion they called her Katie and me KC, which the way us Leicester folk pronounce it sounds like Kacie.' She gave a chuckle. 'My parents are the only ones who ever use my full name now.'

'DC,' Dennis mused over his own initials. 'No, that's no good. People would think I was something to do with the police service.'

Brenda looked at Diane questioningly. 'As a matter in interest, what is your full name, Di?'

'Diane Una Morris,' she answered proudly.

Brenda pressed her lips together to suppress an eruption of mirth. 'Well, I'd think twice about wanting to use yer initials if I were you.'

'And that's enough from you,' Kacie scolded again. 'But she's right, Di. If you're hell-bent on lumbering yourself with another name then I think you need to give the idea a lot more thought.' She turned to face her husband. 'Do we have to discuss a name for the band right now?' she asked. 'After all, you've been trying for God knows how long to come up with something catchy.'

'Well, not right this minute, but as it's a big night for us tonight I thought it'd be a good time to announce our new name.'

'And just what is it yer call yerselves now?' asked Mrs Brown.

'Well, nothing at the moment as we couldn't agree on anything that goes with our image.'

'The Nothings,' the old lady muttered thoughtfully. 'I see what yer mean. You can't really call yerselves The N'otes, can yer, when yer trying to create an image?' They all looked at her blankly. 'N'ote' being Leicester dialect for 'nothing'. She then asked, 'What's an image?'

They all pretended they hadn't heard her question, knowing she'd have difficulty understanding the answer.

'Oh, I know,' Brenda spoke up, 'as you're the leader of the band, what about Dennis and the Denboys. I think that name's rather good meself.'

Dennis vehemently shook his head. 'No self-respecting pop star has Dennis for a name. That's why I've got to change it.'

'I shouldn't let your mother hear you say that, Dennis,' Kacie warned. 'I happen to know she's quite proud of the name she picked for you. She told me you were named after your dad's brother, who was a lovely man, by all accounts. Oh, what about Victor?' she offered, as she had rather a fancy for the film star Victor Mature.

'Victor,' Dennis mused. 'It's all right, I suppose, but it's getting something to go with it to call the boys.'

'Vic and the Vicars,' offered Brenda.

'Oh, don't be funny, Bren,' Dennis growled. 'You might think this is a joke but it's a serious business picking a name for a band.'

Kacie sighed as her thoughts thrashed around in the hope of coming up with something else that might be worth considering. In her desire to get this problem solved once and for all she wondered if Verna would have anything suitable to offer. At the thought of Verna the name Vernon sprang to mind. 'What about Vernon? That's a starry kinda name. Vernon and the er . . . V . . . V . . . Vipers,' she said, the name springing from nowhere. 'It has got a ring to it. Mind you,' she then added, giving him the once-over, 'you don't look much like a Vernon to me, Dennis.'

He eyed her, surprised. 'Vernon and the Vipers,' he repeated slowly. 'Oh, yeah, I like that, Kacie. That's the best one yet. I'll run it past the boys. You're a little wonder, you are.' He threw his arms around her, giving her a bear hug.

She pushed him from her. 'I'm glad that's settled. Now if you want me to be ready in time for your big night you'd better let me finish up here. There's eggs in the pantry. Fry those up and have them on bread.' She gave him a friendly push towards the door. 'And make sure you do 'cos I don't want you playing tonight on an empty stomach, not with all the beer I know will end up down your neck.' She turned to Diane. 'Can you shampoo Brenda for me while I finish off Mrs Brown and comb out Mrs Hackett and Mrs Downs?' She smiled across at the two women sitting patiently under the dryers. 'Won't keep you much longer, ladies.'

Chapter Two

Much later Kacie hurriedly cleared away the remains of her makeshift meal, and flashed a glance across at the clock on the mantel above the old-fashioned black cast-iron fireplace. It was just approaching seven forty-five. She'd better get a move on if she was to catch the start of the performance. She knew Dennis would be very disappointed if he didn't spot her in the audience and, besides, he'd want a blow-by-blow account of how their performance had gone, and she couldn't do that if she'd missed half the show.

She inspected her appearance in the oval mirror hanging above the fireplace, glad to see she looked very presentable in a pretty, scoop-necked blouse just showing the top of her cleavage, pink cardigan with embroidered flowers scattered over it and red A-line skirt. Her hair was, as usual, perfectly groomed again after the rigours of the day and, while checking the seams in her stockings were straight, she smiled happily to herself.

Brenda had looked a treat, and had left delighted after Kacie's hurried but expert thirty minutes' titivating for her date, and Kacie sincerely hoped the evening was going well for her. No doubt she'd find out soon. Mrs Brown, after much dithering, had decided on the wig Kacie had recommended, and the other two ladies, despite being kept waiting longer than usual, had given her a thrupenny tip – not everyone was so generous. She had split it with Diane, feeling the girl had done more than her bit towards making the customers comfortable by plying them with tea, coffee and magazines, plus clearing up after them.

Finally and thankfully, all clients dealt with and desperate to get home, Kacie and Diane, joined by Verna had beavered together to get the salon readied for the next day's business.

Remembering her tips, Kacie retrieved them from her purse, putting them along with the rest she had accumulated over the past weeks in an old Bisto tin in the pantry. When she had enough saved

21

she planned to buy a Formica kitchen table and set of matching chairs she had her eye on to replace the worn old-fashioned drop-leaf type Dennis's mother had given the pair as their wedding present, a piece of furniture Kacie had never been particularly fond of but had been grateful at the time to accept from her much-loved mother-in-law.

Before she gathered her coat to leave, she gazed proudly around the tiny flat she shared with Dennis, which was sited above a busy greengrocer's conveniently located several doors down from Verna's salon and only a few streets away from the factory where her husband worked.

What a state it had been in when they had come to view it, full of excitement at the prospect of having their first home together. 'A well-situated, homely, compact one-bedroomed flat,' the advertisement had read. It was well-situated for them both, but homely it was not, and 'compact' in this case meant tiny. Nor was it anywhere near as clean and tidy as the landlord had led Kacie to believe when she had first made enquiries.

It was in a disgusting state: ancient wallpaper faded and torn in places, well-worn holey linoleum covering creaking floorboards. The living room and bedroom were larger than expected, but the kitchen was tiny. All it contained was a chipped and stained stone pot sink, an old geezer hanging precariously from the grimy whitewashed wall, and a filthy lime-green-coloured kitchenette with doors hanging off, which the landlord assured them he'd fix before they moved in, and which he didn't. The toilet facilities were housed in a drafty dimly lit room out on the landing, and the ancient equipment groaned and grumbled loudly in protest as it flushed, the fresh water coming from a rusting tank above, which was actioned by a length of fraying string, the chain long gone. The cracked toilet bowl was caked in years of dirt and ingrained lime scale.

Kacie remembered only too vividly the hard labour that had gone into making their first home presentable enough to invite family and friends back to. The wallpaper, having been repaired as well as possible using flour and water paste, had been given thick coverings of cheap emulsion, different bright colours of yellow, blue and purple, for each area; the holes in the linoleum were now concealed by cleverly arranged furniture and the scattering of clippy rugs.

The odd assortment of furniture the couple possessed consisted of a thirty-year-old moquette settee, kindly donated by Dennis's Aunty Gladys, which had a plain blue candlewick bedspread thrown over it in order to disguise the bare patches, and co-ordinate it with the two odd armchairs positioned either side of the fireplace. These they had, on separate occasions, bought with hard-earned pennies from a second-hand shop down the road, both of them giggling helplessly in their struggle to carry each home, just as they had the ugly sideboard which housed their precious record collection and on top of which sat their record player. The standard lamp had been rescued from a waste tip, and Kacie had covered and fringed the lampshade herself, very proud of her efforts, as sewing wasn't one of her talents.

Their bed, the springs of which Kacie had laughingly declared played more in tune than the band, had belonged to Dennis's grandmother, who, sadly had passed away just prior to their wedding. They had also inherited the old lady's oak wardrobe, a monstrosity which nevertheless served its purpose.

In the kitchen the old kitchenette had been scrubbed clean, repaired as well as possible and painted bright orange. An aged electric stove – the back plate having long ago stopped functioning, needing a new element that they could never seem to afford – cooked all their meals. Baths were taken weekly at Dennis's mother's in an old tin bath in front of the fire in her parlour.

In some people's eyes the flat may have looked shabby but the two people who lived in it were very happy, very much in love, and to them that was all that mattered.

Realising the time was passing rapidly, Kacie grabbed her coat and had just taken a step towards the outside door when the knocker rapped loudly, making her jump. On opening the door, she found her parents standing in the dimly lit hall outside, their faces displaying the expectant look they always wore whenever they came into contact with their daughter.

Kacie groaned inwardly. She neither had the time nor was in the mood for them. There was only one reason why they had come: to check for cracks in her marriage; hope they were going to achieve their wish of it breaking apart.

From the moment she had introduced her future husband to her parents they had made it apparent they totally disapproved. It had been expected of Kacie to follow her older sister, Caroline, and settle for what they termed a suitable young man with good credentials and decent prospects. Dennis, as far as they were concerned, possessed none of these qualities. He was from the wrong end of Orson Street. Should Kacie saddle herself with this man she'd be condemning herself to a life of drudgery and misery.

In Kacie's opinion her parents' view was totally unwarranted and utterly misguided, and she defied them blatantly, continuing to court Dennis. Despite the Carters doing their utmost to end the liaison, they failed miserably, bargaining without their daughter's steely determination to be with the man she loved. Their relief was most apparent to Kacie when Dennis went away to do his national service but instead of the distance between them causing the relationship to fade, it made it stronger, and when Dennis returned the pair carried on as before.

For Kacie and Dennis their wedding was such a special occasion, marred only for Kacie by the knowledge that her mother's tears were not ones of joy but of sorrow for the dreadful mistake she thought her daughter was making. Even three years later, despite how happy she and Dennis were, Kacie knew her parents still hoped her marriage would fail so they could be proved right. But it was not going to fail. She and Dennis were partners for life.

She forced a bright smile on her face. 'Hello, Mam, Dad. It's lovely to see you both.' She hoped she sounded suitably sincere.

'I do wonder,' said Freda Carter, a sixty-year-old woman who would appear quite pleasant-faced if she smiled more often. She was thin, of medium height, her greying hair pulled tight and knotted in a small bun at the nape of her neck – a hairstyle Kacie itched to get her hands on to modernise, feeling her mother would benefit from a more flattering style. It was an offer she never made, though, knowing it would be flatly refused as it would mean her mother had finally come to accept her daughter's choice of profession.

Kacie frowned at her remark. 'Sorry, mam? Wonder what?'

'If you're pleased to see us. We haven't seen you for over a month now. In fact we did wonder if you were still alive.'

'Well, as you can see, I'm very much so,' she said with forced lightness, then added uncomfortably, 'Look, I haven't been to see you because er—'

'You've been too busy,' her father cut in. 'Or you didn't want to. You don't have to make excuses, Kathryn.'

'I'm not, Dad,' she lied. 'Time flies, that's all. Are you coming in?' she asked reluctantly, standing aside.

Norman Carter, a tall, angular man of sixty-two, shoulders

stooped through years of labouring over company ledgers for the hundred-year-old shoe firm he worked for, poor eyesight aided by thick pebble glasses, fixed his gaze firmly on the coat draped over his daughter's arm. 'You're going out?' It was more of an accusation than a question.

'Well, I am, yes. But I've time for a cuppa.'

Kacie followed her parents through to the living room, extremely glad she had taken the trouble to tidy up. 'I'll just put on the kettle,' she said, heading off into the tiny kitchen. Moments later she came back armed with a tin tray, carrying the tea things. Her parents, by now having unbuttoned their coats, were perched ramrod-straight in the armchairs either side of the fireplace. 'The kettle won't be long. Sorry I've no biscuits,' Kacie apologised, putting the tray down on the table she had not long cleared. Her eyes flashed to the clock on the mantel, acutely aware time was passing, knowing that Dennis would be keeping an eye out for her. She also wondered how long an ordeal of her parents' visit she was going to suffer.

'Where's Dennis?' enquired Freda. 'Working late?'

Kacie's face paled. 'Er . . . no . . . er . . . actually he's—'

'Oh, don't tell me he's still singing with that band. Oh, Kathryn, when is he going to grow up and realise his responsibilities towards you?'

Before she responded Kacie took a deep breath in an effort to control the rising anger that had been bubbling for years under the surface. 'Mother, please don't start,' she said, fighting to keep her emotions in check. 'Dennis enjoys playing in the—'

'Playing,' Freda cut in sternly. 'Yes, *playing* is the right word, Kathryn. But may I remind you that playing is for children? You've been married for three years and by now you should be living somewhere decent, with some nice things around you, and your husband shouldn't be harbouring childish dreams over something that will never bring the riches he seems to think it will.'

'Some make it, Mother.'

'I grant you they do. But not anyone from Evington, and especially not from that end of Orson Street so far as I am aware.'

'There's always a first time,' Kacie retorted more sharply than she intended.

Freda gave her a look as though she was a silly schoolgirl with ludicrous ideas. 'I'm extremely concerned you're in for one awful disappointment. It seems such a pity to me that he doesn't put as much effort into improving his job prospects as he does into that

25

band. He'd be well up the ladder by now if he did.'

Kacie fought hard not to respond, although she desperately wanted to instil in her parents the truth that her husband was a very conscientious worker and they should know that it wasn't easy to get promotion. He was in a queue and would get it come time, and there was plenty of time; they were both only young. An idea suddenly struck her. If she could persuade her parents to come and watch Dennis and the band perform, somehow it might help break barriers down. Well, it was worth a try.

'Actually the boys are playing tonight at the local pub. That's where I'm off to. Why don't you come? I'm sure you'll enjoy yourselves,' she added, despite knowing very well they wouldn't.

Freda pursed her lips, disapprovingly. 'Thank you for asking but I don't think so. Me and your father's idea of a night out is nothing like sitting in a smoky public house with all those inebriates, listening to the row you youngsters call music these days. I'm surprised, myself, anyone truthfully enjoys it.'

Kathryn wanted to say she did and so did lots of other people, but thought better of it. She wondered just what her parents' idea of entertainment was, because as far as she knew they never went out.

Her mother glanced her up and down. 'Are you going out in that blouse?'

'Yes. Why?'

'It's far too revealing for a respectable married woman, Kathryn.'

'It's the latest fashion, Mam, and it isn't revealing at all. You'll be telling me next I'm wearing too much makeup – for a respectable married woman, that is.'

'Your mother's only trying to keep you right, Kathryn,' her father said sharply.

'Yes, I know, but things have changed since your day, Dad.'

'Far too much in my opinion,' Freda said. 'For a married woman to dress gaudily and plaster herself in makeup meant only one thing in our day: that she was a loose woman.'

Kacie knew she looked neither gaudy nor had her makeup plastered on, and she bit her tongue in her effort not to respond to what she saw as her mother's narrow view on life.

'So, how are you, Kathryn?' Freda asked.

'I'm very well, thank you,' she said shortly.

'And your husband – he's treating you all right?'

Kacie glared at her. 'Of course he is,' she snapped.

26

'There is no need to use that tone with me. I'm your mother, Kathryn. I'm concerned for your welfare and so is your father.'

'Why are you so concerned?' And before she could stop herself she blurted, 'Do you think Dennis gets blind drunk and beats me up or something?'

Kacie could tell by her mother's face that that was exactly what she suspected Dennis did.

Freda eyed her daughter stonily. 'I asked if Dennis was treating you well. I meant in general, that's all. As I don't see you that much I wouldn't know, would I?'

Kacie sighed. Surely her mother knew only too well why the pair didn't visit very often and that was because her parents never made Dennis at all welcome, and consequently the visits were purgatory for them both. They called upon her parents when it was absolutely necessary, such as Christmas, Easter and birthdays, using any amount of, she hoped, plausible excuses for their lack of attendance otherwise. 'We'll come soon, Mam,' Kacie promised falsely.

Freda looked at her, unconvinced, as she ran her hand over the arm of the chair. 'Your sister found the time to pay us a visit the week before last and told me they have a new suite. Not second-hand, brand new. Black vinyl it is, with tapered wooden legs and a glass-topped coffee table to match. Of course Malcolm can afford to buy Caroline nice things as he's doing so well in that job of his.'

Kacie was mortally fed up with her own marriage being compared to her sister's and controlling her rising emotions was proving very difficult. 'You keep telling me how well Malcolm is doing and how lovely Caroline's house is, and I'm pleased for them both. But me and Dennis are doing all right and we have a nice home too. You both know how hard we worked to get it nice and it'll do us just fine until we can afford to move to somewhere better,' she said brusquely. She wondered what Caroline had done with her old suite, knowing it would be in far better condition than the odd assortment she herself possessed, and although she wasn't on close terms with her sister it didn't stop her wondering, if her old suite was going begging, whether somehow she could acquire it. 'What did Caroline do with her old suite, Mam? Did she say?'

'No, she didn't. Why? Oh I see—' her mother began.

'Don't say it, Mother,' Kacie interrupted, unable to control her tongue any longer.

'Don't say what?'

'You know perfectly well. That if I'd not married Dennis but someone who had "better prospects" to use your terms, then I wouldn't be enquiring after my sister's cast-offs.'

'Well, that is true, Kathryn. Your husband doesn't seem to provide very well for you, does he?'

Kathryn's tempered flared. 'Only according to your standards. I think Dennis provides for me very well and I wish you'd stop looking down your nose at him.'

'There's no need to speak to your mother in that tone, Kathryn,' Norman said icily.

'Oh, isn't there?' she cried, her self-control breaking. 'I'm sick and tired of hearing you pull Dennis to bits. Whatever he does he'll never be good enough in your eyes, will he? He's a good man, I love him and he loves me. Can't you both just accept that we're happy together instead of constantly reminding me how much better I could have done if I'd married someone else? I couldn't have got better than Dennis, not if I looked for a month of Sundays I couldn't. For God's sake, it's not like we're royalty or anything. And you keep going on about Dennis's lack of promotion when you're not much more than a glorified clerk yourself, Dad, are you? Just because you managed to buy your house and move away from Evington and Dennis's mam still lives here and rents hers, you think you're better than them. Well, you might see that as being a cut above others but let me tell you it makes no difference to me. I don't care whether I own my own house or not or if Dennis stays in his job as he is for the rest of his life. As long as we're together that's all that matters. Now put that in your pipe and smoke it.'

At her daughter's outburst, Freda set her face stonily. 'Are you finished?' she demanded.

'Yes!' Kacie cried.

Freda rose, buttoning up her coat. 'Come along, Norman. I'm not staying here to be spoken to like this by my own daughter. You, madam,' she snapped, wagging a warning finger at Kacie, 'can come to me and apologise because I won't speak to you again until you do. And just for your information, your father is supervisor of his department, not just a glorified clerk, and we scrimped and went without to buy our house and move to what we felt was a better area to improve ourselves, and I look down my nose at your husband because I feel so strongly you could have done so much better for yourself, Kathryn. Why on earth you decided to move back here when you married is beyond me. But me and your father are proud of what we did. And whatever you might think, we have

28

only ever tried to do our best for you.'

'Your mother's right, Kathryn,' Norman said, standing up and joining his wife. 'We've only ever tried to do our best.'

He took his wife's arm and together they left.

As she heard the door shut, the kettle starting whistling and Kacie rushed to switch it off and it was then it hit her full force what had just transpired. Her face crumpled, fat tears of shame rolling down her face, streaking her mascara. Oh God, what have I done? Her mind screamed.

Leaning against the old pot sink, she allowed her thoughts to race wildly. Despite how much she felt her parents were in the wrong, her father was right: they were her parents and as such she should never have spoken so venomously to them. But then were they being fair in showing their dislike and disapproval of the man she had chosen to be her partner in life, who surely over the past three years had more than proved what a good husband he was?

What an awful dilemma she was in.

Part of her wanted to run after her parents to apologise for her behaviour, but the other part felt the strong pull of loyalty towards the man she loved. She knew, though, that should she go after them, nothing would change; that they would continue their regime until she herself caved in and they got their wish. But should she not go after them, she risked the rift never healing, as she knew her mother had meant what she had said: she wouldn't speak to Kacie again until she had apologised.

She suddenly felt the desperate need to discuss this dreadful situation with someone. But who?

One thing she wouldn't do and that was mention any of this to Dennis. Although he always made light of it, she knew deep down her parents' unyielding attitude towards him upset him greatly. No, she must keep this from him to spare his feelings.

Brenda? No. She thought life a joke, and Kacie knew without asking what Brenda's answer to her problem would be: 'Ignore 'em. Parents are just a hindrance, anyway. Look at mine. The only time me mam teks an interest in me is on a Friday night when I hand me board money over. Yer best off without parents, gel, in my opinion.'

She pondered over several other girlfriends to confide in but each had something about them – either personality-wise, or enough problems of her own to deal with – without her burdening them further.

Then she thought of her sister. Prim and proper, Caroline, only two years older than herself, but in all things the sisters were opposites to the extreme. It was an odd state of affairs, she thought, that two people who shared the same parentage and who had been raised by the same set of rules could be so different in nature and such total strangers to each other. Because that's what they were. And it was a great pity that their relationship was so non-existent, as it was at times like this that Kacie would have liked nothing more than a close sister to discuss family problems with and seek advice on how best to handle them. Kacie suddenly realised she couldn't remember the last time she had seen Caroline. Grandmother's funeral or her own wedding? It was one or the other, and both over three years ago. As matters stood between them she may as well not have a sister.

Kacie knew for this particular problem Verna Kozlowski was her obvious choice to turn to for advice. Her mature wisdom and own emotional travels through life meant she would be better able to offer advice to Kacie on how she could sort this mess out. But the poor woman had enough of her own problems to cope with in the strain of running a business and caring for her sick husband without Kacie burdening her further.

Kacie knew she'd have to decide herself what to do. Despite staying away from them as much as possible to avoid the grief they gave her over Dennis, she did love her parents and she hated the thought of being totally estranged from them.

After pondering deeply she decided to give herself time for a suitable answer to present itself. Though God only knew what that answer would be.

Chapter Three

As Kacie arrived at the pub she could hear the strains of music and she realised she had missed the beginning of the band's performance. She hoped Dennis had been too pre-occupied to notice.

As she pulled one of the double doors open to make her entrance, loud music blared out and she was delighted to see the place was packed, and judging from the look on people's faces they seemed to be enjoying themselves. As she pushed her way through the crowd towards the back of the room where a stage had been erected, she felt a hand grab her arm, pulling her to a halt, then the voice of the person the hand belonged to spoke loudly over the din.

'Why, there yer are, Kacie, love. I was thinkin' yer weren't comin'. I've saved yer a seat. D'yer wanna drink? I was just off ter the bar for a stout.'

Kacie beamed in delight. In contrast to her own parents, Dennis's mother, Doris, on her very first meeting with Kacie had welcomed her into the family with open arms and those comforting motherly arms had stayed open ever since. Dotty, as all who knew her affectionately called her, was utterly delighted with her only son's choice of wife, and nothing was too much trouble for her where the young couple were concerned.

She was a tiny woman, four foot ten in her stockinged feet, as rotund as she was tall; face jolly; cheeks rosy; mountainous chest that wobbled alarmingly whenever she laughed, which was often. She supplemented her widow's pension by serving behind the counter of the local bakery situated several shops down from Verna's salon. The customers loved her, especially when she managed to slip a couple of stale buns into a bag and not charge for them when the owner wasn't looking.

'Hello, Mrs C,' Kacie said, bending over to give her mother-in-law an affectionate peck on her cheek. 'I didn't expect you to be here.'

'Me not come to my son's big night?' Dotty said, aghast. 'I'd have to be on my deathbed to miss this, so I would. Even then I'd get the neighbours to push me bed down,' she added, her eyes lighting in amusement at the thought. Then a brief flash of sadness filled her face. 'Just a pity his dear old dad wasn't still with us to see this night, God rest him. So proud 'e would've bin. Knowing my Cyril 'e'd 'ave probably been on the stage with 'em. Mind you, 'e couldn't sing for toffee, had a voice like a gravel pit, so our Dennis must have inherited his talent from me,' she explained chuckling. 'Anyway, there's a load of us sitting right up front. We came early to mek sure we got the best seats. I rallied all me neighbours for support. Well, yer gotta, ain't yer?' And she added puffing her chest out proudly, 'No one else I know of can say they've a son who's a budding pop star, can they?'

Pity her own parents were not more supportive, Kacie thought. Thinking of them, Kacie's face momentarily saddened as thoughts of her encounter with them and the problems she now faced flooded back.

'Are you all right, gel, only yer looks upset?' Dotty asked, her face filled with concern.

'Eh? Oh, no, no,' Kacie fibbed, mentally pulling herself together. 'I've had a long day. Just a bit tired, that's all. I'll be OK after I've downed a barley wine or two.'

'First one coming up then. Oh, that reminds me, you and Dennis are still coming as usual for yer bath on Monday night, are yer?'

'Yes? Why, is it not convenient? We can change it to another evening.'

'Course it's convenient. I always keep Monday night free for you two to have yer ablutions. In fact if yer ever moved to a place where you 'ad room to keep yer own bath or afford the luxury of yer own bathroom, I'd be glad for yer, course I would, but I'd be very upset 'cos I'd miss our bath sessions. I know it'll happen one day, though, but I'm happy to accommodate yer both all I can in the meantime, yer knows that.'

Kacie laid an affectionate hand on her arm and smiled warmly. 'Yes I do, Mrs C, and me and Dennis are very grateful. So why were you asking if we're still coming?'

'I wondered if you'd 'ave time ter gimme a trim?'

'For you, any time. I'll bring my scissors and come straight from work.'

The older woman beamed happily. 'I'm like royalty, ain't I, 'aving me own personal 'airdresser? I'll cook yer both yer dinner by way of saying my thanks. Faggot and chips do yer, and roly-poly ter follow?'

'It's a deal,' Kacie said, grinning. 'But don't bother asking Dennis to bring the spuds 'cos he'll forget.'

'Eh?'

'Nothing. Come on, let's get that drink, and it's my treat,' she said, hooking her arm through Dotty's and leading her towards the bar.

The crowd were clapping enthusiastically. Vernon and the Vipers had just finished their own interpretation of 'All I Have to Do is Dream', by the Everly Brothers, and Kacie had to admit it had been very passable. Dennis, dressed in his best, blue drape suit, light blue winkle-pickers, dark hair styled as immaculately as always, had hugged the mike as though he was making love to it and his hips had swayed sexily to the beat as he had sung. Kacie hadn't witnessed this provocative performance by her husband before and she didn't know whether or not she liked it being displayed to others. She did notice several women nearer the stage ogling him and she didn't know whether she liked that either.

'Oh, ain't our Dennis good, Kacie?' shouted Dotty, clapping hard, nudging her daughter-in-law in the ribs with her elbow.

Kacie agreed with her, thinking it was a pity someone in the music industry couldn't have witnessed the band's performance tonight. 'Yes, it's the best I've seen them,' she replied, clapping as enthusiastically.

Dotty beamed proudly as she inclined her head towards a couple of women standing nearby. 'They think so, 'an all. Fancy Dennis rotten by the way they're looking at him. Mind you, I ain't surprised, him being so good-looking. He gets his looks from his dad. Dead ringer my Cyril wa' for Rudy Vallee when he wa' young. Well, I think so. But you needn't worry, gel, about your 'usband straying. Dennis only 'as eyes for you. I noticed the way he kept winking at yer when he was singing "Living Doll". Good job yer both married, that's all I can say, or I'd be thinking there wa' summat going on between yer both.' She gave Kacie a suggestive wink.

Kacie had known Dennis had sung the song especially for her, even though he knew she detested being called Doll. Two young women whom Kacie knew via their custom at Verna's salon came up to her breathless, 'Eh up, Kacie, your old man ain't bad, is 'e?

I'd say the band's good enough ter give Elvis a run for his money.'

Kacie beamed proudly. 'I'll tell him you said so.'

The last song over and bows taken, a sweating Dennis fought his way towards Kacie and his mother, the delight on his face at the pats on the back he was receiving from members of the audience very apparent. 'Well, what did you think then, Kacie? Hello, Mam,' he said, leaning over to kiss her cheek before he sat down next to his wife, and looking at her expectantly.

'I thought yer were smashing,' said his delighted mother.

'I thought you were all great,' enthused Kacie.

'Great? Really? Oh, good. I thought myself it was going fabulous. I couldn't remember some of the words when we sang that Emile Ford number. Jed lost his drumstick when he did that roll during "Great Balls of Fire", but I don't think anyone noticed. I just hope Reg liked us,' he said, turning his head to see if he could spot the landlord of the pub through the dispersing crowd. He couldn't so he turned his attentions back to Kacie. 'The lads like the name you came up with so that's what we're going to call ourselves in future.'

'Good, I'm glad that's sorted.'

'And to celebrate I've invited the lads back to our place. OK by you?'

'Fine, only we have no drink and we can't feed them.'

'No, probs. I'll chat Reg up for a few bottles to take out and we'll get chips on the way home.'

'Remember you've work in the morning,' she reminded him.

'I know, but work is the last thing on my mind at the moment. Give us a kiss,' he said, puckering his lips at her.

'Get away with you,' she said playfully, pushing him off. 'You're sweating like a running tap and you'll ruin my hair.'

He planted a hurt look on his face. 'Those women over there wouldn't turn me away, Kacie.'

'Oh, you noticed them, did you? Well, you make sure looking is all you do or you'll have me to deal with.'

'Oh, she's a hard woman, ain't she, Mam, denying a man a bit of attention from good-looking broads?'

'Good job I know yer only jokin', so, or I'd slap yer arse meself,' responded Dotty, hiding a smile.

He laughed. 'Kacie knows she's the only woman for me. No one else can hold a candle to her,' he said, gazing at her lovingly. 'My old lady's a cut above the rest and more. Ain't that right, gel?'

Kacie gave him a playful tap on his arm. 'I agree with you totally, kind sir. Now go and square up with Reg and get your pay for the night, else we'll have nothing to buy those chips with,' she ordered.

'OK, boss,' he said, rising up. 'Won't be too long packing up.'

'Me and your mam will go ahead and get the plates warmed up. You are coming back, aren't you, Mrs C?' she asked her.

'What, me miss a celebration? Not on your nelly. I'll bring Ada and Vi too, as they love a knees-up.'

The jovial gathering in the small flat above the greengrocer's went on far longer than anyone intended and much more alcohol was consumed than was realised. It was after two in the morning when Kacie and Dennis finally crawled into bed, the springs loudly announcing their presence.

'Good job we don't have neighbours downstairs, isn't it?' Dennis slurred, giving an inebriated giggle as he took his wife in his arms, pulling her close.

'You're right there,' Kacie replied, snuggling up to him. 'The noise this bed makes is enough to wake the dead. The first thing we do if you ever make some decent money from this singing lark is to buy a new one. And we made enough din between us tonight to wake up the whole of Evington.' She started to chuckle. 'Oh, Dennis, your mam and her cronies singing "We'll Meet Again" at the tops of their voices while Jed was banging my saucepans with a wooden spoon was so funny.'

'Eh, you don't think me mam was serious when she kept going on about the three oldies being our backing group, do you?'

Kacie laughed at the absurdity of it. 'Don't be daft, Dennis. Apart from the fact that the three of them sounded worse than a cats' chorus, I doubt your mam will remember much of what she said in the morning.'

'Oh, thank God for that. I told you, didn't I, about Reg giving us another go next week and if the turnout is as good as tonight he'll seriously consider it as a regular thing?'

'Only a dozen times, Dennis. And so he should with the amount of custom the band brought into the pub tonight. It's usually dead on a Thursday. I bet he took more behind that bar tonight than he has all week.'

'Well, let's hope they all come next week then,' he said, a hint of worry in his voice.

'If your mother has anything to do with it, they will. So how much did Reg pay you? You haven't told me yet,' she asked eagerly, thinking of her new Formica table and chairs.

'Er . . . he didn't,' Dennis slurred hesitantly. 'Tonight was just a trial. I didn't tell you before because I knew you wouldn't like it.'

'I don't. Bloody mercenary sod, that Reg is. He never gave you anything?' she reiterated incredulously.

'A couple of free pints each.'

'Oh, very generous of him,' she said sarcastically. 'So how did you buy the chips?'

He replied sheepishly, 'I borrowed a couple of bob from Jed, said I'd square up with him when I get paid tomorrow.'

'Oh, Dennis,' she scolded. 'And the crate of beer? How did you pay for that.'

'Said I'd square up with Reg tomorrow as well.'

She exhaled loudly as the vision of having the finance to acquire her new table vanished. 'Well, Reg better be paying you for next week, because I'm not letting you do any more gigs in his pub just to line his pockets.'

'Oh, he is, Kacie. A quid.'

'A pound! There's four of you in the band. Dennis, that's only five bob each.'

'It might only be five bob, Kacie, but it's not bad for starters, is it?'

She sighed despondently. 'And you said this band would make our fortunes. Some hope, eh, when you end up playing for nothing.'

He gave a loud hiccup. 'What was that you said?'

'It doesn't matter.'

She felt his hand slide underneath her baby-doll nightie and glide its way up to caress her breast. 'Oh, not too drunk for a bit of slap and tickle then?' she said huskily as she snuggled closer to him.

'Never too sloshed to make love to you, Kacie. Just the thought of your voluptuous curves, my darlin',' he whispered provocatively in her ear as his caress turned more urgent, 'are enough to make any red-blooded man's old fellow stand to attention, no matter how much beer he's had.'

'You mucky bugger,' she said, giggling as she eagerly responded to her husband's welcome advances.

Chapter Four

'So what have you planned for this afternoon?' Verna asked Kacie as she locked the salon door and stashed the keys safely away in her handbag. 'Goodbye, Diane,' she called after the young girl, who was already heading off down the street, intent on savouring every minute of Wednesday afternoon early closing.

Diane turned and waved back. 'Bye, Mrs Koz, Kacie. I'm in a hurry 'cos I want to get to the record shop in town to listen to the latest Ritchie Valens. I'm gonna buy it on Friday if I've got enough money after I've paid me dues out,' she shouted, grinning excitedly as she hurried off.

'Oh, to be young without a care in the world,' Verna sighed, looking after her. She then turned her attention back to Kacie, 'It's a lovely day, isn't it?' she said, looking skyward. 'Very hot for September.'

It was boiling as far as Kacie was concerned. She liked to feel the sun on her skin but this intense heat was too much for her. Sticky from the humid atmosphere in the salon, all Kacie felt like doing was having a long soak in a cool bath with a cup of tea and a good book for company, but apart from the fact she had no bath at her immediate disposal, doing anything relaxing was out of the question. 'Hot or not, I've a pile of ironing big enough to frighten even a hospital laundress to death. I don't mind washing but I hate ironing, especially shirts. Good job Dennis isn't a white-collar worker or I'd never have married him. Who said married life was bliss, eh?'

'An idiot. Well, certainly it wasn't quoted by a woman who worked full time as well as looked after a family. So, no feet up for you this afternoon, then?'

'No chance. I could do with it, though. My feet are killing me.'

Verna looked down at Kacie's feet, then back at her face knowingly. 'I have advised you to wear more comfortable shoes in the salon, dear. Those stilettos aren't really suitable. You'll end up with bunions.'

'I'd sooner risk bunions than be seen dead in comfortable shoes, Mrs Koz,' Kacie scoffed.

'Suffer for the sake of fashion, eh? You young ones . . . I dunno,' she said, shaking her head. She then eyed Kacie concernedly. 'You are all right, aren't you?'

'Yes. Why?'

'Oh, nothing. It's just that you've seemed a bit distant since Dennis's big night. But as I heard so many reports via our customers that that went so well, it can't be anything to do with that, can it?'

Kacie eyed her employer, surprised. She had thought she had managed to keep her problem with her parents hidden while she thought of a suitable solution, which still evaded her. Obviously Verna Kozlowski took much more of an interest in her than she had realised. Dennis hadn't made any comment. She wasn't surprised as, since the band's success at the pub, he had been too preoccupied to notice her unusual quietness, and also as much as possible of his spare time was spent with the other band members in a disused factory down by the canal, practising new numbers and polishing the old.

She debated for a moment whether to take this opportunity of unburdening herself upon Verna, as the woman had asked, but then thought better of it. Verna, she knew, would be wanting to get home to her beloved husband and it wouldn't be fair for Kacie to waylay her. Wednesday afternoons had a habit of flying past and with all Verna had to contend with, she deserved some relaxation time.

'I'm fine, thanks, Mrs Koz,' she fibbed. 'When I've finished off the ironing I'm going to put my feet up before I get Dennis's dinner. I hope you don't mind but I've borrowed a couple of magazines from the salon,' she said, patting her bag. 'I'll bring them back.'

Verna smiled. 'I don't mind at all, dear, call it a perk of the job – and, goodness knows, we don't get many perks in our line of trade, do we? Actually, that pile of mags needs sorting through. Many of them are so tattered, what with people ripping articles and coupons out when they think we're not looking. I'll ask Diane to do it tomorrow if we get a lull.'

As they alighted on to the pavement and prepared to say their goodbyes, Kacie politely asked, 'Any plans for this afternoon yourself, Mrs Koz?'

'Oh, nothing special, but I thought being's it's such a lovely afternoon that Jan might be up to going for a gentle stroll in Abbey Park and maybe have tea in the pavilion.'

Kacie eyed her enviously. 'A walk in the park sounds romantic to me. I can't remember the last time Dennis took me for a stroll since this band business started. The last time must have been when we were courting and he was trying to make an impression on me,' she said drily. 'Mind you, doing things together like walking in the park and suchlike seems to stop when you get married. No time, is there, with all the housework and whatever else to do? Mr Koz feeling better, then, is he?'

'He's not too bad at the moment, thank you, dear. Well, I must get off or the afternoon will have gone.'

'Yeah, me too. Have a good time.'

'I will and, despite your ironing, I hope you do too.'

Kacie had walked only a few yards when she felt a presence beside her and turned to see who it was. A woman looked back at her expectantly. Kacie was just about to confront the woman when, like a bolt, recognition struck and she abruptly stopped, her face quizzical. 'Caroline?'

'Hello, Kacie.'

Totally shocked by the unexpected appearance of her sister, Kacie asked, 'What . . . what on earth are you doing around here? It's well off your beat, isn't it?'

'I've come to see you.'

'Me?';

'Yes. I'm sorry I pounced on you like this but I couldn't remember where you lived, but I did remember where you worked. I was across the street, waiting until you'd finished your conversation with that woman. Was she your boss?'

'Yes, Mrs Kozlowski.'

'I thought it was. I remember her from your wedding. A nice woman.'

'Well, as you didn't stay for the reception I wonder how you'd know that,' Kacie said bluntly.

'Oh, Kacie, but I had to leave straight after the church service as Malcolm said he wasn't feeling well.'

'So you say,' she said, matter-of-factly. 'But, yes, Mrs Koz is a lovely woman. I couldn't work for better.' Kacie frowned at her questioningly. 'Look, Caroline, why have you come to see me?' Then a thought struck and her face set hard. 'Oh, I get it. *They've* sent you, haven't they?' she accused. 'Well, you can bloody go back and tell them that until they agree to accept Dennis as my husband and treat him properly I'll not speak to them again. I've had enough.'

Caroline appeared taken aback. 'I don't know what you're talking about, Kacie. No one's sent me. I came of my own accord.'

'Oh, come off it,' her sister hissed angrily. 'You've hardly ever given me the time of day before, so don't try and make out this is a social visit.'

Caroline gave a sad sigh. 'We haven't exactly been sisterly, have we, and I feel mostly to blame for that. That's why I've come to see you, Kacie – to try and change that situation between us.'

Kacie gawked, astounded. 'What, you expect I can just forget all those years you hardly said two words to me? I wasn't born yesterday, Caroline. You haven't all of a sudden decided you want to be sisterly, that's just an excuse. I know *they* have talked you into coming as another ploy to try and get me to leave Dennis. Well, you're wasting your time. Now if you'll excuse me I've things to do.'

She made to walk off but Caroline grabbed her arm. 'You couldn't be further from the truth, Kacie.'

She shook free her arm. 'Couldn't I? Well, from where I'm standing my reason for you coming sounds more likely than what you've given me.'

'I have told you the truth. Please believe me, Mother and Father have nothing to do with my being here. Well, not in the sense you think. Look, please, could we go to your house and talk?'

'Flat,' Kacie corrected stonily. 'And it's rented, Caroline. You sure you want to be seen dead in it, someone like you with a big house and all the best furniture?'

'It's not big, Kacie, it's a small semi off the Blackbird Road. Hardly the grand palace you're making it out to be.'

'I'm going by what Mam says because, as I've never been invited, I wouldn't know, would I?'

'Point taken. But as you've never showed an interest in coming, what was the point of inviting you?'

Kacie stared at her blankly. Caroline spoke the truth.

'That's exactly what I've come to try and put right – this estrangement between us. I'd love to come to your flat, Kacie.

Please hear me out, that's all I ask. I swear Mother and Father haven't sent me. Please?'

Her tone was begging and Kacie stared at her, bemused. The sudden appearance of Caroline was still taking some getting used to, and despite her sister's plausible excuse Kacie couldn't shift the feeling there was another motive.

'You sure Mam and Dad have nothing to do with you being here?' she reiterated.

'On my honour.'

She stared at Caroline for a moment, deep in thought, then sighed resignedly. It wouldn't hurt to listen to what Caroline had to say. After all, as far as matters stood between them, Kacie herself had nothing to lose. And it was an excuse not to do the ironing. As she remembered the ironing, a vision rose of the disorganised state of the flat that morning as she had hurriedly departed for work. The sink was stacked with breakfast dishes and the pile of ironing was strewn over the settee, some of it toppled on to the floor. Oh, sod it, she thought. If her sister was so hellbent on talking to her then she would have to accept her as she was.

'I'll warn you, the flat is in a bit of a mess, as I work, remember. I haven't got all day like you to get my housework done.'

'Kacie, I've come to see you, not inspect your home.'

'It's a good job,' Kacie snapped. 'OK then, if you insist. I just need to pop in the shop to get some milk.'

A while later, still unable to shake the feeling her sister was hiding the real reason for her visit, Kacie placed a mug of tea in front of her and sat down opposite at the table. She took a moment to appraise Caroline discreetly. She was just the same as ever. Appearing just as calm and collected, prim and proper and as unattractive. She was dressed in a straight, below-the-knee-length tweed skirt and a pale yellow twinset – Marks and Spencer judging by the quality of it; her long dark hair, the same colour as Kacie's, pulled back tightly and tied by a thin brown ribbon at the base of her neck. Her eyesight being poor, she wore a pair of thick-framed brown spectacles, an uncomplimentary style. All in all it was an effect that gave Caroline the appearance of a matronly forty-year-old instead of the twenty-six years she actually was.

It was a shame, Kacie thought. Caroline would never be stunning. She was as thin as a clothes prop but, dressed more fashionably, her hair styled more modernly, and sporting more becoming glasses, she'd certainly appear more attractive.

41

Kacie pushed the sugar basin towards her. 'I can't remember if you take sugar or not, so help yourself if you do.'

She gave a grateful smile. 'I don't, but thank you all the same.'

'I'm sorry I've no biscuits. If there's any in the house Dennis eats them all – well, you know what men are like.' Kacie was babbling, she knew, but didn't really know what else to say.

'Malcolm doesn't eat biscuits.'

Kacie's eyebrows rose, surprised. 'He doesn't eat biscuits?'

'No. He says they're bad for your digestion.'

'Really? Oh! I dread to think what Dennis's digestive system is like then, because he can eat a whole packet at a time, two if I'd let him.'

'How is your husband?' Caroline asked.

'He's fine, thanks, and yours?'

'*He's* fine.'

Kacie flashed her a questioning look, feeling there had been a hidden meaning in her sister's tone and her emphasis of 'he'. Then she mentally shook herself. According to her mother, Caroline and Malcolm were the perfect couple living the perfect life and couldn't be happier. She was imagining things. 'Er . . . more tea?' she asked.

Caroline smiled appreciatively. 'I haven't finished this one yet.' As she took a genteel sip of her tea, she glanced around her. 'You have this place looking nice, Kacie.'

'Well, according to Mother it's nothing compared to yours, but we've done our best,' she said sharply.

Caroline appeared not to have noticed her abrasive manner and said, smiling, 'You certainly have. It's very homely.'

'Thank you. Mam tells me yours is like a show home.'

Caroline sighed. 'I might have nice furniture but nice things don't make a home, do they? It's the people that reside in it that do that.' She placed her cup back in its saucer – the only one without a chip somewhere on it out of the set bought off the market as a wedding gift from clients at the salon – and looked at Kacie meaningfully. 'You're still not sure whether to believe me or not about my reason for coming here, are you?'

Kacie fixed her firmly in the eye. 'You're very observant. I'm not convinced you told me the truth.'

'Kacie, I meant what I said. I'm here to sort things out between us.'

Kacie puckered her lips. 'And how do you propose to do that? You made it very clear when we were young you thought I was a pain in the arse and you never seemed to change your opinion as we got older. Face it, Caroline, we're practically strangers.'

Caroline removed her spectacles, gave them a wipe with a handkerchief she removed from her sleeve, then placed them back. 'Have you thought that that was because you didn't seem to need an older sister?'

Kacie frowned confused. 'What? I don't understand.'

Caroline eyed her tenderly. 'You were always the life and soul, Kacie, so what need could you possibly have for a sister who wouldn't say boo to a goose? You didn't exactly need me to stand up for you, as you were quite capable of doing that for yourself. You proved it often enough. And you didn't need me as a friend; you always had plenty of your own.'

Kacie's face clouded, hurt. 'I often asked you to tag along with us but you always refused.'

'Because I knew it wouldn't be fair on you, that's why. In our situation it wasn't the older sister feeling obliged to drag the younger one with her wherever she went but the other way around.'

Kacie grimaced thoughtfully. 'I don't remember it being like that. I just remember you ignoring me. You used to look at me as though . . . well, as though you wished I'd never been born.'

'That's not true, Kacie,' Caroline vehemently denied.

'Isn't it? I always got the feeling it was.'

'Well, you were wrong. You misconstrued that for the envy I was feeling.'

Kacie eyed her incredulously. 'Envy of me? Whatever for?'

'The strengths you possess that I don't. You have spirit, Kacie.' She pulled a wry face. 'They tried, but Mam and Dad never managed to force you into doing anything you never wanted to do.'

'Not things I was really against, no, I wouldn't let them.' Kacie eyed her sister curiously. 'Are you saying they made you do things you didn't want to?'

'Yes, they did. I never wanted to go to secretarial college but it was expected I would and I hadn't the guts to stand up for myself and insist on doing what I really wanted. I didn't want to accept that boring job I was offered with Crampton and Sons, Solicitors, but Mother and Father were so beside themselves that I had been offered it I felt I couldn't turn it down. Kacie, I hated every minute I spent at college and detested every second I was at work. I never wanted to marry Malcolm either.'

43

'You didn't?' Kacie was shocked to her core at this most unexpected admission.

Caroline shook her head. 'I met Malcolm through working at Crampton's, as you know. He was the only man to ever show any interest in me. Mother and Father thought the sun shone out of his backside, as to them he was perfect husband material for one of their daughters. He came from a solid background and had good prospects, and Mother was planning the wedding almost from the moment I accepted an invitation from him to go to the De Montfort Hall to listen to the London Philharmonic play. His mother had let him down through illness and he had a spare ticket, and I only agreed to accompany him because I felt sorry for him.'

'Did you fancy him at all?'

'He was pleasant enough, but no, I didn't fancy him.'

'But you grew to love him surely?'

Caroline shook her head. 'I married him, Kacie, because I was pushed into it and also I worried his offer might be the only one I'd ever get, and in truth I was desperate to get away from home. What a fool I was. Married life for me is awful, Kacie.'

Kacie was staring at her, horrified. 'But all those things Mother told me – she was always comparing my marriage to yours. She said you and Malcolm were so happy together.'

'She thinks we are. It was all a cover-up. She believed what I told her.' Caroline gave a sad sigh. 'I lied because, despite what they'd done to me, I couldn't bring myself to hurt them.'

Kacie's face filled with sadness. 'Oh, Caroline, this is all so dreadful. I never realised.'

'How could you, Kacie? You were young, with so much going on in your life and, besides, you had your own battles with Mam and Dad to deal with to have much room left to notice what I was going through.'

Kacie sighed, shocked rigid by these revelations. 'That was so selfish of me, Caroline. You're my sister; I should have noticed. I'm mortified, really I am.'

Caroline leaned across the table and placed a reassuring hand upon Kacie's. 'Oh, Kacie, I'm sorry if you think I'm trying to blame you in any way. I'm not, not at all. If this situation is anyone's fault it's mine for not having the guts to stand up to Mam and Dad.'

Kacie eyed her warily. Despite her sister's reassurances that she laid no blame for what had transpired in the past on Kacie, Kacie couldn't help but feel a huge amount of responsibility for being oblivious of her sister's plight and misery.

'Would you like more tea?' she asked.

Caroline smiled warmly at her. 'I'd love some, thank you.'

As Kacie passed Caroline her replenished cup, she asked, 'So . . . what did you want to do for a living if it wasn't office-related, Caroline?'

The elder sister gave a distant smile. 'I wanted to work in a shop. A newsagent's. I dreamed of serving the customers with their papers and tobacco, helping all the children choose their sweets. I'd have relished it, been really happy. Instead I earned my living working for a self-important man who treated me like I was his slave, barking orders at me from morning until night and woebetide if I made any mistakes, but I didn't dare leave for fear of the repercussions from Mother and Father.'

Kacie was now staring at her, bewildered. 'Repercussions or not, if you were that unhappy you should have found the courage—'

'Don't you think I wanted to, Kacie? But you can't summon up something that isn't there. As I've already said, I don't possess your strong will.' Her eyes glazed distantly. 'I remember vividly the time you announced you wanted to be a hairdresser when you left school. Mother was furious, a most unrespectable profession for a daughter of hers. They took it for granted that you'd follow their wishes and go to college, then get yourself a respectable job just like I had done.'

Kacie grunted. 'I remember Mother saying that going to college and getting office skills had far more potential rewards than she felt hairdressing would ever give me. I wasn't interested at the time in what she had to say. The thought of ending up working in a stuffy firm for stuffy people filled me with dread. I had the chance to do something I really wanted to do for a living and something I knew I'd be good at. What Verna Kozlowski was offering me was such a great opportunity, I'd have been mad to turn it down. Even now I know Mam and Dad still think I made the wrong choice. And Mother thinks I don't realise that her way of showing her disapproval is never asking me to do her hair. But that's her loss.'

Caroline clasped her hands and looked intently at Kacie. 'And you stuck out over Dennis. They put you through hell but you never gave him up.'

'I couldn't give him up, I loved him too much. When we decided

45

to get married, Dennis was insistent he ask Dad for permission out of respect, even though I was of age. But I wouldn't let him; I knew World War Three would erupt. So I told Mam and Dad of our arrangements and said I'd be upset if they didn't come to my wedding but it was up to them if they came or not as we were going ahead with it anyway. It was a hard thing to do, believe me.'

Caroline looked at her admiringly. 'Now can you appreciate why I was envious of you?'

Kacie stared at her thoughtfully. 'I wonder if Mam and Dad realise how unhappy their rigid rules made us, especially you. The trouble with them is that they still live in the past, when children did exactly what their parents told them.'

Caroline sighed despondently. 'I don't expect they have any idea. I think they saw you as a very rebellious child and were glad I was so amenable. I'm just so angry with myself because if I hadn't been such a coward I wouldn't be in this mess now.'

Kacie tightened her lips as her self-imposed guilt for her sister's situation heightened. 'Is there anything I can do?' she offered, but at the same time wondering what on earth she could do.

Caroline eyed her eagerly. 'Do you mean that, Kacie?'

'Yes, of course I do. I'd be glad to do anything.'

'I was hoping you'd say that. You see, I need somewhere to stay for a few days.'

Kacie gawped at her. 'Why?'

Caroline took a deep breath. 'Because I've finally decided to take my life into my own hands and I'm leaving Malcolm.'

'Leaving him?' Kacie was stunned.

'Don't look so shocked, Kacie. If things weren't right between you and Dennis, and you were so miserable you dreaded getting up each morning, you'd do something about it, wouldn't you, and to hell with the consequences?'

'Yes, I would,' she replied with conviction.

'Well, then, how can you be so flabbergasted that I would? I've given this a lot of thought and what I'm doing is right for both of us. Malcolm will be upset, not because I've left him but because his dinner won't be on the table when he gets home from work, or his washing, ironing and cleaning done.'

'That's a bit harsh, Caroline. I don't know him very well but Malcolm seems a nice chap.'

'Most people who meet him think he is, Kacie. A charming man, they say, and aren't I a lucky wife to have such a husband? But that charming man doesn't exist behind closed doors. He treats me worse than a servant. As for money, I have to account for every penny I spend, produce receipts for everything. It's very humiliating, Kacie, not to be trusted with your housekeeping money. How I've managed to save the few pounds I have is a feat in itself, and has taken me years, penny by penny. I'm not allowed to do anything on my own – join any women's groups, that sort of thing. Malcolm says they are a waste of time, time that women should spend doing what men married them for.'

As Caroline was speaking something was niggling away at Kacie. Suddenly she realised it was what her mother had told her the last time she had seen her. 'If Malcolm is so mean how come you have a brand-new suite and coffee table? Mother told me. The latest fashion in black vinyl, she said. Gushing about it, she was.'

'And it's horrible, Kacie. I hated it the moment I set eyes on it.'

'So why did you buy it?'

'I didn't. Malcolm's mother gave him the money as a gift. She said the one we had was a disgrace, although it was perfectly all right. He bought the suite without even consulting me.'

'Oh, Caroline, that's awful. I'd go mad if Dennis bought anything for our home without involving me. Do you think Malcolm has any idea that you're thinking of leaving him?'

'It wouldn't enter his head that I would dare do such a thing.'

'How do you think he'll react when he finds out, then?'

'I expect he'll be angry, but only for the disgrace this will cause him. Don't worry about Malcolm, Kacie, he'll soon find someone else. Someone who'll be quite happy to devote her life to caring for a boring husband and having every minute of her day organised for her. Because that's what Malcolm does. He writes lists of things I'm to do that day as if I'm not capable of organising myself or planning my own time.'

Kacie was horrified. 'That bad, eh? I'd like to see my Dennis try that on with me. He'd soon get his comeuppance.'

Caroline's eyes suddenly sparkled. 'You live such an exciting life with Dennis, don't you, Kacie?'

'Exciting?' Kacie blew out her cheeks and exhaled sharply. 'You're the second person to tell me that. I'm beginning to think I must do, although I wouldn't describe my life as exciting. Eventful, maybe.'

'I don't suppose my life will ever be exciting,' Caroline said wistfully, 'but I'd happily settle for eventful.'

47

'So what are your plans for this new eventful life, then?' Kacie asked.

'First, to get myself somewhere to live.' She gazed around her. 'A little flat like this would do me.' Then her face clouded. 'Trouble is, I've no money to speak of, just the few pounds I managed to save to tide me over until I get a job. I shouldn't have too much trouble with my qualifications, although I'm a bit rusty, not having worked these past six years I've been married.' She leaned over and placed a hand on Kacie's arm. 'I wondered what you'd think about me moving around here. That way we'd be closer and we could get to know each other. What do you think?'

Kacie wasn't sure what she felt about Caroline living so near by, but overriding this was her guilt for not realising how much in the past her sister had needed her. 'I . . . think that's a great idea. But flats around here aren't easy to get, Caroline.'

'Oh. Well, I can try.'

Kacie frowned anxiously. 'You are sure you're doing the right thing? I mean, leaving home is a pretty final thing to do. Have you tried talking to Malcolm, tell him how you feel?'

'I've tried on many occasions, Kacie.' Caroline gave a sad sigh. 'But you get to a stage where you don't really care about putting things right. I mean, what is the point when you don't love someone enough to make the effort? I remember looking at Malcolm one day, he was voicing his opinions on something or other I'd done that he wasn't happy with. What was it now . . . Oh, I know, I'd ironed creases down his shirt sleeves and he didn't like that. As he was telling me how his mother used to do them it struck me that I didn't actually like him. That's an awful thing to admit, Kacie, that you don't like your husband as a person, and over time it eats away at you until you hate being in the same room.' She took a deep breath and raised her chin defiantly. 'I don't care about what trouble this will cause – Mam and Dad disowning me or the disgrace of what I've done in other people's eyes. I can live with that. I want it to be final. I want a divorce.'

'A divorce? Oh! You have really decided, haven't you?'

'Oh, yes.'

'Well, going on what you've just told me I can't say as I blame you, Caroline,' Kacie said. 'Dennis annoys me something rotten sometimes, but I like him and he's my friend as well as my . . .' She blushed and said coyly, 'Well, you know, my lover.'

A deep sadness filled Caroline's face. 'I never ever enjoyed that side of things. It was performing a duty for me. I was so thankful that Malcolm wasn't demanding in that department.' Gnawing her bottom lip she eyed Kacie worriedly. 'There is something I haven't been entirely truthful about, Kacie.'

'Oh?'

'When I said I was leaving Malcolm, well, leaving was the wrong word. I've already left. I've left him a letter on the kitchen table. Cowardly of me, I know, but I couldn't face him. So there's no going back. My belongings are at the bus station in left luggage. Can I . . . can I please stay here for a few days till I get myself sorted?'

So Kacie's initial suspicion that Caroline had an ulterior motive for her visit was right. 'So that's why you really came here today, Caroline, to get a bed for a few nights because you had no one else to turn to?' she accused.

Caroline looked her square in the eyes. 'Yes.'

Kacie tightened her lips, hurt. 'You should have just told me the truth in the first place.'

'And would you have entertained me, considering how we have been with each other, if I hadn't approached you the way I did?'

'I would have listened to you after you'd convinced me your visit was nothing to do with Mam and Dad.'

'I couldn't take that chance, Kacie. But please believe me, I was telling the truth about wanting us to be proper sisters. I really want that, Kacie.'

'Huh.'

'Kacie, I do. Honestly I do.'

Kacie eyed her for several moments, then her face broke into a warm smile. 'Yes, so do I. It'll be nice getting to know each other properly. I'm just sorry it's in these circumstances.' She paused and eyed Caroline worriedly. 'But offering you a bed is another matter. Under normal circumstances, I'd welcome you with open arms but, as you can see, there's hardly room for me and Dennis, let alone—'

'It's only for a few nights,' Caroline implored. 'I wouldn't be putting you out like this if I had any other choice. You know I can't go back to Mam and Dad's. I'd sooner stay with Malcolm than live with them again. I won't take up much space and the settee will be fine. You and Dennis won't know I'm here. I'm sure Dennis won't mind, me being family.'

'Well, er . . .'

'Oh, thanks, Kacie, thanks so much,' Caroline cried ecstatically.

49

'For the first time in my life I'm so excited. This is a brand-new start for me and you're helping me do it.'

Kacie sighed resignedly. Her sister looked so happy she hadn't the heart to dispel her good humour, not with all that she was facing. She just worried what Dennis would say about this turn of events.

Caroline suddenly eyed Kacie, bothered. 'You won't mention any of this to Mam and Dad, will you? They'll cause a stink, keep at me until they wear me down into going back to Malcolm. You know what they're like, Kacie.'

'Oh, surely they won't force you to do anything of the kind once they know how awful it's been for you.'

'I can't risk that, Kacie, so please don't mention anything. I will tell them when I'm ready to. I just need some time to build up the nerve to face them. Making the decision to leave Malcolm has taken such a lot out of me, you see. One step at a time, eh?'

All Kacie's thoughts were centred on the fact she had a house guest for a few days and wondering how on earth they were all going to live together compatibly in such tiny surroundings. 'I, er . . . can't see that being a problem as we're not speaking at the moment, and as things stand I can't see that changing during the time you'll be with us.'

Caroline sighed, hugely relieved.

A thought struck Kacie. 'What about Malcolm? Is he likely to come here and cause trouble?'

'No. This is the last place Malcolm would think to come, so don't worry. But if by chance you should see him you won't tell him anything, will you? Please say you won't. I couldn't face him hounding me.'

'All right. I'll cover up for you, but you'll have to face all of them sooner or later.'

Caroline leaped up from the table, raced round and threw her arms around her sister in a bearlike hug. 'Thank you. This is what sisters do, isn't it – help each other?'

Despite her deep concerns over her enforced involvement in her sister's affairs, Kacie managed to put a smile on her face. 'Yes, yes, they do. Well . . . you'd better go and fetch your bags, then.'

Chapter Five

'Hiya, Doll . . . er . . . sweetie,' Dennis called as he entered the flat at just after six that evening. In the living room he stripped off his donkey jacket, flung himself down in an armchair and, pulling off his work boots, glanced across at his wife, who was sitting at the table, her chin in her hands staring blankly into space. 'God, am I glad today's over,' he said, wriggling his toes inside heavily darned socks, then stretching his feet out to rest on the hearth. 'Nonstop it's been, and one of the lads had to pick a really busy day to have an accident. A drill bit went straight through his hand. You should have seen the blood. Kacie? *Kacie*, are you listening to me?'

'Eh? Oh, sorry, Dennis, I didn't hear you come in. Oh God,' she cried, jumping up. 'Is that the time? I haven't started the dinner yet.'

'Or done the ironing,' he commented, noticing the pile still strewn over the settee and on the floor. 'Decided to put your feet up this afternoon? Well, I can't say as I blame you. Don't worry about dinner. I'll throw us something together if you like. What's in the pantry?'

'Oh, I dunno. Er . . .'

Concerned, he jumped up and went over to her, placing a hand on her shoulder. 'Kacie, what's wrong?'

She took a deep breath, before looking up at him. 'I think you'd better sit down.'

'Why?'

'Just sit down, Dennis,' she ordered. 'I need to talk to you.'

He did as he was told and when she was sitting down opposite he asked, worried, 'Well?'

Anxiously, she ran her hand over her chin. 'How do you feel about someone stopping with us for a couple of nights, Dennis?'

He laughed. 'You are joking, Kacie?'

'I'm not, Dennis.'

He laughed again. 'And where are they gonna sleep exactly?'

'The settee.'

His mouth dropped open. 'You're serious, aren't you?'

'Deadly.'

'Who are we talking about?'

'My sister.'

'Caroline?'

'I haven't got another sister, Dennis, so yes, Caroline.'

He grimaced, confused. 'But you don't see Caroline. You haven't seen her to my knowledge since our wedding, when neither she nor that husband of hers stayed for the reception so you didn't even talk to her. That was over three years ago, Kacie.'

'Well, I talked to her today. She came here. She's left Malcolm and has asked if we can put her up until she sorts herself out.'

'Left Malcolm?'

She nodded.

'Well, she should have thought about her sleeping arrangements before she did something so stupid. We can't put her up, can we? You did tell her no?' He saw the look on her face. 'Don't tell me you agreed, Kacie? There's no room to swing a cat in here so how are we going to accommodate her? I don't even know her. I can't walk around in my underpants with a stranger here, can I? You don't like her anyway.'

'Well . . .'

'Well what?'

She clasped her hands, distraught. 'I think I've been wrong about her all these years, Dennis. I never realised how selfish I've been towards her until now. We have to help her, Dennis,' she pleaded. 'I have to try and make up to her somehow.'

He was staring at her, bewildered. 'Kacie, you haven't got a selfish bone in your body. You might be as stubborn as a mule and lash out with your tongue but you're *not* selfish.'

'Oh, Dennis, I think I have been,' she whispered, tears springing to her eyes.

Face stern, he leaned forward and fixed her with his eyes. 'I think you'd better tell me from the beginning.'

A while later he shook his head disbelievingly. 'What a mess. I can't think how your sister let herself be bullied by your parents into marrying a man she didn't love – like even.' He eyed her sharply. 'Are you sure she's telling you the truth, Kacie? After all, you don't know her all that well, considering she's your sister.'

She shrugged. 'She didn't give me any reason to doubt her, Dennis.'

He issued a deep sigh. 'I dunno, Kacie, this is all beyond me. But why does Caroline have to come here? Why can't she go back home to your Mam and Dad? After all, there's more room for her there.'

Kacie looked at him, aghast. 'Be serious, Dennis. I wouldn't put a dog through the hell my parents are going to give her when they find out what she's done. We might be practically strangers but she is my sister.'

He pulled a grim face. 'Yes, I suppose so. I know first-hand what your parents are like. They don't give up easily, do they?'

'Caroline has been through enough already so us putting ourselves out for a few days isn't much to ask is it, Dennis?'

He scratched his head, then smiled at Kacie tenderly. 'She's family, I suppose, and if I had a sister in the same situation, you'd help her out. Where is Caroline now?'

'Collecting her belongings from the bus station.' She looked at the clock. It was gone seven. 'I must say, she's been gone a long while.'

'I'm sure she's OK, Kacie.'

'So you don't mind if she stops?'

'I didn't say I didn't mind, but if it makes you happy I'm sure I can manage for a couple of days. Anyway, once she's had time to think things through she'll probably go back.'

From the way her sister had spoken Kacie severely doubted that, but nevertheless said, 'Yes, she might.' She leaped up and rushed over to him, throwing her arms around his neck, hugging him tightly. 'I do love you,' she whispered huskily.

'Well, I sure must love you to go without walking about in my underpants for a few days. I'll ask around at work if anyone knows if there's any lodgings going.'

'Thanks, Dennis,' she said, kissing him on his cheek before she straightened up. 'Anyway, she'll be company for me on the evenings you're off practising with the lads. Or should I say drinking?' she added, a twinkle in her eyes.

'Practising, Kacie, with a few pints to keep our voices lubricated,' he said, grinning back mischievously.

'Oh, Dennis,' she said, clasping her hands together in delight, 'it'll be nice having a proper sister.'

'Yes, I can imagine it will be for you. I quite like the idea of having a proper sister-in-law too. As long as that sister-in-law is under her own roof and not ours, though,' he added. 'Let's just hope we don't get a visit from your folks whilst she's with us. They'll blame us, Kacie, say we encouraged her to do what she has being's we're letting her stay with us.'

Kacie frowned, worried. 'I hadn't thought of them blaming us.' Then a thought struck and her face brightened. 'Still, them finding out she's with us isn't very likely—' She stopped mid-flow, realising she was about to blurt out her recent run-in with her parents, something she had promised herself to keep from Dennis to save his already hurt feelings in that department.

'Why isn't it very likely?' he asked.

'Oh, er . . . I was just going to say it's not very likely Mam and Dad will find out Caroline is staying here being's they only venture down this part of Evington when they come and see us. And they don't come here very often, do they, because they're too stubborn to admit what a great husband you are and that they were wrong about you? Mind you, they'd better get around to admitting their mistake sooner or later because I'm never going to give you up,' she said, looking at him lovingly. 'I'll get the dinner started,' she said, heading off into the kitchen. 'I hope Caroline likes chips and mushy peas.'

Chapter Six

'So how's your lodger, Kacie?' asked Verna three weeks later as the pair were checking the stock in the cluttered room above the salon.

'Still lodging,' she replied flatly. 'We could do with half a dozen number two perm lotions. We've nine of number one and seven of number three so we've enough until next week.'

Verna added the items to the list. 'I thought your sister only intended staying with you for a couple of nights.'

'So did I. And cotton wool wadding, as we're nearly out. Oh, and a couple of gallons of lacquer powder, and we'll need more white spirit to mix it with. We're really going through that stuff at a rate of knots. As you know, Mrs Koz, if we don't send our clients out of the salon with their hair as stiff as a board they think they're not getting their money's worth of lacquer and expect a reduction in the price of their hairdo. Especially the younger ones.'

'We could still cut back. Those extra squirts all add up. Shampoo?'

Kacie flashed her a worried look. It was most unlike her employer to be stingy. Never before, to Kacie's knowledge, had Verna asked her staff to be sparing with the sundries, and it crossed her mind that despite their seeming busy enough, maybe the salon wasn't doing as well as she thought. She bent down and counted the containers by her feet. 'We've three Winchesters full of green soap and several large bottles of our quality shampoo, so we've plenty. Oh, just a thought, any news on that other hairdresser's opening, or was it a rumour?'

'Well, it doesn't appear it was gossip after all. The shop is indeed in the process of being refitted into a hairdresser's.'

'Oh, I see. Well, I shouldn't worry, Mrs Koz. Your salon has years of good reputation behind it, and it's not like this salon is opening next door, is it? You've nothing to worry about, believe me.'

'I'm not so sure, Kacie, dear. As I said when we first talked about

55

this, people like to try new things, and it might be that they like the new salon more than mine and don't come back.'

'Well, we'll have to hope they don't like it better than yours. And, let's face it, they've one big disadvantage to start with. I'm not working there,' Kacie said, grinning mischievously. Then added, tongue in cheek, 'We can always hope something goes drastically wrong on opening day and the shop is forced to shut before it's had a chance to steal your customers. I think you're worrying unnecessarily, Mrs Koz. Is this anything to do with why you've just asked me to be sparing with the lacquer?'

'Well, I thought it wouldn't hurt to economise a bit in case we have to pull our horns in later. Mind you, that practice would soon drive customers away if they thought they were being short-changed.' She smiled. 'You're right, Kacie, dear. I'm worrying unnecessarily. Right, do we need anything else or are we finished making our list of requirements?'

'No, not quite. We need some setting lotions, a box of perming papers, kirby-grips and a selection of hairnets. Bleach powder and peroxide,' she said, checking them off. 'We're all right for that too. But we need sterilising solution for the perm rollers and combs. A gallon at least. No, as we're on an economy drive half a gallon will do.'

Verna flashed her a grin. 'You do push your luck sometimes, Kacie, with that mouth of yours. Right, rinses and tints we've already gone through so that's about it then for this week,' said she, folding up her list. 'Unless you can think of anything else?'

Kacie thought for a moment. 'I do need a new overall. I've sewn the bib pocket on this one that many times the material underneath has worn away and my combs and grips keep falling out, but I suppose I can make it do me a little while longer.' She smiled at her employer. 'Just about time for a cuppa before my next lady is due so do you fancy one?'

'Never say no to a cuppa, you know that, Kacie.'

'Then I'll put the kettle on. I'll just check Di is all right and bring the tea through to your office.'

'I've took three bookings,' Diane said proudly when Kacie popped her head through the door leading into the salon to enquire how she was fairing. 'Two perms and a trim. All fer termorra. Apart from a couple of spare slots that's us booked up fer the day.'

'You haven't put the appointments too close together, have you?'

Kacie asked, joining Diane at the little counter just inside the door where they received their clients. 'You have given Verna and me plenty of time to do them properly?'

'They didn't ask for Mrs Koz to do their hair, they both wanted you. I had to tell one of 'em yer were too busy, so she settled for Mrs Koz but she weren't too pleased, Kacie; said Mrs Koz ain't got your knack.'

'Don't tell Mrs Koz that, will you?'

Diane vehemently shook her head. 'Course I wouldn't, Kacie. I wouldn't upset Mrs Koz fer the world, you know that.' Diane's face suddenly filled with shame. 'I'm sorry about the other day, Kacie.'

Kacie grinned. 'It wasn't my intention to bring up that incident, but two perms, a tint and a trim all booked within the same hour is too much even for me to cope with when Mrs Koz is otherwise occupied. We all make mistakes, Di, and let's hope you learned from that one.'

'Oh, I did, Kacie, I did.'

'Good, then that's all that matters,' Kacie said, giving Diane a reassuring pat on her arm. 'And I don't think our clients noticed I was running around the salon like a blue-arsed fly, and Mrs Koz is none the wiser.' She started to chuckle. 'The look on my face when they all trooped in at the same time must have been a picture.'

'It was,' Diane readily agreed. 'As me mam would say, "Yer looked like you'd just 'eard a 'owling gale was on the way and remembered you'd a great 'ole in yer knickers." '

Kacie looked at her blankly. 'Your mother and her sayings,' she said, shaking her head, mystified. 'I'm not quite sure of that one's moral but it'll come to me in time. Anyway, we've finished checking what supplies we need from the wholesaler's this week, so are you all right to hold the fort for a few more minutes while I snatch a cuppa with Mrs Koz before my next lady is due?'

'I'm fine, Kacie, honest. I love answering the telephone. Hheel-loo,' she mimicked a BBC radio announcer. 'Verna's Hairstylist, har may I be of hassistance?'

Kacie guffawed loudly. 'Putting that voice on, you could teach them a thing or two at the railway station as one of their announcers. I defy anyone to make out what they are saying.'

'Oh, I wouldn't like that, Kacie,' Diane blurted, alarmed. 'I want to stay here. I love me job, really I do.'

'I was joking, Di.'

'Oh! Oh, right,' she said, mightily relieved.

'I'll leave you to it,' said Kacie. 'I'll bring you a cuppa through. Oh, and don't forget, besides putting all the towels into soak you have to mix up a bucket of lacquer and bottle it up before you go home tonight as we're running low. I'll give you a hand if I can. Please give me a shout when Mrs Bedoes arrives, will you?'

'I will, Kacie.'

When she went through to join Verna in her office, Kacie found her sitting behind her desk, staring blankly into space. She put the cup of tea in front of her and, as she sat down in the chair opposite, asked, 'You all right, Mrs Koz?'

'Eh! Oh, Kacie, dear, I didn't hear you come in.' She spotted the cup and saucer before her. 'Oh, my tea, thank you. This is most welcome, I must say.' She took a sip of the steaming liquid, then cradling the cup between her hands asked, 'Well, what are you going to do then?'

'I'm sorry? About what?'

'Your sister?'

She frowned. 'What do you mean, what am I going to do?'

'Well, she can't stay with you for ever, can she?'

'No, but I get the impression she thinks she can. I thought she'd soon get fed up sleeping on our lumpy settee but she doesn't seem to mind.'

'Oh dear,' Verna said gravely.

Kacie sighed despondently. 'I know I'm not going to make any sense when I say the better I'm getting to know her, the more I regret us not being closer when we were younger. I really got it wrong about her. She's nothing like the haughty, stuck-up cow I thought she was. She's just the quiet type and has hardly any confidence in herself.'

'Unlike you,' said Verna, smiling warmly.

Kacie laughed. 'Yes, I don't lack much in that department, do I? It's just a pity some of my traits weren't shared out a bit more equally between us. Anyway, I enjoy having Caroline around but at the same time she's driving me mad, Mrs Koz. She's so obliging and she's really got herself into a routine. The dinner's ready when I get home, then before I've laid down my knife and fork, she's already rushing about collecting the dishes. I've tried to tell her not to, but she takes no notice. She does the washing on Monday, the ironing on Tuesday, the flat cleaning on Wednesday, toilet, outside landing and stairs on Thursday. I've never seen the flat look so spotless and I'm not a complete slouch where housework

58

is concerned. Friday she does the weekly bake. Oh, and she shops every day.'

'Sounds like heaven,' Verna said wistfully. 'I'd give anything for someone to do all that for me.'

'It is heaven in a way. It's great going home knowing I've nothing to do, especially after some of the busy days we have. I have to say Caroline's good at shopping. She manages to get some really good bargains and she won't let me pay for the food she buys. She insists it's her way of contributing.'

'That's something, I suppose,' said Verna. 'In my experience, visiting relatives don't offer a penny towards their keep.'

'Yes, some people can be thoughtless, but without a job and money coming in, Caroline's few pounds she arrived with will soon be gone, and then what will she do? We can't afford to keep her and, more to the point, I don't suppose Caroline realises but she's taken over the running of my home.'

'Mmm, but she's only trying to make herself useful.'

'Yes, but there's being useful and doing everything. I know I sound ungrateful but I'd sooner her concentrate all her efforts into getting herself a job and somewhere to live than duties for me.'

Verna took a sip of her tea before asking, 'Have you spoken to Caroline about it?'

Kacie sighed. 'I keep meaning to but when it comes down to it I haven't the heart. She's so eager to please that I just can't bring myself to have words with her 'cos she'll be upset, I know she will, and I couldn't bear that, not on top of what she must already be feeling from her leaving Malcolm.'

Verna looked at her thoughtfully. 'Now she's had time to think about the implications of what she's done, does she have any regrets about leaving her husband?'

Kacie shrugged. 'If she has she's not said anything to me. She hardly ever mentions Malcolm. In fact, she hasn't talked about her marriage at all since she first arrived.'

'Mmm. It doesn't look like she's going to go back to him then, does it?'

Kacie shook her head.

'What's Dennis saying about this state of affairs?' Verna asked.

'It's what he's not saying that worries me, Mrs Koz. I know it's only a matter of time, though, before he does speak his mind. I have noticed he's going out more nights to practise with the lads since Caroline moved in. Normally I'd be kicking up a stink about that but at the moment I'm grateful because I know she's getting on his nerves. And the time we do spend together we're not alone, as Caroline never goes out. And when we go to bed . . .' She cast her eyes down and said coyly, 'Well, since Caroline's arrival that side of things has stopped. I mean you can't, can you, knowing your sister is on the other side of the wall?'

'Mmm,' Verna mouthed again, her face set grimly. 'Has Caroline made any efforts to look for a job and somewhere to live at all?'

Kacie shrugged again. 'I've no idea. I didn't push her at first, just to let her settle herself a bit and to get used to what she's done. Now I don't like to ask in case she thinks I want rid of her.'

Verna eyed her knowingly. 'But the truth is you do, Kacie.'

'Yes, I do.'

Verna took another sip of her tea, eyes glazed thoughtfully. 'Er . . . just a thought, Kacie. You haven't considered visiting her husband, have you?'

'Me visit Malcolm? Whatever for?'

'Just to check a reconciliation isn't out of the question. What I'm getting at is that Caroline has obviously got her own reasons for what she's done but you know how we women can blow things out of all proportion sometimes. Maybe things aren't as bad as she sees them. By what she's done her husband has had a good sharp shock and it just might have knocked some sense into him – if he's as bad as Caroline says he is, that is.'

Kacie frowned. 'Do you think Caroline has made all this up about Malcolm?'

'Not made it up, no. Obviously things between them aren't right and whatever is wrong was bad enough for Caroline to feel she had no alternative but to leave. What I'm trying to say is that her absence from the marital home has given her husband time to take a long hard look at himself and just maybe he's decided to do something to put matters right. Caroline might be prepared to forgive and forget if she thought that their lives in the future were going to be happier all round.'

Kacie pressed her lips together. 'Oh, I never thought of that. Do you think it would be worth me paying a visit, then? You don't think I'd be seen as interfering? I'd hate to turn into my mother, Mrs Koz.'

'I don't think you'll ever do that, dear. And interfering can be a good thing sometimes. I certainly do think it worth you going to see him. After all, it's not like he knows that your sister is with you so he could approach her himself, and I know it might not seem right but you don't have to tell Caroline what you're actually up to, do you? You don't have to tell her husband either. You could just go to see him, pretending you're paying your sister a visit, and suss matters out for yourself, so to speak.'

Kacie gnawed her bottom lip in contemplation. 'Yes, I could, couldn't I? And if my going does manage to save her marriage then it's worth it, isn't it?'

'Be worth it to save yours,' Verna said meaningfully.

'Eh?'

'My dear, marriages are fragile at the best of times and your sister outstaying her welcome could certainly put a strain on yours if you're not careful. It does sound to me like it's already beginning to.'

'Mrs Koz, I appreciate your concern but it'd take a lot more than accommodating my sister for a while to come between me and Dennis. But I do think you have a point in me going to see Malcolm. I could go tonight.' Then she frowned deeply.

'What's wrong, dear?'

'Eh? I'm sure we're supposed to be doing something tonight, but for the life of me I can't think what it is, so it can't be that important, can it? Anyway, I've made my mind up. I'll go and see Malcolm tonight before I go home.'

'I'll keep my fingers crossed all goes well. Now, dear,' said Verna, placing her empty cup back in its saucer, 'two things I need to discuss with you.'

'Oh?'

She laughed at the look on Kacie's face. 'Don't look so worried, dear. Neither of them is sinister. Firstly, and I should have mentioned this to you several weeks ago but it completely slipped my mind, what with Jan taking unwell again, but Wella are having a competition evening a week on Friday at the Bell Hotel and, of course, anybody who's anybody will be sending their best stylist as it's quite prestigious. I've entered you for two sections.'

'Two!'

'Yes, and you'll win them easily, Kacie.'

'I'm glad you have that much confidence 'cos I'd hate to disappoint you. I haven't entered a competition since my college days.'

'Then it's about time you did. This'll be good publicity for the salon, Kacie, and we need all we can get in consideration of this new salon opening. The *Leicester Mercury* is covering it as well as the hairdressing journals.'

Kacie inwardly groaned, thinking of all the practice she'd need to make sure she was up to scratch with the latest techniques. 'So what sections have you entered me for?'

'The one entitled "The Professional Woman", the other "Creative Evening Styles".'

'Oh, nothing simple then.'

'Don't be sarcastic, Kacie. As I've said, it's nothing you can't handle. Now you could use Diane for one of your models and I'm sure you have a friend who'll be delighted to be the other. What about Brenda?'

'I could ask her.'

'Good. Now I picked up some hair mags for you to get some ideas,' Verna said, pushing a pile over. 'You've nearly a fortnight to decide what you're going to do. When you get some firm ideas you could run them past me, if you like. Now to the other matter. I wonder if you'd mind handling the salon on your own on Saturday morning as my sister had decided to pay me a visit from Northampton. I haven't seen her for an age and it appears she's got some business in Leicester and wants to pop in. I've checked the appointment book and we're fairly evenly spread so do you think you'll manage?'

'If I can do two perms, a tint and a trim all together then I can manage anything.'

Verna frowned. 'When did you do that?'

Kacie realised she was about to land Diane right in it. 'Oh, I didn't. But I'm sure I could if I was pushed. Yes, of course I'll manage. I've just realised how important it is to keep on friendly terms with my sister and you must with yours. I'd be delighted to help out so you can see her.'

Verna smiled gratefully. 'I knew I could rely on you, Kacie.'

Chapter Seven

Early that evening, Kacie rapped purposefully on the door of Caroline's marital home. As she waited for an answer she glanced around her. The garden was neat and tidy, not a weed in sight amongst the carefully arranged shrubs and perennials, and every blade of grass on the patch of lawn appeared to be trimmed to exactly the same length. The nets at the windows were snow-white, the folds evenly spaced. They were expensive nets too, unlike the cheap market end-of-roll ones that hung in her own flat.

Kacie was immediately struck by how tired, drawn and over-weight Malcolm looked when he opened the door, and her heart went out to him. She judged he was obviously missing his wife dreadfully.

His small grey eyes flashed quickly over his visitor before snapping at her brusquely, 'You're late. I was expecting you at six. It's now a quarter to seven.'

She stared at him, taken aback. 'Pardon?'

He issued an irritated sigh. 'Look, just come in. I've my dinner on the stove and I'm in the middle of trying to iron a shirt for work tomorrow. Leave your shoes inside the door.'

'Pardon?'

'Shoes,' he said, pointing at her feet.

She looked at him, shocked. 'You want me to take off my shoes?'

'I've no intention of having my carpets ruined by your stilettos,' he said, turning from her and heading off down the passage.

Slipping off her shoes, hoping her feet didn't smell after the busy day she had had in the hot salon, she obediently followed him down the thickly carpeted hallway and on into the lounge. There, she automatically cast her eyes around. Her mother hadn't exaggerated. The room was indeed like one of those pictured in women's magazines as a modern 1959 house, and was like nothing she had ever been in before. She knew of no one who could afford to deck their homes out with such up-to-date, quality furniture and accessories. But what struck Kacie most was that, like the front garden, this room was so neat and tidy, as though no one actually lived here.

The cushions adorning the black vinyl suite her mother had told her about were placed just so, the lava lamp on the occasional table at the side of the settee matched the colour of the cushions. Modern pictures on the walls were hung perfectly square. Ornaments were few but tasteful and placed just right to catch the eye. And as well as a radio, they had a television.

Kacie realised Malcolm was talking to her. She turned her attentions fully to him. 'I'm sorry, what were you saying?'

He smiled at her. It was a satisfied smile. 'You're admiring the room. Yes, it is nice and so is the rest of the house. I'd be obliged, though, if you'd put everything back exactly where you found it and be careful when handling the ornaments. They are expensive, some of them heirlooms. Breakages will be docked from your wages. Now I'd like a good going-over once a week and I expect corners to be done. I will inspect, so be warned. I want my bed linen changed once a fortnight and fresh towels put out every other day. We'll discuss meal arrangements, my likes and dislikes in a minute, but first the laundry.' He noticed the look on her face and frowned. 'You do do laundry?'

As he had addressed her, Kacie, wondering what on earth he was going on about, was staring at him blankly. 'My own, yes,' she answered.

He gave an exasperated sigh. 'I asked the agency to send me someone who'll do everything. If you don't do laundry then you're not what I requested and you're no good to me.'

Oh, so that was it. Malcolm was assuming she had come about a job. She felt a deep warming to this man. He had taken stock of himself; he must have, to consider employing a domestic to help Caroline around the house. Maybe that was so she could join some of the women's organisations that Malcolm had refused to allow her to join before, saying that time spent there was time she should be spending looking after him. It was just like Verna had suggested. His wife's abrupt departure had resulted in him taking a long hard look at his marriage and he was sorting matters to make Caroline's life far more fulfilling. She gave him a warm smile. 'I'm not from the agency,' she said.

He scowled, bewildered. 'You're not? Then who are you?'

'Don't you recognise me, Malcolm? No, I expect you wouldn't, all things considered. I'm Caroline's sister.'

He gawped at her, shocked. 'Oh! Oh, I, er . . . recognise you now.' Kacie knew he was lying, but didn't pass comment. 'Why are you here?' he asked, frowning.

Her mind raced frantically, mentally scolding herself for not having the foresight to think of a plausible excuse for her visit. She had automatically thought that the door would be opened to her and she would be asked in for a cup of tea, not mistaken for a daily. But then she should have expected her brother-in-law's reaction, as the last time he'd seen her was over three years ago, and that was only briefly at her wedding. Then it came to her: she would take the same approach that Caroline had. After all, it had worked for her. 'I've come to make amends with Caroline. Well, it's silly this situation between us. After all, we are sisters and we're adults now, not children. I thought I'd make the first move by coming to see her.'

'Oh, I see,' he said, raking his hand through his thinning hair. 'Well, I'm sorry you've had a wasted journey as she's not here.'

Kacie acted surprised at this news. 'Oh, will she be long? I can wait,' she said, determined not to leave until she had accomplished her task.

'Yes, she could be. She's, er . . . gone off to one of her meetings. Women's Voluntary or Institute, something like that.'

Kacie planted a look of acute disappointment on her face. 'Oh dear, and I'd set my heart on talking to her.' She then smiled at him winningly. 'I don't mind waiting. You and me could have a chat and, in the meantime, Caroline might return.'

To her utter bewilderment she watched his face twist into a look of contempt. 'Yes, she might grace us with her presence,' he snarled sarcastically. 'But I wouldn't advise you to be here when she does.'

Kacie's mouth fell open at his venomous tone and she was shocked at how swiftly his whole persona had changed from someone she had thought to be deeply distressed at the terrible situation that had befallen him, to one filled with anger. 'I beg your pardon?' she uttered, astounded.

With narrowed eyes, he thrust his face into hers, growling thunderously, 'I don't believe your cock-and-bull story of wanting to be sisterly. I doubt you know the meaning of the word. You've come to cadge something. Money, I expect. Well, you've wasted your time. Apart from the fact I'm not in the habit of playing banker to family or otherwise, for your information your dear sister has left, the stupid woman.'

Although outraged by his totally unfounded accusation, Kacie still managed to appear shocked by the news that her sister had departed. 'Caroline has left you? Why?'

'Because she doesn't have the sense to know a good thing when she's got it, that's why,' he snarled, his face growing purple as his anger intensified. 'I plucked her out of that hovel she lived in with your parents and gave her the kind of life other women in her position would grab at.'

Kacie gawped, fishlike. 'Hovel! How dare you refer to my parents' home—'

'How dare I?' he erupted. 'You might not think it a hovel but compared to where I come from and this house, it is. Obviously you're as ignorant as your sister in your appreciation of fine things. How many women do you know who have such furniture to clean? And as for clothes, how many do you know who have husbands who pick a respectable wardrobe for them to wear? Which didn't come cheap,' he added.

'Well, maybe Caroline wanted to pick her own clothes,' Kacie said defensively.

'Caroline pick her own clothes?' he repeated incredulously. He mockingly looked Kacie over. 'Before I got hold of her, Caroline's dress sense was worse than yours.'

Kacie knew she looked perfectly respectable in her black Capristyle pants and pink gingham checked blouse, and at his unjust remark her temper flared. 'Now just a minute—'

'No, you listen to me,' Malcolm growled, wagging a warning finger. 'Your sister wanted for nothing, but was she grateful? Was she hell. She had the nerve to leave me a note on the mantel saying I'd treated her badly and that she was leaving me. How dare she? Well, I tell you this, she won't have it so easy when she decides to come crawling back. Oh, no. I'll be keeping a tight rein on her in future. If I'd realised how selfish she was then I would never have married her.' He smirked maliciously. 'But then I haven't decided I want Caroline back yet. She wasn't particularly good at anything she did. Fancy ironing creases down shirtsleeves. And the number of times I've had to remind her that I like my vegetables with a bite in them, not soggy like she dishes up. And she's always moving things around when she knows I expect everything to be left when I put it.'

He suddenly stopped his tirade and eyed her contemptuously. 'I expect you're delighted to hear this news. I expect you're as jealous as hell that Caroline managed to make herself such a good bargain when she married me. Unlike you, eh, who married a man who can't even afford to keep you at home where you should be, not out working. Nor can he rent somewhere decent, let alone actually buy his own house and furnish it like I have.'

Clenching her fists in an effort to control her rage, Kacie eyed him coldly. 'Far from it, I was thinking how lucky I am to have married a man who loves me and treats me with respect. Not like you, eh? All you wanted was a dumb housekeeper. I'm glad to hear Caroline has had the sense to leave you. My sister and I never hit it off, but regardless, I was happy for her, thinking that she'd married such a nice man. I was wrong. You're not nice at all. You're just a bully. It's a pity Caroline didn't see through you before she tied herself to you. She's well shot of you and if she's any sense she'll never come back. And you be warned,' she cried, wagging a menacing finger at him. 'If Caroline applies for a divorce and you contest it, I'll personally tell your employers, neighbours and everyone else the truth about you, how you virtually kept my sister a prisoner in her own home, her sole purpose in life drudging for you. By the time I've finished you'll never hold your head up in this town again.' She suddenly stopped and sniffed the air. 'Is that your dinner burning?' She gave a laugh, then spinning round, head held high, she marched out of the house, grabbing her shoes en route and slamming the door shut behind her.

So consumed was she by her encounter with Malcolm, it wasn't until she had almost arrived home that the damage she could have caused hit full force. After her choice words to her sister's husband there was a good possibility she had ruined any hope of a reconciliation, should Caroline have wished it. But she was glad that she had given that awful man a piece of her mind. From what Kacie had witnessed, Caroline hadn't been exaggerating, but actually had been very conservative in her description of him.

Malcolm Pargiter was a thoroughly nasty piece of work and it was her opinion that her sister was well justified in wanting a divorce, and to hell with the stigma that would bring.

Caroline jumped up from the chair the moment Kacie shut the front door on entering the flat.

'Oh, there you are, Kacie. I was worried because you're so late. I hope your dinner isn't ruined. I've cooked you a nice piece of liver and fried onions.'

Caroline's delight at her appearance was not lost on Kacie, and it heightened the guilt she was feeling for what she'd just done. As she stripped off her coat she debated for several seconds whether to come clean or not, then, deeply concerned about how her sister would react, decided against it, shoving it all to the back of her mind.

She smiled at Caroline. 'That sounds grand. I'm sorry I'm late – got waylaid at work and I'm that hungry I could eat a scabby cat. Not that what you dish up resembles that,' she hurriedly added, remembering Malcolm's unwarranted ridicule of her sister's cooking. 'I think you're a grand cook, nearly as good as me,' she added, a mischievous twinkle sparkling her eyes. 'Has Dennis eaten yet?' Kacie asked as she hung her coat on the rack on the wall just inside the door.

'Er . . . yes, and he's already gone out.' Caroline gnawed her bottom lip anxiously. 'Had you forgotten him and the Vipers are playing at the pub again tonight? Dennis is expecting you there, Kacie, but you've already missed the start. It's gone eight.'

Her face fell. 'Oh God, so that's what I was supposed to be doing tonight,' she uttered, mortified. 'By the time I eat my dinner and get myself ready I'll not only have missed the start but possibly the end too.' She sighed resignedly. 'Oh, never mind, I'm sure Dennis won't miss me for one night, and to be honest I could do with soaking my feet in a bowl of hot salt water. They're killing me,' she said, thankfully slipping off her stilettos.

Caroline smiled warmly as she pushed her unflattering glasses further back on her nose. 'Dennis will understand, Kacie, I'm sure he will. And I'm glad you're not going out because there's something I want to talk to you about.' Before Kacie could ask on what subject, Caroline was heading off into the kitchen. 'Sit yourself at the table and I'll bring your dinner through,' she called.

'That was delicious,' Kacie said a while later as she placed down her knife and fork and pushed away her plate. 'I can never get my liver so tender, so how did you do it?'

Caroline shrugged. 'I've no idea. I just threw it in the frying pan. Oh, but I did soak it in milk first as it does help to make it tender.'

'Oh, that's a new one on me. I'll do that in future. Will you sit down?' she ordered as Caroline jumped up and was busying herself collecting Kacie's used dishes.

'But I was going to make you a fresh pot of tea.'

'The tea can wait, so can clearing the table. You wanted to tell me something, so sit down and tell me.'

Face grave, Caroline tightly clenched her hands and sank back down on to her chair. Taking a deep breath, she raised her head. 'I've . . . I've decided to go back to Malcolm.'

This was the last thing Kacie had expected to hear, or wanted to after what she had just done. But far more of a worry for her was the thought of her sister returning to such a terrible life. Malcolm had treated his wife badly before her visit; there was no telling how diabolically he would treat her after Kacie's interference.

Before she could check herself she blurted, 'But why in God's name do you want to go back to living like that? I mean, I know he's your husband, Caroline, but he's just a bully, he's treated you awful, and his mother sounds as bad. Malcolm's not ever going to let you have any life to speak of except drudging for him. He's not changed, Caroline. People so full of themselves like he is don't, believe me. Your house is lovely but it's so . . . so . . . unlived in. I doubt a speck of dust is allowed to land before Malcolm is barking orders for you to gut the place out. How can you possibly want to go back? You just can't,' she cried.

Caroline eyed her suspiciously. 'Have you . . .? No, I'm being silly.'

Horrified at her outburst, Kacie gulped and asked worriedly, 'Have I . . . er . . . what?'

Caroline mentally shook herself. 'I'm being stupid. By the way you spoke it crossed my mind that you must have been to see Malcolm and see for yourself his true side.'

'Eh! Oh, no, no,' she lied. 'I'm just going on what you've told me.'

She gave a wry smile. 'I painted a very vivid picture then, didn't I? Anyway, it doesn't matter what he's like. I've no choice, Kacie. I have to go back.'

'No, you don't.'

Caroline's eyes filled with sadness. 'But I do. I can't stay here for ever. In fact I'm already worried I've outstayed my welcome.' Her eyes filled with tenderness. 'I have enjoyed being here with you and Dennis, I can't tell you how much. I can't remember the last time I've felt so . . . so happy and at peace with myself, but I know it can't go on. You want your flat back to yourselves and I'm not too blind to realise that Dennis goes out a lot more to practise with the band since I arrived, because I'm getting in the way, and I don't blame him. He married you, not you and your sister. Please don't suggest I go back to Mam and Dad. I doubt they'll even speak to me after what I've done.'

Kacie pulled a face. 'I'd never suggest that, Caroline. You could no more go back there than I ever could. I tell you something, Caroline, when I have children me and Dennis will back them in anything they do and, should they make mistakes, then we'll be there to pick up the pieces, not make them feel like criminals like Mam and Dad made us feel.'

'Yes, that's how parents should be, isn't it?' Caroline said wistfully. 'I've always wanted children but I have to say I'm thankful now Malcolm and me never had any.'

'Yeah, but you never know, in the future you could meet some lovely chap and have a houseful.'

Caroline gave a distant smile. 'That would be nice, but after my experience with Malcolm if I'm ever lucky enough to meet someone who I know will treat me properly I still won't commit myself to him until I'm absolutely sure. Anyway, that's the future and it's now I'm worried about. I've nowhere else to go so, whether I like it or not, I have to go back to Malcolm.'

Face set stern, Kacie folded her arms, rested them on the table and leaned forward. 'Now you listen to me, Sis. Dennis hasn't said a word about you getting in the way. I admit the flat is small and sometimes we get on top of one another but we're managing, aren't we, and we can manage for a while longer. Dennis is going out more because he *is* practising with the band, not because *you're* getting in the way.' She grinned, a twinkle of amusement in her eyes. 'Let's face it, they do need to keep practising if they're going to become the famous pop stars they reckon they are.'

'But it's not just that, Kacie. I know I acted so full of bravado when I first came here and said I didn't give a damn what I'd done to Malcolm, but since then it's been preying so heavily on my mind. It's unforgivable of me, walking out like that. What will people think of him when they find out his wife has left him? It could affect his promotion at work – you know what bosses are like about that sort of thing. The shame this will—'

'Shame!' Kacie exclaimed. 'It's no more than a man like him deserves, treating his wife like he did. Do you think he's losing sleep over what he's done to you or how people will treat you when they find out you've left your husband?'

'No, I don't suppose so,' she said softly.

'No, neither do I. You told me when you first arrived that all he'd be concerned about was that you weren't there to do for him. Well, in that case let Malcolm pay someone to clean his immaculate palace and wash his dirty underpants and hopefully he'll treat them a damn sight better than he ever treated you. But I doubt it,' she added, remembering her encounter with him. 'You'll go back to that man over my dead body. Now you're staying put until you get yourself sorted, and that's that.'

Caroline looked at her gratefully. 'Are you sure, Kacie?'

'Positive.' And she added, grinning mischievously, 'I only wish you'd brought your television with you when you left.'

Caroline was frowning puzzled. 'Television? What television?'

Kacie eyed her as though she was stupid. 'The one in your . . .' Her voice tailed off as it suddenly struck her she was about to divulge the fact she had visited her marital home. 'Er . . . didn't you tell me you had one?' she said lightly.

'No. Definitely not a television. Malcolm wouldn't allow such a thing. His opinion is that televisions are an unnecessary evil, the programmes transmitted nothing but drivel aimed at the lower classes. Besides, he said he wasn't going to pay out good money just so I could sit all day watching it when I should be occupied elsewhere.'

Kacie's eyes narrowed, disgustedly. 'He did, did he? So you think Malcolm would never consider getting one?'

'Oh, no. Definitely not.'

'Mmm.' Kacie mouthed, fighting hard to keep her own counsel. The bastard, she thought, guessing that as soon as Caroline had departed he had gone out and purchased this *unnecessary evil* and was glued in front of it at every opportunity. This revelation made her even more determined Caroline was not going back. She raised her head and looked her sister in the eye. 'What exactly have you done towards getting yourself a job and somewhere of your own to live?'

Caroline's face filled with shame. 'Nothing,' she whispered.

'Why not?'

'I can't, Kacie,' she answered softly.

Kacie was bemused. 'What do you mean, you can't?'

Caroline anxiously gnawed her bottom lip. 'I tried, Kacie, believe me, but I can't summon the courage.' She took a deep breath, clasping her hands nervously. 'Malcolm made me feel so useless.

71

He was always criticising everything I did and now I feel I can't do anything right. I feel safe and secure in your flat, Kacie, but going out into the world scares me to death at the moment. I don't mind shopping for you and Dennis, but the thought of attending an interview for a job fills me with dread. I'd never get through it, and I know that anyone considering employing me would think me a blithering idiot.' She gave a helpless shrug. 'And besides, what could I offer them? I haven't been near a typewriter for years. I doubt I could type one sentence correctly, let alone a full letter.'

'Don't be silly,' Kacie scolded. 'Of course you could. It's like riding a bike, isn't it, you never forget? You might be a bit rusty at first but it wouldn't take long for you to get back into the swing of it. Anyway, I thought you wanted to work in a newsagent's?'

'I did. It was my dream.'

'Then forget office work. You hated it anyway. I bet there's newsagents all over the place that would grab at someone like you behind their counters.'

'I wish I had your confidence.'

'Confidence be buggered. If I was in your position where I had the choice of returning to a life of misery or summoning up the courage to attend a few interviews then I know which way I'd go. You can't give up just like this, Caroline. It took a lot of courage to do what you did, now all you have to do is summon it again but for different reasons this time.' She eyed her sister. 'Answer me truthfully, do you really want to go back to Malcolm?'

Caroline shook her head vehemently. 'The thought makes me cringe.'

'Then get out there and get a job. After that you'll have the money to rent a place of your own. I'll help you.'

'Help me? You've given me more than enough as it is. Anyway, how will you help me get a job?' Then a thought struck her. 'You're not thinking of attending the interviews with me, are you?'

'That's an idea,' Kacie said, laughing. 'You'd be bound to get it if I came along and did the talking for you. But you're quite capable of talking for yourself. As I said, you just need some confidence and that's what I'm going to help you get.'

Caroline eyed her quizzically. 'How?'

'For a start,' she said, scanning her over, 'I could do wonders with your hair. And your clothes don't exactly do anything for you, Caroline, except make you look years older. Sorry if I'm being blunt,' she added.

Caroline gave a wan smile. 'You speak the truth, Kacie. What I wear might be top quality but I know the styles make me look like an old frump. But I can't afford to come to the salon or buy new clothes. The few pounds I brought with me are nearly gone,' she added softly.

'Who said anything about either? A woman doesn't need Lady Docker's hundreds of thousands to make her look good. I do quite a bit of home hairdressing, but for God's sake don't mention that to Mrs Koz when you get to meet her, though I'm sure she suspects, as all hairdressers moonlight for a few extra shillings. But anyway, I don't charge family. As for clothes, if I remember right you're a dab hand with the sewing machine.'

'I am, or I used to be before I married.'

'Same as typing, it's like riding a bike. Mrs C, Dennis's mother, will be glad to lend us her old treadle. You can buy material off the market and run yourself up some new gear. I'm no good at sewing but I can pin a pattern to fabric and cut it out. When you're working the first thing you can do is save some money towards a new pair of specs. We'll have you looking a million dollars in no time.'

Kacie noticed Caroline's doubtful look. 'Oi,' she scolded, 'have faith in yourself. If I tell you you'll look a million dollars by the time we've finished, then you will.'

Caroline stared at her for a moment, then her face split with a happy smile. 'OK, Kacie. I'm in your hands.' Then her face clouded, worried. 'But . . .'

'But what?' Kacie demanded.

'I was just going to mention Dennis. Don't you think you ought to ask him if it's all right if I stay a bit longer?'

Caroline was right, Kacie should discuss this with Dennis, but she felt sure he'd be in agreement under the circumstances and, after all, it wasn't for ever. 'You didn't think of him when you arrived out of the blue the other week so why now?' Kacie said, tongue in cheek.

'I know, and really that was unforgivable of me, but I wasn't thinking straight. All I could think of was getting away from Malcolm before I went completely doolally, and you were the only one I could turn to.'

'I'm glad you did,' Kacie said. 'Leave Dennis to me. He's OK about you being here, really, so don't give it another thought. Right,' she said, rising from her chair, 'get a towel and pull the chair out under the light.'

'Why?' Caroline asked bewildered.

'You want your hair doing, don't you? I'll just get my scissors,' Kacie said, looking around for her handbag.

'You have them with you?'

Kacie spotted her handbag at the side of the armchair, picked it up and rifled through it for her scissors. She pulled them out and waved then at her sister. 'Caroline, a hairdresser's precious tools of her trade never leave her side, as they have a habit of disappearing. A hairdresser's scissors are like a new bed, not that I've ever had one, but you have to get used to them, bed them in, so to speak, as each pair is unique and has its own peculiarities. Besides, my scissors cost me ten pounds to buy when I qualified and I can't afford to replace them.'

'Oh, Kacie. Oh, Kacie,' was all Caroline could murmur when she scrutinised herself in the mirror a while later. 'I look a different person. I can't believe it's me.'

'Do you like it?'

'I love it,' Caroline cried jubilantly. 'Kacie, it's wonderful. I can face the world looking like this. What's this style called?'

'An urchin cut. I'm glad I was right that it suits your face. Been a bit too late if it hadn't, mind,' she said, grinning. 'You do have the same shaped face as Audrey Hepburn, so I took the chance of styling the fringe like she wears hers.'

'You're so clever, Kacie,' Caroline cried, throwing her arms around her sister and giving her a hug. 'I can't thank you enough.'

'You can, by helping clear up the mess we've made,' she said, surveying the offcuts of her sister's hair scattered on the floor. She looked across at the clock. It was just after ten thirty. 'In fact, if you don't mind I'll leave you to it. I'll walk down and meet Dennis and see how they got on tonight.'

'I don't mind at all, Kacie. It's the least I can do. I'll have the kettle boiling for when you get back.'

Dennis was just saying his goodbyes to the rest of the band when she arrived at his side outside the back entrance of the pub where the band had not long finished their stint.

'See you Friday night then, seven o'clock sharp,' Jed was saying to Dennis as the pair loaded the last piece of his drum kit into the back of the old rusting Commer van they had borrowed for the night from Jed's brother, who worked as a carpet fitter. 'I can't wait meself, mate. We'll go down a storm, you see if we don't.' Jed

74

slapped Dennis on the back. 'Here's to stardom, eh?' he said excitedly, eyes shining.

'Too right,' Dennis replied, equally elated, slapping him back.

'You've got another gig?' Kacie asked Dennis, delighted, linking her arm through his.

He spun his head to face her. 'Eh? Oh, hello, D— Kacie,' he said, planting a kiss on her lips. 'No, not exactly.' His face was wreathed in excitement and, unlinking his arm from hers, he placed both hands on her shoulders, beaming into her face. 'You know how you've always wanted to go to Butlin's? Well, how do you fancy going with all the gang this weekend?'

She stared at him, stunned, as what he said sank in. Then her face lit, thrilled. 'Butlin's!' she exclaimed, jumping up and down, clapping her hands in glee. 'Really? Oh, Dennis, you know how long I've wanted to go there. If all the rest of the crowd are going we'll have a brilliant time. I hope Brenda will lend me her polka-dot bikini. I've heard they have some smashing games around the pool. And the dancing – they say the dance halls are all decked out in different themes, and I think the one in Skeggy is Hawaiian,' she said, wriggling her hips hoola hoola style. 'Me and you can enter the rock-and-roll contest. Apparently they have some great bands playing. I wonder who's on when we're there? Hey, maybe they'll let you and the boys play a few songs. Oh, I can't wait . . .' Her voice trailed off as a worrying thought suddenly struck and her face contorted questioningly. 'Hang on a minute. How are we going to afford it? Unless you've won the pools and haven't told me?'

'I wish. I . . . er . . . thought you wouldn't mind dipping in to your table fund.'

'Dipping in!' she exclaimed. 'You mean using all of it and more besides.'

'Yeah, well, we can somehow cut back to find the extra. Besides, it's all in, so no extras like food to find. Jed's brother has just come back from the camp in Skeggy and told him about the talent contests they have. Apparently the one they're holding this week-end is so big they come from all over to take part and, best of all, talent scouts might be there.'

She shook her head at him, pretending annoyance. 'I should have realised there'd be an ulterior motive.'

He grinned at her. 'You don't mind, though, do you?'

She laughed. 'No, course not. It'll be great. Me and the other girls will cheer you and the Vipers on that loud you'll be bound to win.' A thought suddenly struck her and she froze. 'Did you say this weekend?'

'Yeah. I know it's short notice but Mrs Koz will let you have the day off, won't she?'

Her face fell. 'Ah . . .'

'Kacie, come in, it's not like you have any time off. Mrs Koz can manage for one day, surely?'

'Well, Saturdays are usually our busiest day and this is not giving her any warning to get help in or juggle the appointments so she and Diane can manage themselves, but apart from that Mrs Koz's sister is coming up from Northampton on Saturday morning and she's asked me to hold the fort so she can see her. I promised her I would.' Her face filled with disappointment. 'Oh, Dennis, I've always wanted to go to Butlin's. Does it have to be this weekend?' she pleaded.

'I've already told you it does. They won't hold another contest like this one until next year, Kacie, so we can't miss out on it. Jed's making the booking first thing tomorrow and apparently you get a large discount for parties over six. They'll be eight of us, so hopefully we'll get it even cheaper. We're all chipping in for the petrol so the weekend won't be that expensive. If you don't come, Kacie, I'll be the only one of the band without their other half. Besides, I want you there.'

She gave a helpless shrug. 'But I can't let Verna down now.'

He looked at her hard. 'But you can me?'

'You're being unfair,' she snapped. Her mind flashed wildly for a moment, desperate for a solution so she could go on the trip. 'Look, if we're not too busy in the afternoon maybe I can get off early and catch the train down. That way I'd still be in time for the contest.'

'We're all cramming in the van to save money,' he snapped, 'and I want you there from the start, not for part of the time.'

Kacie became aware of passers-by taking an interest in their rising voices. 'Can't we discuss this at home in private?'

He gave a grunt. 'How on earth can we discuss anything in private with your sister there?'

She clamped her lips tight, knowing he was right. 'I'll speak to Mrs Koz tomorrow and see what I can do,' she said. Then, thinking it better to change the subject, asked, 'Did it go well tonight?'

'It went great, and if you'd been here you'd have seen for yourself,' he answered sulkily.

Kacie eyed him sharply. 'Don't be like that, Dennis. It's only one gig I've not managed to come to.'

He pouted. 'I suppose. But I missed you.'

'I've missed you too.' And before she could stop herself, she added, 'Now you know how I feel when you go out several times a week, sometimes before I get home from work, and I'm in bed by the time you get back.'

'Yeah, OK, but I have to practise.'

'I know and I don't complain, do I?'

'No, I suppose not. Anyway, you haven't told me why you didn't show tonight? Where were you?' he asked as they began to walk home, side-stepping inebriated stragglers still tumbling out of the pub doors.

She hated lying to Dennis but to tell him the truth would be worse, she felt. 'I got waylaid at the salon.'

'No you didn't. I came to collect you on my way to the pub and it was all closed up.' He stopped and faced her fully. 'So where were you?' he demanded.

She eyed him for a moment. If she continued lying she'd be digging herself a deeper hole. Best to come clean. 'OK, if you want the truth I went to see Malcolm.'

'Malcolm?'

'Caroline's husband.'

'Oh, that Malcolm.' He frowned, bewildered. 'Whatever did you want to go and see him for?'

'Well, I just thought I might help them get back together.'

His eyes lit up. 'And it worked? She's going home?'

Kacie shook her head. 'No.'

He studied her for several long moments. 'You made things between them worse, didn't you?' he accused.

'That was impossible, Dennis. The man's a pig and I'm glad Caroline's left him.'

'That might be so, Kacie, but now Caroline's got her feet under our table. You should have left well alone – if anything, encouraged her to go back.'

She looked at him, astounded. 'Dennis, you don't mean that. My sister's marriage was nothing but misery, and after my visit I saw for myself that it's far worse than ever she made out. She did the right thing in leaving that brute, I've no doubts on that. I thought you didn't mind her staying with us.'

'When I agreed I thought it'd only be for a couple of nights. I've done my best to keep quiet on the subject but, as you mentioned it, she's getting on my nerves, Kacie. She's always there, always running around after us. I can't even put my cup down before she's whipped it away and washed it up. And we haven't made love since she moved in. That's not right, Kacie; it's driving me crazy. She's got to go.'

'Oh, but, Dennis, she can't. I've told her she can stay until she gets a place of her own.'

'You told her what?'

'Dennis, please try to understand. What else could I do, apart from chuck her out on the street?'

'And when is she likely to get herself a job?' he demanded. 'As far as I can tell she's made no effort whatsoever.'

'That's because Malcolm knocked the stuffing out of her. She's lost her confidence, Dennis. Well, lost it is the wrong thing to say. I don't think she's ever had any. But I'm going to help her feel better about herself. I cut her hair tonight. If I say so myself she looks great, a different person. With some decent clothes she'll soon get a job and be out from under our feet, I promise.'

Dennis shook his head doubtfully. 'And how long is soon? In this case as long as a piece of elastic, I imagine. Face it, Kacie, it's gonna be months before this is all settled, and I can't stand the thought of her living with us any longer.'

Kacie couldn't believe she was hearing Dennis talking like this. 'So what do you suggest I do?' she demanded.

'Well, Kacie, let's face it, if you hadn't put your oar in she could have gone back to her husband and, if she was still hellbent on leaving him, done it properly from there instead of dumping herself on us. Sort this out, Kacie, and quick before . . .' His voice tailed off.

'Before what?' she demanded.

Dennis pressed his lips together, knowing he was about to say something he would regret. He stared at his wife. How much he loved her. She was everything to him, and had been from the minute he'd first seen her, and she'd made such sacrifices in respect of her relationship with her parents in order to marry him. She was looking at him, her pretty face contorted, shocked, her brown eyes full of hurt by his seemingly uncompromising attitude towards her sister, whom he knew Kacie wanted so much to help. He didn't begrudge Kacie doing that, he just didn't want it to take place under his own roof. Caroline's presence was disrupting his home life and he didn't like it. Fuelling his annoyance was also his distress that Kacie wasn't going to be able to come with him to Butlin's, wouldn't be beside him as she should be, and in turn he wouldn't be able to give his beloved wife a much-coveted break, which under normal circumstances they wouldn't be able to afford. Also, she wouldn't witness the band's success in the contest, which he felt positive would happen. All things considered, he couldn't help himself but blurt, 'Before I go.'

She gawped at him, shocked. 'You don't mean that?' she gasped.

He took a deep breath. 'I do,' he said stubbornly. 'I can go and stay with Jed or one of the other lads in the band. If Caroline's not gone by the time I get back from Butlin's on Sunday night then it's me that'll be packing my bags and I won't come back until she's gone.'

Kacie's temper flared. 'You might as well go and live with Jed or one of the other lads now then, because, let's face it, you spend more time with them than you do with me through that stupid band of yours. But I really can't believe you're going to go to Butlin's without me,' she cried.

'You won't let people down but you're expecting me to, Kacie. If I don't go then "the stupid band", as you call them, can't enter the contest. I'm the lead singer, remember. You know I want you to come, but if you can't I'm still going. As for your sister, if she won't go back to Malcolm she should go to your parents. At least they have more room than us.'

'We've already covered that ground, Dennis, when Caroline first arrived. You of all people know how my parents can be, and I'm shocked that you'd even consider putting Caroline through the hell you know they would create. They'd never leave her in peace until she went crawling back to Malcolm.' She looked at him searchingly. 'I can't believe you're being so pig-headed about all this, Dennis. I can't believe you're putting me in such a terrible position.'

He shifted uneasily on his feet. He knew he was being unfair but had gone too far to back down now without severely bruising his male pride. 'A wife is supposed to put her husband first, Kacie. You've put your sister and employer before me. I find that hard to accept. Maybe you don't love me as much as you say you do.'

She gasped. 'Oh, Dennis, how could you say that? Against my parents' wishes I married you. If that's not enough to tell you how much I love you then I don't know what is. And in all the time we've been together I've never refused you anything before now. I'd

79

love to go to Butlin's, you know that, and don't you think I want our flat back to ourselves? But I've promised to help my sister and I've promised Verna to take charge of the salon on Saturday morning. It's not fair that you're asking me to let them down when you won't consider letting your friends down.'

Face stony, he stared at her. 'You seem to have made your choice so I might as well pack my bags now, mightn't I?'

She stared at him, unable to believe that meeting her husband for a leisurely walk home together was ending so disastrously. Did Dennis really mean what he had said? He couldn't possibly – he loved her, he was bluffing, had to be. She was so upset she obstinately said, 'If that's what you want.'

He had thought she'd back down and the shock that she hadn't, stunned him rigid. Spinning on his heel he stalked off in the direction of their flat, leaving her gawping after him.

'Why is Dennis packing his holdall?' Caroline whispered to Kacie as she entered the flat a short while after Dennis. 'And he seems to be in such a bad mood, which is not like him. He never said a word to me when he came in, just stormed into the bedroom and began banging about. I'd made some sandwiches and a pot of tea, thinking he'd be hungry after the show tonight.'

Kacie froze. Dennis really was carrying out his threat. A rush of dread mixed with pain and hurt filled her being. This wasn't happening. It was a nightmare. Any minute Dennis would realise how stupid he was acting and relent, come through, grinning boyishly at her as he always did when he'd done something he knew she'd be annoyed about, and apologise.

She was to be cruelly disappointed. Next she knew, he came storming out of the bedroom, bulging holdall slung over his shoulder, his stage attire on a hanger over his arm, and, without even acknowledging her or Caroline, strode out of the flat, slamming the door as he went.

Bewildered, Caroline looked in horror at her deathly pale sister. She desperately wanted to know what had caused Dennis to act so uncharacteristically but thought it best to sit Kacie down before she collapsed. 'I'll pour you a cuppa,' she said, taking Kacie's arm and guiding her to the living room.

'Thanks,' Kacie uttered gratefully as Caroline put a mug of sweet tea in her hands a short while later. 'It's just a tiff,' she said, looking up at her sister through watery eyes.

Caroline's experiences of life were not so limited that she didn't realise whatever was behind the scene tonight had not been caused by a mere tiff but thought it best not to pass comment. 'Well, in that case it will soon blow over,' she said lightly.

'Yes, it will,' a subdued Kacie replied. She awkwardly rose, placing her cup on the table. 'I'm going to bed, if you don't mind, Caroline. I'll see you in the morning.'

Sleep did not come easily to Kacie. Since they had married, this was the first night she had not shared her bed with Dennis, and on top of the terrible despair she was suffering, she felt lost and lonely, cocooned inside the great folds of the lumpy old mattress.

She reached over, grabbed Dennis's pillow and pulled it to her, burying her face in it. Odours of him still lingered, and fat tears of desolation rolled down her face. 'Oh, Dennis,' she sobbed. 'How could you leave me?' Where was he? Had he gone to Kevin or one of the other lads, as he'd threatened to, or to his mother's, or was he aimlessly roaming the dark, deserted streets, wanting to come home but pride stopping him? Was he as upset as she was at what had taken place between them, the hurtful words they had shouted at each other. 'Please come home, Dennis,' she chokingly whispered.

She convulsed into sobs again, which took an age to subside. Finally cried out, she began to think with a certain amount of logic. Knowing how much he loved her, she realised Dennis would be as upset about this situation as she was. He would come to the salon tomorrow, tail between his legs, his boyish smile splitting his face, eyes filled with tender love, and beg her forgiveness. Then she in turn would beg his, and they would fall into each other's arms, hug each other tightly, and sort out this mess. Yes, that's what would happen, because neither of them would allow such a silly disagreement to come between them.

With this happier thought she finally fell into a fitful sleep.

Chapter Eight

But Dennis did not appear the next day as Kacie had hoped, nor the day after, and by the time Saturday morning arrived she had not seen or heard from him.

'Ouch, that 'urt, Kacie, ducky. A' yer tryin' ter scalp me? I've 'ardly any 'air as it is, wi'out you pulling out what's left.'

At the boom of Mrs Addison's baritone voice, Kacie jumped, jerked from her private thoughts, every one of which was centred on her terrible situation. 'Oh, I'm sorry,' she apologised to the large lady whose fine greying hair she was in the process of styling. Trying to force herself to concentrate she finished what she was doing and held a mirror at the back of the woman's head so she could check her handiwork. 'All right for you, is it?' she asked.

'Mmm,' Mrs Addison mouthed in a displeased tone. 'It's OK, I suppose, but not up ter yer usual, me duck.'

'Isn't it?' Kacie frowned, dismayed, and on closer inspection agreed entirely with Mrs Addison's opinion. Her work was passable but not up to her usual high standard. 'Let me dress you out again,' she offered, as she fished her tail comb back out of her overall pocket.

The old lady vehemently shook her head, 'No thanks, Kacie. You've pulled and tugged me 'air enough for one day. I'll mek do with this, if yer don't mind,' she said, rising and undoing the coverall placed on every client by way of protection. 'It's not as though I'm going anywhere special, just off ter bingo tonight, and whether me 'air looks posh or not don't mek no difference to me luck. I ain't won 'ote fer weeks.' Handing Kacie the coverall, Ivy Addison leaned over and whispered in Kacie's ear, 'I guess it's yer curse time that's put you outta sorts. I understand, me duck, as I suffered for years. Could've killed my old man when *that* time came around each month. To be honest I could 'ave killed 'im when it wasn't me monthly time too.' She gave a toothless grin. 'Good job

83

'e passed on early, else there was a danger I'd 'ave spent me old age banged up for murder. Oh, he was a bisom, was my old man. Drive a saint to drink, 'e would've. I wonder who 'e's tormentin' up there,' she said, casting her eyes upwards. 'Whoever it is, I pity the poor beggars, really I do. Anyway, must be letting you get on and I'll see yer in a fortnight.'

Despite her wretchedness, Kacie managed a smile. 'Bye, Mrs Addison, and I'll keep my fingers crossed you win the jackpot.'

'Shouldn't waste yer energy, Kacie, ducky. In my experience, luck only happens to those that's either as crooked as a corkscrew, which I'm definitely not, or to those that's led a blameless life, and I've not exactly done that,' she said, winking mischievously. 'Remind me to tell you one day what me and Gladys Islop got up to in the air-raid shelters, but don't tell Gladys I told yer 'cos she likes ter play the lady. But lady she ain't, far from it.' She gave a loud guffaw as she waddled off over to the counter where Diane was waiting to take her money.

When she'd finished with Mrs Addison, Diane, armed with her sweeping brush, came up to Kacie. 'Are you all right?' she asked concernedly.

Kacie spun to face her, annoyed. 'Why does everyone keep asking me that?' she said tartly.

Diane gulped. 'Er . . . 'cos yer don't look as if yer are all right, Kacie. And you're biting everyone's head off, which ain't like you.'

'Well, that's because everyone keeps asking how I am,' she hissed. 'I'm fine, and I won't tell you again. Who's next?' she snapped shortly.

Diane looked across at the clock. 'Mrs Wilson's got another fifteen minutes to go on her perm before she needs rinsing off and the neutraliser applying. Another ten minutes for Mrs Green under the dryer, so that means Mrs Biddles is next.'

'Then you'd better get Mrs Biddles, hadn't you?'

Diane flinched at her abrupt tone. 'Will do, Kacie. Oh, by the way, there's a young gel at the counter asking if someone could trim her hair.'

Kacie sighed, thinking that Mrs Koz's sister could have picked a better day to visit than a busy Saturday morning. 'I can, but she'll have to wait about three-quarters of an hour.'

'I'll ask 'er if she wants ter wait and I'll fetch Mrs Biddles over.'

Kacie was just finishing off Mrs Biddles when the young girl who was waiting patiently for a trim came up to her. 'Could I use your lavy?' she asked.

Concentrating hard on her customer in an effort to avoid any more mishaps that day, her eyes flashed quickly to the girl, then back to her client. 'Yes, certainly. It's through the door at the back, past the stairs and out in the yard. The chain is a bit temperamental so give it a good tug when you've finished. There, Mrs Biddles,' Kacie said, showing her her handiwork. 'All right for you?'

The woman frowned. 'What colour did yer say you were tinting me?'

'Er . . . chestnut, wasn't it?' she said quizzically.

'Well, you should know, ducky, as you're supposed ter be the hairdresser, but if this colour is chestnut then I'm a monkey's uncle. Chestnut is a reddy brown, in'it? This is just brown. In fact the same colour brown as my privy door.'

'Oh!'

'It'll have ter do,' she said crossly, rising from her chair. 'I've no time for you to do me again. I've me meat ter get before the butcher closes fer lunch and me family's descending this afternoon for their tea and I've still baking ter do, but next time I want tinting chestnut that's what I expect to get. I shan't be leaving a tip. I'm sure you understand why.'

As she walked away Kacie inwardly groaned. Everything she was tackling today she was making a muck-up of. If she carried on like this Verna would have no clients left and she'd be out of a job.

Just then the door burst open and Brenda charged in. She stopped in her tracks, eyeing Kacie surprised. 'Hiya. I didn't expect you to be here. I thought you'd already be gone with the rest of 'em last night. Packed like sardines in that old van, so they were.' She gave a chuckle of mirth as a memory rose up. 'It was ever so funny. Jed's cymbals were sticking out the front side window 'cos they couldn't fit everything in the back. Loads turned out to wave 'em off and wish 'em all good luck. Wouldn't it be summat if they won the contest?' She looked at Kacie enquiringly. 'As you weren't there I thought they'd be picking you up on the way, and it crossed my mind how on earth you'd get in, being's the van was packed so tight. Did they forget you or summat?' she asked, laughing.

Kacie's heart plummeted so low at this devastating news she thought it had fallen out of her. As the previous evening had worn on and Dennis hadn't appeared at the flat, her hope of him coming to make amends before the trip had faded, and now what little hope she had left had been brutally dashed. 'Some of us have to work, Brenda,' she said tartly. 'I can't take time off willy-nilly for no good reason.' Then a thought struck. Brenda hadn't mentioned Dennis had been there, not by name. Maybe he hadn't gone after all, maybe he was coming round to the salon later to see her. Her hopes rose as she asked Brenda hesitantly, 'Was, er . . . Dennis there?'

Brenda scowled at her as though she was stupid. 'Be pointless the rest of the band entering a contest wi'out the lead singer, Kacie. Of course he was there. Why are you asking? You should know his whereabouts being's 'e's your old man.'

'Yes, of course I knew he'd gone,' she snapped defensively. 'I'm that busy I'm getting myself all confused, and I was working late last night, that's why I never managed to see them off. What I meant to ask was if Dennis seemed all right.'

Brenda nodded. 'Fine to me. They were all larking about like they do, it's a wonder they got the van packed up and set off in time.'

Kacie's heart thumped painfully. Larking about. That didn't sound as though Dennis had a broken heart. Fighting to control her emotions, Kacie asked abruptly, 'Look, what is it you want, Brenda?'

'Eh? Oh, I wondered if you can fit me in for a shampoo and set?'

'No.'

'What?'

'You heard.'

'I heard but there was no need to be so rude. You can usually fit me in,' she sulked.

'Well, I can't today. I'm run off my feet as it is.' And that was the truth, but in all honesty she didn't want to be here at all. She wanted to be curled up in her bed, to nurse her misery.

'I'll have ter settle for Mrs Koz then, like I thought I was gonna have to when I thought you'd gone off to Butlin's,' Brenda sulked. 'But she ain't half so good as you.'

'Mrs Koz has the morning off and I'm trying to manage here all on my own,' Kacie snapped.

'Oh? Well, can I come around yours tonight and get a foreigner done? I wouldn't ask only Jim's taking me for a meal at the Imperial Hotel. Sounds posh, dunnit, and I wanna look nice. I think . . . Oh, Kacie, I'm hoping Jim's gonna ask me to get engaged so yer will mek me look extra nice, won't yer?'

'No.'

Brenda gawped, astonished. 'Eh?'

'I said, no.'

'No! This in't like you, Kacie. What's up?'

'Nothing's up,' she fumed. 'I just can't do your hair today, that's all – either here or at home.'

Brenda's face contorted angrily. 'Call yerself a friend – well, some bloody friend you are,' she hissed. 'I'll find somewhere that *will* do me hair, then.'

'You do that,' Kacie snapped back.

'Right, then. I will,' she cried as she spun on her heel and stalked off.

Diane came up to her. 'Kacie . . .?'

'For God's sake, Di, what is it now?'

The girl flinched at Kacie's manner. 'I . . . I just wanted to know if yer'd like a cuppa?'

'Oh!' she exclaimed, shame filling her. 'I'm sorry, Di. Yes, please, I'd love one.' She rubbed her aching head. 'Before you put the kettle on can you hold the fort for a minute while I nip upstairs and get some Aspro out of my bag? My head's about to explode.' I hope to God I've got some, she thought as she hurried off.

Kacie was so preoccupied that she had almost reached the small cupboard Verna had provided for the staff to keep their personal belongings in whilst working, when it registered she wasn't alone, and she froze in shock as she spotted someone hunched down, rifling through the open cupboard. The Kacie recognised the girl who was supposed to be waiting to have her hair trimmed and who had asked to use the toilet minutes ago.

The intruder realised she was being observed and jerked round, Kacie's purse clutched in her hand. 'Oh!' she cried, staring wildly at Kacie. 'I . . . I wasn't doing anything.'

'It doesn't look like it,' Kacie replied stonily, her eyes fixed on her purse. She quickly appraised the girl. She looked in dire need of a wash and change of clothes but her youthful face looked honest, which surprised Kacie, considering the situation she had caught her in. 'So that's how you were going to pay for your trim, was it, by stealing from me?'

The girl flashed her eyes to the purse in her hand, then back up to Kacie. 'No.'

'Oh, don't waste your breath,' Kacie hissed. 'I'm in no mood. We'll just see what the bobbies say about this.'

'The police!' the girl exclaimed in horror. 'Oh, no, please don't fetch the rozzers,' she begged, thrusting Kacie's purse towards her. ''Ere, 'ave the bleddy purse.'

Kacie snatched it from her, opened it up and checked the contents, which were practically all of her wages she'd received yesterday morning. It was all still there.

'I ain't taken 'ote,' the girl spat.

'Only because I caught you, you haven't. It's my guess you had no intention of getting your hair trimmed, you saw how busy we were and just waited for the opportunity to find where the staff keep their bags. If I hadn't come up here when I did then you'd've been away with the lot,' she accused.

'I only need a pound, and that's all I'd'a took.'

'Oh, just a pound,' Kacie said sarcastically. 'And I'm supposed to be grateful, am I?' Then out of curiosity, she asked, 'Why just a pound?'

The girl looked at her hard. 'You're a nosy sod, ain't yer? If yer must know I need a pound ter pay fer lodgings fer the week and ter buy some food. If I've got lodgings I can get a job. Nobody'll employee me whilst I've nowhere to live, see.'

Kacie could see the girl's unshed tears and, despite her offensive manner, knew there was more to this situation than met the eye. 'Why have you nowhere to live? You must have family.'

To Kacie's horror the girl's face crumpled. 'Oh, I've family, all right, and some bloody family they are. If yer must know, me dad chucked me out.'

'Chucked you out? Why on earth did he do that?'

The girl sniffed loudly and fixed Kacie in her eyes defiantly. 'If me family don't care a toss for me then why should you?'

Kacie gasped at the harshness of her tone.

'Is everything all right, Kacie?'

Kacie spun round to find Diane behind her, looking suspiciously at the girl. Diane then noticed that Kacie was clutching her purse and the truth of the situation struck her. 'She was stealing your purse, wasn't she? I thought she looked shifty when she came in the salon. I'll fetch the bobbies, Kacie. You leave it ter me.' She made to hurry off.

Kacie grabbed her arm and pulled her to a halt. 'You'll do no such thing. I'll sort this out, Di. You get back down to the salon and tell the customers I won't be long.'

Diane looked at her, astounded. 'But—'

'Di.'

'OK, Kacie, OK.' She eyed the girl darkly. 'But you just call if she starts 'ote.'

Kacie turned her attention back to the girl. 'What's your name?'

'Eh?'

'Your name. I presume you have one.'

'Course I 'ave, but I ain't telling you.'

'Suit yourself but I do want to know why your dad chucked you out. Was it because he caught you stealing from him?'

'No, it wasn't,' she shouted indignantly. 'I ain't never stole 'ote before in me life. Me dad chucked me out 'cos his lady friend didn't like me around after she moved in. She told 'im lies about me. Said I swore at 'er, threw things at 'er and went through 'er stuff.'

'And did you do any of those things?'

'No, I didn't,' the girl fervently denied. 'I wanted to swear at her, 'cos she was an 'orrible old cow, only sucked up to me dad 'cos she was being evicted from 'er home, which she doesn't know I know, but I 'eld me tongue because I didn't want to upset me dad. Silly bugger thinks 'e loves her. If me mam could see what were 'appening she'd be turning in 'er grave.'

Kacie sighed. 'Oh, I see. And is there no hope of patching things up by speaking to your dad?'

'I've tried but 'e teks 'er side. They say love's blind, don't they? Well, it's made me dad deaf as well.'

'Mmm. You say you need the pound to get lodgings and then a job?'

She nodded. 'I do.' Her face filled with shame. 'I didn't want to steal it, misses, but I'd no other choice. No one was going to give it ter me, was they?'

Kacie shook her head. 'No, I suppose not.' She took a deep breath. She could ill afford to lose that amount of money but the girl's plight had touched her. Momentarily she forgot her own terrible trauma, and deep sympathy rose. She opened her purse and took a pound note which she held out towards the girl. 'Just take it and make sure you do with it what you told me.'

The girl's mouth fell open. 'You mean it?' she uttered, snatching the note from Kacie's hand.

Kacie nodded. 'Now skedaddle before I change my mind.'

The girl's face beamed in delight. 'I'll pay yer back, misses.'

'You make sure you do. You know where to find me.'

With that, the girl kicked up her heels and fled across the room. As she reached the doorway near the top of the stairs she stopped and looked back at Kacie. 'Me name's Mel, short fer Melanie.'

With that she was gone.

Diane looked at Kacie worriedly when she returned to the salon a few seconds later. 'That gel went flying outta 'ere like the devil himself was chasing 'er. I tried to stop 'er, Kacie, honest I did, but she wa' too quick fer me.'

'That's all right, Di. I let her go.'

'Yer did?' she said, eyes wide in disbelief. 'Why?'

'Because I did.'

'But she was stealing from yer.'

'I know. But sometimes, Di, due to circumstances beyond our control, we're reduced to doing things that normally we wouldn't. Now I want to hear no more of this and I certainly don't want Mrs Koz hearing about it, OK.'

Diane looked at her for several seconds before sighing resignedly. 'If yer say so, Kacie.'

'I do. Now let's get on.'

Not long after that Dotty Cooper charged through the door, evidently deeply bothered. 'Is it true what I 'eard, our Kacie?' she shouted.

Kacie lifted her head and wearily looked across at her. 'And what's that, Mrs C?'

'That our Dennis 'as gone off ter Butlin's and left you behind?'

Kacie sighed. 'Well, it wasn't quite like that, but yes he has.'

'Well, the little so and so,' his mother fumed. 'What the 'ell does my son think 'e's playin' at, actin' like 'e's a single man?' She came up to Kacie and laid a plump hand on her arm. 'I'll give 'im what for when 'e gets back, don't you worry, gel. I can't believe 'e's done such a thing. I really can't.'

Kacie pulled her mother-in-law out of earshot of the array of customers whom she knew all hoped to hear some juicy gossip. 'Dennis had no choice but to go without me, Mrs C,' she said in hushed tones. 'I couldn't get away from work at such short notice and Dennis couldn't let the band down. If he hadn't gone then the band couldn't have entered the contest.'

Dotty gave a haughty sniff. 'Mmm, I suppose. But, all the same, I can see that you ain't exactly 'appy about him goin'. It's my guess you didn't sleep much last night.' Her shrewd eyes scrutinised her

90

daughter-in-law closely. 'Is there anything you ain't tellin' me, gel? Is there more to this?'

'No, no,' Kacie lied, not wanting to upset her beloved mother-in-law unnecessarily by divulging the awful row they had had, which would all be forgotten once Dennis returned. 'I didn't sleep much because I missed him, and that's natural, isn't it?'

'Mmm, I suppose. But I still don't think it's right. If Dennis's dad had gone off anywhere wi'out me he'd not have lived to tell the tale. You know what they say about Butlin's, don't yer? Drunken parties, and people ending up in others' chalets. Men easily get led astray, yer know, by young hussy types 'ellbent on a good time.'

'You listen to too much gossip, Mrs C. I've heard of Butlin's reputation too but I happen to think it's been blown out of proportion. Dennis wouldn't do anything like that to me. Besides, the other lads girlfriends are with them, so they're not going to let anything untoward happen, are they?'

'No, I s'pose not.' Dotty's face filled with shame. 'I'm sorry, gel. I didn't mean to cast nasturtiums on me son. It's just that, in my experience, give a married man a bit of rope and he stretches it like 'lastic. Away from their wives they seem ter think they can act single again. I wa' lucky with my old man: 'e never strayed once and never gave me any reason to suspect 'im, not like some 'usbands. Yeah, yer right, my Dennis is a good lad. 'E teks after 'is dad, and doing anything against yer wouldn't enter his 'ead. 'E loves yer too much. It's just that it would break me 'eart if 'ote should 'appen ter you two. I've witnessed so many marriages break up through silly things – usually the man's to blame, not being able to keep 'is privates private, if yer get me drift.'

A happy smile broke her aged face. 'Oh, wouldn't it be just summat if the lads won the contest? Is there a prize, d'yer reckon? Money'd come in 'andy for yer, wouldn't it? I'll keep everything crossed for luck. Listen, send young Diane down ter the shop in a few minutes and I'll put a couple of nice sausage rolls aside for yer. My treat,' she added, grinning meaningfully at Kacie.

'Thanks, I'll do that as soon as we get a lull.'

'That sister of yours still with yer?' Dotty asked.

'Yes.'

'Mmm, 'bout time she moved on, in'it, and left you both in peace? Well, I must get back ter the shop as I never told me boss I wa' popping out.'

After she had waddled out of the salon Kacie stared after her, deep in thought. Her mother-in-law's fears on supposed goings-on at the holiday camp had not entered Kacie's head before, but now she felt a desperate urge to chase after Dennis, even though she had a salon full of customers who needed her attention. But common sense took over. She trusted Dennis. Like she had said to Dotty, he would never betray her.

Shoving her mother-in-law's fears aside, she got on with her job.

Chapter Nine

The meal Caroline had prepared that evening looked delicious, but Kacie was so consumed by misery that she couldn't face it.

'I'm sorry, Caroline, I'm not hungry,' she said, pushing away her plate. 'I'll cover it up and maybe have it later,' she added, not wanting Caroline to think she was ungrateful but, feeling as wretched as she was, doubtful she would want to eat again until she had sorted matters out with her husband.

'I'll do it, Kacie,' Caroline offered, picking up the plate before Kacie could stop her and disappearing off into the kitchen. Moments later she returned, armed with a fresh pot of tea, and sat down opposite.

'It was a lovely drying day today,' she chattered as she put milk and sugar into the cups, 'so I got some washing done and ironed it. Oh, and I swept and polished the flat and scrubbed the oven out so there's nothing for you to do but put your feet up for the rest of the weekend.'

Irritation filled Kacie. She knew Caroline meant well, but occupying herself tackling jobs around the flat was a far better option to her than sitting moping, waiting for Dennis's return. 'Thanks,' she said through clenched teeth.

Caroline eyed her hesitantly. 'Have you heard from Dennis?' she asked tentatively.

'That's not likely, being's he's in Butlin's,' Kacie snapped.

'Oh! Oh, he actually went then?' Caroline was shocked.

'So Brenda says.' Then, unable to control her emotions any longer, she allowed her face to crumple, tears of desolation rolling down her cheeks. 'He never even came to see me, Caroline, never tried to make things up before he went,' she sobbed. 'For all he knows I could have changed my mind and decided to go with him, the stubborn so and so.'

'And you're not stubborn?' Caroline commented as she pushed a cup of tea towards Kacie. 'I realise I don't know exactly what's gone on between you, but one thing I do know, Kacie, is that when you dig your heels in, you're unmovable.'

'Yes, it's one of my good points, isn't it?' she said, giving a sarcastic laugh as she wiped her eyes with a sodden handkerchief. 'But why should I be the one to make the first move when Dennis was wrong to put me on the spot like he did? He just wouldn't understand I couldn't go to Butlin's with him after I'd promised Mrs Koz I'd look after the salon for her while her sister visited.'

Caroline pressed her lips together tightly. 'Mmm, I see. So that's what caused your row. Excuse me for saying but it's a pity you couldn't have compromised before it got so out of hand.'

Kacie sighted. 'I tried my damnedest, said if I could get off early I'd catch a train down, but Dennis was having none of that. Anyway, it's too late for the whys and wherefores, Caroline. Dennis has hurt me more than I can ever explain.'

Gnawing her bottom lip anxiously, Caroline looked at her for several long seconds before asking worriedly, 'Was that all your disagreement was about?'

Blowing her nose, Kacie eyed her sister, puzzled. 'What do you mean?'

'Well . . . I just wondered if it had anything to do with my being here and you're not telling me in case I get upset.'

Kacie averted her gaze. How could she tell Caroline that she was right, and that the argument with her husband had indeed escalated to its awful climax because of her? Should she divulge the whole truth she knew Caroline would immediately pack her belongings and return to that terrible husband of hers, to a life of utter misery and drudgery. She couldn't do it. 'It was nothing to do with you,' she lied. 'I've told you what caused it.' Suddenly something Brenda had said flashed into her mind. She saw Dennis larking about as they packed the van, pictured him along with the rest of the gang enjoying himself at Butlin's, and her temper flared to override her trauma. 'Sod, Dennis,' she hissed. 'I hope he's having a bloody miserable time and they come last in that contest.'

Caroline gasped at the viciousness of her tone. 'You don't mean that, Kacie?'

'I bloody well do.' She looked across at the clock and made a decision. 'Well, if he can enjoy himself then so can I. Anything has got to be better than sitting here moping. Come on, you,' she ordered her sister. 'Get your glad rags on. Me and you are going out.'

'Out? Out where exactly?'

Kacie gave a nonchalant shrug. 'Oh, I dunno. To the pub, a coffee bar, dancing. Yeah, we'll go to the Palais. Saturday night is great. You'll love it, and it's been ages since I went.'

Malcolm had told Caroline that dance halls were dens of iniquity, and that, in his opinion, no respectable woman would ever contemplate stepping over such an establishment's threshold. She had believed him and was horrified that her sister seemed so keen to go. The thought of spending time surrounded by people whose devil-may-care behaviour left much to be desired terrified Caroline witless. Her mind raced, searching for a plausible excuse to refuse. Then relief flooded as the answer presented itself. 'The Palais? Oh, but I couldn't. I've never been dancing before.'

'What, never?' Kacie exclaimed, horrified. 'Well, it's about time you bloody did then.'

'But I . . . Well, I can't dance.'

'Dancing is easy, it's just moving your body in time to the beat. Rock and roll is harder, I grant you, but you'll soon get the hang of it. And, Caroline, I promise you, after tonight you'll want to go dancing every week. Dancing takes you out of yourself and that's just what I need right now – to forget about Dennis for a couple of hours.' That's if I can, she thought.

After Malcolm's explicit descriptions Caroline still wasn't convinced. 'I still can't go, Kacie. I have no glad rags. I shall be quite happy here. I've a good book to read.'

But Kacie was not accepting her excuses. 'I'm not going without you. I'll find you something to wear in my wardrobe. I know I'm bigger than you but we can pin or tack whatever you want to make it fit.' She jumped up from her chair, leaped over to Caroline and, grabbing her arm, pulled her upright. 'Come on,' she commanded, giving her no option.

One hand clutching the back of Kacie's pretty blue blouse, her other clamped around a glass of barley wine – which she was dubious of tasting – Caroline, dressed in Kacie's rose-patterned full skirt, black belt, white slashed-necked top and over-sized stilettos, followed her sister as she weaved her way through the thick crowds of revellers towards a row of tables and chairs on the other side of the large dance hall. Miraculously, Katie spotted two chairs just being vacated and dashed across to make a claim before someone else occupied them.

At her sister's sudden departure Caroline's heart raced in sheer panic, the swirling crowds around her seeming suffocatingly close. Frantic at being alone she dropped her drink, which splattered over the carpet, glass rolling away and disappearing. The next thing she knew a hand grabbed hers and she was being pulled on to the middle of the packed dance floor. Once there the person who had done the deed turned her to face him, beaming broadly. Before she could stop him he had taken her in his arms and began to lead her around in time to the music.

She stole a glance at his face and caught her breath. The man whose arms she was in was so good-looking, and she realised that he must have made a mistake in taking her for a dance, had grabbed the wrong hand. To her amazement, though, she found she was easily following his steps.

'Me name's Clive,' she heard him shout above the music. 'I haven't seen you here before.'

She gulped. 'Er . . . no. It's my first time.'

He smiled down at her. 'You can't be from Leicester then, not having been to the Palais before. What's yer name?'

'Er . . . Caroline.'

'Pretty name, like you. I spotted you when you came in with your friend and I followed you. I hope you don't mind. Wanted to get you on the floor before any other chap beat me to it.'

She was looking up at him, dumbstruck. No one had ever called her pretty before. 'No . . . no, I don't mind,' she uttered. So this man hadn't made a mistake after all. She couldn't quite believe it. She glanced around at the couples dancing close by, noted their happy faces and she knew then that Malcolm's interpretation of dance halls had been so misleading, he had lied in fact. This place was no den of iniquity. The hundreds of people here were all good-natured types, their only intention to enjoy themselves after a long week at work. Her eyes travelled up to gaze at the huge rotating crystal ball above her head, sparkling as it reflected the lights, and she felt a glow of happiness. This was as near to heaven as she had ever experienced. Round and round in the stranger's arms she danced in a dreamlike trance.

The music died away and everyone released their partners and clapped enthusiastically, but Clive's arms remained fixed tightly around Caroline. 'Would you like another dance?' he asked.

'Oh, yes, please,' she breathed ecstatically.

Several yards away, obscured by the crowds, Kacie sat nursing a glass a barley wine, lost in her own thoughts. It had been a mistake to come. She wasn't enjoying herself, had no heart for dancing. All she could think of was Dennis and in her mind's eye could see visions of the last time that had come to the Palais together, and remembered the good time they had had dancing the night away, to hurry home after to make passionate love in their ancient bed. She wondered what he was doing now. If he was missing her at all. Or was he enjoying himself so much he'd forgotten his wife existed?

Instead of the carefree mood of the dance hall lifting her spirits, it was having the opposite effect. She desperately wanted to return to the comfort of her own home to wallow in her misery, but couldn't because she'd promised her sister a good night out and wouldn't let her down. Regardless, Caroline had disappeared off somewhere and Kacie hoped she was not queuing for the toilet but was on the dance floor enjoying herself with some chap whose fancy she'd taken. After much titivating her sister did look lovely, nothing like her former old-fashioned appearance, and Kacie knew she'd attract attention. It was about time she experienced how good life could be, and if the evening achieved only a night of fun for her then Kacie felt her sitting it out until the finish would we well worth it.

Just then she felt a hand clamp her arm and a deep voice said, 'Well, hello, Doll.' Her heart leaped with excitement. It was Dennis. She spun her head round, eyes full of expectation, and as she looked into the face of the stranger leaning over her, her own fell in utter disappointment. He looked the jack-the-lad type, cigarette dangling from the corner of his mouth; shabby Teddy-boy-style grey jacket over far too tight drain-pipe trousers. The pint of beer he was holding in his other hand looked in danger of slopping over her and she leaned away from him, wrenching her arm free from his grasp.

'Who the hell do you think you're calling Doll?' she hissed indignantly.

The man grinned leeringly at her. 'You. So, Doll, where 'ave you been all me life?' he said, winking at her suggestively.

'Hiding from you,' she rebuffed him. 'Now if you don't mind I'd like to enjoy my drink in peace.'

He laughed at her comment and after resting his eyes for several seconds on her shapely legs, he brought them back to fix her in the eye. 'Wow, not only a looker but like to play hard ter get. Good, I like a woman with balls. Shall we go outside now or d'yer wanna drink first?'

She flashed him a look of total disgust. 'Bugger off, you cretin. Go and crawl back into the hole you crept out of. By the way, do the asylum guards know you've escaped?'

The leer left his face and it filled with contempt. 'You cocky cow,' he spat before he turned and swaggered off.

The whole incident upset Kacie greatly and her desolation deepened. Oh, Dennis, she inwardly screamed, how could you do this to me?

Just then she saw Caroline approaching, and she had a man in tow.

With all the effort she could muster Kacie forced a smile on her face. 'Hello. Enjoying yourself?' she greeted as jocularly as she could manage.

'I am,' Caroline proclaimed excitedly. 'You were right, Kacie. The Palais is a wonderful place. Oh, this is Clive,' she said, introducing her new friend.

Kacie held out her hand. 'Nice to meet you,' she said, appraising him. He looked a nice type – not that good-looking, in her opinion, but very pleasant-faced, smartly dressed in a dark blue suit, his fair hair worn very short, parted at the side and plastered down with Brylcreem. He obviously liked her sister and, judging by her happy face, Caroline had taken a fancy to him. Kacie was pleased for her.

'You all right, Kacie?' Caroline asked her.

'I'm fine,' she lied. 'I'm glad I came, aren't you?'

Kacie might have a bright smile on her face but Caroline knew her sister was far from fine. It was her eyes that betrayed the truth. They were full of despair. She made a hurried decision and, pushing her own new-found pleasures aside, sat down next to Kacie, leaning over to whisper in her ear, 'I've a headache, Kacie, would you be very upset if we went home?'

Kacie looked at her. Yes please, she felt desperate to say but she knew Caroline was suggesting this selfless sacrifice on her behalf. Her sister was having a great time and the last thing she wanted to do was go home. A deep warming towards Caroline filled her. What a lovely woman she was turning out to be. 'Go home?' she scoffed. 'I've not paid good money to go home after less than an hour. Now get back on the floor with Clive before I drag you on there myself.'

'But, Kacie—'

'No buts, just do as I say. I brought you out to have some fun and we're not going home until you have. Get her back on that dance floor, Clive, before some other chap snaps her up,' she ordered him.

Clive didn't need another telling, and before Caroline could refuse he had grabbed her hand and pulled her away.

Settling back in her seat, preparing herself for a long wait, Kacie took a sip of her drink and glanced around her. Not one miserable face did she spot, and she wondered how it was that everyone appeared so happy apart from her.

''Ello, Kacie. Fancy seeing you 'ere.'

Her head jerked round at the mention of her name and she inwardly groaned to find Brenda at her side.

'Hello, Bren,' she said, as pleased as she could manage. 'I didn't know whether you'd still be talking to me after our argument this morning.'

'Well, I don't 'old grudges, you know that, Kacie,' she said, sitting down in the vacant chair next to her. 'I won't say you didn't upset me 'cos yer did but I appreciate you were busy and I did drop it on yer at the last minute. I did me own 'air, and if I say it meself I don't look too bad. Anyway, wadda you doing 'ere?'

'What does it look like? I'm enjoying myself, that's what I'm doing here.'

Brenda pulled a wry face. 'I see, while the cat's away, is it? I bet your Dennis won't be happy when he finds out you've been gallivanting in his absence.'

Kacie flashed her a withering look. 'And what exactly do you think Dennis is doing at Butlin's, attending a church service?'

'Well, no, but—'

'But, what?' Kacie cut in. 'Brenda, Dennis is my husband, not my jailer, and what's good for him is good for me, and if he gets the hump when he finds out I've had a night down the Palais while he's been away then that's his problem.'

Brenda pursed her lips knowingly. 'Oh! Like that, is it? Tit for tat.'

Kacie's brow furrowed. 'Oh, for God's sake, Brenda, grow up. Just because I couldn't go to Butlin's with the gang doesn't mean I have to act nunlike all weekend. Tit for tat didn't enter my head. I fancied a night out and what's wrong with that?'

'But you are married, Kacie.'

Kacie looked at her incredulously. 'So is Dennis, and I don't suppose that fact will stop him from enjoying himself tonight with the lads after the contest,' she said tersely.

'No, no, I don't suppose it will.' Brenda realised she ought to get off this line of conversation as it was obviously angering her friend. She'd already had one upsetting incident with her and she didn't want to be the instigator of another and risk losing Kacie's friendship. 'Eh, Kacie, I'll introduce yer ter Jim when he comes back from the lavy.'

'Oh, that'll be nice,' Kacie said, hoping she sounded suitably interested, as being introduced to someone new and having to make amenable conversation was the last thing she felt like doing. But then she realised she should try to make an effort. After all, Brenda was a friend of long standing and was obviously smitten by this man. 'So, did he ask you to marry him when he took you for that meal?'

Brenda woefully shook her head. 'Well, we didn't exactly end up going for a meal. I could have sworn he said he was tekin' me to the Imperial Hotel but we ended up in the Imperial pub with a gang of his mates. I know e's the one for me, Kacie, and I know 'e'll pop the question sooner or later. I just hope it's sooner, as I've seen this fabulous wedding dress in C & A. Ah, 'ere 'e is.' Her face lit up as she stood and hooked her arm through that of the lanky, pale man who swaggered up to join her. 'Jim, this is me friend Kacie I told yer about.'

He scanned Kacie over, his eyes lingering on her chest and legs a little too long for her liking before he spoke. 'Nice ter meet yer at long last. Bren's told me so much about yer. 'Airdresser, ain't yer?'

'For my sins.'

'Well, maybe I could come and get me hair cut by yer sometime.' And leaning over so Brenda couldn't hear, he added, 'We could get to know each other better under the hair dryer, you being a friend of Bren's. I bet you've a lovely touch with yer 'ands and I ain't bothered where yer put 'em.'

Kacie shuddered, shocked and insulted by this man's unwarranted suggestion, and fuming that he had made it to a friend of his girlfriend while she was with him. Before she could stop herself, Kacie threw back her head and responded mockingly, 'Oh, you fancy sitting with a load of old ladies having your hair permed, do you? That type, I see,' she said, winking at him knowingly. 'I'd watch him if I were you, Bren. You'll be catching him wearing your underclothes next.'

He disdainfully curled his lip at her, then turned to Brenda. 'Hilarious, your friend, ain't she?' he hissed.

Brenda flashed Kacie a furious scowl. 'Yeah, she can be funny, can our Kacie, but I'm not so sure she's me friend any more. Come on, Jim,' she said, dragging him away.

Kacie sighed despondently, her shoulders slumping. Despite feeling her response to Jim had been totally deserved, she knew she should have kept her own counsel out of respect for Brenda. The poor girl couldn't have heard what he had said and so was bound to think that Kacie's response had been totally untoward, and in the circumstances she couldn't blame Brenda for reacting as she had. She would have to go and visit Brenda with some plausible excuse for her conduct that wouldn't blacken her boyfriend, hope Brenda believed her and was forgiving. But she did hope that Brenda saw this man for the sleazy type he was and came to her senses over him before it was too late.

How Kacie wished the evening would hurry up and end before she upset anyone else.

Finally, an hour later, having had several acquaintances come up to greet her, and managing to hold polite conversations with them, and also having been asked to dance several times and politely refusing, Kacie couldn't stand it any longer. She had to go home; her longing to escape overwhelmed all else. Without further thought, she retrieved her coat from the cloakroom and departed.

A frantic Caroline found her sister curled up in bed asleep a couple of hours later. Looking down at her, she gave a tender smile. Best thing for her, she thought. Tomorrow afternoon, Dennis would be back and the pair could sort out their differences, this dreadful estrangement between them would be over.

Chapter Ten

When Caroline rose at nine the next morning she found Kacie sitting ramrod straight in a dining chair by the living-room window. As she entered the room, Caroline was shocked at how ashen and drawn her sister looked.

'I owe you an apology,' Kacie said softly.

'You do?' Caroline asked, bewildered, advancing further into the room.

'Yes.' Kacie shuddered, pulling her shabby dressing gown around her. 'It was unforgivable of me, abandoning you in the Palais last night. I'm sorry, Caroline, I don't know what came over me.'

Caroline walked across to her and laid a reassuring hand on her arm. 'I understand. I have to say I was worried when I returned to the table and you'd disappeared. I thought you'd gone to get a drink or to the toilet, but I started to panic as the time passed and you didn't return. We searched high and low for you, even got the bouncers and manager involved, and it was Clive who insisted you'd probably gone home. I can't tell you how relieved I was to find you in bed.' It was a stupid question she knew, but still she asked: 'Did you manage to sleep, Kacie?'

She gave a wan smile. 'A little, thanks.'

And spent the rest of the night sobbing, by the looks of her, Caroline thought, but decided it was best not to comment. 'Thanks for taking me out last night, Kacie. I really enjoyed myself.'

'Good, I'm glad,' she said sincerely, and made an effort to ask, 'And what about Clive?'

Caroline frowned, perplexed. 'What about him?'

'Are you seeing him again?'

'Oh, no. He did ask me, and under normal circumstances I would have liked to very much, but I'm still a married woman, Kacie, and it wouldn't have been right. He saw me back here and after I knew you were safe I thanked him for a pleasant evening

103

and for the help he'd given me in looking for you and that was it.'

'Oh, what a shame. Never mind, there's plenty of more Clives about.'

'What do you mean?'

'I mean, Caroline, that you might still be legally married to Malcolm but having a few dances and possibly accepting a date now and then is not committing a cardinal sin.'

'It is in my eyes, Kacie,' Caroline said with conviction.

'Then it's about time you stopped thinking like that or you'll never forge a new life for yourself. Look, I'm sorry, I don't mean to have a go at you, it's just that Clive did seem nice.'

'Yes, he was.'

'Then next time don't let a chance like that pass you by.'

'I'll try not to. Would you like a cuppa? And some breakfast? You must be hungry.'

'A cuppa would be lovely, but no breakfast, thank you.'

'Oh, but you must eat,' Caroline insisted. 'I'll do you some toast.'

Kacie eyed her sharply. 'Caroline, will you stop fussing? I said I'm not hungry. All I want is Dennis to come home so we can sort out this mess.'

Caroline swallowed hard. 'I'm sorry, Kacie. Yes, of course that's what you want. What time is he due?'

'I don't know. Late afternoon, about fiveish, I should think. It's a five-hour journey or thereabouts. They won't be able to travel very fast in that old van, it being so loaded, and I suppose they'll stop at a couple of pubs on the way back. What time is it now?' she said, looking over at the clock. 'Only a quarter past nine.' Her eyes filled with tears. 'Oh, Caroline, what am I going to do for all that time? Five o'clock seems days away, not hours.'

'It'll soon pass,' she soothed. 'We could . . .'

'We could what?' she blurted. 'Play dominoes? You don't get it, Caroline. I don't want to do anything. I just want Dennis back,' she wailed pitifully.

'And he'll be here before you know it,' Caroline smiled at her kindly. 'Look, I'll make some toast and by the time I have you might feel like eating.'

'And I asked you to stop fussing,' Kacie shouted angrily. Immediately she felt a rush of shame for her outburst. She knew Caroline was only acting with the best of intentions but Kacie wished she would just leave her alone. Suddenly the thought of moping around the flat and putting up with Caroline's constant well-meaning attentions filled her with dread, and a great urge to flee overwhelmed her. She jumped up from her chair and headed off into her bedroom to pull on some clothes, then a minute or so later headed for the front door.

'Where are you going?' Caroline called after her.

'For a blow of fresh air,' Kacie tonelessly responded.

The weather was changing. Autumn was rapidly approaching and a cold nip stung the early October air. Kacie shuddered as she tightened her coat around her, then dug her hands deep into her pockets. Her search for solitude so she could decide how best to treat Dennis on his return had brought her to the Spinney Hill Park, a large enclosed oasis of grass, trees and beds of shrubs, breaking an otherwise condensed area of red bricks and mortar.

Solitude she wasn't to have, though, as on this Sunday morning the park was filled with all manner of individuals. Some were taking pleasurable strolls, others walking offspring in prams, or their dogs. A filthy tramp was stretched out on one of the numerous benches, covered in old newspapers, his life's belongings in a tattered brown carrier bag being used as a pillow. Two winos were slumped in oblivion under a tree, still clutching empty bottles of cheap alcohol and white spirit. Clusters of shabby children were playing games. The girls, armed with lengths of their mothers' washing lines or old ropes, were skipping or, with stones for markers, playing hopscotch. Some boys raced around, kicking tin cans as footballs; others, with pieces of old wood scavenged from rubbish heaps for use as bats and stumps, played cricket and rounders.

The jovial atmosphere, though, did not help to lift Kacie's sombre mood.

She sought a vacant bench and sat down to gaze absently around her. Normally a Sunday morning for herself and Dennis was spent enjoying the total freedom of their one day off a week together: a late lie-in and, finances allowing, a visit to the pub for a drink with friends before a tasty Sunday dinner of a small joint of brisket or shank of pork, roast potatoes and vegetables, leftover hot Yorkshire pudding topped with jam or butter and sugar for afters; then dozing in the armchairs listening to the radio, reading the papers, before both preparing themselves for the week of work ahead. This was the first Sunday she had spent since she could remember without Dennis by her side and she didn't like it, vowing not to spend another without him again.

Her whole attention then turned to how she was going to deal with Dennis on his return. That's if he did return, bearing in mind his threat not to do so until Caroline had left. But she felt sure that threat had been said in temper. At heart Dennis was a compassionate man and wouldn't really expect his wife to throw her sister out until she had somewhere else to go.

She felt a great desire to lash out at Dennis, leave him in no doubt what anguish and misery this situation had caused her, but more confrontation was not the answer. All it would achieve was antagonising the situation and prolonging it further. She decided it best to put a smile on her face and welcome him home with a nice meal ready on the table and show keen interest in how his weekend had gone. He'd most likely be upset at the band's failure to succeed in the contest – after all, it had been a huge event – and would need her full sympathy and comfort, which she would readily give.

A thought suddenly struck her. Not that she wished Dennis's future dreams to be shattered – she of all people would have been thrilled and delighted for them to have succeeded – but just maybe the band's failure to win such a high-profile contest might make all the members take stock and rethink the band's future. Maybe even disband, which in turn would mean Dennis would turn all his attention to their future as a couple, which, while the band had been in formation, had taken a back seat.

She also felt awful to think it, but it was a pity she couldn't ask Caroline to make herself scarce so Dennis and she could do their making-up in private. But she couldn't upset Caroline by pointing out so blatantly that her presence wasn't welcome. Besides, her sister had nowhere else to go.

She hitched up her sleeve and looked at her watch, a small-faced cheap Timex Dennis had saved hard for two Christmases previously. It read two minutes past eleven. Still at least six hours before Dennis's expected return. Too much time left to mope aimlessly around the flat after she'd spruced herself up and got everything ready.

She was getting chilly sitting on the bench. She could always go and visit Dennis's mother, where she knew she'd receive an enthusiastic welcome but there was a danger the full truth behind her son's trip alone to the holiday camp in Skegness could come out via a slip of the tongue, so she decided a visit was unwise. She didn't want to upset Dotty unnecessarily or risk pitching mother against

106

son, which could also antagonise her own situation.

She should visit Brenda and try to put right what had transpired between them the previous evening but then she decided against that too, as until she had sorted matters out with Dennis she hadn't the energy to make the effort on anything else of an emotion nature. Her friendship with Brenda had survived many years, so making amends over a simple misunderstanding she felt could wait a day or so until she herself was in a better frame of mind. Besides, Brenda was more than likely spending the day with her future intended, it being Sunday, and Kacie had no desire to encounter Jim so soon after his lurid suggestion to her, worried that should he make such comments again she couldn't trust her own retaliation. In the circumstances she felt it best to catch Brenda on her own to deal with this.

She suddenly thought of her parents but again, that situation was something she'd give her full attention to once matters were resolved with her husband, which was paramount to Kacie.

She gazed around. The park was beginning to empty as people dispersed to their various destinations, more than likely to have their dinner. She was beginning to feel nauseated through lack of food, but not enough to return home to Caroline's fussing. She was, though, desperate for a cup of tea. Then she remembered a little café several streets away that catered for factory workers. She had heard that the owner, a kindly middle-aged woman who'd lost her husband in the war and had never remarried, opened on a Sunday. She would take a walk down that way and it would pass some time.

It was a welcoming sight for Kacie to spot that the café windows were steamed up as she approached, and she could smell cooking food. They dusty bell over the door clanged dully as she entered and she spotted several tables were occupied by shabby-looking creatures, each cradling a mug of something hot, she presumed tea, some with plates before them, on which was what looked to Kacie like stale slab cake, and most unappetising. She found a vacant table and as soon as she sat down an elderly lady sitting at the table adjacent rose up from her seat and shuffled across.

''Ello, me duck,' she cackled, giving Kacie a broad black-toothed grin. ''Ave yer seen me daughter? Beryl, 'er name is. She's comin' ter collect me 'cos she's teking me out fer the day. I'm waitin' for 'er. Did yer see 'er on yer way 'ere?'

Kacie eyed her blankly. 'Er . . . well, er . . .'

A matronly woman emerged from behind the counter by the back of the room and hurried over, pulling a tattered notepad from the pocket of her stained large white apron. 'Now, now, Gracie, don't you go 'arassing this young lady. She didn't see your Beryl but she'll be 'ere soon, so get back to yer seat and let this young lady make 'er order in peace.'

Kacie watched as silently the old lady obeyed. 'Has she been waiting for her daughter long?' she asked the owner out of interest.

The woman began to wipe the table with a grubby dishcloth she'd pulled out of her apron pocket. 'She ain't got a daughter, dear. Well, not living. Her Beryl died in childbirth over forty years ago, and her husband not long after in a terrible accident involving a lorry, and the poor old duck has never got over it. Gracie comes here every day. Same as George and Albert over there,' she said, nodding her head in the direction of two old boys, their shrunken bodies lost inside huge well-worn overcoats. 'And a few others. If I didn't open they'd 'ave nowhere to go – poor old sods, they are. At least here they get a bit of warmth and company. And so do I, 'cos I ain't got no one either, so it suits all round, dunnit? Now, what canna get yer, ducky?' she asked, beaming broadly.

Kacie suddenly felt so humble. To be alone in the world with no one to care what happened to you must be so dreadful, she thought, and vowed most vehemently to sort matters out with all those she cared for, not wanting at all to end up like these poor unfortunates. She smiled back at the owner. 'A cup of tea, please.'

'Can I tempt yer to a nice bit of slab cake? I've currant and Madeira.'

Kacie shook her head and said hurriedly, 'No, thank you. Just the tea.'

The tea was weak but hot and sweet, and Kacie gratefully sipped on it, feeling it taking the chill from her bones after she'd sat so long in the park. By the time her mug was empty the clock on the wall read just approaching one o'clock and she deduced that if she took a slow walk home she would have over three hours to do all she needed in plenty of time to welcome home Dennis.

'Thank you,' she called to the café owner as she made to depart.

'You're welcome, dear. Come back any time.'

'If yer see my Beryl will you tell 'er I'm waitin?' the old lady asked.

Kacie smiled kindly at her and nodded. 'I will.'

She met Caroline at her door when she arrived home. She was dressed for outdoors and Kacie's spirits soared, thinking that her wish had been granted and that Caroline was going to make herself scarce, allowing herself and Dennis to make up in private.

'Going for a walk?' she asked casually, not wanting Caroline to get an inkling she was keen to see her off the premises.

'No, I've just come back. I was looking for you,' Caroline replied earnestly. 'I've searched high and low. Where have you been Kacie?'

Kacie sighed in deep irritation. Caroline really was beginning to suffocate her in her insistence to administer sisterly protection. 'I told you I was going for a blow of fresh air, and coming to check on me is going a bit too far, Caroline. I'm old enough to look after myself. Did you think I'd been murdered or was going to throw myself in the canal?'

'Don't be silly, Kacie,' Caroline snapped. 'And I wasn't checking up on you.' She eyed her sister gravely. 'You'd better take your coat off and come and sit down.'

'I've no time for relaxing; I've loads to do before Dennis gets back. I can't let him catch me looking like this, can I?'

Caroline shifted uneasily on her feet. 'Well, that's just it, Kacie.'

Kacie frowned at her, suddenly noticing how upset she seemed. 'What's just it?' she demanded. 'What's happened, Caroline?' Then a horrifying thought struck. 'Has Malcolm been here?'

Her sister gulped hard. 'No, not Malcolm.'

'Who then? Oh, no, not Mam and Dad?'

'No, not them. Dennis.'

Kacie's heart raced wildly. 'He's back! He's here!' she cried, thrilled, pushing past Caroline and on into the living room, forgetting all her plans for his welcome home or that she looked a mess. Dennis had returned and that was all that mattered. Her eyes flashed around in excited expectation but the room was empty and she spun to face her sister. 'Where is he?' she cried, bewildered.

Clasping her hands tightly, her face wreathed in worry, Caroline uttered, 'He's gone, Kacie.'

'Gone? What do you mean, he's gone.'

Caroline laid a hand on her arm. 'Kacie, please come and sit down. I have—'

'I don't want to sit down,' she cried, frenziedly shaking free her arm. 'For God's sake, Caroline, tell me where Dennis has gone.'

She took a deep breath. 'To London.'

Kacie stared at her, thinking she must have misheard. 'London?

What on earth are you talking about?'

'Oh, Kacie, he burst in here about an hour after you'd gone out, so excited you'd have thought he'd won the pools. I suppose it's like he has. The band won the competition.'

This news stunned Kacie rigid, knocking the breath from her body. 'They did!' she exclaimed. 'Why, that's wonderful, brilliant! God, I bet Dennis was beside himself.'

Caroline nodded vigorously. 'Oh, he was, Kacie, he was. There were several talent scouts there from record companies. The one from Decca approached them with an offer to go to London and cut a demo record – I think that's what Dennis said it was called. Well, they had to catch the afternoon train to be down there to report to the company first thing Monday morning. They set off back here from Butlin's at the crack of dawn.'

'Really,' Kacie gasped, astounded. 'Oh, my God! This is just what he always dreamed of, something I thought never would happen. Oh, Caroline, I should have had more faith. But why didn't Dennis wait to tell me all this himself?' she demanded, confused.

'He couldn't wait to tell you, Kacie – was frantic to know where you were. I told him you'd gone for a blow of fresh air and he said you'd probably be around Brenda's or his mother's, and he'd try Brenda first. He came back not long after, barging in here in a furious temper.'

Kacie was still trying to digest the news of the band's success and the fact her beloved husband had gone haring off down to London without waiting to see her and, stupefied, asked, 'Why? Why was he in such an awful mood?'

Caroline shrugged. 'I don't know. He never spoke to me, Kacie. Just charged in the bedroom, collected some things and left.'

'What?' She grimaced, totally bewildered. 'He never left word where he was staying? A message for me? Anything?'

Caroline shook her head. 'No, I'm so sorry, Kacie. I'm as confused about all this as you are.'

Kacie stared at her, a hollow feeling filling her as she desperately tried to fathom what had changed Dennis's mood from jubilation to consternation in just a matter of minutes, sending him off on his exciting new venture without even seeing her. The cause, then, had to be something terrible to make him act in such a way. But what? She had to find out. The fear of God upon her, she spun on her heels and ran out of the door.

'Where are you going?' Caroline called.

'To see Brenda,' Kacie shouted back as she raced down the stairs.

Brenda stood on her threshold, her face scowling fiercely when she saw who was there.

'Wadda you want?' she demanded nastily.

'Dennis came to see you, looking for me?'

Folding her arms under her shapely bosom Brenda took a stance. 'Yeah, that's right.'

Kacie's brow furrowed, eyes narrowing. 'And what did you tell him, Brenda?'

'The truth,' she spat. 'He asked me if I'd seen yer and I told him the last time I had was at the Palais last night, and that you were fornicating with any man you could lay yer 'ands on and I said I hoped he'd realised he'd married a jezebel.'

'What? You told my Dennis, *what?*'

'It's true.'

'Brenda, you know it isn't.'

'Oh, yes it is. I saw yer wi' that bloke just before I came up ter yer. All over yer, he wa'. And I'll never forgive yer, never, fer what you said ter my Jim. I hope yer pleased wi' yerself 'cos it caused an awful row and 'e's finished wi' me, Kacie, 'cos I called 'im a liar. So tit for tat, eh? You ruined my relationship and I've definitely put a spoke in yours.'

Kacie's whole being filled with fury. 'Now you listen here, Brenda. That bloke you're saying was all over me, well, whatever you might think you saw, I was actually telling him where to get off, and as for what I said to Jim, it's only what he deserved after propositioning me like that. I didn't want to tell you, but that's what he did.'

Brenda's face darkened thunderously. 'Liar,' she spat. 'Jim wouldn't do that to me. He said you'd propositioned him. I asked him what was said between yer when he leaned over and whispered to yer. He said he asked yer if there were any chance of getting a discount if he paid you to give me a posh 'air do as a treat 'cos he wanted ter tek me somewhere special. He said you'd said you'd treat him any time, and that you looked at him in a suggestive way. I told him you'd never do such a thing and that he must have got you wrong. I stuck up for you, I did, and what an idiot I was to do that. He shouted at me, said you did say and do what he said, and that I wa' callin' 'im a liar so obviously didn't trust 'im, and as far as 'e wa' concerned we was finished. And it's all your fault, Kacie. How could you do that to

111

me?' she bellowed, tears of distress spurting from her eyes.

But Kacie had stopped listening to Brenda's tirade. All that was thrashing through her mind was that Brenda had told Dennis she had been flirting outrageously with other men and it appeared that Dennis had believed her without giving his wife a chance to defend herself.

Without another word to Brenda she rushed off. She had to see Dennis and straighten things out. Jed's girlfriend, Tessa, would be able to tell her their whereabouts, as she had been one of the women that had accompanied them to Butlin's.

Tessa shook her mane of carrot-red hair. 'I dunno where they're staying, Kacie. All I know is that they had to catch the one thirty to London. They were being met at St Pancras and taken to a hotel.'

'But you were there, Tessa, you must know more,' Kacie implored.

'No, I don't. After the contest – and, oh, Kacie, you should 'ave bin there. It was terrific. The lads won easily and we gels were so proud. Your Dennis was sensational. I've never heard him sing so good and the band played the best I've ever heard 'em too. The scout from the record company was all over 'em, said he thought they'd a real chance of making the big time, all depending though on the quality of the demo.' She scowled. 'I dunno whether to be excited or not about all this. I mean, the lads have dreamed of something like this happening. I never thought it would meself so I'm as shocked as the other girlfriends and, I expect, you. Fame and fortune is one thing, but I didn't like all the women screaming at them and giving them the come-on, and neither did the other gels. Still, Jed said we'd have to get used ter that sort of thing when they did make it big. Mind you, it was your Dennis that received the most attention so it was probably a good job yer weren't there, Kacie, 'cos yer wouldn't 'ave liked it.'

Kacie's face clouded. 'And did he—'

'Eh, don't start that, Kacie,' she cut in. 'Your Dennis played up to it, 'course he did, but it wa' only an act. He loves yer too much to ever do the dirty on yer. Anyway, most of the women were just scrubbers, in my opinion, Kacie, so yer've no need ter worry.'

Good-time girls or not, Kacie did not like what she was hearing.

'I have ter say, though, Kacie, you wouldn't 'ave thought your Dennis was off on a chance of a lifetime today, he was in such a bad mood when I saw them go at the station.'

Kacie already knew why. 'So when will we have news on what's happening and where they're staying? I need to speak to Dennis urgently, Tessa.'

Tessa shrugged. 'Jed's gonna ring me tomorrow as soon as he knows 'ote. But yer know what work is like, Kacie. If they've a hint it's a private call they won't let me take it. I've told him to pretend he's a customer with an enquiry, and I hope with all that's going on Jed remembers.'

At the mention of work a thought struck Kacie. 'What about their jobs? What will happen when none of them turns up tomorrow?'

'I think that was the last thing they care about,' said Tessa.

Kacie's shoulders sagged in despair. 'Will you get word to me as soon as you hear anything?'

'Course I will, but Dennis will ring the salon, surely.'

Hopefully, Kacie thought. 'Yes, of course he will, but, all the same, you will let me know?'

Tessa nodded.

With a heavy heart Kacie returned home.

'Any news?' Caroline asked as soon as she opened the front door. She then noticed the look of doom on her sister's face. 'Good grief, you look like death.'

'So would you if your supposed best friend had just told your husband that you were a slut.'

Caroline gasped, mortified. 'Oh, Kacie, she didn't? So that's why Dennis was in such a foul mood.'

Kacie nodded sorrowfully. 'Brenda told Dennis such a fabricated story of what I was doing in the Palais, which, coming on top of the row we'd already had, well . . .' Tears of distress filled her eyes. 'Oh, Caroline,' she wailed, 'this is such a mess. He's already on his way to London and I've no idea where he's staying so I can't put any of this right.'

'But you will, Kacie. Dennis is bound to be angry and hurt by the lies Brenda told him but when he starts thinking straight he'll realise that none of it's true. He's going to get caught up with all that's happening on the band front but I'm positive he'll find time to call you tomorrow at the salon, you'll see.' She forced a reassuring smile on her face. 'If all goes well he'll be making arrangements for you to join him in London, if not, he'll be back home before you know it.'

Kacie wished she could summon up her sister's faith. 'I hope you're right, Caroline, 'cos this is killing me,' she sobbed.

113

Chapter Eleven

All night long Kacie tossed and turned, and, feeling absolutely dreadful, had to drag herself out of bed when the alarm shrilled at seven the next morning. She took one look at herself in the mirror and hardly recognised her reflection: eyes red and swollen from crying, pallor tinged grey, face etched by deep pain. Her whole body felt leadlike and the great urge to crawl back into bed overwhelmed her, but she knew she couldn't. She had a job to go to which she couldn't risk losing.

'Kacie, there's something wrong so don't fob me off with a denial. I must say, you look a sight and it's unlike you not to pay meticulous attention to your appearance.'

Through gritty eyes Kacie looked at her employer sitting behind her desk, hands clasped, face set stern, staring at her intently. She knew Verna spoke the truth. Beneath her overall her clothes were crumpled, as she'd thrown on the ones she had worn yesterday, which had been discarded in a heap on the floor in her haste to get to bed to nurse her misery. Her hair had been hurriedly brushed and pushed behind her ears. She'd had no incentive or energy to style it into its usual becoming modern beehive. Her face, although washed, was devoid of its light application of makeup. But she didn't care. All Kacie cared about was the telephone ringing and Dennis being at the other end.

It had rung several times that morning and each time she had jumped in expectation, and each time she had been cruelly disappointed.

'I'm fine,' she insisted, more brusquely than she intended. 'Just missing Dennis, and I didn't sleep last night.'

Verna's shrewd eyes stared at her scrutinisingly. 'Are you sure there's nothing more to it than that? I have noticed our clients you attend don't leave the salon so chirpy and full of praise for you as they normally do. For most of last week you were like a bear with a sore head and it doesn't seem to me that the weekend has improved your mood, Kacie. You've always had a sharp tongue on you, not one afraid to speak your mind, but I've never heard you be so blatantly rude like I have on more than one occasion last week. Today you jump out of your skin every time the telephone rings.'

Kacie shifted uncomfortably on her feet. Never before had she been on the receiving end of a dressing down from her employer and she felt deeply humiliated. 'Well, that's because I'm waiting to hear news of the record company's assessment of the band,' she tried to excuse her despicable conduct.

'Mmm, yes, I can appreciate you being edgy over that but that doesn't excuse you being so . . . so . . . obnoxious. Poor Diane is so scared she's tiptoeing around you. Kacie, news regarding the band might take a while to come through. I've no idea how the music industry operates but finding out if they have the makings will surely take a few days to establish, so you're going to have to be patient. Now how you act in your own time is your business but when you're at work I won't have you upsetting the clients, or staff, and neither will I accept any more slipshod work. The reason I've held my tongue for this long is because I have such a high regard for you, but enough is enough.'

Kacie looked at her shamefully. 'I'm sorry, Mrs Koz.'

She smiled at her kindly. 'Apology accepted. Now what you need to do to take your mind off personal things is to concentrate your efforts on your work. What have you planned for the competition on Friday evening?'

Kacie looked at her blankly. 'Eh?'

Verna eyed her back, shocked. 'Oh, Kacie, don't tell me you've forgotten?'

Kacie had – hadn't given it another thought after Verna had told her about it nearly a week ago. At this moment the last thing she felt like doing was entering a contest – had no enthusiasm for it at all – but she really didn't have any choice unless she refused and risked upsetting her employer and possibly losing her job. 'I've, er . . . one or two ideas but nothing definite,' she fibbed.

'Well, please, give it more thought, Kacie. Time is moving on and you need to practise the styles you're going to enter with. This is very important for the salon. I'm relying on you to do your best. The publicity this will generate when you win will give the salon a good boost. Wella is a hugely respected company and

116

the winners of this competition will be featured in all the hairdressing magazines.'

Kacie felt the burden of responsibility Verna was heaping on her weighing heavily, wishing her boss didn't have such high expectations. Under normal circumstances she'd have been excited and full of enthusiasm at the prospect of pitting her skills against the cream of Leicester's hairdressers, but at this moment she severely doubted she would be placed very high in a tea-mashing contest. She realised Verna had asked her a question. 'Pardon?'

Verna sighed, irritated. 'I asked if you've another model lined up besides Diane. Did you ask your friend Brenda?'

Kacie inwardly groaned. After yesterday, Kacie doubted she and Brenda would ever speak again. 'Er . . . she can't. She's busy that night doing something important.'

'What could be more important than the competition? Well, have you anyone else in mind, Kacie?'

She shook her head. 'I could ask Tessa but I doubt she'd let me restyle her mane of red hair she's so proud of.'

'Mmm. Well, just a thought, but what about your sister? Would she be willing, do you think?'

'I've already restyled her hair,' Kacie said.

'Oh, well, surely you know someone else who will oblige, and in the meantime you promise you're going to concentrate your efforts on the competition?'

Kacie's mind had strayed once again to her own predicament. Her mind's eye pictured Dennis revelling in the attention he was receiving down in London and her thoughts settled on the possibility that in all the excitement of what was happening he'd no time to give his wife any thought.

'Kacie?' Verna barked.

She jumped. 'Pardon?'

'The competition?' she sharply prompted.

'Oh, yes, the competition. I'll do my best, Mrs Koz,' wondering who she could get to agree to model for her at such short notice.

As she left Verna's office she bumped into Diane coming to fetch her.

'You coming, Kacie, only the customers are getting fidgety?' she approached her timidly.

'Eh? Oh, yes, Di. Oh, by the way, you are all right for Friday evening? The competition?'

'Oh, yes, I'm looking forward to it.' She eyed Kacie warily. 'I ain't mentioned it to yer 'cos you seemed to have other things bothering yer. D'yer know what yer gonna do with me yet?' she asked, excited at the prospect.

'I'm working on that but you'll look the business, trust me. Er . . . you don't have a friend that fancies being a model, do you?'

Diane looked shame-faced. 'I dun't 'ave many friends, Kacie – well, no close ones to ask a favour like that – but I could ask me sister if yer desperate, only I don't recommend her 'cos she can't sit still for five minutes and she's a gob on 'er worse than a navvy and that could be embarrassing.'

Kacie had met Diane's sister, whom she felt was far worse than Diane's description, and to use her would definitely have to be the last resort. 'Then it's a miracle we need,' she muttered to herself, severely doubting she'd get anyone at such short notice, and considering the way her life was heading at the moment.

Kacie was wrong, though. Her miracle was waiting for her out in the salon at that very moment. It was Diane who spotted her first, loitering by the counter.

'You've a bleddy nerve coming in 'ere after what Kacie found you doing,' Diane hissed, outraged as she strode across. 'Wadda yer want?'

'Not to see you,' Mel tartly responded. 'It's 'er I want,' she said, nodding her head in Kacie's direction.

'Well, she's busy,' Diane snapped, 'so you'll 'ave ter mek do wi' me. Now wadda yer want?'

Kacie heard the commotion that was building by the counter and glanced across. She was most surprised to see Melanie and, excusing herself from her customer, made her way over. 'Well, hello, this is a surprise. It's all right, Di, I'll deal with this. Can you just go and finish taking Mrs Green's rollers out and tell her I won't be a minute?'

Diane flashed Mel a scathing scowl before doing as she was told.

'What can I do for you?' Kacie asked Mel.

'It's what I can do for you,' she said, beaming broadly. She held out her hand. 'The quid I owe yer.'

Kacie looked in shock at the two ten-shilling notes the girl was holding out, which in truth she'd forgotten about with all else that was occupying her. She hadn't really expected to see the money again. 'Are you sure you can afford to pay me back?'

'Well, no, not exactly. It's skint me, but me landlady, Mrs Bunting, reckons before I do 'ote else me debts should be paid. So

I'm paying 'em. If it weren't for you I wouldn't have such lovely lodgings or a job, and I'm bloody grateful.'

Kacie smiled, glad to hear some nice news for a change. 'I'm so pleased. What is your job?'

Mel grinned proudly. 'In a warehouse, packing shoes, and I love it. I've made a friend already and we're going out next week.'

'Good. And your lodgings are lovely, you say? Your landlady sounds nice.'

'Oh, she is. She's like a mother ter me. I've told 'er all about me, even that you caught me nickin' yer purse.' Her chin raised proudly. 'She said she admired me for being 'onest.'

'And so do I. Well, thank you,' Kacie said, taking the money. She made to say her goodbyes when she suddenly noticed how thick and long was Mel's mane of hair, ideal for the sort of style she hoped to create for the competition. An idea struck. Mel was the miracle she was desperate for and she just hoped the girl was receptive. 'Er . . . you said you can't really afford to pay this all back in one lump?'

Mel looked bewildered. 'Yeah, I did, but so what?'

Kacie smiled at her. 'I'm going to offer you a deal.'

'A deal?'

Kacie nodded. 'How do you fancy being a model for me on Friday night for a competition I'm entering? If you do, I'll pay you ten shillings, so that's only ten shillings you'll owe me and you'll get a free hairdo into the bargain. The only trouble is that you'd have to be here no later than four so we can get there on time to set up.'

Mel stared blankly at Kacie whilst her offer sank in, then her face lit brightly. 'Bleddy 'ell,' she exclaimed. 'I like the sound of that. OK, yer on. We finish early on a Friday so I can make it, no sweat.'

Kacie's face lit up. At least one of her problems had been solved. 'Great, and I'm much appreciative. Oh, I don't suppose you've an evening-type dress, have you?' She thought this a silly question and her mind was already trying to fathom where she could find a suitable dress to fit Mel at this short notice. She was most surprised by the young girl's answer.

'Matter of fact I have. I used ter do ballroom dancing till all me trouble started. It's a lovely dress, pink chiffon and sequins what me mam made for me. Me dad never liked me in it, said it was too old for me.'

'But it'll be perfect for the competition,' Kacie said, relieved.

'Mel, you won't let me down, will you?' she asked, handing back one of the ten-shilling notes, which was snatched from her hand.

'I sure won't. Mrs Bunting said that you're me guardian angel, so I can't let you down for fear of rotting in damnation. See yer Friday then,' she said gleefully, slapping Kacie on her arm in a familiar gesture before she galloped out of the door.

'Did I 'ear yer right, Kacie, and yer gonna use 'er as a model?' Diane asked disbelievingly as Kacie went over to join her to reclaim her client. 'If yer are, yer must be mad.'

'You have big ears, Di,' she scolded, 'and who I use as a model is none of your business. Now go and put the kettle on and mash a cuppa.'

Just then the telephone shrilled and Kacie jumped. 'I'll get it,' she cried, leaping over to the counter, grabbing up the receiver. Once again her hopes were dashed. It wasn't Dennis but a representative from a manufacturer of brushes, wanting to know if they could sell Verna some wares.

Kacie didn't go home straight from work that night, deciding to take a walk to try to sort out her muddled thoughts. On finally arriving home well after eight, Caroline pounced upon her in the passageway by the door. 'Oh, Kacie, I was so worried about you. Thank God you're home.'

Kacie was about to tell her to stop being so over-protective when she noticed there was something different about her sister. She was highly charged about something. Automatically she thought Caroline's state had something to do with Dennis and she looked at her expectantly. 'Is . . . Is Den—'

'No, I've heard nothing,' Caroline cut in. 'I was hoping you had, though, and that's why you were late.'

'No,' Kacie snapped abruptly, swallowing her bitter disappointment. 'But you're bursting over something, Caroline,' she said, stripping off her coat, kicking off her painful stilettos. She eyed her, bothered. 'I hope it's something good you've to tell me. I couldn't bear to hear anything awful.'

Caroline beamed excitedly. 'Oh, it is, Kacie. I was going to break the news over dinner. I hope you're hungry as I've cooked corn beef hash. I hope it's not too dried up.'

Kacie wasn't hungry but didn't want to offend her sister. 'I could manage a small helping. Well, are you going to tell me or what?'

'I've got myself a job,' Caroline erupted.

'A job? Really! Oh, Caroline, that's wonderful,' she said, leaping up to hug her fiercely. 'I'm so pleased. Doing what?'

'In a newsagents and tobacconist's. I woke up this morning and gave myself a good talking to, Kacie. I thought of all the things you've said to me, and since you cut my hair and we've discussed me changing my style of clothes I feel so much better about myself. I had to do something, Kacie. I'm running very low on money and I know you can't afford to keep me. So today I took the plunge, did myself up as best I could and set off not long after you'd left for work. I borrowed your ecru A-line skirt and yellow blouse. I hope you don't mind. I've hung them back up in your wardrobe. Anyway, I can't say it wasn't nerve-racking but I promised myself I wasn't coming home until I'd found something, anything – even office work as a last resort. I must have been in a dozen different shops, a few factories and other businesses around the area and made enquiries if they needed any help. Most of them did but I wasn't suitable for their needs . . .

'I'd just about given up when I came across a newsagent's in a row of shops by the General Hospital. I took several deep breaths and went in. Oh, he's a lovely bloke who owns the shop, Kacie. Really nice, friendly. A widower with two young children that his mam helps him look after. He said he'd been looking for someone for a while, had had a lot of trouble getting someone suitable since his last assistant left because she was just far too old and the job was too much for her. It was on my mind to walk away then, as the other places I'd tried turned me down because I'd not the right experience but he insisted I told him all about myself, which I did, and I also said how I'd always wanted to do this kind of work. I was so shocked when he said he'd given me a month's trial. I start next Monday morning at six, on four pounds, seventeen and six a week.'

Kacie pulled a grim face. 'Six. That's the middle of the night.'

'On the week it's my turn to do the papers, when I'm trained, it'll be a five o'clock start. But I'm not complaining, Kacie. It's just part of the job and I've always known it's long hours.' A smile of pride lit Caroline's face. 'So from now on I'll be able to pay you whatever board you require and I'll soon have the means to look around for a place of my own. I have you to thank. I hope you know how grateful I am, Kacie?'

'I only helped change your appearance, Caroline. The rest you've done by yourself. You're on your way to your future,' her sister uttered emotionally, eyeing her proudly. 'Come on,' she said, linking her arm, 'let's go and have a celebration cup of tea.'

It's been a day for miracles, Kacie thought as they made their way through to the living room, and wondered if she'd be pushing her luck to wish for a third. As she was making her wish there was a loud bang on the door and she jumped. Dennis, she automatically thought, her heart pounding rapidly as she imagined her wish had been granted. But her heart plummeted as she realised Dennis had a key; he wouldn't be hammering on the door expecting to be let in.

'I'll go,' offered Caroline.

'No, I will. You make the tea.'

As soon as Kacie turned the knob of the Yale lock, releasing the catch, the door was thrust open so violently she landed against the wall, banging her head.

'WHERE IS SHE?' a deep voice bellowed. 'I KNOW SHE'S HERE.'

The knock she had received momentarily dazed Kacie and she fought to regain her wits. She was aware that someone had entered the flat, someone big, a man, who was heading down the short passageway towards the living room. Next she knew, all hell was breaking loose. Screaming and shouting was filling the air. Faculties regained, she raced into the living room and the sight that met her stunned her rigid. A drunken Malcolm in a raging fury held the screaming, helpless Caroline by her hair with one hand and was slapping her around her face with the other.

'You bitch!' he was roaring. 'How dare you make a laughing stock of me? I'll teach you. I'll bloody teach you a lesson you'll not forget. The neighbours raised the alarm because they hadn't seen you for a while and I had the police waiting for me at the house when I got home from work this afternoon. They think I've bloody murdered you, you stupid cow.' He suddenly sensed Kacie's presence and swung to face her, taking the still-screaming Caroline with him. 'You think you're so fucking clever, don't you, eh?' he spat at Kacie, eyes murderous. 'I suddenly realised tonight, when the police were questioning me, just where Caroline was and always has been. Here with you. It was when the police asked me what family she had. Well, I knew she'd never go back to her parents but then I thought, what about you? You came to see me. Then I thought, why? Why out of the blue like that just when Caroline had left me? That cock-and-bull story you told me about wanting to be sisterly never made sense. You came to suss me out, see if I was going to kick up a fuss about this bitch leaving me.'

'No, no, Malcolm, it wasn't like that,' Kacie tried to soothe him. 'I told you the truth.'

'Shut your lying fucking mouth,' he bawled. 'I'm doing the speaking. It was exactly as I say. You came to find out if I'd guessed where she was and was going to come around and cause trouble. Well, for your information, I couldn't have given a toss where she was,' he hissed, giving Caroline a frenzied shake, which made her yelp. 'I'd have gladly divorced her and good riddance. But I do care now the whole neighbourhood is talking about me. I might as well give them something to talk about. I'll swing for this bitch,' he said, shaking her again, 'and see if I care.'

Forgetting her own safety Kacie was filled with an intense rage and, clenching her fists, she shouted, 'Let her go or I'll—'

'You'll what?' Malcolm laughed, a deep callous chuckle. 'You're no match for me. When I've finished with her, I'll deal with you. I might as well be hanged for two as for one.' He swung back his hand and made to smash it in Caroline's face. Simultaneously Kacie's fury reached fever pitch and without a thought she leaped across and threw herself bodily upon him. Her unexpected attack took him off guard and the three tumbled over, falling heavily on the floor. Kacie quickly gained her senses, raised herself on her haunches and started to beat her fists furiously into Malcolm, screaming at him to leave her sister alone.

The next she knew she was being hauled to her feet and a male voice said, 'We'll deal with this, Mrs Cooper.'

She flashed her head round to look straight into the stern face of a burly policeman. Her mouth opened and closed like a fish's. 'He . . . he . . . was going to kill my sister,' she cried frenziedly.

'Not if you could help it, eh?' the police said, his eyes twinkling. 'Take him to the station, constable.'

The constable, restraining a now quietened Malcolm, nodded. 'Right you are, Sarge.'

As they passed Kacie on the way out, Malcolm gave her a murderous glare. She gave him one back of utter contempt. Then she leaped over to Caroline, still prostrate on the floor. 'Are you all right, Caroline? Caroline, are you all right?' she demanded, helping her to sit up.

Shaking, she nodded. 'I'm fine, Kacie, honest.'

A while later Sergeant O'Connor looked at each in turn, then settled his eyes on Caroline. 'You had us worried, Mrs Pargiter. It was the neighbours who raised the alarm, very concerned that they'd not seen hide nor hair of you for over three weeks they went to enquire and your husband told them you'd gone away to stay with a sick aunt, but they then thought it odd when they saw him burning belongings of yours on a bonfire the night before last, so they contacted us.

'Mr Pargiter was very straight with his answers. He told us you'd left him and he hadn't a clue why. That as far as he was aware, you were happy and the marriage was good. He'd lied to the neighbours to save embarrassment when you came back, which he said he was convinced you would. I have to say he seemed very upset about the whole affair. But when I insisted there must be a reason for your leaving, and obviously we'd have to find you to confirm your safety, he couldn't look me in the eye and got very agitated. That raised my suspicions. It's apparent now he didn't want you found because the truth of his real character would come out and that was the last thing he wanted people to know.'

'How did you know to come here?' Kacie asked.

'We managed to get out of him that Mrs Pargiter had a sister but he insisted he didn't know where you lived. Obviously that was a lie. But we had to go back to the station and make enquiries about your address, Mrs Cooper, and in the meantime your husband, Mrs Pargiter, got himself very drunk and took matters into his own hands. More than likely his intention was to frighten you, Mrs Pargiter, into not revealing his true character. I'm just sorry we didn't arrive earlier and save you this . . . well . . .'

'That's OK, Sergeant,' said Kacie. 'We're just glad you came when you did.'

He smiled kindly at her, then addressed Caroline. 'Do you want to press charges against your husband, Mrs Pargiter?'

'Charges!' she exclaimed.

'Yes, she does,' said Kacie.

'No, I don't,' insisted Caroline. 'I don't want any more to do with Malcolm, Kacie. Can you warn him to stay away from me, Sergeant, please?' she implored.

'I can certainly, and I'm sure when I'm finished with him he won't dare come near you ever again,' he said sternly.

'Then that's fine.' Caroline said, relieved.

'Now are you ladies sure you're both all right? Is there anyone you want me to send for? Your parents?'

'No, no!' they both cried.

'They must not know about this, Sergeant,' said Kacie.

'No, they mustn't,' Caroline insisted.

'Only because . . . er . . . it will really upset them,' Kacie said.

'If you're sure . . .' He stood up. 'Well, thanks for the tea. We'll be keeping Mr Pargiter in the cells overnight to calm down and I'll be cautioning him in the morning. You won't hear from him again, you have my word.'

Kacie saw the sergeant to the door and, after giving him her profuse thanks, returned to the living room. She sat down next to Caroline on the settee and put her arm around her. 'Are you mad with me?'

Caroline eyed her, bewildered. 'Mad with you? Why should I be?'

'Well, you now know I went around to see Malcolm. I didn't mean to cause any trouble, Caroline, I just went—'

'It's all right, Kacie, I know whatever reason you went for you'd only have my best interests at heart. I'm not annoyed, honestly.'

Kacie sighed, relieved, then turned to scrutinise her sister. Caroline's face was red where Malcolm had slapped her, but apart from that there was no other physical signs of his brutality. 'Are you really all right?' she asked.

'Yes, Kacie, yes, really I'm fine. Apart from being shaken up, and my head hurting where he nearly wrenched out my hair, I've never felt better. Malcolm's despicable behaviour tonight has confirmed that I've definitely done the right thing. I married a horrible man, Kacie, horrible and I'll never regret leaving him. I've a new life now. I'm starting a new job on Monday and I'm not going to let Malcolm spoil that.'

Kacie smiled at her, hugging her tightly. 'That's my girl.'

Chapter Twelve

By the time Friday dawned Kacie was beside herself. She still had not heard a word from Dennis and having gone through so many scenarios trying to lend valid reason to his silence, she'd come to the conclusion that he'd been so devastated by what Brenda had told him and so consumed by winning the contest and being approached by the scout, it had all been too much for him. Also, since his arrival in London, with doing what was expected of them by the record company, it wouldn't be that easy for him to get to a telephone during salon opening hours.

Her urgent longing to sort out matters between them was driving her crazy and it was only Verna's severe reprimand and the dreadful thought that she could possibly lose her job that kept her functioning.

Each night, though, she had, full of hope, called upon Tessa on her way home and had been terribly disappointed to find that there was still no news from Jed, and as neither had the other girlfriends had word of any kind from the rest of the band members, still no one had a clue how matters were progressing. The other three women, although not at all happy about the lack of contact, were obviously not as distressed over this state of affairs as Kacie was. But she kept telling herself, tomorrow, Dennis would make contact tomorrow, and it was only that hope that was allowing her fitful sleep.

Maybe the cold snap they were having had something to do with it, but all day the salon had suffered a steady stream of customers complaining about anything that took their fancy, from the poor quality of coal they were paying top prices for to the cost of bread, which had just risen a halfpenny a loaf. Very aware that her employer was keeping a watchful eye on her, and with all credit to herself, Kacie had listened politely and not passed comment. She was thankful when ten minutes to four arrived and Verna, having

127

finished off a customer, took Kacie into the office.

'Confident about tonight, are you, Kacie?' she asked.

Against the odds she was hopeful that the styles she'd managed to sketch out and, after work practised on Diane and wigs in the salon, would raise a few eyebrows, and she nodded. 'Quietly confident,' she responded. 'Unless another salon has an ace up their sleeve.'

Verna pulled a wry face. 'Well, let's hope they haven't.' She laid a reassuring hand on Kacie's arm. 'I'm still of the opinion that you're a cut above anyone else, Kacie, so I'll be very disappointed if you don't come in to work tomorrow with at least a first in one of the two entries. Now, dear, I'm sorry I can't come tonight and give you moral support but Jan has picked up a chest infection and I'm not happy about leaving him longer than I absolutely have to.'

Although not liking to hear this news about her employer's husband's failing health, Kacie was relieved that Verna wouldn't be there breathing down her neck, heightening her pressure to succeed.

'Right, we'd better get together the equipment you'll be needing, and as soon as your other model arrives you can get off. What time did you say that young girl was coming?'

'Four.' Kacie prayed Mel hadn't changed her mind.

'Well, let's hope she's on time because you need to be at the Bell to set up and use every minute of the allotted time to create your styles.' She smiled broadly at Kacie. 'All I can wish you is good luck and I'll make room for the trophy – or should I say trophies – in the salon for all our customers to admire.'

Kacie groaned inwardly. Did Verna realise what a terrible strain she was under?

Thankfully Mel was true to her word and, dress over her arm and a crumpled carrier bag carrying her ballroom evening shoes, was waiting for Kacie out in the salon. Balancing everything between them the three set off to catch the ten past four bus to take them into town.

The atmosphere in the large room at the Bell Hotel that had been set aside for the entrants to labour over their creations was highly charged. There were prestigious judges, and the audience was made up of hopeful salon owners and their respective guests from around the city and shires. A dozen or so highly skilled hairdressers were huddled in their individual groups, concentration etched deeply on

128

their faces, the air alive with shouts of instructions as they ordered their models and assistants.

Having found her allotted space, which consisted of a couple of chairs for the models to sit on and a socket at the end of a long cable in which to plug the cumbersome stand hair dryer, Kacie set about her task. Within fifteen minutes she had dampened and set in large rollers Diane's hair, positioned the dryer over her and was tackling Mel.

'This is so excitin'!' Mel exclaimed, her eyes darting all ways.

'Will you please keep still?' Kacie scolded.

'Oh, yeah, I'm sorry,' Mel said, pulling her tongue out at Diane, whom she'd noticed giving her a look of distain.

Kacie was very aware of the rivalry that was rapidly developing between the girls. She guessed that Diane was the main culprit for this growing tension, as she knew the young girl idolised her and was probably resentful of the attentions that Mel was receiving from Kacie. Also, she deduced that Diane was envious of the fact that she had picked Mel as the model for the evening creation, meaning Mel got to dress glamorously, whereas Diane's style was intended for businesswomen, and Kacie had managed to get hold of a second-hand plain blue suit for her to parade in before the judges and audience, which wasn't pleasing her at all. On the bus the girls had sniped constantly at each other and several times Kacie had had to intervene. Now her patience was growing very short.

'Listen, you two,' she snapped, wagging a warning finger at each in turn. 'This bickering stops now. I've enough on my plate getting your hairs perfect without you two having a go at each other. Mrs Koz is expecting us to return with a trophy and I'll have no chance unless I get full co-operation from the pair of you.'

They both looked deeply ashamed. 'Sorry, Kacie,' they muttered solemnly, heads bowed.

'I should think so,' she said sternly. 'Now you're as daft as each other because I'm sure that if you gave each other a chance you could become good friends and, knowing what I do about you both, you could each do with all the friends you can get.'

They exchanged looks. It was Mel who spoke up first. 'Kacie's right, so I've got no objection if you ain't,' she said, speaking loudly so Diane could hear her over the noise of the hair dryer she was sitting under, as well as the commotion being made by the rest of the ensemble. 'You could come out wi' me and me friend on Friday if yer want?'

Diane's face lit up. 'I'd love to.'

Kacie exhaled, relieved. Thank God for small mercies, she thought. Then suddenly jumped, spinning around to face the perpetrator of a loud 'Oh, bugger!'

The woman grimaced apologetically at Kacie. 'Sorry,' she said. 'I've forgotten to bring my box of hairpins and I don't know what I'm going to do now.'

She was a very attractive woman, not much older than Kacie and was obviously very upset by her lapse. Kacie instantly felt sorry for her, knowing if she'd done the same thing on such an occasion how mortified she would be. She reached over and picked up the box Verna had supplied her with. 'Use whatever you need,' she said, offering them to her. 'I've plenty.'

The woman eyed her, shocked. 'You mean it?'

'Yes, why?'

She gave Kacie a grateful smile. 'Well, it's just that you don't expect such a gesture in situations like this, do you? Everyone out for themselves, if you get my meaning.'

Kacie cast her eyes around, noticing the determination on all the other hairdressers' faces. She gave a wry laugh. 'It's like pitting yourself against the enemy, isn't it?'

The woman nodded. 'Isn't it just?' She held out her hand. 'Myrna Jenson, pleased to meet you, and before you ask the question, Myrna Loy was my mother's favourite film star.'

Kacie chuckled, grasping her hand and shaking firmly. 'Kathryn Cooper, Kacie to my friends and, before you ask, nickname courtesy of my school mates.'

'They picked a good choice. I haven't heard it before and it suits you. What salon are you with?' she asked.

'Verna's on St Saviours Road. And you?'

'I'm not. I'm just opening up my own on Green Lane Road. That's not far from you, is it?'

So this was the woman who was causing Verna such sleepless nights. 'My employer is very concerned we're going to lose customers when your salon opens.'

Myrna shook her head. 'Then she's silly to think that. Green Lane Road might be in the same vicinity but it's far enough away not to cause your employer any headaches. And you can please tell her from me I am not the type to go poaching other businesses' clients. My aim is to build my own clientele with my own reputation.' Her eyes lit excitedly. 'I'm going to name my salon Cut and Curls – what do you think?'

'I think that's a great name,' Kacie agreed.

'I'm so glad. I've been agonising over a catchy name for ages. You're the first one I've let in on it. Oh, I can't wait to get started. I'm only managing to do this from money I've saved whilst I was working in London. I just hope I'm going to have enough to buy supplies after the refitting of the shop.'

Kacie looked at her curiously. 'You worked in London, you say?'

Myrna nodded. 'I was so lucky to do my training under a man called Vidal Sassoon. A genius. I've never seen another hairdresser who can cut and create like him. Believe me, soon we're all going to be wearing his hair designs and us as hairdressers are going to have to be able to cut them because that's what the youngsters are all going to be wanting. London is fantastic. It's the place to be if you want to make a name for yourself. I used to love window shopping down the Kings Road. Have you ever heard of Mary Quant?'

'I've read about her in magazines. She's got a shop or something, hasn't she?'

'Boutique. That's what shops selling the kind of clothes for us young ones are called nowadays. You should see the stuff she has in there. It's fantastic. Trouble is, I can only afford to buy little bits and pieces. But when my money is rolling in from the salon that's where I'll be shopping for my clothes in future.'

Kacie was puzzled. 'If London is so fantastic, why open your salon in Leicester?'

'It all boils down to money. I couldn't afford London prices. Besides, Leicester is my home and it's not until you go away and live somewhere else that you appreciate your home town.' She gave a sudden grin. 'And my mother was nagging me to come home.'

'How did you come to do your apprenticeship in London?' Kacie asked curiously.

'I've always wanted to be a hairdresser but I couldn't get an apprenticeship in Leicester, not a decent one with a reputable salon, because when I was trying everyone wanted to be a hairdresser and girls were cutting each others throats to be awarded training. Luckily I had an auntie who lived in Neasden, and she suggested I tried my luck down there, which I'm glad to say I did. Best of all, after I qualified I earned much more money in London and, because I lived with my auntie, managed to save quite a bit out of my wages as well as still having fun.' Myrna giggled. 'Opening my own salon has always been my dream so I thought, why not take the plunge while I had the means to do it and I'd no other commitments, like a husband and kids? Being placed in this competition is so important to me because of the huge publicity it would bring. To get a first would be a great. I understand the *Mercury* is here tonight.'

At the mention of the competition Kacie suddenly realised the time. 'Good God!' she exclaimed in horror. 'We've been standing here gossiping for well over five minutes and neither of us will be entering anything if we don't get a move on. Anyway, good luck with the salon, I do hope it goes well,' she said sincerely, and before she hurried back to her task added, a twinkle of mischief sparking her eyes, 'And yes, I understand the *Mercury* is sending a reporter and photographer, as well as the hairdressing magazines. I bet you a tanner it's my photograph they'll be taking, not yours.'

Myrna raised her tail comb in a gesture as if to do battle. 'You're on.'

For the next hour and a half Kacie managed to concentrate all her efforts on the task in hand and finally stood back to admire her skills. Diane's usual bouffant had been softened and styled more around her face, the ends to flick out around the sides and back of her head, an easy but becoming style for the young fashionable working woman to create quickly each morning.

Mel's style was far more elaborate, and her thick locks had been backcombed hard to create volume, then smoothed up and secured on to her crown, the ends of her hair then pinned and tweaked into large loops and curls. The effect was stunning. Although meant for a much older person, Kacie hoped that with careful application of makeup, and wearing her dress, the judges would not notice how young Mel was and down-mark Kacie for not using an older model.

She nodded, satisfied. 'Not bad, if I say so myself, and with a good twenty minutes to spare. Right, all I need is to give you both a good blast of lacquer, put your makeup on and you change into your clothes and we're all set for the judging. And you two keep everything crossed,' she added, reaching down into the box by her feet for the spray bottle of lacquer. She gave each of the girls a liberal spray and another couple of squirts for luck. She quickly glanced around the room and was glad to see that, although very passable, no one else's came up to her own high standard, she felt. Then she looked over to see how Myrna was progressing and her face fell. Myrna's creations, although totally different from her own, were just as stunning. The woman certainly was gifted and maybe Verna was right to be worried.

Myrna looked over at Kacie's handiwork and smiled. 'You're giving me a run for my money, Kacie. You're good, I'll say that.'

'So are you. But we'll let the judges decide who's the best.' Kacie then noticed the look of horror growing on Myrna's face. 'What's wrong?' she asked.

'Your hairdos, they're . . . well, dripping,' she said, pointing over at Mel and Diane.

'Eh?' Kacie turned to see what Myrna was pointing at, and gawped in horror. 'Oh, my God, what on earth . . . But I don't understand . . .' She gingerly felt the ends of Diane's hair, then lightly patted Mel's. 'Why, they're wet!' she exclaimed, mortified.

'I thought I wa', only I thought it was the lacquer not drying very quick as yer did spray a lot on, Kacie,' said Diane.

'So did I,' said Mel.

Kacie looked at the bottle of lacquer in her hand and it was then she saw that it was not the type used in Verna's salon. Then the truth hit full force. Someone had switched her bottle of lacquer for one filled with water. 'I've been sabotaged,' she uttered, her eyes flashing around to see if she could spot a likely saboteur amongst the other hairdressers. But everyone seemed to be busy labouring away. Whoever was guilty wasn't going to show themselves.

Myrna came over. 'The bottles must have been swapped over whilst we were talking. This is outrageous. We should report it to the judges.'

Kacie shook her head. 'We can't prove it. I saw nothing. Did you, girls?'

They both solemnly shook their heads, having been happily chatting, getting to know each other whilst Kacie had been talking to Myrna.

Kacie's shoulders sagged. 'Well, that's me scuppered and my boss is going to be livid. She was convinced I'd come first in both entries and has practically told all the neighbourhood. I should have been more vigilant. I know this sort of thing happens.'

'Yes, but you never think it will to you. All I can say is, Kacie, that you had whoever did it scared when they saw your efforts taking shape.'

'That's no comfort,' Kacie uttered. 'It was the judges I was hoping to impress. Now I've no chance.'

Myrna sighed. 'I feel partly to blame,' she said gravely. 'If I

133

hadn't kept you talking, bragging about my salon, then this might not have happened.' She looked hard at Mel and Diane, then fixed her eyes determinedly back on Kacie. 'Come on, we're wasting time.'

Kacie eyed her blankly. 'Wasting time?'

'Yes. You've a competition to enter, remember. You're not going to let whoever did this get away with it, are you, without doing nothing? You've worked too hard not to. Two hair dryers are better than one,' Myrna said, grinning.

Kacie looked at her, shocked. 'You'll help me?'

'After what you did for me? Now, are we going to try or not?'

'We are,' Kacie said with conviction. 'But we'd better watch out because the judges don't like collaboration between contestants. Keep your eyes peeled, girls, for anyone official-looking.'

The two women beavered away and with just two minutes to spare Kacie and Myrna stood back to scrutinise their hurried rescue efforts. Both knew they had done an excellent job between them in the circumstances but both also knew the results were not up to competition standard. Mel's hair was still damp and wouldn't hold the loops, which were already flopping, and some of Diane's flicks were insisting on turning under and not out, which ruined the total effect.

'Well, at least we've tried,' said a despondent Kacie. 'But the judges will laugh at this. I might as well go home now.' She turned to Myrna and looked at her gratefully. 'I want to thank you though, very much so.' She turned to the girls. 'And you both for sitting so patiently.'

'I'm so sorry, Kacie,' Myrna uttered, upset.

'And so are we,' said Mel and Diane.

Kacie looked hard at Myrna. 'Will you do me a great favour?'

'I'll try.'

'Come first in your entries. Then at least whoever did this won't have got away with it.'

Myrna gave a tight smile. 'I'll do my best, Kacie.'

'Good. I'll look out for you in the *Mercury*. Right, girls, let's get packed up and out of here.'

Outside on the pavement after their hurried exit Kacie stared at the pile of items they had brought with them from the salon. With all that was happening to her she hadn't thought her life could get any worse and she was feeling absolutely drained, not at all looking forward to facing Verna in the morning. 'I don't fancy lugging this lot home, not the way I'm feeling tonight. I wonder if the hotel would keep it safe in a cupboard until tomorrow. I'll get up early and fetch it before starting work.' That idea didn't appeal either, but better than the alternative.

She went back inside the hotel and was surprised when the woman behind the reception desk readily agreed. 'People leave things with us all the time. We have a special cupboard. It'll be quite safe.'

After depositing the equipment and supplies with the receptionist, outside on the pavement Kacie made to say her goodbyes to the girls.

'Me and Di are goin' fer a drink, Kacie, a'yer gonna join us? It might do you good.'

She smiled gratefully at them. 'The way I feel at the moment I could drink a bucketful, and thanks for the offer but I really just want to get home. You two enjoy yourselves. I'll see you tomorrow, Di, and you soon, Mel?'

'Yeah, I'll pop up the salon when I've saved some more money and yer can do me 'air.'

Kacie watched as the two girls happily trotted off up the Humberstone Gate, their belongings swinging on their arms. She shuddered, the cold evening air chilling her. Suddenly she envied them. Although both in their own way had personal problems, in reality neither had anything of a serious nature to worry about except whether they had enough money on them for the price of their drinks. Sighing miserably, she made her way to the bus stop.

As usual Caroline pounced on her the minute she opened the front door. 'You're early. I didn't expect you for at least another hour or so. I was going to do you a sandwich. I'd better put the kettle on. Oh, how did it go?'

'Don't ask and, for God's sake, stop fussing, Caroline.' And before she could stop herself Kacie blurted, 'You're really getting on my nerves.'

Caroline's face fell, deeply hurt, and Kacie immediately felt ashamed for her outburst. 'I didn't mean it, I'm so sorry. It's just, just . . .' Suddenly her self-control collapsed, face crumpled, eyes filled with huge tears of misery, which rolled down her face. 'Oh, it was dreadful, Caroline,' she sobbed. 'I didn't even get as far as the judging because someone switched my bottle of lacquer for water and the hairdos were ruined.'

Caroline threw her arms around her and hugged her protectively.

'I'm so sorry, Kacie. Did you find out who did it?'

'No,' she blubbered. 'Verna will be furious. She was banking on me winning something. She'll blame me, say I should have been more vigilant. I could lose my job.'

'Oh, it won't come to that, Kacie.'

Just then the front door knocker sounded loudly and both women turned, startled. 'It's gone eight, a bit late for callers,' said Caroline, releasing her sister. 'You go on through, I'll see who it is.'

For once Kacie was glad to let her sister take charge. 'I don't care who it is,' she said. 'I'm not at home.'

Caroline nodded in understanding. 'All right, Kacie.'

Her back against the well-banked-up fire, Kacie heard the mumble of voices, then the click of the front door closing and presently Caroline came in. 'It was Tessa, Jed's girlfriend. She was sorry to hear you weren't feeling well but said this would cheer you up.' She handed Kacie a scrap of paper with writing upon it.

Kacie looked at it. 'It's the address of a hotel,' she said, puzzled. 'In London.' Then its significance registered. 'Oh, she must have had a call from Jed and this is where the band is staying. Did she say anything else, Caroline? Anything at all?'

Caroline shook her head. 'No. She asked to see you. I said you weren't well and I did lie and say you were in bed. She told me to give you that bit of paper and said it would cheer you up. Oh, and she hopes you're feeling better soon.'

Kacie's mind was racing. She had the address of where Dennis was staying. She couldn't wait another minute. She had to go and see him. Now. She turned and rushed into her bedroom, flung wide the wardrobe doors and began gathering her clothes.

'What are you doing?' asked Caroline, framed in the doorway.

'Can I borrow your suitcase?' Kacie asked. 'It'll be too big for all the clothes I've got but it doesn't matter. And I'll need my toiletries, and what else . . .?'

'Kacie, what on earth are you doing?' Caroline asked again.

Kacie momentarily stopped what she was doing and looked across at her sister incredulously. 'Going to see Dennis, of course. Now can I borrow your suitcase or what?'

'Yes, of course. But it's gone eight, Kacie.'

'So? There'll be a train. I'll catch the mail train if necessary. I have to see Dennis, Caroline, surely you understand?'

'Yes, yes, of course I do. But can't it wait until tomorrow? London is not the place to be in late at night, Kacie. You don't know your way around, for a start. And what about your job? What will Mrs Koz say when you don't turn up for work in the morning?'

'That's the last thing on my mind at the moment, Caroline. Anyway,' she said ironically, 'after tonight, if I manage to keep it it'll be a miracle. Oh, Mrs Koz will understand when I explain, I know she will. I just have to see Dennis and straighten this mess out, then I'll be back. You can go around and explain to Mrs Koz for me, Caroline. It's only one day she'll have to manage without me.' She leaped over to her tallboy, pulled open the middle drawer and grabbed out her baby-doll pyjamas, then quickly changed her mind and snatched instead her best night-dress, a flimsy creation she'd worn on her wedding night. 'I'll need this,' she said, confident that once Dennis and herself had talked matters out they'd be spending the rest of the night making passionate love. 'And this,' she said, picking up her bottle of Estee Lauder's Youth Dew she kept for special occasions. She spun to face her sister. 'Now will you fetch your case for me, please?' she said frantically.

Sighing resignedly, Caroline did as she was asked.

'You're taking everything?' Caroline asked as she helped with the packing.

'I haven't got that much and I haven't time to stand and sort through it,' she gabbled, her mind on other things. 'Just throw everything in, Caroline. Lucky I got paid today. The rent and all else will have to wait until I get back. It won't hurt as I'm up to date with everything. Can you fetch my makeup bag, please? It's on the table in the kitchen.'

Case packed, dressed for the off, and precious scrap of paper tucked safely in her handbag, Kacie opened the front door and said goodbye to her sister.

'I wish you'd change your mind,' Caroline begged her.

'Caroline, I'm going to London, not Timbuktu. I have an address. It's not like I'm going on a wild-goose chase. Now for God's sake stop worrying. I'm a grown woman, not a child.'

'And as stubborn as a mule. Are you sure you don't want me to see you off at the station?'

'I'm positive. It's cold and I don't know how long I'll have to wait for the train.' She leaned over and kissed Caroline's cheek. 'Thanks for your help,' and with a twinkle in her eye said, 'I'll take care of your case, so don't worry.'

'It's not the case I care a damn about, but I do you, Kacie.'

'I do you too, and don't worry, I'll be fine. Look, I'd better dash. Tarra.'

'Tarra, Kacie,' Caroline uttered worriedly, as she watched her sister rush down the stairs before she closed the flat door.

Chapter Thirteen

Thinking it an extortionate price for such a short ride, Kacie handed over half a crown and thanked the taxi driver. Luck had been with her, and by the skin of her teeth she had managed to leap on the nine o'clock train that was just departing. The journey had seemed to take for ever, at last, though, she was outside the hotel where Dennis was staying. She just hoped that with the lateness of hour he wouldn't already be asleep. But then he wouldn't be annoyed, not when he knew who it was that was disturbing him. She was his wife, after all, and despite their temporary estrangement she knew after his initial shock he'd be overjoyed to see her.

Picking up her suitcase she glanced the hotel over. It was situated in a side street off the Euston Road, adjoining other premises consisting of several restaurants; pub on two of the corners; business premises; a drinking club and another hotel; all built from pale creamy coloured stone. The Grafton Hotel's outward appearance certainly didn't conjure up the inside plushness of the Grand Hotel in Leicester, but judging by the drapes and ornate lamps Kacie could see at the large downstairs windows it did seem a cut above the Bell Hotel where she'd been earlier that evening. She was gratified to note that the record company people seemed to be looking after Dennis and the boys well.

She made to ascend the stone steps leading up to the rotating entrance door when a young night porter, appeared from nowhere, looming before her.

'Can I 'elp yer, madam? Only we ain't expecting no guests at this hour. 'Ave yer a bookin'?'

She looked up at him, startled. 'Well, no, I've no booking. I've come to visit someone. My husband. I understand he's staying here.'

'Oh?' The porter eyed her warily. 'Who's that then?'

'Mr Cooper. Dennis Cooper.'

He shook his head. 'That name don't ring any bells. I pride meself on knowing the names of those staying. You sure yer got the right hotel?'

'Positive,' she answered. 'This is the Grafton Hotel on Tottenham Court Road?' she asked, wondering if the taxi driver had dropped her off at the wrong place.

'It is,' he confirmed. 'But as I said, I know all the names of the guests what's staying and there's no one of that name registered.'

'Oh?' Her mind raced frantically, then a thought struck. 'He might be booked in under the name of Vernon something or other. The rest of the band is staying here. They're called Vernon and the Vipers. The record company will have made the booking and be paying the bill, I should think.'

'Ahh.' His face was knowing and he eyed her scathingly, folding his arms in a defensive manner. 'We've been warned about the likes of yerself showing up – had experiences before, in fact.'

She frowned at him puzzled. 'Sorry? I don't understand.'

He made a sudden leap towards her, grabbed her arm and propelled her forcefully back down the steps and on to the street. 'You think I'm fick or wot, lady? Fans trying to get in. Use any number of crafty ways. It's happened before when Kathy Kirby stopped 'ere. Screaming gels and blokes all over the place. Some even tried to shin up the drainpipe to catch a glimpse of 'er. Never had a fan pretending to be a wife before, though. Mad you all are. Come on, off yer go,' he said, giving her a forceful push.

She staggered backwards, losing her grip on her case, which skidded across the pavement to clatter against the hotel wall. She quickly regained her composure and took a stance. 'Now you look here—'

'No, you,' he cut in. 'You've been rumbled, misses. Now bugger off before I call the scuffers and 'ave yer physically removed.'

With that he turned and ran back into the hotel.

Kacie stepped across to the dark shadows of the building wall to reclaim her suitcase but instead leaned herself against it, her mind racing. This reception was the last thing she had expected. How was she going to convince the young porter she wasn't a fan but genuinely Dennis's wife? Well, there was nothing for it, she had to cause such a fuss the porter would have no alternative but to wake Dennis and confirm her story. And he could call the police if he liked. That would soon show she was telling the truth. She made to pick up her suitcase and go and tackle the porter again when a taxi

140

drew up. She decided it best not to cause a scene in front of other guests, so slunk back into the shadows to wait until they had gone inside.

A young woman alighted from the taxi and as she turned and became illuminated by the streetlight, Kacie could see how good-looking she was, her mane of ash-blonde hair cascading to her shoulders. Her slim, shapely body was dressed very fashionably in a short, blue taffeta, bell-skirted evening dress with a low-cut strapless top, a wrap of the same material draped around her shoulders. All very tasteful and very expensive, Kacie judged. So this was how people in the capital city dressed of an evening, and she wondered where the woman had been. Remembering articles she had read, awe-struck, in magazines, on young London socialites, Kacie assumed the woman had probably been to the opera or the ballet.

Then a tall man got out and joined the woman. He was smartly dressed too, the light from the streetlamp shimmering the sheen on his very up-to-date well-cut silver-grey suit. The fringe of his dark hair flopped well down over his forehead and from what Kacie could see of the man's feature's, she thought him to be very attractive.

The handsome couple were both unaware they were being watched and out of respect Kacie pressed her back right up against the wall so as not disturb their intimacy. The man turned his head slightly, most of his features now on view to Kacie, and to her absolute astonishment she realised it was Dennis. An outwardly different Dennis to the one who had left her to go for the weekend to Butlin's. In Kacie's eyes, the new haircut he was sporting enhanced him drastically from ruggedly good-looking to devastatingly handsome, and his new clothing seemed to have given him a confident air. She made to announce her presence but what Dennis did next made her face drain ashen, her hand shooting up to cover her gawping mouth, glaring eyes wide in shock.

He put his arms around the woman and gave her a tight embrace. 'Thanks, Abbey, you've been wonderful,' he said, then kissed her cheek affectionately.

She looked up at him, her beautiful face wreathed in deep concern. 'You are sure about this, Dennis? Positive you're doing the right thing?'

'I've never been so sure about anything in all my life. We've done nothing but discuss this all night, Abbey.'

'I know, but I still feel this is all so sudden.'

141

'Some might see it like that but I knew instantly, Abbey, and I don't see any point in carrying on with this charade any longer. Do you?'

'No. As you said when we first talked about this, people know their own feelings and we know when something is right for us.'

'Right, we've agreed what we're going to tell the record company but first I'm going to go and see Kacie. I'm going to travel up tomorrow morning. She deserves to be told about this before anyone else and I'm not looking forward to it, believe me. I haven't worked out how I'm going to break this news to her yet, either. This decision has got to be the most difficult I've ever made in my life, and I'm hoping Kacie will be very understanding and let me leave without a fuss. I'm sure she will be when she hears my reasons and knows I won't change my mind, and I think she'll be relieved it's all over, if you want the truth, and she can settle down and live a normal life. Hopefully I'll be back before I'm missed by the chief at Decca. It hasn't stopped since we got down, has it? I never realised how much was involved in all this fame business. If they call for us to come into the office for any meetings and I haven't arrived back, will you cover for me, please?'

'Of course I will. After all, it is my job to look after the band's interests.'

'You've more than done that with me.'

'Mmm, I have.' She eyed him worriedly. 'Because of my involvement in all this I feel hugely responsible for your decision. Are you sure you wouldn't like me to come with you and help you explain to your wife? I know it's not quite the done thing, but I will.'

'That's taking your job a bit far, isn't it?' he said, grinning at her.

'This is no time for flippancy, Dennis. We both know our relationship has gone much further than me being assigned as the band's personal assistant.'

'I'm sorry, yes it has, much further, and that's my fault entirely, Abbey, as it was me who approached you first. I appreciate your offer, but Kacie and me weren't on the best of terms when I came down here so I'm not sure how she's going to react when she sees me. I've witnessed Kacie in full flight and I wouldn't want you to be in the firing line. Best I deal with this alone.'

She leaned up and kissed his cheek. 'I hope you're right, Dennis. I'll be thinking of you. Best of luck. You'll need it.'

Before she climbed back aboard the taxi they hugged again and kissed each other on the cheek tenderly. Dennis shut the door, waved the cab off and ran up the hotel steps to disappear through its rotating door.

In the dark shadows, Kacie stood frozen rigid, stunned senseless by what she had overheard. Her mind frenziedly went over and over the conversation, dissecting every word that she had heard, trying to make another reason for it other than the one that was glaringly obvious to her, one which she was resisting to acknowledge. But try as she might, there was only one explanation. Her Dennis, her beloved husband, the man she adored, had planned to spend the rest of her life with, in the space of less than a week had fallen in love with another woman and was planning to tell Kacie he was leaving her. And how could Dennis say she herself would be relieved that their marriage was over and that she could settle down to a normal life without him? Did he not realise how much she loved him and how much the loss of him would affect her whole existence? And was that hussy really offering to accompany Dennis to break the news of their illicit relationship?

Her body started to shake, and a great wave of desolation flooded through her. As tears of utter misery filled her eyes a low moan of grief escaped her lips. If anyone else had repeated this conversation to her she wouldn't have believed them – scoffed at the absurdity at the very idea that Dennis would deceive her. But she had to believe it, she had heard it with her own ears, her own eyes witnessed the affectionate way in which the two had acted.

As fat tears of devastation rolled down her face she felt the great desire to race to him, beg him not to leave her, plead with him to forgive her over anything she had done to cause him to seek the comforts of another woman's arms. It was her pride that stopped her. She was terrified at the thought of humiliating herself in front of a man whose love she'd once had, risking him acting pityingly towards her and losing the last bit of respect he may still harbour for her.

As she sniffed back the river of snot that was pouring from her nose and mingling with her tears, a great surge of desolation and loneliness overwhelmed her and her eyes darted frighteningly around, suddenly alarmed by this alien city she was in. She had to get out of here, away from where she was most definitely not wanted.

An approaching taxi caught her attention and, grabbing up her suitcase, she darted into the middle of the road to flag it down.

'Whoa there, misses,' the driver shouted at her. 'I nearly ran you over.'

Wishing vehemently that he had, thinking that at least dead she wouldn't be suffering such indescribable pain, Kacie flung open the door and jumped inside. 'St Pancras, please,' she choked, her destination being the only other address she knew in this strange place.

Chapter Fourteen

On looking back, Kacie couldn't remember much about the journey home – just asking a station porter the time of the next train to Leicester, and the long wait in a freezing waiting room for the six a.m. departure.

Her body heavy with fatigue, she dragged herself out of the station into the buzzing atmosphere of the busy Leicester day. Putting her suitcase down on the pavement, she gazed blindly around at the familiar red-brick buildings, at the people she felt so akin to, as they scurried about their business. She was home. But to what? This city that had held so much for her, now she felt held nothing. Dennis was planning today to tell her their marriage was over. Was he already travelling up on the train to do so?

The thought of returning to the flat, waiting for his knock to sound on the door, she knowing what he was about to tell her, filled her with absolute dread. She couldn't face it. And once he had gone from her for ever to another woman's arms, what would she do then? How would she carry on with her life, living inside walls that held so many happy memories for her, every nook and cranny a reminder of him?

She suddenly felt an overwhelming sense of worthlessness, unimportance. If Dennis, a man who had promised to love and cherish her for the rest of his days, could so easily cast her aside, then what meaning did her existence hold to anyone else? Then the very thought of facing those she knew, having to explain what had transpired and then suffering their inevitable pity, the whispers behind her back, made her shudder in trepidation. Caroline she knew above everyone else would suffocate her with her sisterly protection. She couldn't face any of it.

She made her decision there and then. She wasn't going back. She had nothing to go back to. She would start afresh, where no one knew her, in unfamiliar surroundings affording her no reminders whatsoever of her previous happy life. All she needed she carried with her in Caroline's suitcase. Caroline had managed without Kacie until recent weeks and now she was freed from the misery of her marriage, had her own bright future to look forward to, had no need of Kacie any longer. As far as Kacie was concerned, Caroline was welcome to the flat, should she wish to stay on in it, and all that was in it.

As for Kacie's job, she felt that after her surly behaviour of late, her drop of standard, the happenings at the competition and then her being absent without permission, she would be lucky if Verna would ever actually talk to her again, let alone allow her to keep her job. Probably she would be very glad to be rid of her. Also, she hated the idea of being at the salon, where Dennis could come and find her at anytime.

Then she remembered her mother-in-law, that lovely woman whose welcome into her family had been given so generously and unconditionally. Kacie would miss her dreadfully, but sadly she was no longer part of that special circle. Her place now belonged to the woman she had seen Dennis acting so intimately with only hours ago, and although the old lady's heart would be broken she felt the least Dennis could do was be the one to explain to his mother of their break-up, and she hoped Dotty would understand the reason for her own absence.

Her own parents – well, they could bask in their own glory when they eventually did find out that they had been right all along, their only upset that they wouldn't be able to tell her themselves as she wouldn't be around.

She took her purse from her handbag and counted her money. After spending a pound on train and taxi fares on her ill-fated trip, she had four pounds and a few coppers left from her wages. It would have to stretch until she found herself work but, more importantly, at this moment she needed somewhere to stay.

Chapter Fifteen

The small room she was being shown was no palace, far from it, the landlady definitely not the friendly warm Mrs Bunting kind that Mel had been lucky enough to find.

She had chosen the area of the West End of Leicester as being as far away as she could possible get from Evington, somewhere she wouldn't be likely to cross paths with anyone she knew.

The three-storey bay terrace, overgrown scrap of garden at the front, had very apparently lost its glory decades ago and there were no surprises in store for Kacie when, having spotted the tatty vacancy sign pinned to the peeling brown front door, she knocked on it and it was opened by a slovenly middle-aged woman. She looked Kacie over suspiciously before bluntly asking her what she wanted. Neither was Kacie surprised by the state of the vacant room she was being shown.

With her present low esteem and traumatised emotions, none of this was of importance. She needed somewhere to rest her head of a night and this shabby room on the second floor at the back of the property would suffice. The walls were covered in grimy wallpaper, the once-white paintwork was grey with age. The glass in the window that looked out on to a jungle of a back garden was so filthy hardly any light came in. In the far corner was a cracked pot sink above which hung a doubtful-looking geezer. By the side of it sat a worn oak cupboard, inside which the landlady had generously supplied one of each of the most basic kitchen equipment. It was also where tenants were expected to keep all the rest of their domestic items. On top of the cupboard were two greasy gas jets on a metal ring, provided for cooking. The covers on the rickety-looking bed which was against the main back wall had definitely seen better days and were desperate for a wash. A piece of rodding, spanning the alcove by the boarded-up fireplace in front of which was an old electric fire, had been provided to hang clothes and was covered by a moth-eaten piece of curtaining. A gate-legged table marked by scratches, cup rings and cigarette burns; two dining chairs, the stuffing protruding out of their plastic seating and one uncomfortable-looking easy chair completed the sparse furnishing. The floor was covered by cheap lino, so worn the pattern was hardly visible.

'Fifteen bob a week, plus gas and electric,' the landlady said off-handedly, the ash from her cigarette dangling from the corner of her thin lips falling on the floor. 'You've a ring on,' she observed suspiciously through her beady icy grey eyes. 'Are yer married? This is a single occupancy, yer know.'

'I am aware this room is for one person and I might wear a ring but I'm no longer married,' Kacie answered tonelessly.

'I don't allow visitors after eight at night.'

'That's fine, there won't be any.'

'No pets.'

'I have none.'

'No loud music.'

'I've no radio or record player.'

'What d'yer do for a living?'

'I'm a hairdresser.'

'Huh, well, that's better than n'ote I suppose, but as long as yer can pay the rent I don't really care how yer earn yer money. D'yer want the room or not?'

'I'll take it. I'd like to move in straight away.'

As she suspected, the bed was most uncomfortable but before Kacie would consider actually sleeping on it she gathered the bedding together and, whilst it was running through a cycle in the machine at the local Launderette she went to purchase some necessities, being very frugal with her spending.

Back in her new abode she swept, scrubbed and polished until not a cobweb remained, nor a speck of dust, and after she'd hung up her clothes, hoping the creases would drop out after her hasty packing, and having no iron as yet at her disposal to smarten them up, she remade her bed with the freshly laundered bedding. Then she prepared herself a meal of potatoes and corn beef, only eating in order to keep up her strength. Crockery washed and put away in the now cleaned cupboard, she then sat down on the bed and took a look around her.

Despite now smelling much fresher and looking far cleaner, this room was still depressing but it would have to do until she was in a financial position to find somewhere better. She lifted her hand to remove a stray strand of hair that had fallen into her eye and as she did so she caught sight of her wedding ring and she stared at it. This token of his love Dennis had so tenderly put on her finger whilst all those gathered around them had witnessed their union was now meaningless. He didn't love her any more and they might still be tied in the eyes of the law but that was all they were tied by. With a distressed lump in her throat, eyes filled with tears of misery, she slowly eased the ring off. Knowing she would never bring herself to part with it, she fetched her handbag, took out her purse and tucked it right down into one of the corners. She then collapsed back on to the bed, dissolving into heart-rending sobs.

Finally cried out, Kacie raised her head as a cold icy grip enclosed her heart. Grieving over her loss of Dennis was not going to bring him back. She had somehow to push all thoughts of him to the back of her mind; needed to concentrate all her efforts on her immediate future. She had to decide what best to do about getting herself some work, as the money in her purse would only last her a week at the most.

The last thing she felt like applying for was a job with another hairdressing salon. She had loved it at Verna's, being part of a small but happy staff, and knew that she'd never be that contented again. But hairdressing was all she knew. It was such a shame she had not the means at her disposal either to open her own salon, like Myrna had done, or to operate another alternative which was becoming very popular over the last couple of years, a mobile hairdresser – the hairdresser going to the clients' houses.

She then explored other occupations but none appealed in the slightest. But she had to do something.

She felt the urgent need for a walk, feeling a blow of fresh air might help her think clearer. If nothing else it would start to familiarise her with her new surroundings.

Picking up her coat she quietly left her room and made her way down the dimly lit stairs. Just as she reached halfway down, she heard a door click shut and she paused for a moment, all her senses telling her that someone had been watching her. She mentally shook herself: she was being silly. She was in unfamiliar surroundings, the most terrible situation had just befallen her, and she wasn't exactly feeling her normal self. The noise she had heard was just another lodger returning back to his or her room.

As she arrived on the street Kacie turned and looked back at the house, and, as she saw the curtain of the bay window of the room at the front move, she knew that she had been right. Someone had been watching her – still was, in fact. But then, she reasoned, whoever they were must just be wondering who the new occupant of the room upstairs was, and would be wanting to catch a glimpse of her out of curiosity. She suspected she'd do the same. With that comforting thought, she continued on her way.

At the end of the dismal street to the left was a large park, almost identical in appearance to the Spinney Hill Park in Evington. To the right was the busy thoroughfare of King Richard Road which eventually led to the West Bridge on the outskirts of the town. The long parade consisted of numerous assorted terraced shops, pubs, a couple of cafés and the odd business operation. Situated immediately behind was a large maze of interwoven terraced streets, the people who resided in the dilapidated near-slum dwellings no better off than those in the area she had come from.

She had happy memories of strolling in Spinney Hill Park whilst courting Dennis and, fighting hard to avoid any situation that resurrected reminders of him, chose to window-shop down the King Richard Road.

For half an hour she managed to lose herself amongst the throng of shoppers on this late Saturday afternoon, looking at the goods on display. A few items caught her eye. A pretty red jumper in the Three Sisters haberdashery; a pair of black courts in one of the two shoe retailers; a nice table lamp that would help brighten her room in one of the second-hand shops – all of which she made a mental note of, she hoped, to purchase when she had the funds. She did, though, purchase from a fusty-smelling junk shop a much-needed iron, though from its condition she didn't feel it would last her long; an old Oxo tin in which to keep her rent money and shillings for the gas and electric meters; and a mirror which unfortunately had a crack in it, but all for the price of sixpence. Kacie congratulated herself on her bargains.

She was nearing the end of the parade of shops and about to turn and make her way back when she saw a card in a café window advertising for a waitress, and although the job didn't appeal to her, it was work after all and she was in no position not to consider it. She was just about to go inside and make further enquiries when someone spoke to her.

'Excuse me, but can you tell me where the Sunny Side Residential

Home for Retired Ladies is? I know it's around here somewhere but damned if I can find it. I've been wandering around for ages. My elderly aunt has just moved in there and I'm paying her a visit, seeing if she needs anything, her hair washing or whatever. She's crippled with arthritis, poor love, and can't manage much by herself. If I don't hurry up and find the place I'll not have time to do much for her before teatime. I understand meals are very punctual in these sort of places.'

Kacie looked at the woman addressing her. She was smartly dressed and appeared pleasant enough. She certainly liked to talk, that was obvious. Kacie shook her head. 'I'm sorry I haven't a clue. I'm new around these parts myself.'

The woman smiled apologetically at her. 'Then I'm sorry to have bothered you. Good day.'

Kacie watched as she walked off, then tackled another passer-by. That person pointed her in the Fosse Road direction and, glad to see the woman had seemed to have discovered her destination, Kacie turned back to look once again at the card in the café window. Then something the woman had said struck her and her face screwed in deep thought. She had said that amongst other things she was going to wash her aunt's hair. Kacie wondered why the staff at the home didn't do it.

She pictured all those women under one roof. It was such a pity she couldn't offer to do their hair. The money she made would buy her time to look around for a suitable way in which to earn her living.

Then suddenly a vision of the equipment from Verna's salon she had left at the hotel after the competition rose tantalisingly before her. Had anyone been to collect it? Probably not, as without Kacie they would be short-staffed whilst Verna got someone to take her place. Her mind then whirled as an idea began to take shape. If she borrowed the equipment she could offer to do the old ladies' hair for them. Surely the person in charge of the home would jump at the prospect of a very skilled hairdresser offering her services at a much lower rate than a salon charged. Whatever sundries she used from the stock Verna had supplied for the competition, glad to remember her ex-employer had been most generous with the amounts, she could replace before she returned the equipment back to the hotel.

Her heart pounded with anticipation. It was such a good plan – one that could give her an encouraging start on her solitary road to her future. She just hoped the person that ran the home was receptive to her idea. There was no time like the present to find out, and she hurried off in the direction she had seen the woman heading.

The matron was just the type Kacie would expect to be running a home for the care of the well-to-do elderly. Nicely rounded and pleasant-faced, her dark blue and white uniform spotlessly clean and crisp, she smiled warmly at Kacie.

'Well, my dear, we've never been approached by a hairdresser before. I'm sure my ladies would be delighted to have their hairs done. Some poor dears we have here are quite infirm and cannot get out. We do what we can ourselves, of course, but sometimes time doesn't allow for us to get around to doing all the little extras that make life so much pleasanter for them. So what would you be offering?'

Kacie took a deep breath before replying. Obviously she was restricted by what she could do by the supplies Verna had furnished her with for the competition. 'I thought for a start so you can try me out, I'd concentrate on trims and sets.'

'Mmm, seems reasonable enough. And your charges?'

Her mind whirled. She hadn't thought about that. She did a quick calculation, hoping her figures were not too expensive to outprice herself and not too cheap to forgo any profit. 'Two shillings for just a trim. Three for a shampoo and set. A special rate of four shillings for both.'

The matron looked impressed. 'Very reasonable. I wouldn't mind you doing mine at that price. I'm sure the other members of staff would be interested too. I have twenty-five ladies here at present and I'm sure half if not more will jump at this. Well, jump is the wrong word to use – some of my ladies can hardly walk.'

Kacie couldn't believe her good fortune and just prayed the equipment stored away in the hotel cupboard for safekeeping had not been collected.

'Monday would be a good day for us. Could you manage so soon?'

Kacie fought not to appear too eager. 'Yes, that would be fine.'

'So we'll see you about eight thirty, then? Oh, is there a limit to how many bookings you can take?' the matron asked.

Kacie quickly did a calculation in her head. If she started at eight thirty and worked like a Trojan all day she could probably get through as many as wanted her service, plus possibly the staff. It would be no mean feat but, thinking of the money she could earn, a challenge she couldn't afford to turn down. 'I'll do my best to get through all those that want their hairs doing. If I run out of time I can always come back.' She held out her hand. 'I'll see you Monday morning at eight thirty, and I'll look forward to it.'

Outside the nursing home, Kacie caught the bus into town, all the journey worrying what she would do if the equipment had been collected. Luck was with her and the equipment was there, and how she managed to lug it all back, the cumbersome stand hair dryer and the heavy bags of sundries, was a miracle in itself. Several thoughtful people did give her a hand getting on and off the bus, for which she thanked them profusely.

Every muscle in her body groaning, she finally and with much relief arrived back at her new abode. As she pushed open the gate with her foot she was most perturbed to notice a chink of light showing through the drawn curtains of the downstairs window, which then suddenly disappeared as the curtaining fell back into place. Someone had been watching her again. A surge of indignation and annoyance reared. She didn't like the thought one little bit that someone was spying on her comings and goings. She wondered how long the person behind those curtains was going to do this before he or she got fed up.

Kacie decided she couldn't wait that long. She had enough on her plate dealing with her own problems without some faceless person adding to them by their mindless actions. Dragging the equipment and supplies up the short path to the front door, she let herself in and deposited everything by the bottom step of the staircase. She then took several deep breaths, raised her chin and rapped purposely on the door of the room to the front of the house.

Nothing happened, but she knew someone was in there, so she rapped again, harder this time. She thought she heard a noise coming from immediately behind the door and she pressed her ear to it and listened intently. She could hear breathing, she knew she could. Determined not to go away until she had addressed this unpleasant situation, she stood back, clenched her fist and gave the door two good thumps. Again nothing happened. Then a sudden sound made her jump and her eyes shot down to see that the knob on the door was slowly turning. The door inched open a crack and she stepped back in shock when she saw an eye peering at her.

'What can I do for you?' a deep voice asked.

An overwhelming feeling of foreboding filled her, her mind conjuring all manner of visions of the person the eye belonged to – none of them pleasant. She suddenly wished she had left well alone. Fighting to calm a sickening apprehension that was whirling in her stomach, she took a very deep breath and said far more confidently than ever she felt, 'My name is Kacie Cooper. I've just moved into the room upstairs. Now what else do you want to know?'

There was silence for several long moments, during which time Kacie began to be gravely concerned that whoever was behind the door would suddenly leap out at her, brandishing a knife, or something equally terrifying. Finally a reply was issued. 'It's very nice of you to introduce yourself. But I don't understand what you mean by what else do I want to know?'

The polite response after what she had expected took her by surprise and quashed any terror she was feeling, replacing it with annoyance. 'You know perfectly well what I mean. You've been watching me. I don't like it.'

There was silence again. Then slowly the door opened further to reveal fully the man standing behind it. Kacie's face filled with astonishment. He resembled nothing at all of the terrifying visions her mind had concocted. He was, she judged, in his late twenties, maybe younger, of medium height; sandy-coloured short back and sides neatly combed. The clothes he was wearing, although of the style of the 1940s, were clean and pressed. Although by no means handsome, his was a pleasant, wholesome face that was looking at her ashamedly. 'I'm very sorry if I upset you. I didn't mean to appear as if I was checking your moves.'

His voice had an educated edge, not at all the type of person she expected would be living in these dire surroundings.

'Well, you did,' she snapped.

'I apologise again. It's just . . . just . . .'

'Just what?' she demanded.

His face suddenly reddened with embarrassment and he averted his gaze. 'I saw you when you first arrived and I wanted to introduce myself but then I thought I might be imposing, so I didn't. I have to admit, I was looking out for you . . .' His voice trailed off, his whole persona displaying his discomfort. 'I think you're so pretty.' Then he added hurriedly, 'I hope I haven't embarrassed you.'

His admission stunned Kacie, and she found herself smiling at him. 'Well, thanks for the compliment. To be honest, it's just what I need right now.'

His relief was most apparent. 'You're not going to complain to Mrs Slattery about me, then?'

'Not this time but I will if you peep at me behind your curtains again. Anyway, I personally suspect Mrs Slattery wouldn't give a monkey's. She's only interested in the rent. Well, it's nice to have met you. At least now I know there's other life in this place besides myself and Mrs Slattery.'

He looked at her searchingly. 'I've been here a few years and you're the first other lodger I've spoken properly to.' He eyed her hesitantly. 'Er . . . you wouldn't like to come in for a beverage, would you?' he asked, opening the door wider in an inviting gesture.

Kacie stared at him unsurely.

'I'm not going to bite you, I promise,' he said. 'I really would be honoured if you would take tea with me.'

He was so well mannered, his request to her so old-fashionedly put, and she hesitated, thinking how would she manage to make polite conversation with this man when it was obvious they had nothing in common. But he was looking at her so hopefully, almost pleadingly, and suddenly it struck her that he was terribly lonely. Her heart went out to him. It wouldn't hurt her to take a few minutes of her time to have a cup of tea, and his suggestion was a preferable option to returning to her dismal room and possibly brooding over her recent emotional events. 'A cuppa sounds grand.' Temporarily forgetting she had abandoned the hair dryer and bag of sundries at the bottom of the stairs, she went inside.

Slipping off her coat, Kacie sat down in one of the comfortable chairs by the side of the modern electric fire, and as he busied himself mashing the tea, she stole a glance around. The room was much larger than her own, and had been made very comfortable considering a man on his own lived here. None of the furniture was that supplied by the landlady either. It was obviously second-hand, but in a far superior condition than that which Kacie was paying for the privilege of using. And most noticeable to Kacie was that not only did he have an electric fire that actually produced a decent amount of heat, he also had a proper gas cooker fitted and a proper kitchenette in which to store all his food and equipment, although she did notice that one of the sliding glass doors of the cupboard was cracked.

'You've made it nice,' she said, impressed.

He turned and smiled across at her. 'I've done my best. I do apologise but I've just realised I've no fresh milk, only condensed. Will that be all right?' he asked.

She nodded. 'Fine, thank you. Er . . . I don't know your name . . .'

'Oh, how thoughtless of me, I haven't introduced myself properly.' He walked across and placed a china cup and saucer on the small table to the side of her, then held out his hand. 'Richard Proctor. I'm very pleased to meet you, Miss Cooper.'

She accepted his hand and shook. 'My friends call me Kacie as in K.C.'

He looked at her expectantly. 'Do you think we might become friends?' His tone had a hint of plea in it.

She smiled at him mischievously. 'Well, now I know you're not a Peeping Tom or, worse, a mass murderer, I don't see why not. Unless, of course, there's something you're hiding?'

'I can assure you there isn't,' he insisted. 'Not at all. I'm just a simple man, living a simple life.' He sat down in the chair opposite, placing his cup down on the floor beside him. Leaning forward he clasped his hands and looked at her. 'It'll be nice not to feel so alone here, knowing I've a friend upstairs. It's very difficult getting to know people living in a place like this.'

'Yes I suppose it is,' she agreed. 'Once we're inside our rooms, we're very isolated, aren't we?' It had been Kacie's choice to isolate herself but she realised it could be a very lonely kind of existence for others, and probably would be for herself when finally she managed to lay Dennis's memory to rest. 'Do your friends and family visit often?' she asked.

He shook his head.

She eyed him, surprised. 'What, hardly at all?'

He looked uncomfortable. 'Not at all, actually. Er . . . truth is, I haven't actually got any proper friends and this is not the kind of place my father would visit.'

She grimaced. 'Oh, I see. But everyone has at least one proper friend.'

He eyed her for several moments before saying, 'Unfortunately I haven't. People are wary of me, you see, Kacie. Because I pronounce my words differently to them they think I'm something I'm not.' He could see she was looking very bewilderedly at him. 'I suppose I should explain.'

156

'You don't have to, Richard.'

He eyed her expectantly. 'I'd really would like us to have a chance of becoming friends. Maybe if I told you a little of my background then you'll know there's nothing peculiar about me or anything to be frightened of.'

She picked up her cup of tea and took a sip. That's exactly how she was beginning to think of him. An oddity. A recluse. Definitely someone with something to hide, despite his reassurances that he hadn't. She was intrigued to hear what had landed him at this address when it was obvious he didn't really belong in such surroundings. 'OK,' she said, settling back into her chair.

'Do you mind if I light my pipe?' Richard asked.

Kacie shook her head. 'Not at all.'

He took several moments to pack it and get it lit, then sat back, his eyes glazing distantly. 'I'm one of life's misfits, Kacie. I was born into one society but felt far more comfortable in another.'

She was eyeing him, bemused. 'I'm sorry, I don't understand.'

He smiled apologetically at her. 'I'm not making much sense, am I? I'll try to explain better. I come from people who are not rich by gentry standards but comfortably off. My mother died when I was only two years old, too young for me to remember her, but from her photographs I know she was a very beautiful woman. My father was devoted to her and was so grieved when she died he threw himself into his work by way of coping. He was hardly ever at home, out before I was up in a morning and not back until after I went to bed of an evening. I lived quite a lonely existence, my only companion being our elderly housekeeper. She was a kindly enough old body but she wasn't cut out to raise a young boy and I was very much left to my own devices. As a consequence I was very shy around people, especially those of my own age. At five I was sent to a private day school in Leicester. It was purgatory for me, Kacie. I'd never mixed with children of my own age before and hadn't any idea how to make friends.

'Then when I was about eight a miracle happened. Our old housekeeper retired and that was when Jenny came into my life. She was like a breath of spring air – young and pretty, and life radiated from her. She was appalled at what little outside interests and contacts I had and immediately set about changing that. Gradually, with her gentle coaxing and influence, I came out of my shell.

'Jenny lived with her family at the other end of the village. She had two young brothers, and after school, when my homework was done and her chores finished, she took it upon herself to take me down to her house to play with them. To this day I have no idea whether my father had given Jenny his authority to do so. We always returned in time to get me cleaned up and made presentable to say my goodnights to my father should he return before my bedtime.

'Jenny's own father was a miner, her mother undertook cleaning jobs and whatever else came her way. They had hardly a penny to their names but their house was always filled with such love and laughter and I was always made to feel so welcome there. They were such happy times for me, Kacie. My life suddenly became full of all sorts of things that I had never been allowed to do before or, in truth, actually was aware went on: running barefoot through fields; scrumping for apples; scavenging for coal off the slag heaps. We played cricket with home-made bats, football with a blown-up pig's bladder; made a cart from old wooden boxes and wheels from a rusting shell of a pram we'd found on the tip. They kept pigs and a goat, and I loved to help muck them out and feed them. Jenny's mother would let me watch her baking, and Jenny's brothers and I would squabble over the bowl to lick out. So many adventures, Kacie, so many experiences I would have missed out on if it hadn't been for Jenny coming into my life, or her family giving me so much of a welcome into their home.'

Richard's face clouded grimly. 'Then my happy world suddenly changed again so drastically. I was coming up for twelve. Jenny told me she was getting married and moving to another village several miles away and wouldn't be coming any more. At the same time my father told me I was going away to boarding school. I can't tell you how desolate I was.

'The school was good, the masters kind enough, but I never really got on with the other boys. I always felt I was an outsider and I could never understand why until one day it struck me. I didn't relate to their moral standards. I didn't like the way they conducted themselves, especially how they sneered on those less privileged, the sort of people who'd shown me such kindness, readily sharing their last crust of bread with me. When I tried to point out what I saw as their errors, I was ostracised even more, and to an extent bullied for my principles. I was so relieved when my school days finally ended when I was sixteen.'

Kacie was listening intently, feeling a great sadness grip her as Richard's sorry story unfolded.

'It was then that my father really began to take notice of me,' he continued. 'It was as though he'd suddenly woken up from a long sleep and realised he had a son. I accompanied him to musical evenings, the theatre, dinner with his friends.'

'Did you enjoy those times?' Kacie asked.

He shook his head. 'I hated every minute. I wanted to be back in that little house with Jenny and her family. I had nothing in common with the people my father introduced me to and I felt awkward in their company. Then my father informed me I was to be enrolled in university to study law. I should explain my father comes from a long line of solicitors and it was expected that I would follow him into the family firm. It was the first I knew of his plans for me and I was horrified, Kacie.'

This story was sounding very familiar to Kacie. 'I know what you're going to say,' she said. 'You didn't want to study law, did you? You wanted to do something else and your father wouldn't entertain the idea.'

He eyed her surprised. 'Yes, that's exactly it. But how did you know?'

'You don't have to come from a well-to-do family to have parents that have set ideas how their children should behave. My parents had very clear ideas what they wanted me and my sister to do. My sister, to her cost, allowed them to rule her life but I didn't. I stuck out for what I wanted and it wasn't easy.'

'No, it's not, is it, standing up for your rights? It takes much nerve and courage. My father tried his hardest to make me follow his wishes and when I wouldn't the gulf between us widened again. It wasn't a pleasant time.'

'Oh, how sad,' Kacie said in genuine sympathy. 'My parents too made life very difficult for me when I wouldn't follow their wishes. Especially in who I chose to marry.'

'You're married?' he asked, and Kacie detected a morsel of dismay in his voice.

She hadn't meant to mention a word on that subject, it just happened to slip out, and a sudden rush of sadness at her recent trauma flooded her face. 'I was,' she said sharply, then with great effort forced a smile on her face. 'I didn't stick around long enough for my parents to tell me they had told me so,' she said lightly.

He looked at her in understanding. 'So you've run away, have you?'

She looked at him quizzically. She hadn't thought of what she had done in that way but he was right. She had run away from everything in order not to face it. 'Rightly or wrongly, yes, I have. So what happened to you next?' she asked.

'As matters stood, if I wasn't going to university to study law then my father refused to finance me studying anything else. He thought that would change my mind, you see. Only it didn't. I was more determined than ever to do what I wanted.'

'And what was that?' Kacie asked.

'I had pondered several occupations but what I had really set my heart on was becoming a vet.'

Kacie looked impressed. 'A vet, eh? That's a good occupation. As good as being a lawyer.'

'That was my way of thinking too, but my father insisted I was to study law or nothing. He said I'd not the makings of a vet. Trouble is, he was right. The doctoring of animals was an idea that was nurtured during my childhood when I helped Jenny's family to care for their animals. Only I was too naïve to realise that mucking out and feeding are entirely different matters to administering to medical needs. I applied for many positions and finally was granted an interview for a vet's assistant at a practice out near Oakham, in Rutland.'

'Oakham? Where is that?' she asked.

'It's a very pretty market town about twenty-odd miles away, and Rutland is the smallest county in England. It's very rural, lots of farms, idyllic location. The countryside is so beautiful but, most importantly to me, it was far enough away from my father not to risk the prospect of bumping into him and eventually wearing me down into changing my mind, which I was very fearful of him doing. I was overjoyed to get the job. Mr Dennison, the vet, was very reticent about taking someone on who had no experience but I think I was so enthusiastic that he eventually agreed to give me a trial.'

He issued an ironic laugh. 'It was disastrous from the beginning. During my first week, I'd managed to poison a dog, which luckily didn't die, by mouth feeding it medicine that I'd been told to insert in its rear end. I don't know how it happened, to be honest. I think that by the time I caught the dog, which was running around, snapping at my heels, I'd forgotten which end I'd been told to put the suppository in. I was chased across a field by a bull with an acute ear infection that I was supposed to be holding steady whilst Mr Dennison did his business, and landed up jumping in a river to save myself being gored to death, and I nearly drowned because I can't swim. Then I set fire to a barn.'

His face was so serious as he related his story and Kacie was trying very hard to hold back her mirth, which was threatening to erupt at the comical vision he was conjuring up. 'How on earth did you manage to do that?' she asked.

'Quite easily really. There are strict rules to be adhered to when out in the countryside and I forgot one of the most important ones. My boss had been called out in the middle of the night to attend a sick calf and while he went inside to talk to the farmer and to get warm, as it was freezing cold, he asked me to keep an eye on the patient. I decided to have a smoke of my pipe whilst I was waiting and I'd just got it going when I heard my boss coming back. I quickly tapped it out, completely forgetting I was emptying the still smouldering tobacco on to dry straw. We'd only managed to walk as far as my boss's old jalopy when all hell broke loose. I've never seen flames like it. The barn burned to the ground in practically the wink of an eye. Lucky all the animals escaped unharmed, apart from a couple of unfortunate chickens.'

'Oh, dear,' Kacie said, still fighting to control an explosion of laughter. 'So that was the end of your veterinary career?'

'Well, it never really got started, did it, but yes it was. My boss took me aside and said he didn't think I was really suited to it.'

Lips pressed tight, Kacie said, 'I can see his point. So what did you do then?'

'Took a long hard look at myself and made the decision to find myself an occupation that was more suitable for me. I hadn't much money then, hardly any, in fact, without asking for my father's help, which I was very loath to do. I just about managed to scrap together the rent for this place. Then fortunately after a few knock-backs I got myself a job as an accounts clerk with GEC on the Blackbird Road and I've been there ever since.'

'Do you like your job at GEC?'

Richard stared at her thoughtfully, before saying, 'Yes, yes I do. I seem to have a knack with figures.' He eyed her, surprised. 'Maybe I've found my niche after all. I've never realised that before. Yes, maybe I have.'

'What about your father?' Kacie asked. 'Have you ever made it up with him?'

'It's taking time, but yes, we are getting to know each other at long last. I visit him once a month and we have dinner together. It's

161

a very strained relationship which I hope will gradually become closer when he finally accepts me for what I am.'

Richard's relationship with his father sounded much like that Kacie had with her own parents. 'I'm so sorry,' she said sincerely.

He frowned, puzzled. 'Sorry for what?'

'The way you're being forced to live because your father doesn't allow you to live your life the way you want to.'

'Oh, Kacie, you have missed the point entirely. This *is* the life I have chosen for myself. I might not have much to my name but at least I'm a free man, in control of my own destiny, such as it is, but having said that, it can only get better. The only sadness I have is that people that I'm amongst now seem reticent to accept me but hopefully, given time, that situation will change. I do hope so, anyway.'

She smiled at him kindly. 'Well, consider yourself accepted by me.'

His delight was most apparent. 'Thank you, Kacie. You don't know how much your gesture means to me.' He picked up his cup and downed the contents before replacing it in its saucer. He looked across at her. 'So there you have my life story. It's as I said: I have no skeletons in my cupboard, nothing about me that you should be wary or frightened of. I'm just a simple man, living a simple life.' He eyed her enquiringly. 'So what about you, Kacie? What brings you to Slattery Mansions?'

She took a deep breath, knowing it was inevitable he would ask that particular question and still very unwilling to bare her soul by answering it. 'Circumstances brought me here,' she said shortly. 'Sometimes our lives don't work out exactly as we thought they were going to.'

The expression on his face told her he understood she didn't want to talk about it. He just smiled and said, 'What do you do for a job?'

'I'm a hairdresser.'

'Oh, really?' He was impressed. 'So that's why you came home tonight dragging a hair dryer with you. It looks very heavy.'

'It is. Actually, it's not mine. I've, er . . . borrowed it.'

'Hairdressing,' he mused. 'Now that's a good skill to possess. Everyone needs their hair cutting, don't they? Do you like your profession?'

'I love it. Being a hairdresser is the only thing I ever wanted to do. But like you, my parents had other ideas. Secretarial, to be exact. There is no way I could stomach the thought of sitting in a stuffy office taking dictation all day.'

He looked at her. 'No, I can't see you being the sort to do that. I know I haven't been acquainted with you for much more than an hour or so but I think I'm right when I say you've a lot of life about you, Kacie, and being imprisoned inside an austere office would drive you mad.'

She smiled. 'Your observations are absolutely spot-on.' She picked up her cup of tea and took several large sips. 'So what are the other lodgers like, then?' she asked.

Richard pulled a wry face. 'I don't know much about them but there's six in total. You and me. Then there's a chap who lives in the attic room. He's very tall and thin, and wears only black. Comes and goes at strange times. I've no idea of his name or what he does for a living.'

'Cat burglar, do you reckon?' Kacie said, a twinkle of amusement sparkling her eye.

He stared thoughtfully at her. 'I never thought of that.' Then he realised she was being flippant. 'Oh, you are naughty, Kacie, but come to think of it he does have that look about him. Mmm, now you've got me wondering what he really gets up to.'

'He's probably perfectly respectable. A night watchman or something. What about the other lodgers?' she prompted.

'Oh, yes. On the middle floor, you're in the room at the back, of course, then there's an old lady who lives in the middle. She doesn't go out much, except shopping on a Friday morning and church twice on a Sunday. Two spinster sisters live in the room above mine. They dress identically and you never see one without the other. They go out most days – I haven't a clue where. They nod a greeting if you happen to bump into them, but that's all.

'Behind me on the ground floor there's a young woman who I think is a waitress in the Turkey Café in town as I'm positive I've seen her working there. Her boyfriend stays some nights, even though Mrs Slattery has a strict rule about visitors after eight. He sneaks out about six in the morning and I only know that because I hear the doors opening and shutting and it's too early for anyone else to be about.

'Then that leaves Mrs Slattery herself, who lives in the two rooms at the back of the house leading on to the back garden. I don't think there is a Mr Slattery still living but knowing what I do of Mrs Slattery, I suspect her husband didn't have much of a life with her. She goes out every night to play bingo in the working men's club down the road. So that completes the residents of number seventeen Danehill Road. Quite an odd collection, don't you think?'

Kacie nodded. 'You observe a lot behind your curtain, don't you?' she said, tongue in cheek. 'So what do you get up to in your spare time?'

'I wouldn't say I get up to much at all. I read a lot and enjoy puzzles but my passion is the radio.'

'Oh, I love listening to the radio too. The Goons make me howl with laughter. *Around the Horn* is funny too, but best of all I love popular music shows.'

He looked a morsel uncomfortable as though he didn't know what she was talking about. 'I listen to the Home Service myself,' he said. 'Plays and concerts, that kind of thing.'

She thought his choice of listening sounded very boring. 'Oh! I see.' And as she had never listened to the Home Service she couldn't carry this line of the conversation on so she said, 'Well, I haven't got a radio at the moment but it's going to be one of the first things I buy when I get some money together. So, what about girlfriends? I mean, I know you said you don't have any actual friends that visit but you must have a girlfriend you take out?'

He sadly shook his head. 'I haven't had one for years. Well, at all, really,' he said wistfully. 'Women don't go for men like me, do they?'

'Don't they?'

'No. Well, I've no illusions about myself, Kacie. I'm not the dashing, cavalier sort of man that women hanker after.'

Kacie hid a smile at his use of such old-fashioned terminology, though finding it quite an endearing, innocent quality that was most refreshing in comparison with some of the brash types of men she was acquainted with. For a brief moment she wondered what Dennis would make of Richard. Then she hurriedly squashed that thought, to avoid spoiling her pleasant evening by tumbling into a mood of depression.

'It's not that I wouldn't like a girlfriend,' Richard was saying, more to himself than to Kacie. 'I'd love to get married some day and have children, but women . . . well . . . the majority seem to give me a wide berth. The ones that do give me the eye aren't really the type I'd like to go out with, if that's not an unkind thing to say.' He suddenly looked her straight in the eye. 'Take you, for instant. You wouldn't look at me twice, would you, Kacie?'

His blunt question took her temporarily by surprise and for several long moments her mind whirled as she tried to think of an answer that wouldn't hurt him. She couldn't, so decided to speak honestly. 'If you want the truth, no. I'm sorry if I'm being blunt but you did ask. Not that any man is of interest to me or ever will be again for reasons I don't wish to discuss at the moment, and while we're on that subject, I warn you not to get any ideas on me in that direction, Richard. I'd really like to be your friend but that's as far as it goes. Anyway, you're . . . well, what I call square.'

A look of bewilderment crossed his face. 'Square?'

'Old-fashioned. Very.' She ran a critical eye over him. 'Richard, Fair Isle V-necks went out during the war and so did those Oxford bags you're wearing. And as for short back and sides – my dad has his hair cut like that and he's twice your age.'

'Oh? But I've always dressed like this.'

'Then it's time you modernised yourself. Even a bit would help.' She suddenly thought of her sister and realised this situation she was in with Richard was exactly the same as she had been with Caroline. What she had done with Caroline had done wonders for her, so there was no reason why it shouldn't be the same for Richard. 'A few alterations here and there and we'll soon have the women flocking after you,' she said.

He was eyeing her, dumbstruck. 'Do . . . do you think so?'

'I'm positive. You're not a bad-looking bloke. I've seen much worse,' she said, grinning at him mischievously. 'For a start you could grow your hair and I'll restyle it for you. I won't charge,' she added, tongue in cheek.

'Really? You'd do that for me?'

'Friends help each other, don't they?'

He gave a delighted smile, which lit up his face. 'Yes, yes, they do, don't they? I'd be very grateful if you could do something with me. I'll start letting my hair grow straight away. If you don't think it presumptuous of me, will you help me pick out some new clothes? Only when you've spare time, of course.'

'I'd be delighted.' Kacie took a moment to look at her new friend and then she realised that during all the time she had been talking to him she had, for the most part, managed to push aside her own heartache and associated problems.

She was still having difficulty taking on board how much her life had changed in such a short space of time. Yesterday morning she had risen thinking that the only problem she had in the world was resolving her petty estrangement with her beloved husband. Now she had no husband and had turned her back on everything associated with him and her past, and through her own decision found herself facing God knew what, and all alone. She was suddenly glad Richard had taken it upon himself to spy on her. His actions were turning out to be a blessing in disguise.

'I want to thank you for tonight,' she said sincerely.

He eyed her, bemused. 'Thank me? Why? I should be begging your forgiveness for watching you like that. It was most ungentlemanly of me. But I hope you understand why I couldn't help myself.'

'I'm glad you did because if you hadn't have spied on me both of us would be sitting on our own now, wouldn't we, and maybe the chance of us getting to know each other might never have happened. And I tell you something, Richard. Me moving into Slattery Mansions is going to be one of the best things that happened to you,' she said, laughing.

He looked at her searchingly. He knew her remark was tongue in cheek, but he wondered if the lovely young woman sitting before him, who had so unexpectedly entered his life, had any real idea how much her coming inside his room for a cup of tea and the hour or so she had spent in his company had meant to him, let alone the offer of developing a friendship. Even just the thought of having a real friend was making him feel needed again, wanted. He smiled warmly at her. 'I do believe you're right. More tea?'

'I don't mind if I do, thank you.' She looked at him for a moment as she mulled over an idea. She wanted to extend an offer for Sunday dinner, but watching her pennies she had only purchased a quarter-pound of sausages and two slices of corned beef from the butcher's, both to eke out for several meals. Oh, to hell with it, she thought. She'd be glad of his company and she thought she wasn't wrong in deducing that he'd be glad of hers. 'Would you like to come up for your dinner tomorrow? I can't promise you much but it'll be hot and filling.'

Richard's delight was most apparent. Regardless, though, of her generous offer Richard doubted his new friend had much money. 'I'd love to. Thank you so much for asking me. But on one condition?'

'Oh?'

'I provide the meat. I have a small beef joint which will do two

166

admirably. I also have first-hand experience in knowing that our landlady is not very generous in the crockery and cutlery department so I shall bring with me a plate, knife and fork.'

Kacie laughed. 'Then you can definitely come.'

Chapter Sixteen

Miss Regan, matron of Sunny Side Residential Home for Retired Ladies, popped her head round the door to check on Kacie's progress. 'How are you getting on?' she asked.

Kacie wiped her hand across her forehead to mop a film of sweat. It was very cold outside, a bitter late October afternoon, people huddled inside their winter woollies, but Kacie was far from cold. The small room she had been allocated had built up a significant amount of heat from the continual running of the stand hair dryer in order to dry the hair of her constant stream of customers. It was coming up to three in the afternoon and she had lost count of the number of ladies she had attended to. Was it ten or fifteen or more – she had no idea. All she was aware of was that each had gone away very happy with her service, and she herself was so fatigued she wondered how she was going to find the energy to keep going until all those that wished her to do their hair had been done.

'Very well, thank you,' she said, smiling.

'Good. I'll send a cup of tea through for you.'

'That'll be much appreciated, Matron, thank you.' Kacie turned her attention back to the very severe-looking elderly lady she was dealing with, who all the time Kacie had been talking to Matron had continued reminiscing over her past, blissfully unaware that Kacie's attentions were elsewhere.

'Then out of the blue I was promoted to headmistress,' she was saying. 'Well, it was such a difficult choice. Did I marry Sebastian or accept the job? It was one or the other. Such a difficult decision. I chose my career and Sebastian married someone else.'

'And you never regretted that?' Kacie asked, as she felt was expected of her, as she took the last roller out of Miss Amelia Gilbert's hair and began to brush her out.

'Of course I did, very much so, but I thought at the time teaching young ladies was my calling. I had a wonderful career, but at the end of it I had nothing except the money that enabled me to live out my remaining years in a place like this. No husband, children, no one to mourn me when I finally go. Oh, that looks very nice, dear,' she suddenly exclaimed as she caught sight of herself in the mirror. 'I do like the way you've waved that bit round the front of my ears. I do believe you've made me look much younger.'

'Well, in that case, I'll have the same style,' a voice piped up.

Miss Gilbert spun her head around, her face indignant. 'You will not, Miss Carson. I don't want anyone else looking like me.'

'Well, in that case, dear,' Miss Carson said, addressing Kacie, 'can you make me look like Rita Hayworth.'

'This young lady might be very talented,' Miss Gilbert erupted, 'but I'd hardly call her a miracle worker, Miss Carson. Besides, you'd look ridiculous with her style of hair as she's at least forty years younger than you. I would say Gracie Fields is more in your line myself.'

Kacie was very fearful of a huge jealous row brewing. 'We'll discuss a suitable style when it's your turn,' she said to Miss Carson, hoping to defuse the situation. 'Now, Miss Gilbert, are you happy with your hairdo?'

'Delighted, dear, most delighted,' she said, preening herself. She rose stiffly, unfastened the protective cloak Kacie had wrapped around her and handed it to her. 'Now I've seen what you can do I think I'll risk a tint next time.' She handed Kacie a sixpenny piece. 'Matron told us Nurse Grey is collecting the money all together as she felt you'd have enough to do. Very thoughtful of her. Matron is like that. This is just a little extra from me to show my appreciation. It's been a long time since I've had my hair done by a professional. The nurses are very obliging when they get the time, but professional hairdressers they most definitely are not. But don't tell them I told you that.'

'I won't,' Kacie assured. 'Thank you very much for your gesture,' she said, putting the tip into her pocket.

Finally there were no more ladies waiting and Kacie gave a weary sigh of gratitude. She had had some very busy days at Verna's salon but nothing of this magnitude. But then she wasn't complaining, just very gratified that the money she had earned was well worth the back-breaking work. By the time she replaced the supplies she had borrowed she calculated a tidy sum would be left over, enough, she hoped, to give serious thought to being able to do mobile hairdressing for a living in future.

After packing up and making a great effort to leave the room as she found it, she made her way to the matron's office in search of Nurse Grey, to collect her dues. Nurse Grey was seated behind Matron's desk, drinking a cup of tea and leafing through a copy of the *Picture Post*. She was a pretty young woman, with the face of an angel, and Kacie judged she was very popular with her charges.

'All the ladies have been attended to, Nurse Grey, and as far as I'm aware they are all very happy with my service,' Kacie said, smiling.

'Yes, so it seems. The common room is abuzz with it all. Matron told me to extend her thanks for the hairdo you gave her. It's a pity I was too busy elsewhere for you to do mine, but never mind. Well, thank you for all you've done. I expect you'll be wanting to get home and put your feet up after the day you've had.'

'That's exactly what I do want to do.' Kacie looked at her and gave a discreet cough. 'Er . . . I'll be off then.'

'Right oh,' she said smiling.

Kacie shifted uncomfortably on her feet. Not a mention of her payment had been made. Obviously it had slipped Nurse Grey's mind and Kacie felt very awkward asking for it. 'Er . . . I don't like to mention this, Nurse Grey, but my money . . .?'

She eyed her blankly. 'Money? Oh, but I gave that to you over an hour ago. You thanked me and put it in your handbag.'

Kacie stared confusedly at her. 'Forgive me for contradicting you, Nurse Grey, you did bring me a cup of tea, but you didn't give me any money.'

The nurse looked at Kacie as though she was stupid. 'I can assure you I did. In a large envelope it was – just over three pounds in total. Matron and I counted it to be sure it was all present and correct before she went home. She said she thought you'd done extremely well and worked very hard to make all that.' She eyed Kacie disbelievingly. 'Don't tell me you've mislaid it?'

Kacie frowned, trying to recall the events as Nurse Grey was telling them, but she couldn't. Then suddenly she knew why. Because they had not happened. Suddenly the terrible truth hit Kacie and she blurted, 'You know perfectly well I haven't mislaid an envelope containing my money, because you never gave it to me, did you, nurse?'

The woman's pretty face suddenly turned ugly. 'Just what is it you're accusing me of?'

171

'Theft. Because that's what you've done. You've stolen my money,' she cried.

Nurse Grey rose to stand before Kacie, her baby-blue eyes boring icily into hers. 'It's your word against mine.' A mocking smile twitched her full lips. 'I've worked here for years, have the full trust of Matron. If I say I've given you the money, Matron will believe me without question. Close the door on your way out.'

Kacie stared at her, frozen rigid, having great difficulty believing this innocent-looking woman, who was in a very trusted position, a woman who had also taken an oath to care and protect other human beings, had so blatantly stolen all she'd laboured so hard for. And she was right, there was absolutely nothing Kacie could do about it. It was Kacie's word against hers and Matron was bound to take the nurse's side in the circumstances.

'You'll get your just deserts,' Kacie hissed.

Nurse Grey grinned at her, a mocking grin, full of spite. 'You're right there, I will. With my little windfall I intend to treat myself to a day around the shops. That's very nice *just deserts*, don't you think?'

'Take a large gulp, Kacie, please. Come on, it'll do you good.'

'I can't, Richard,' she chokingly sobbed. 'I feel sick already. Brandy will make me worse.'

'It's not brandy it's Cognac – and a good one at that. It won't make you feel worse, trust me, it will help calm you. Come on, Kacie, please, just a sip.' Richard held the glass of Cognac to Kacie's mouth and she had no alternative but to comply with his wishes. She coughed and spluttered as the liquid hit the back of her throat. 'There, now, what did I tell you? You feel better already, don't you?' he soothed.

She shook her head and looked at him through swollen red eyes. 'How could that woman do that to me? How could she sit there and so smugly admit she'd stolen my money and – oh, Richard, I needed it so badly. For the whole day all I've come away with is half a crown in tips.'

'Well, she has, Kacie. She's obviously a very clever woman because she's right in what she says and that it's her word against yours. All you can do is be wiser in the future. You upsetting yourself like this won't bring that money back, it'll only make you ill.'

Richard eyed his new friend tenderly. He'd known her such a

short space of time, knew so little about her in reality, but regardless, already was a great admirer. He knew she had suffered a great sadness, some dreadful loss – and very recently if he wasn't wrong. It was so very apparent by what she said and didn't say; by an ever-present glisten of pain in her lovely brown eyes, despite her constant endeavour to conceal her true feelings by her ready broad smile which he instinctively knew took great effort on her part to display. He did suspect that the cause of her great heartache was something to do with her husband but would never be so impolite as to ask. Kacie would tell him if she ever trusted him enough to want him to know. Seeing her in such a state of distress was upsetting him greatly.

Yesterday she had been so excited about the forthcoming day and what she hoped it would bring. As they had shared their Sunday dinner, he having roasted the joint in his oven; she boiling the potatoes, vegetables and gravy as best she could on the two aged gas rings which spluttered and hissed and kept going out – she laughing at her poor results which, regardless, they had both eaten with relish – she had been so full of expectation, and had talked of nothing else. Now in one fell swoop, at the deceitful hands of another, she had lost all hope of securing not only her immediate future but possibly financing a new venture for herself. His heart went out to her, wishing there was something he could do to salvage the situation; at least give her some hope.

Then an idea struck him and for a moment he explored it and was satisfied it would work. 'Kacie?'

'Mmm?' she blubbered, wiping her eyes on her handkerchief as she looked up at him.

'How much money would be needed to start you off on your own?'

She looked at him blankly and shrugged. 'I don't know.'

'Well, you must have some idea?'

'Why are you asking?'

'If you answer my question first, then I'll tell you.'

She gave a loud sigh. 'I'd need to buy a portable stand hair dryer. As I've already told you, the one I used today was borrowed and I have to take it back. A good second-hand one would do me, which at a rough guess would cost about ten pounds, maybe less if I'm lucky. I'd need a wraparound to protect customers and they cost about fifteen shillings from the wholesaler's. Then a supply of sundries, just enough to start me off. A decent bag to carry it all in. That's about it.'

'Not a lot then. I mean I don't know how much the sundries would cost but all in all do you reckon fifteen pounds would be enough?'

'Maybe give or take.' She looked at him bewildered. 'But I don't see the point of this conversation.'

He smiled secretively at her. 'There's a point to it, Kacie. I have that amount and I want you to have it to get yourself up and running.'

She gawped at him. 'But I can't let you do that. It wouldn't be fair.'

'It's not fair for a friend to help another?'

'Well yes, of course it is, but fifteen pounds is such a lot of money and you need that to buy your new clothes, and besides I don't know how long it would take for me to pay you back.'

'Paying me back isn't an issue, Kacie. My wages more than cover my needs and I've managed to save a little. That money is sitting in the bank doing nothing apart from earning a small amount of interest which is neither here nor there. As for my change of image, I've dressed in this fashion for such a long time that a while longer will make no difference, not when the money could be used for something far more important.'

She was looking at him, stunned. 'You would do this for me?'

'If you'll allow me to, it would give me so much pleasure. So will you?'

She was unable to take his generous offer on board, reluctant to take advantage of his good nature even though the money would be the answer to her financial problems. She'd never be given such an opportunity again. It would take her years to save enough from whatever she earned to enable her to set up on her own. She'd be a fool to turn Richard's offer down and she knew he'd be so hurt if she did. She'd make a go of it, she had no doubt about that, if only to pay him back the money he was lending to her.

'Good. I'll take an early lunch hour, draw the money out and give it to you tomorrow night. I am positive there are many ladies living around these parts who would be delighted for you to visit their homes and do their hair. All you have to do is let people know you're available.' Her eyes followed him as he rose and walked across to his kitchen area. 'I'm going to make you scrambled eggs on toast,' he said. 'And you'll eat it, Kacie.'

As he busied himself with her meal and mashing a pot of tea,

Kacie's mind began to formulate a plan of action. Tomorrow she would set about the purchase of her requirements. Hairdressing establishments continually advertised in the *Leicester Mercury* the sale of their unwanted items that they had replaced with more updated models. She could pay a visit to the wholesaler to price her sundry needs.

As she was excitedly planning the operation of her business venture, she suddenly thought of Myrna, who was doing the same. She wondered if she had opened her salon yet and how well she was getting on. If she had time after all her chores tomorrow she would pay the woman a visit and find out. It would be nice to see her again and renew their acquaintance.

But the very first thing she must do before anything else was to return Verna's equipment she had borrowed back to the hotel, hopefully before anyone turned up to collect it.

Suddenly her future didn't look quite so bleak. Working for herself she felt would do much to take her mind off her terrible heartache. And she had her new friend, Richard, to thank. She squashed an urge to rush over to him and give him a hug of gratitude, feeling it best to avoid such an intimate display, not wanting him to get any ideas that their friendship would ever be any more than platonic, as her feminine intuition was telling her that he liked her very much. Instead she said, 'I don't know how to thank you, Richard.'

He turned and smiled across at her. She had no idea, he thought, that to him her offer of friendship far outweighed the money he was helping her with. 'You making a success of this will be thanks enough.'

As she closed her eyes that night, lying on her uncomfortable mattress, thin blankets pulled right up under her chin, despite her fight against it she could not stop her thoughts focusing on Dennis. She had loved him for such a long time, cared for him, worried for him, and even though his feelings were now for another, she found it impossible to cut off her feelings for him. She still couldn't accept what he had done to her, and as on every night since she had uncovered his deception, she cried herself to sleep.

Chapter Seventeen

Kacie was most surprised to enter the premises of Cut and Curls to find the place absent of any sign of customers, or hairdressers for that matter. Then through a door at the back Myrna emerged and immediately Kacie thought how striking she looked, dressed in a very fashionable pair of tight-fitting black pedal pushers and a three-quarter-sleeved forest-green blouse with matching flat pumps, which looked far more comfortable to Kacie than her own stilettos. Her shoulder-length thick blonde hair, which she had worn loose for the competition, was pulled up into a ponytail, making her appear much younger than her twenty-five years.

'I'm sorry,' Myrna said, advancing towards her, her pretty face apologetic. 'I've had to delay the official opening until . . .' Her voice tailed off as she recognised Kacie and her face broke into a broad smile of welcome. 'Kacie!' she exclaimed, walking over to join her. 'God, it's great to see you.' She flashed her a wicked smile. 'I trust you've come to pay me the tanner you owe me?'

Kacie looked at her nonplussed. 'Sorry?'

'The competition. I won a first in the evening section and a second in the fantasy class.'

'You did! Why, that's brilliant. Well done.'

Kacie unclipped her handbag and took out her purse, attempting to pay over her dues, but Myrna stopped her. 'I hardly won it fair and square so the bet is void. I doubt I would have if you hadn't have been sabotaged. The styles you created definitely had the edge over mine.'

Kacie smiled at her. 'It's very good of you to say so, even if I don't agree with you.'

'You didn't see me in the *Mercury* then, posing with all the bigwigs from Wella and our local dignitaries?'

'Er . . . no, I'm sorry I didn't. I've, er . . . been a little preoccupied since the evening of the competition and haven't read any papers.' Desperately wanting to change a subject that resurrected her past, she took a look around. 'Are those the new style of sinks you've had installed?' she asked admiringly.

Myrna nodded. 'Back washes are so much more comfortable for the clients. The old-style sinks were cheaper, of course, but I decided the extra cost was well worth it.'

'I agree with you. You've got the place looking really bright and trendy,' Kacie said. 'I love the way you've put American film star pictures around the walls. Tony Curtis,' she uttered rapturously. 'Isn't he just divine? He's got those eyes that just make you melt, hasn't he? Charlton Heston, Kirk Douglas, Marlon Brando, James Dean . . . Oh, Natalie Wood. She's so pretty. Hey, and that's a great picture of Marilyn Monroe. Isn't it from *Some Like It Hot?* I want to see that as I've heard it's so funny. I'd do anything to look like Marilyn,' Kacie said, sighing wistfully.

'Oh, I don't know,' said Myrna, looking at the picture. 'I think our own Diana Dors is just as stunning and sexy. As for Joan Collins – well, wouldn't you give anything to look like her? Anyway, I wanted to achieve a sort of American coffee-bar feel to the place. It's all the rage at the moment down in London. That's why I chose red vinyl chairs and the black-and-white tiles for the floor. When I can afford it I want to get a juke box installed.'

'A juke box! Wow! Women of our age are going to love coming here. It's about time someone catered for us and not just for the oldies. This place is going to go down a bomb, I know it is.' Kacie squashed a feeling of sadness, remembering her dream of having her combined establishment with Dennis of a record shop, coffee bar and hairdresser's, which would now never happen. Regardless, she was genuine in her wish to see Myrna succeed.

'I do hope so,' said Myrna. 'I've ploughed every last penny I have into this place and I'm banking on it. In truth, I wouldn't have been able to do some of the finishing touches if it hadn't been for the most amazing bit of luck I had.'

'Oh, and what was that?' Kacie eagerly asked.

'Well, out of the blue a huge box was delivered last week containing everything I need in the product line to last me for months, and I've no idea who sent it. There was just a note inside wishing me good luck.'

'Really?'

Myrna nodded. 'I was so shocked. I'll be eternally grateful to whoever my benefactor is.'

'I'd want to kiss their feet if anyone did something like that for me.' Kacie looked quizzically at her. 'Er . . . I thought you said at the competition that you were opening today?'

'That was the plan but I had to put it back until tomorrow as the sinks decided to leak and I needed the plumbers back in. It's been a nightmare, to be honest. They said they'd come last Friday and didn't arrive, and it wasn't until I screamed blue murder at them that they finally came today and finished off the job they should have done properly in the first place. Thank God it's all over now and I'm ready to go.'

'Well, that's why I came, to wish you good luck.'

'Thank you,' Myrna said, smiling warmly. 'Any time you want a hairdo you know where to come.'

Kacie laughed. 'Actually, I'm working on a little operation myself. I'm planning to go mobile. Not in this area,' she hurriedly added. 'So you've no need to be concerned.'

'I've told you before, Kacie, that in my opinion all competition is healthy. But you're really going mobile? Why that's great. You'll be a success too, I know you will.'

'Not if what happened to me yesterday happens again, I won't.'

'What do you mean?'

Kacie told Myrna her sorry tale of her day at the retired ladies' home.

'Why, that's awful!' Myrna exclaimed, horrified. 'I can't believe that woman had the bare-faced cheek to admit she stole your money, and after all your hard work too.'

'Well, believe me, she did.'

Myrna shook her head, appalled. 'Well, just thank God you weren't relying on that money to start your new business up.'

'Mmm,' she mouthed, not thinking it right to divulge Richard's generous offer. It was a private matter between him and herself. 'Like you with this salon, I'm banking my idea pays off, as after what happened I've only so much money to get it off the ground. I'm going to the wholesaler's now to see what I can afford to buy to get me started. To be honest I spent more than I planned on a portable hair dryer so I will have to be very selective on what I buy.'

Myrna eyed her questioningly. 'What happened to your job at . . . Verna's Hairstylist, wasn't it? Did you leave it, then? You seemed so happy working there.' Then a thought struck and her face clouded. 'Oh no, your boss didn't sack you after what happened at the contest?'

179

'Er . . . not exactly,' replied Kacie cagily. 'We, er . . . just parted company.'

'Oh, I see.' Myrna looked at her thoughtfully. 'Look, I had a damn good stroke of luck happen to me and I'd like to share some of that with you. You needn't bother going to the wholesaler's to buy your start-up stock, you can have what you need from me.'

Kacie was astounded. 'You mean that?'

'It'd be my pleasure. If I ever find out who my benefactor is I will be so happy to tell them that they were responsible for helping two hairdressers get started and not just one. You go through to the back and put the kettle on whilst I sort you a good mix of products out.'

Kacie was reeling from Myrna's kind gesture. 'I don't know how to thank you, Myrna.'

She smiled warmly at Kacie. 'You making a good go of your business will be thanks enough.'

'I can't believe it, Richard,' Kacie said later that evening as she was sharing a pot of tea with him in his room, bringing him up to date with all her news. 'I can't believe how generous Myrna was, and she insists she doesn't want replacing what she gave me. I'm so pleased as well with the stand dryer I got, despite it costing more than I bargained for. But, still, it is one of those new types that come apart to make it easier to carry about.' She pulled a wry face. 'Mind you, it's still just as heavy and bulky, so how they get away with describing it as being easily portable is beyond me. Anyway, with the money I didn't have to spend on stock I was able to go to the wholesaler's and buy lots of little extras, like assorted coloured hairnets and packets of kirby-grips and pins that I can sell on to my customers, and I bought a nice container to put them in. It all helps build my profits.'

Richard smiled, impressed at her. Kacie was bubbling over at the prospect of making a success of her venture and it was a joy for him to feel he was a small part of it all. 'You've had a busy day, and very productive by the sounds of it.'

'I have and I'm bushed. Now I have all my equipment and solutions tomorrow I'm going to concentrate on drumming up business.'

'I've been giving that some thought, Kacie.'

'You have?'

'Yes.' He rubbed his hand across his chin. 'While I was at work this morning it struck me that you'd need the use of a telephone to operate your mobile hairdressing business so clients can ring you to make their appointments.'

'Yes, I will,' she said, wondering what he was getting at.

'But you haven't access to one, Kacie.'

She eyed him blankly for a moment, then her face fell, and she slapped her forehead in dismay at her oversight. 'Oh, Richard, how could I overlook something so important as that?' Then a thought struck. 'Oh, wait a minute. I can make use of the public telephone in the hall for now.'

'I think Mrs Slattery will kick up rather a stink if that continually rings day and night, and she'll soon put a stop to you using it for your business. Besides, if you're out working how are you going to answer it? Of course, I'd be delighted to, but I'm out during weekdays too.'

Kacie gave a heavy sigh. 'I can't believe I never realised this. What the hell am I doing to do?'

'I do have a suggestion.'

'You do?'

'Well, it's only a suggestion, but until you're in a financial position to either open your own salon or move to a flat or something where you can have your own telephone installed, why not continue your business the way you've started out, by concentrating on retirement homes?'

She flashed him a look of disparagement. 'And I made a huge success of that, didn't I?'

'Kacie, just let that incident be a lesson to you. You'd be silly to give up because of one woman's callous actions. The retirement home got you all excited in the first place because of all those ladies under one roof and, apart from having your money stolen, look how well you did. The old dears were delighted, you said. It still makes great sense to go down that route, at least for the immediate future.'

She looked at him very thoughtfully for several long moments, then nodded. 'You're right, Richard. What you suggest makes absolute sense.'

He smiled at her. 'I'm glad you agree because while my boss was out I made a couple of telephone calls on your behalf. I've arranged an appointment for you with The Glades Retirement Home on Glenfield Road at two o'clock and The Pastures on Narborough Road South at four tomorrow.' He pulled a face. 'How on earth owners come up with the names for their establishments defies belief, as both these places are in built-up areas with not a glade or a pasture for miles. Still, both seemed very interested in your services and very keen to see you.' He suddenly looked at her, worried. 'I hope you're not annoyed?'

'Annoyed! Richard, I don't know how to thank you,' she cried in delight.

'No need for thanks, Kacie. The pleasure is all mine.'

Kacie covertly studied Richard from beneath her lashes. She felt she was so lucky to have him as her friend at a time when she needed one so badly. He was such a dear man, so thoughtful and very kind. He'd make some woman a wonderful husband. It suddenly struck her that Caroline would like him and she felt positive he would like her. They'd make a lovely couple. It was a shame that she couldn't introduce them but Caroline was in her past, a past she'd walked away from.

She suddenly felt a wave of sadness flood over her and was overwhelmed with a great longing to see her sister, which was rapidly followed by a terrible desire to see everyone she cared for that she'd walked away from: her parents, mother-in-law, Verna and Diane, her numerous friends and acquaintances, even Brenda, despite the fact she had instigated the split between Dennis and herself.

But she couldn't go and visit any of them, not yet, not for a long time – the reasons she had walked away in the first place were still far too painful for her to face up to. Her wellbeing depended on her coming to terms with it all and healing her wounds, and she felt she had been right to do what she had, knowing she could only move forward by removing herself from painful memories and reminders of the man who had smashed her world to pieces, and yet a man she still loved so much.

She realised Richard was talking to her. 'Pardon?'

He was looking at her worriedly. 'I asked if you were all right, Kacie. You look . . . well . . . sad.'

Despite the growing friendship between them she still couldn't bring herself to discuss with him the true reasons behind her arrival here. She took a deep breath and planted a smile on her face. 'I'm not sad not at all, Richard,' she lied. 'I was just, er . . . picturing in my mind what you'd look like in your new clothes once I've paid you back – and I will, Richard. It's the first thing I intend to do.'

182

'Don't worry yourself, Kacie. All in good time.' He gave her a doubtful look. 'Now I've had time to think about this change of image, I'm really not sure.'

'Oh, cold feet, eh? Stop worrying, Richard. We're just going to buy a few clothes which will make you look trendier. You want a girlfriend, don't you? Well, you won't get one dressing like a granddad.'

He burst into a fit of laughter. 'Oh, Kacie, you do have such a way with you. After what you've just said, how can I refuse?' He eyed her tenderly. 'Do you know how much my life has changed since you entered it? For the better, I may add.'

She smiled. 'Well, I'm glad I make someone happy. And I hope you're going to be even more so with this.' From behind her back where she'd hidden it earlier, she produced a bottle of port. 'It's not Cognac, I'm afraid, and it wasn't expensive either. It's just a gesture to express my gratitude for all your help. I paid for it with my own money.'

His initial look of surprise quickly turned to one of appreciation. 'There was no need, but as you've bought it I'll fetch two glasses and we'll make a toast to your future. I also took it upon myself to cook you dinner. Just a simple chicken casserole, nothing fancy. I would lay a bet you haven't eaten much today.'

'You're right, I haven't, except for a slice of toast this morning, which is very difficult to cook over those confounded gas jets. The bread kept falling off the fork and I burned two slices to a cinder before I actually managed to make an eatable piece.'

They both giggled and Richard went to fetch the glasses.

Chapter Eighteen

After her disastrous start at Sunny Side, Kacie couldn't believe that her new business now seemed to be running so smoothly. The two interviews she had had with the owners of the retirement homes Richard had set up for her had proved a great success, both readily agreeing to give her service a trial, both having the foresight to suss out their residents before she arrived, and each had a list of potential customers for her, with others to follow once the more reticent residents witnessed for themselves Kacie's skills, which the owners, after interviewing her at length, had no doubts she possessed.

The one and only stipulation Kacie made was that she herself would collect payments from her customers when each hairdo was completed.

Her only disappointment was that neither of the owners of the homes could accommodate her until the following week. For monetary reasons she needed to be working immediately. After paying out her lodgings last Friday and putting aside a couple of shillings for the gas and electric she only had a few coppers left which she would have to eke out until some money came in.

For the rest of the week she busied herself uncovering addresses of other retirement homes in the city to which she could travel. She was surprised to find there were quite a few such places in Leicester and around the shires, many not the type she was after, but at least five seemed possibilities. On paying them a visit, walking the distances to save money on bus fares, she tried not to be dismayed when the first three she called upon showed no interest at all in what she had to offer, saying that the staff attended to that kind of thing. The other two displayed a mild curiosity and after much work on Kacie's part, eventually agreed to arrange a more suitable time to discuss matters further when they were less busy. Unfortunately they were for the following week, but at least Kacie felt that

185

she had two possibilities, which, if she could secure them, would mean four homes on her books. The money she could make, depending on how many clients she had, would, she hoped, at least pay her rent, buy her food and pay Richard back bit by bit for what she owed him.

Each evening Kacie found herself rushing to Richard's room as soon as she heard him return home from work to update him on her news, and very soon, without either of them realising it, a routine was established and they were spending their evenings together. As the days passed the most unlikely friendship between two people of the opposite sex, with such diverse backgrounds, brought together by the circumstances of their past, continued to grow.

For Kacie, Richard was turning into the close brotherly type she had never had, and she found herself looking forward to spending time in his company, knowing with his presence in her life she had much to be grateful for, not only in the way he had rushed to her rescue financially, but that he was there to offer her support when she needed it. She was still having terrible difficulty accepting Dennis's betrayal of her and all emotions relating to it were still as raw as when she first found out. That dreadful happening outside the hotel in London seemed as though it had taken place years ago, not the two weeks it actually was, but she kept instilling in herself that if she concentrated all her efforts on her future, as time passed her pain would lessen, her wounds heal.

Richard, knowing that his relationship with the very attractive woman who had moved in upstairs would never be any more than very trusting friendship, found to his utter joy his life had taken on a whole new meaning. When he had made his choice to go his own way in life, it had never occurred to him that not all people's attitudes mirrored that of Jenny and her family. He hadn't realised how much his privileged background ostracised him from a world he had so wanted to be part of. Now, through Kacie, he no longer felt an outsider. A doorway was being opened into the society he so desperately wanted to belong to. He had much to thank Kacie for in making this possible.

Kacie rose early Tuesday morning. After checking her appearance, making herself as presentable as she could, she then checked several times that she had everything she needed. She was to be at The Glades at nine o'clock and, in order to be punctual, set off earlier than she needed to catch the Outer Circle bus that ran around the outskirts of the city and would take her the few stops she needed to reach Glenfield Road a few streets away.

When the bus arrived it was loaded with workers and she was afraid for a minute the conductor would not allow her passage when he spotted the dismantled but still cumbersome hair dryer she was trying to get on with, as well as her bulky bag full of sundries., Much to Kacie's relief, the handsome West Indian gave her a great big smile and his help, stowing the dryer and bag safely into the luggage compartment under the stairs.

Kacie was fortunate to slip into the only seat vacant as the occupant rose to get off at the next stop. In the front of her two teenage women were loudly chatting and Kacie could not help but overhear their conversation.

'The *Mercury* wa' full on it last night,' one of the women was saying. ' "Sons of Leicester on verge of being latest pop sensations", the headline went. There was pictures and everythin'. That lead singer ain't 'arf good-looking. I can't wait for the record to be released at the end of the month. I'm gonna start saving now to buy it.'

'Funny name they've got, though,' her companion commented.

'No it ain't. No more stupid a name than Conway Twitty. I think Vernon and the Vipers has a ring to it.'

Sitting behind them, Kacie felt suddenly drained pale at the mention of the band's name, and all painful emotions concerning Dennis returned with a vengeance. She fought the great urge to scream at the women to stop their chatter. Did they not realise how much torture their conversation was causing her? But how could they? Her head flashed around in a desperate search for a means of escape but there was nowhere else to sit, no room to stand, and the bus had still a way to go before it reached her particular stop. She was trapped, forced to listen to more.

'I fancy the drummer meself. D'yer reckon he's married?'

'Nah. *Mercury* said none of 'em are. There's 'ope for us then, eh?' the girl said, giggling. She delved into her handbag and pulled out a newspaper clipping which she carefully unfolded. 'I've cut the article out. Gonna stick it on my bedroom wall along with all the rest I collect. I can fall asleep then gazing into Vernon's dreamy eyes. He has got dreamy eyes. Look.'

'Oh, he has, yeah,' said her mate. 'But I still fancy the drummer. Eh, I thought yer said none of 'em was attached. Well, who's that woman Vernon's with, then?'

'What woman?'

''Er,' she said, pointing. 'In the picture that says they're just going into a 'otel. Posh-looking doss'ouse, in'it?' she said sarcastically.

'Oh, that picture. I didn't see a woman lurking behind 'em. It's all right, it says 'er name is Abigail Tomlinson and she works for the record company. She's the band's personal assistant. Fancy 'aving a personal assistant to do everything for you. I'd quite like one meself, wouldn't you, eh? And that's no doss'ouse, you ignorant clot. It sez 'ere that it's the Dorchester, and Vernon and the Vipers are attending a press conference prior to the launch of their first single. Ohh, it's great in'it, a band from yer own town splashed all over the papers? They'll be on the *6.5 Special* soon.'

'That's all well and good but we ain't got a telly so we can't watch 'em anyway.'

'Me Auntie Elsie has. She'll let us watch it if we bung her a shilling for a 'alf-of bitter. We'll go 'alves, eh?'

'Yeah, we will. Oh, I can't wait.'

Thankfully, Kacie's stop came into view and gratefully she made her escape.

Hair dryer propped against a wall, bag of sundries on the pavement, Kacie stood for a moment to calm her raging emotions. The conversation she had overheard had knocked the stuffing from her, temporarily lowering the imaginary protective steel-hard barrier she had wrapped around her heart. In her mind's eye all she could picture was Dennis and Abigail Tomlinson entering a hotel together. The newspaper might have reported that they were attending a press conference but newspapers were notorious for getting their facts wrong. More than likely they were having an intimate meal together, possibly planning their future, and the thought brought tears of misery to her eyes, a terrible gnawing pain in the pit of her stomach.

Also she had overheard the woman say that Vernon and the Vipers were very soon going to be released upon the public. That would mean every record shop, popular radio station, club, pub and coffee bar would be playing their music; magazines and newspapers carrying their pictures. Not that she begrudged Dennis his fame for a minute. After all, he had worked hard and lusted after it for long enough, but the possibility of seeing his face every time she read a trendy magazine, or hearing his voice each time she switched on the radio, or blaring from a juke box in a variety of drinking establishments, was something she dreaded. All it would achieve for her would be a constant reminder of the man she still loved desperately and had lost for ever, never being allowed to let his memory fade and heal her pain.

Then the solution of how best to handle this came to her. At least until she felt strong enough to cope, she would lead a nunlike existence. She'd read no more newspapers or magazines nor listen to the popular music stations on the radio; neither would she enter a record shop, pub, club of coffee bar. Considering her love of music, a self-imposed ban would be an extremely difficult thing to stick with, but a small price to pay to avoid causing herself unnecessary grief.

Her hard decision made, she brought the mental barrier protecting her heart back into place, took several deep breaths, with great effort forced a smile on her face, gathered her equipment and bravely continued on her way.

The owner of The Glades gave her an enthusiastic welcome. 'The residents are so excited, my dear,' she said as she guided Kacie down a long corridor. 'I can't remember them all being so lively since Russ Conway did us the honour of coming to play for us on the piano one afternoon. Mind you, that was before he was famous. I doubt we could afford him now. Now, my dear, you've ten ladies that want you to do their hairs and I've told all of them of your prices, which I have to say I think are very reasonable. I will advise you that several of my old ladies can be rather cantankerous, so should any start playing you up or try to leave without settling their bills, you send for me and I'll deal with them.' They arrived at a room right at the back of the large imposing Victorian building. 'This is the room I've set aside for you. I hope it's all right? It's the old washroom, I'm afraid, but it's the only place not used frequently with a sink and an electric socket in it for your hair dryer so you'll not be disturbed.'

'It'll do me perfectly,' said Kacie. 'Thank you very much.'

'Shall I send the first one through? Mind you, you'll probably find them all trooping in to watch once you get started.'

Kacie smiled. 'I don't mind, they're all most welcome to come and watch. Please give me five minutes to set up and then you can send them through.'

Kacie knew something was wrong immediately she tried to lather her first client's wet hair. Whatever was in the bottle might be the normal green soap colour, but green soap it most definitely was not. The stuff she had put on her customer's hair was of a cloggy

189

consistency and an awful smell was coming from it, like bad eggs.

Head over the sink the client piped up, 'Goodness me, just what is that terrible smell?'

Kacie was baffled herself. She grabbed up the container and looked at the label. It clearly read Green Soap and the name of a well-known manufacturer. 'I'm sorry, Miss Harris, but I must have opened the wrong bottle of shampoo,' she fibbed, in an effort to smooth over the situation whilst she sorted it out. Hastily she dug around in the sundries bag and unearthed a bottle of lanolin shampoo she had bought for those customers who wished to pay extra for a better-quality product. As soon as she untwisted the lid and poured a little of the contents into her palm she saw to her horror that this was definitely not what the label depicted. It was creamy in colour but again the consistency and smell was the same as that in the green soap container.

Heart thumping erratically, mind racing frantically, she hurriedly rinsed Miss Harris's hair clear of whatever was on it, wrapped a towel around her head and moved her away from the sink. She quickly grabbed up her bag of products and accessories and, with her back to her waiting clients so they couldn't see what she was doing, she tested, by squirting it on her hand, a spray bottle of lacquer she had mixed up herself the previous night from the powder in the large tub and gallon of white spirit she had brought from Myrna. Its sticky consistency felt about right but then as it dried instead of it being clear her hand was showing a white residue which was hardening rapidly. She couldn't work out what it was but a large quantity of something else had been added to the lacquer powder. Something like starch. Why?

A great foreboding filled her as she randomly checked her other stock and to her great bewilderment and shock found the small bottles supposedly containing cold waving perm lotions actually had been filled with water; the setting lotions the same but they had been coloured with, she guessed, food dyes to give the appearance of being what they were supposed to represent.

Her heart thumped painfully, her legs buckling. She had been sabotaged again but on a far grander scale. Why had Myrna done this to her? Kacie represented no threat to her business. She slapped her hands to her face in a helpless gesture, a groan of despair escaping her lips. There was nothing she could do about it. She couldn't abandon these ladies whilst she raced off to purchase kosher supplies. Besides, she had no money, having used every last penny of what she had been given by Richard setting up her business. Having paid her lodgings last Friday, bought a few necessities and splashed out on the bottle of port, she had only a few shillings of her own left, which would go nowhere at the wholesaler's.

Face a deathly pale, she rapidly bungled all her belongings together and after making a very embarrassed excuse for her sudden departure, she fled from the premises.

Fully expecting to be greeted by an exhilarated Kacie, rapturous after her successful day, Richard was most shocked to have Kacie finally open her door to him and he immediately saw her distressed state.

'Kacie, what on earth has happened?' he demanded, entering, her room and shutting the door behind him.

She collapsed down on her bed and through choking sobs related her dreadful tale. When she had finished he sat down next to her, his own face bewildered, as he placed a comforting arm around her shoulder. 'But this doesn't make any sense, Kacie. Why would Myrna doctor the commodities she sold you?'

'I don't know? I wish I did. I can't help wondering if it was Myrna behind what happened at the competition, but if it was, Lord knows how she managed to switch those bottles. The only time I didn't have that bag of hair products in my sight was when I was talking to her, and to be honest I can't work out how she did all this either. She wasn't gone long enough to do it.'

He rose. 'I'll make you a cup of tea, then we'll try and rationalise this.'

'What is there to rationalise? I've been stupid enough to have the dirty done on me again and it looks like it was done by someone I thought was my friend.'

Richard was concentrating on trying to light one of the gas burners and failing badly. 'Oh, for goodness' sake, Kacie, I don't know how you cope with this old thing,' he erupted. 'It's more than likely a death trap. Come on, we'll go down to my room where it's more comfortable and at least I have a cooker that works, even if I had to buy it myself.'

Too drained and dispirited to refuse, Kacie obediently followed.

Huddled in one of Richard's armchairs by a fully turned on electric fire, cradling a cup of scalding hot tea, she looked at him hopelessly. 'I've lost all your money, Richard. I'm so sorry. I'm going to have to get myself a job and on the wages I'll be earning, it'll take me ages to pay you back.'

'That money is not important. If you remember right, it was you that insisted on paying it back. I was quite happy just to give it to you. Now,' he said, sitting down opposite, 'you must confront Myrna with this.'

She gave a heavy sigh. 'What's the point?'

'The point is, Kacie, that you find out the reason why she did such a diabolical thing.'

She eyed him wanly. 'Richard, I've no energy to face anything at the moment. Whatever I can summon up I need to put towards getting myself a job.'

'I can see your reasoning, but I still think you should go and see her. Find out why, if nothing else. I'd come with you, Kacie, but unfortunately I have to go to work tomorrow.'

She sighed. 'I suppose you're right. I should go and see her. I could go around tomorrow morning before I start looking for work. I thought I'd make a start at the labour exchange.'

He looked at her, taken aback. 'You surprise me, Kacie. I would have thought you'd be better going to actual salons yourself and enquiring after work sooner than wait for hours for someone to see you at the labour exchange. I mean, all you have to do is show your certificates of qualification and someone like you will be inundated with work. Well, I would have thought so. And it's my opinion that only firms that are desperate for people resort to asking the labour exchange to send them possibilities. You know, the sort of places that don't pay so well or where the conditions of working leave much to be desired.'

She looked at him stupefied. Her certificates of qualification that she was so proud of were hanging in Verna's salon. She had been so occupied by other matters that having to produce them as confirmation of her skills when she applied for jobs had never crossed her mind. The superiors of the homes hadn't asked to see them – luckily they'd taken her at face value – but any salon of repute wouldn't. Proof of her training would be one of the first things they would ask for. It wasn't as though she could breeze into the salon and expect Verna to hand her certificates over without demanding a detailed explanation for her sudden disappearance, and also there was the risk of bumping into numerous others she and Dennis were acquainted with. She still couldn't bring herself to face it.

Her unwillingness to collect her certificates until she felt strong enough mentally to confront her past meant she had only one option at this moment and that was to pay a visit to the labour exchange and hope they had a salon on their books that needed a stylist so desperately they wouldn't ask too many questions. If not, then she'd have to resort to other means in which to earn herself a living.

She realised Richard was talking to her. 'Pardon?'

'I asked if sausage and chips would do you?'

'What! Oh, I couldn't eat anything, Richard, but thanks for the offer.'

'You will by the time I've cooked it,' he insisted.

Chapter Nineteen

Cedric Brindle was not in the best of moods. He was a tall man, skeletally thin, possessing no sense of humour whatsoever. He hated his job, despising the people he had to deal with. A confirmed bachelor, his only joy in life was carrying out his duties as a lay preacher, and he lived for Sunday Worship when he could force the Gospels according to himself down the throats of his unfortunate congregation, none of whom dare not attend for fear of his retaliations. He had been known on more than one occasion to drag a deserter out of bed and shame him before the horrified gathering.

All day, as usual at the labour exchange, he had dealt with what he deemed to be the dregs of the earth, seeking the kind of work he felt they were most unsuitable or unskilled for, expecting him to produce these jobs like magic. When he bluntly pointed out their errors they were usually most uncooth with their responses, some even threatening violence. Cedric felt great satisfaction and did not bat an eyelid as he had them forcefully removed.

His opinion of Kacie as she had sat down before him had been made by a flash across her so quick it went unnoticed by her. Cedric disapproved of her, of her modern style of dress which he thought trashy, and she didn't seem to have much life about her, no visible signs of enthusiasm that he could see for getting herself work at all. His assessment was that she was typical of the majority that came into the labour exchange on the pretext of looking for work when their true aim was to keep the officials happy so they could collect their dole.

Without appearing even to look at her he brusquely asked, 'I trust you're here to seek work?'

Feeling that death would be a blessed relief from the seemingly never-ending catastrophes being heaped on her of late, Kacie had had to drag herself here and the long wait to see this man had not helped to lift her dampened spirits in the slightest. His surly manner offended her and she eyed him sharply. 'This is the labour exchange, isn't it? Why else would I be here if it wasn't for a job? I'm a hairdresser by trade and I'd be obliged to know what vacancies are on offer.'

The manner of her response to him did not help her cause. Cedric did no more than pull a card randomly from the pile dedicated to vacancies for women, glanced it over, then proceeded to fill in a form.

'What are you doing?' Kacie asked.

He raised his head and looked at her nonchalantly. 'Filling in an interview form.' He spoke to her as though she was stupid.

'An interview for what?'

He gave an irritated sigh. 'For a filing clerk in the records department at the Leicester Royal Infirmary.'

'But that isn't for a hairdresser.'

'It's a job,' he snapped. 'Someone in your unemployed position cannot afford to be choosy.'

Her hackles rose at his impertinence and she couldn't help but say stonily, 'Excuse me for my ignorance but aren't your sort employed by the Government to help people out of work look for jobs that are suitable for them?'

'Yes,' Cedric replied, his sour face frowning as he wondered where this line of conversation was leading.

'Well, in that case I suggest you check your cards again to find something that'll suit my skills before I demand to see your superior and tell him exactly what I think of the help you've giving me.'

Cedric's bony face turned a deep colour of purple. 'I don't appreciate your manner,' he hissed.

She fixed him straight in his eyes. 'And I don't appreciate yours. Now are you going to look again or do I speak to your boss?'

Lips tight, he snatched up his cards again and flicked through them. He'd teach this madam for daring to confront him and threaten his livelihood by reporting him to his boss. Several vacancies for leading salons in town and a couple of others not far from where Kacie lived, the family type of establishment that would have suited her down to the ground, were passed over as there was one particular vacancy Cedric Brindle was looking for. Ah, there it was. He pulled the card out and hid a smirk as he studied it.

Madge Benson, owner of Florentina's salon. The most detested woman in Leicester's hairdressing history. She ruled her staff with a rod of iron and ran them ragged for as little as she could get away with paying them. Only those unfortunately not acquainted with Madge Benson's reputation took a job at Florentina's, and they never stayed longer than they absolutely had to. Consequently, Florentina's always had vacancies for staff.

'This should suit you,' he said. 'A stylist is required at a salon on Narborough Road. Wage negotiable, according to your skills. I suggest you take it as it's all I've got on offer in your line.'

She glowered at him. 'Thank you,' she said icily. 'I'd be very obliged if you could fill me out an introduction form.'

His eyes darkened menacingly as he grabbed a form and, completed, he thrust it at her. 'Good luck,' he said, a smirk of malice twitching his lips. You'll need it, he thought.

She gave him a look of contempt as she departed.

As soon as she walked through the front door of her lodgings, Richard came out of his room to greet her.

'I was looking out for you,' he said.

'I thought you weren't going to peep at me from behind your curtains again?' She frowned at him quizzically. 'Anyway, what are you doing home in the middle of the afternoon?'

'I've taken the afternoon off. Have you been to see Myrna?'

Taking a deep breath, she shook her head. 'Not yet.'

'That's what I thought, and that's why I've taken the afternoon off – to come with you. Anyway, come on through, I've the kettle on and I've something to show you.'

'What?'

He gave her a secretive smile. 'It's a surprise.'

She followed him inside his room and immediately saw two large boxes on the table. One had a large red ribbon tied around it. 'That one is yours,' Richard said, pointing to it.

She eyed him, confused. 'For me? But what is it?'

'Why don't you open it and find out whilst I make the tea?'

Filled with curiosity, she carefully slipped off the ribbon and pulled open the leaves of the box, taking a peak inside. 'Why, it's a radio!' she exclaimed.

'Clever girl,' he said, a merry twinkle in his eyes. 'And it's a present for you.'

'Oh, Richard, but you shouldn't have,' she cried. 'Really, it's far too expensive for a gift for me.'

'The cost is not important, Kacie. I got a great deal of pleasure out of buying that for you. I know you miss listening to your favourite popular music programmes and I thought you needed cheering up.'

Despite the fact that she was overwhelmed with her gift and deeply touched by his generosity, she hadn't the heart to upset him by explaining that for the foreseeable future anything connected with the popular music scene was off limits to her. Regardless, she said in delight, 'Oh, Richard, it's wonderful, thank you so much.'

'You do like it and you're not offended?'

'I love it, and I'm not. Now forgive me for being nosy but I'm desperate to know who the other box is for.'

'It's a present for myself. I'll show you.'

He opened the box and she took a look inside. 'It's a record player,' she said.

'It's a beauty, isn't it? As a move in the right direction in respect of my new image that you're going to create for me, Kacie, I thought I ought to accustom myself with the sort of music I'm expected to appreciate in future. I don't know whether you have any records or not but you're welcome to borrow the player any time you like. I've also purchased a selection of the very latest long players too. If you want you can borrow those when I've accustomed myself to my new mode of listening.'

'Oh, Richard, you're too kind, really you are.' She eyed him concernedly. 'But you love your opera and classical stuff.'

'Yes I do and I still will, but I need to broaden my tastes, don't I, if I intend to modernise myself?'

A feeling of gloom began to infiltrate her. This line of conversation was reminding her of Dennis and she prayed none of the LPs Richard had bought was in any way connected with the band. Nevertheless she smiled at him. 'I am impressed.' She forced herself to ask, 'So what records did you buy?'

He picked up a bag and took them out. 'Dickie Valentine, Winifred Atwell, Andy Williams and Harry Belafonte,' he said, leafing through them. 'They're all high in the charts. Have I made a good choice, do you think, Kacie?' he asked eagerly.

She looked at him, mixed emotions racing through her. Half of her was glad his choices were by artists the older generation had made popular, the type Dennis would have cringed at, and he and the band flatly refused to be associated with. The other half was dismayed that his great effort to lift his appreciation of music to the sort the young modern generation were into, the types he was so desperate to become part of, was way off track. She hadn't the heart to dampen his enthusiasm, though, by putting him straight. 'I shall enjoy listening to them with you,' she said diplomatically.

'I'll set the player up and put one on now,' he said. 'Which one is your favourite and I'll put that on first?'

Kacie blew out her cheeks. 'Er . . . they're all as interesting. You choose.'

'All right, er . . . we'll go for Winifred Atwell. I've not heard her sing before. In fact I wasn't acquainted with her at all until I looked at the latest copy of the hit parade that was on the record shop wall.'

'I think you'll find Winifred Atwell plays the honky-tonk piano, Richard. She doesn't sing, as far as I'm aware.'

Richard looked blankly at her, not having a clue what she was talking about. 'Honky-tonk? Really? That sounds very trendy. I made a good choice then. Drat, I can't get the needle in. Ahh, that's got it. Right here we go.'

As the lively sound of Winifred Atwell bashing out 'Let's Have Another Party' filled the room, Richard handed Kacie a cup of tea and, sitting down in the armchair opposite, asked, 'So, what did you get up to today?'

She took a sip of her tea before saying, 'I've got myself a job with a salon on Narborough Road. I start Monday morning.'

'Kacie, that's great,' he enthused. 'So what's the place like and do you think you'll like working there?'

Kacie sighed. She hadn't been impressed at all when she had entered the shop armed with her introduction form. The décor of the salon itself was drab, desperately in need of a lick of paint, and the half-dead pot plants lining the window ledge needed throwing out and replacing, although the outdated hairstyle posters on the walls did help a little to alleviate its overall dismal appearance. The room at the back she had been taken into for her interview was used as the proprietor's office as well as the stockroom, and she had noticed to her horror that the hairdressing supplies appeared to be piled in a haphazard heap, no system of stock control apparent.

Madge Benson herself was a thin woman, nearing her sixties, Kacie guessed. It was difficult to ascertain exactly, her face being covered by a thick layer of makeup, some of it having settled into deep creases crisscrossing her sharp features. Her dyed black hair was piled high on her head in a cottage-loaf-style bun, and she was dressed in long flowing black garments, reminding Kacie of a witch. Around her scrawny neck were several heavy gold chains, bangles on her arms and big-stoned rings on her long bony fingers. All through the interview she had chain-smoked Capstan full-strength cigarettes.

Despite the proprietor's attitude seeming pleasant enough, all Kacie's senses had screamed at her to run, that she'd hate working here, but apart from her desperate need of a job, who else would employ her without proof that she was qualified – which thankfully and for whatever reason, Madge Benson hadn't, and hopefully once she could see what Kacie was capable of would forget to do so.

'It's a job, Richard, and that's what counts,' she said.

He started tapping his foot in time to the music. 'This is good, isn't it?' he said.

It was all right, she thought, if you liked that type of thing, which she didn't, but the old ladies at the home would have loved it. She just nodded.

'Have you finished your tea?' Richard asked.

'Nearly, why?'

'We're going out, remember.'

She eyed him pleadingly. 'Can't we just leave it, Richard? I haven't the energy.'

'If that's what you want to do, I would never force you, but if you don't you'll regret it.' He eyed her gravely. 'It's possible that Myrna deliberately ruined your chances of having your own business, Kacie. If you don't challenge her I fear she could do it to someone else.'

'You're right,' she said, drinking the dregs in her cup and standing up. 'Turn that awful row off and we'll get going before I change my mind.'

He grimaced at her. 'Awful row?'

She gawped, mortified at her thoughtless remark. 'Oh, I'm sorry, that was a slip of the tongue. I meant to say . . . er . . . what did I mean to say?'

'You said what you meant, Kacie. It is an awful noise, isn't it?'

Her face filled with shame. 'But you like it and that's what matters.'

He shook his head. 'Actually I don't, but I'm trying to like it, really I am?'

She smiled at him kindly. 'You shouldn't have to force yourself to like it, Richard. That's not what it's all about. You're supposed to enjoy what you're listening to, whether it's pop, classical, opera or anything else that takes your fancy.'

'But I don't want to be square any more, Kacie. I want to be trendy and with it.'

'Maybe that's not you, though, Richard. Now I know you better, I happen to think I was wrong to encourage you to change. Yes, a new set of more fashionable clothes would do wonders for you and so will a change of hairstyle, but nothing more than that. You're lovely as you are. What do they say, that it takes all sorts to make a world? Well, I happen to think this all sort,' she said, placing her hand on his arm in an affectionate gesture, 'is rather a nice chap and a wonderful friend and, Richard, that's what really counts. One day some lovely lady who likes the same kind of things that you do will come into your life and you'll be perfect together.'

He eyed her hopefully. 'Do you think so?'

'I do. Just be patient. If I happen to bump into anyone that I think will fit the bill, be assured I'll nudge her your way.'

They both laughed.

Kacie stared stupefied at the premises of Cut and Curls. The place was in darkness and the outside door tightly secured. It was very obvious that no business was being conducted here. 'I don't understand,' she uttered, bewildered.

'You have got the right place?' Richard asked.

'Of course I've got the right place,' she snapped, annoyed.

'Maybe Myrna has gone home early,' he suggested.

'I'd hardly think that likely being's she's only been open just over a week.'

'No, I suppose not. Is it early closing day around here then?'

'Not on a Tuesday, Richard.'

'Oh, well, I'm stumped then.'

Just then a middle-aged woman approached, laden down with shopping. Richard waylaid her.

'Excuse me, madam,' he began.

'Madam?' she spat, indignant, giving Richard a furious scowl. 'Madams run brothels, dun't they? I'm no madam, I'll let you know.'

'Misses,' Kacie interjected. 'My friend meant to say misses.'

'Oh, well, that's different. Wadda yer want?'

Richard was very careful with his words. 'My good lady, do you happen to know where the owner of the hairdresser's is, please?'

She pulled a wry face. 'As far away as possible if she's any sense, for fear of being lynched. If she wa' a 'airdresser than I'm the Queen a' Sheba. Now if yer don't mind I've got better things ter do than stand chattin' ter you.'

Kacie and Richard looked at each other, bewildered, as the woman waddled away.

'What do you make of that?' Kacie asked.

He shrugged. 'I'm not sure. Ah, I'll ask this young woman. Excuse me, ma— er . . . miss. Do you happen to know why this hairdressing shop is closed for business?'

The young woman, Kacie guessed to be in her late teens, looked at Richard as though he was stupid. 'If yer ask me, it should never 'ave been opened fer business in the first place,' she said tartly.

'Why do you say that?' Kacie asked.

'Why? 'Cos she were no 'airdresser, that's why. Me three mates are still suffering the consequences. We were all so excited about getting a new trendy style and none of us told our mams but we all took sickies from work 'cos she was offering half-price on opening day. Lord knows what she tried to perm Janet's 'air with but that were no perm she wa' trying to give her, and what she put on Pam's hair ter wash it with stunk to high heaven and her scalp is still itching from it. She tried ter mek excuses, said there was summat wrong wi' the products she was using and asked us to come back the next day. But there was no way we were all going to be taken for a ride again. Word spread like wild fire after that and no one 'ud go near the place. Last Thursday she shut up shop and no one 'as seen 'er since. I'd find yerself a decent 'airdresser, if I were you,' she said, addressing Kacie. 'And thank yer stars you 'ad a lucky escape.'

All through her narrative Kacie was staring at her, stunned. 'Er . . . yes, I will,' she uttered.

'Well,' said Richard, his face set tight, as the young woman continued on her way, 'obviously from what she said it's my guess that what happened to Myrna is the same as what happened to you. Still, now we know that Myrna is not the guilty party. Whoever supplied all the products is.'

'Mmm,' mouthed Kacie worriedly. 'Seems like it, doesn't it? I wonder where she's gone.'

He gave a shrug of his shoulders. 'Maybe back to London, do you think? You did tell me it was London where she had been working before she came back to Leicester?'

202

'Yes, it was. This is so awful, Richard. Myrna put everything she had into opening this salon and now she's ruined. Poor girl,' she uttered.

'Poor you too,' he said. He shook his head, bewildered. 'It still doesn't make sense to me why anyone would go to all this trouble. You told me Myrna said she got sent her opening products from an anonymous well-wisher?'

Kacie looked at him, confused. 'She did.'

Richard exhaled loudly. 'Well, that poses the question, what was this anonymous well-wisher's motive? I don't suppose we'll ever find out now. Best put this all behind you, Kacie, and concentrate on starting your new job on Monday.' He looked at her hard. His new friend needed cheering up. 'Come on,' he said, hooking his arm through hers and propelling her off down the street.

'Where are we going?' she asked.

'Shopping,' he said. 'It's about time you gave me this new look you keep promising me.'

'But you haven't any money. You lent it to me.'

'Not all of it, Kacie. Come on.'

For the next couple of hours Kacie forgot all her troubles as she lost herself happily helping Richard choose his new wardrobe. They visited several men's stores in the town centre that catered for the young modern man, and Richard was very reticent at first, but after much coaxing from Kacie was delighted with the items she picked out for him and amazed at the transformation in his appearance a different cut in clothes could have. By the time they had finished he had purchased two pairs of trousers for smart wear and two for casual, two jackets, an off-the-peg suit, five shirts, two long-sleeved jumpers, a selection of ties and two new pairs of shoes – one a pair of winkle-pickers which Richard said pinched his toes, but which Kacie insisted wouldn't once he'd worn them in. You had to suffer for the sake of fashion. It was the done thing if you wanted to be trendy.

'I can't remember the last time I had so much fun,' he said to Kacie as they came out of the Irish men's shop on Silver Street. 'Are you sure these denim jeans are me, Kacie?'

'You look great in them,' she enthused. 'All the stuff you bought looks great on you, Richard. Stop worrying. All you need now is a nice woman to wear them for. That'll come, believe me.' She looked at him, concerned. 'You have spent such a lot, though.'

He smiled at her, eyes twinkling. 'I'm sure my bank account can stand it. Now what about you?'

'Me? What about me?'

'I bet you'd like a new outfit.'

She would. Several items had caught her eye in shop windows. 'You know what my finances are like at the moment, Richard. Buying clothes is not on my list of priorities.'

'But I'd like to treat you to something, if you'd let me.'

She looked at him affectionately. 'I appreciate the gesture but I've enough clothes to do me at the moment for my lifestyle. Besides, I think you've spent enough for one day. You can buy me a coffee, though, from British Home Stores.'

It would have given him so much pleasure to have treated her to something new to wear but her answer was final and he knew it was pointless arguing with her. 'Would you not sooner go to a coffee bar? The Kenco on Granby Street I've heard is the place the "in crowd" all go at the moment. We can listen to the juke box and you can start teaching me what artists I should be listening to.' The look of horror that flashed across her face shocked him. 'Have I said something wrong, Kacie?'

'Oh, no, no,' she said hurriedly. 'I'm, er . . . not in the mood for loud music in a coffee bar.' Out of the corner of her eye she spotted a woman coming towards them. She froze. It was her mother. The look on her face was one of worry, preoccupation. She was obviously searching for somewhere as she was looking around at the buildings. Kacie's instinct was to run to her, hug her, ask if she was all right, but she couldn't; she wasn't ready to deal with her past yet. She grabbed Richard's arm. 'I want to go home. We can have a coffee there.' She pulled him off down the street. 'Come on, there's a bus in,' she urged, wanting to be on it before her mother spotted her.

Richard had no choice but to obey Kacie as she was gripping his arm so tightly, but that didn't stop him wondering why all of a sudden she was so hellbent on catching the bus and getting out of town when seconds ago she had suggested having a coffee. There had been a frozen look on her face. What had happened to Kacie to bring that sudden change about? He so desperately wanted to question her, to offer his help. On the bus he turned to face her. 'Kacie . . .?' he began.

She turned to look at him. 'Yes?' she said.

The frozen look had now left her face, whatever had upset her so badly no longer apparent, and as much as he wanted to, he couldn't bring himself to pry into her most personal life. She would tell him when she had a desire to. He took a breath. 'Er . . . I just wanted to thank you for a lovely afternoon.'

'You're most welcome,' she said.

Chapter Twenty

Madge Benson paused at the side of the customer Kacie was attending to and, sticking her beaked nose superiorly in the air, asked, 'Everything all right, Mrs Butler?'

The client nodded. 'Very much so, Miss Benson. You seem to have got yerself a little treasure in young Kacie,' she said, winking at Kacie's reflection through the mirror in front of her.

'That remains to be seen,' said Madge, flashing Kacie a look of derision. She leaned towards Kacie and said in hushed tones, 'I've noticed you're being far too liberal with the sundries. Half the amount of shampoo and setting lotion is sufficient.'

Kacie took a deep breath, fighting hard to keep her own counsel. Madge Benson was no Verna Kozlowski in any way shape or form, and not for the first time since she had started working at Florentina's nearly two weeks ago did she have to quash a great longing to be back in Verna's salon, working with people who had become her friends, being trusted and allowed to carry out her profession as she felt it should be done, in pleasant surroundings and in a congenial environment.

Kacie was not used to or appreciated having her skills questioned at every opportunity. Neither was she used to having to use the cheapest quality hair products which she'd have to be an idiot not to know had been thinned down by Madge Benson to eke them out even further. All this was making her job so much more difficult, and achieving the kind of results she expected of herself was proving near on impossible.

'But I had to use that amount of shampoo as I couldn't get a lather, and if I used less setting lotion, Miss Benson, then I might as well not put any on. While we are on that subject, I have noticed—'

'Let me remind you,' Madge cut in sharply, her voice rising, 'that I am the proprietor of this establishment and you are the employee, and as such you follow my instructions unless you want to see yourself out of a job.' Without waiting for an answer she disappeared into the back.

Kacie stared after her, a great surge of annoyance rearing at her employer's unwarranted treatment of her. And how bloody-minded she was, Kacie thought, to give me a dressing down in front of a customer. The only thing stopping Kacie from charging after Madge Benson and telling her just what she could do with her job was the knowledge that without her certificates she would not get another position very easily.

'Tek no notice of 'er, me duck. She thinks what she's just done makes her look important,' Jessie Butler, Kacie's customer, piped up. 'But it don't. It just meks us customers feel sorry for you gels that 'ave ter work for her. She's now gone for a swig out of her hidden bottle. She thinks none of us knows she's a drinker, but we do.'

Kacie was already aware of her employer's secret habit, had realised on her very first day that as well as being a heavy smoker Madge Benson had a penchant for a good quantity of the hard stuff. It was Kacie's guess that she must polish off a half-bottle of vodka during working hours, and she also wondered how much her employer got through at night. To her credit, Madge Benson never appeared inebriated during working hours and was always on time in the morning, even if her mood was not exactly full of spring joy.

Feeling it unethical to pass comment on her employer Kacie turned and addressed Rita, the young apprentice. 'Could you get me a fresh towel to put around Mrs Butler's shoulders, please, Rita. This one is wet.'

Rita, a fifteen-year-old, sullen-looking, plump plodder of a girl, looked blankly at her. 'Don't think there's any dry ones left,' she whined sulkily.

Kacie fought to keep her temper. This slovenly girl was turning out to be the bane of her life. What she would give to have the very willing and capable Diane here now. 'Would you go and check?' she asked evenly. 'And if there's no dry towels I suggest you ought to set about making sure we do have some.' And she couldn't help but add, 'It's not as though you're doing anything else at the moment, despite the fact I did ask you to sweep the floor.'

The girl glowered at her before slopping off.

'Why is someone like you working here, Kacie?'

Jessie Butler's question caught Kacie unawares. 'Er . . . it's a job,

Mrs Butler,' she said as she resumed attending to her hair.

'Not much of one for someone like you, though, ducky, is it? I'd'a thought you'd be snapped up by a posh salon in town.'

'Maybe I don't want to work for a posh salon, Mrs Butler.'

'Mmm, maybe yer don't. But there's other salons better than this who'd grab at yer.'

'If it's that bad then why do you come here, Mrs Butler?'

'Same as the rest of 'em round 'ere do, me duck. 'Cos if note else, Madge's rates are cheaper than the rest and it's all we can afford. Madge might be a boozer but she ain't daft. She knows if she raises her prices then she'll 'ave no custom, then 'ow will she support her drink and fag habit, 'cos it's my guess that's just about all this business does for 'er. She dresses like she does 'cos she thinks it meks her look regal. More like a witch, if yer ask me. And don't be fooled by all that jewellery she wears. All costume and paste, the whole lot of it. She thinks none of us know, silly old beggar she is. It's only folks like me that's bin coming 'ere that long and too long in the tooth to be bothered with change that patronises this salon now. Anyway, it's not as though we want some fancy 'airdo now, is it? Just a shampoo and set once a fortnight and a perm every six months. The types Madge usually employs are just about capable of that.' In the mirror she scanned Kacie's reflection, through shrewd age-faded intelligent blue eyes. 'You're different. I knew the minute I sat down and yer ran your fingers through my 'air and told me its texture and condition, then recommended a more suitable style for me. No other 'airdresser has done that before, not in this salon. Still, why yer 'ere is your business, and please excuse an old lady's nosiness in prying.'

Kacie smiled as she finished trimming her salt-and-pepper hair and prepared to set it in rollers. 'That's all right, Mrs Butler, and no offence taken.' She gave her scissors a wipe and placed them on the ledge under the mirror, then glanced towards the door, hoping to see Rita returning with a fresh towel, and when she didn't, sighed, irritated, knowing the girl had more than likely forgotten all about the simple task Kacie had asked her to do; was probably hiding in the toilet in the yard, engrossed in one of her teenage magazines.

She realised Mrs Butler was talking to her. 'Pardon?'

'I said this wa' Madge's sister's place, yer know.'

'Was it?' Kacie asked as she wound a section of Jessie's hair around a pink plastic roller.

'Mmm. I knew the Benson sisters when they were young. Not a

very nice life, they had. The father disappeared when they were both little, went off with another woman or something like that. I'm not surprised meself as the mother was a huge woman, looked like one of them oriental Buddhas and ugly with it. Ironic really, considering her daughters were both so thin. But she ruled those girls with a rod of iron. They weren't allowed to breathe unless she gave permission. Consequently they both never married. Mind you, neither of them were exactly good-looking so I don't think they had that many suitors.

'It was poor Madge that drew the short straw and had to stay at home whilst Faye went to work to keep them all. Faye trained as a hairdresser with Molly Snedall, who used to have a little place on Tudor Road. I must give Faye Benson her due. She knew how to cut hair. Just after the war, the mother died – and about time too, if yer ask me – and Faye, now not being answerable to the old woman, borrowed some money from the bank and opened this place whilst poor old Madge continued to keep house. Through sheer hard work Faye managed to build up a nice business. N'ote was too good for 'er customers and this salon wa' a joy ter come into.

'Then two years ago the poor sole goes and dies just like that, no warning whatsoever. Heart or something. As her only living relative Madge inherited the place. Well, all us around here thought Madge would sell up. Never having worked in her life what did she know about the running of such an establishment?'

Kacie stopped what she was doing and eyed Mrs Butler in surprise, momentarily forgetting how unethical it was to become engaged in gossip about her boss. 'So Miss Benson is not a qualified hairdresser then?'

Jessie Butler chuckled. 'Not on your nelly. She wouldn't know one end of a hairbrush from another. How long 'ave yer worked 'ere, gel?'

'Nearly two weeks.'

'And in that time 'ave yer ever seen Madge so much as pick up a comb?'

Kacie stared at her. No she hadn't. But then she hadn't thought much, as the number of customers coming in had just about kept her occupied. Besides, she was aware that some proprietors, unlike Verna, who willingly lent a hand when busy, preferred to take a back seat and let their employees do the donkey work. 'Oh, I automatically thought she was a hairdresser,' Kacie said diplomatically.

'Well, now yer know she isn't, and if you ever get busy then yer'd 'ave ter manage by yerself and no mistake. When Madge first took over three hairstylists were employed, besides an apprentice. They soon left. Wouldn't put up with the way Madge thought she could treat 'em. Shameful, it was. She cut their wages, for a start, and lorded over them like she wa' royalty. If Faye could see how all her hard work has gone down the pan, she'd be turning in her grave.

'I've lost count of the number of stylists Madge's employed since she took over. Practically every time I come in there's someone different. Trouble with Madge is, she doesn't seem to learn from her mistakes. I suppose the way she acts if understandable. After all those years of being closeted she suddenly finds she can do exactly what she likes when she likes, but then that's no excuse for her treating people like dirt just because she thinks she's better than them because she has her own business.' Mrs Butler gave a sad sigh. 'I don't suppose I shall see you again, me duck.'

Kacie was looking at her thoughtfully. Learning all this about her employer was making Kacie see her in a new light. She actually felt very sorry for Madge and the austere life she had been forced to lead. But then Jessie Butler was right. Just because Madge Benson was an employer that didn't give her the right to treat her staff as though they should be beholden to her because she had given them a job. 'Don't write me off that quickly, Mrs Butler,' she said. 'I intend to stick around for a while.'

'Why?'

'Excuse me?'

'As I said before, someone like you can have yer pick of jobs. So why stay 'ere? Especially after what I've told yer.'

Kacie smiled at her. 'Maybe I just want to work here, Mrs Butler. And maybe I'm not the type to stand for Miss Benson's ways, whether she's my employer or not. Maybe she won't have her way that easily with me.'

Jessie Butler eyed her, impressed. 'I knew you were different.'

Rita didn't put in an appearance until long after Jessie Butler had left, brimming over with delight at the becoming hairstyle Kacie had created for her.

'Where have you been?' Kacie demanded. 'And what happened to the clean towel I asked you to get?'

'Eh? Oh, I fergot,' she said disinterestedly.

'Forgot!' Kacie sighed heavily. 'Rita, do you want to be a hairdresser?'

The girl looked at her blankly. 'No.'

'No?' Kacie stared at her aghast. 'Then why in God's name did you accept an apprenticeship?'

'But I didn't.'

Kacie frowned at her, bewildered. 'So . . . so just what is it you are supposed to be doing here?'

Rita shrugged. 'I dunno really. 'Elping out, I s'pose.'

'But that's just it, Rita, you don't help out. You hardly do anything. Do you want to keep this job?'

She shrugged again and stared gormlessly at Kacie for several moments. 'Yeah,' she said finally. 'It's the only job I could get and me mother'd kill me if I lost it.'

Kacie eyed her sternly. 'Well, you will lose it if you don't buck your ideas up. You're employed here to help and that's what I expect you to do. I can't do your own job as well as my own. Now I want this place sweeping out, and I mean properly, corners as well. Then I want the mirrors wiping down and the sinks cleaning and around the taps. And water the pot plants. When you've finished that, please tackle the laundry. Each morning we should have enough fresh towels to last the day. As it is, at the moment that is far from the case. And, Rita, be warned. If I have to speak to you again I shall approach Miss Benson and have you replaced by someone who's more willing. Is that understood?'

'I s'pose.'

Kacie's hackles rose. 'There no suppose about it. You'll be out on your ear, Rita, and make no mistake. Er . . . as a matter of interest, how much are you paid?'

'Two pounds a week, less national insurance.'

Kacie inwardly groaned. No wonder the girl showed no interest in her job on the pittance she was getting. Kacie knew instinctively that it was no use approaching Madge Benson about paying her a decent wage as she had no leverage to do so. As matters stood, the girl in truth was not worth the money she was already getting but then maybe she had never been given any encouragement to show her worth, if indeed she possessed any. Most people had written Diane off because she was a little slow on the uptake, but look how she had turned out, encouraged by Verna and Kacie herself. Kacie's thoughts whirled, wondering what she could do to give the girl some incentives. Then an idea struck and she hoped it might work. 'Look, I tell you what, you pull your weight and any tips I get I'll split with you.'

Rita gawped at her in astonishment. 'Yer will?'

She nodded.

'But what's the point? You'll be gone like the rest soon.'

'I won't, Rita. I'm sticking around for a while, you can count on that. You never know, you might find you've an interest in hairdressing and I could begin to teach you bits and pieces.'

Rita stared at Kacie thoughtfully. 'I think I'd like that – yeah, I think I would. But what about 'er?'

''Er? Oh, Miss Benson. As long as we do our jobs Miss Benson has no complaints, and what we do between ourselves is our business, OK?'

The girl beamed happily at her. 'Yer on. I think I like you. You're different, you are.'

Kacie smiled at her.

After closing time, Kacie, having dispatched Rita off to collect her pay from Madge and her belongings to go home, took a look around the salon. Rita had been true to her word and given the room a good going-over and it did look better now the floor was properly clean, and mirrors, sinks and taps gleaming. Even the pot plants looked happier after their water.

Rita came through to join her. 'Miss Benson told me ter tell yer ter go through and get yer wages.'

'Oh, thanks, Rita. I was just having a look around and you've done a good job so you can be proud of yourself.'

The girl grinned happily. 'Ta, Kacie. I 'ave ter say I quite enjoyed meself, and the time went quick when it usually drags summat rotten. I'll see yer termorra then?'

'Yes. Good night.'

Kacie gladly accepted the first pay packet of her employment at Florentina's, having had to work a week in hand. For the last week she had been surviving on the small tips she had received from grateful customers who could afford to slip a couple of pennies her way. She had been very careful not to divulge to Richard her precarious financial situation, knowing her new friend would insist on helping her out, and she felt he'd done enough already. She ripped open the brown envelope and checked the contents, and then she frowned, bewildered. 'I think there's some mistake, Miss Benson.'

'Mistake? I don't think so,' she said brusquely.

'I'm sorry to contradict you, Miss Benson, but I'm fifteen shillings short.'

Folding her arms, Madge leaned on her desk and eyed Kacie intently. 'And how do you make that out?'

'At my interview you said you'd pay me the going rate and the going rate for a skilled stylist is five pounds a week. You've only given me four pounds five shillings, and that's before my tax and national insurance has been deducted.'

Unfolding her arms and leaning back in her chair, Miss Benson smiled smugly. 'You're wrong. I'm only paying you ten shillings below the going rate and in the circumstances you're lucky to only be getting ten shillings less.'

'Fifteen shillings,' Kacie corrected her.

'Ten. Five shillings is a weekly deduction that all senior staff pay towards wear and tear of your overalls, breakages of equipment and cups of tea.'

'But that's outrageous.'

'That's my rules. Take them or leave them.'

'But you never pointed that rule out at my interview, Miss Benson. And what do you mean, I'm lucky to be getting only ten shillings less in the circumstances? What circumstances?'

'Oh, come, come, Mrs Cooper, I thought you were an intelligent woman. You've yet to prove to me that you are qualified. Now usually the first thing a prospective employee throws at me is their qualification certificates but you haven't made any attempt to show me yours. Why's that?'

'Er . . .' Kacie's mind raced frantically. 'Because . . . because . . . I've mislaid them.'

'Oh? Well, when you find them and I check they're genuine we'll discuss your wages.'

'But that's not fair, Miss Benson. My work here this last fortnight is proof enough of what I can do.'

'Yes, I grant you, you're a cut above anyone else that I've had the misfortune to employ but I'm not so fuddled in my brain as not to realise that you're not properly qualified or why else would you give me that cock-and-bull that you've mislaid your certificates. No self-respecting hairdressing would lose something so precious to her.' She looked at Kacie knowingly. 'I'm not so stupid as to know that you're working here because no one else will take you on at the level I have. Now if you're not happy with what I pay, or with my rules and regulations, then you're welcome to leave. I'll always get someone else. I'll warn you, though, that if you do decide to go I will keep your wage of this week in lieu of no notice on your part. So what is it to be?'

Kacie fought a great desire to tell Madge Benson exactly what she could do with her job, but her need of her wage stopped her. But, Kacie vowed, the minute she felt strong enough mentally to face her past and collect her certificates, that's when she would give this odious woman a piece of her mind. Until then she had no choice but to stay put.

She took a deep breath before answering, 'I'll see you tomorrow morning.'

Madge just smirked smugly at her.

Chapter Twenty-one

It was Christmas Eve, and Kacie's mood was like the day outside – dark and gloomy. Try as she might to stop them, happy memories of Christmases she had spent with her beloved husband – and she had so many of them – were constantly invading her thoughts. As Christmas Day had drawn nearer and the festive spirit had become more evident everywhere, her own spirits had sunk deeper.

Until a few days ago she felt she had been progressing so well, managing to fool herself she was coming to terms with her loss of Dennis, her wounds healing, but she had bargained without the effect this time of year would have on her. Today, as she endured having to listen to her clients chatter on incessantly about their festive plans, she was having a job to stop herself from running to her dismal bedsitter, bolting the door and shutting herself away until the whole season was well and truly over.

She had been at Florentina's salon for nearly two months now, and through sheer determination was managing just about to tolerate Madge's ways, but was still striving hard towards the day when she felt strong enough to put her past behind her and secure herself a job where her talents would be appreciated and she'd be treated well by a respectful boss.

Over the past few weeks Kacie had grown fond of Rita. The girl was steadily improving and making herself very useful. She actually appeared to be enjoying her job, which pleased Kacie enormously. If her time here only achieved the rebirth of Rita then she felt it was worth it.

Excited over Christmas herself, today Rita was singing good-humouredly, a song unfamiliar to Kacie. A lover and his rock were all the words she could snatch but it was pleasant enough, and before long Kacie found she was humming the tune herself. Having very quickly learned that the happier the customer then the more likely she was to receive her share of tips, Rita, a bright smile fixed firmly on her plump face, was willingly tackling all that was required of her by Kacie and readily pressing upon customers cups of tea whether they wanted them or not, her desire to purchase extra presents for her family for Christmas, funded by her share of the tips, spurring her on.

Today, even the usually dour-faced Madge wore a satisfied smile as she periodically checked the growing contents in her till, augmented by the extra clients that had come on spec through the salon door, deciding last minute on a spruce-up for Christmas.

It was nearing five o'clock and the last customer had left over half an hour ago. The salon had been cleaned and tidied, dirty towels washed, rinsed and wrung out and put on the cradle dryers in the back.

'We've done well today, Kacie,' said Rita, counting the tips in her hand.

Kacie smiled wearily at her. The number of customers she had attended to today would not be anywhere near the amount she knew would have walked through Verna's salon door, but nevertheless she had had to style them all herself and had had to work nonstop to do so. 'Yes, we did, Rita, and you've been a little treasure. Thank you.'

The delight on the girl's face at Kacie's praise was most apparent. ''Ave I? 'Ave I really, Kacie?'

'Absolutely. I couldn't have managed without you.' She was exaggerating; the girl still had much to learn before Kacie could begin to compare her to Diane, but she was making a very concentrated effort, that was the main thing. 'Can't you tell by the tips we made?'

Rita nodded vigorously. 'I've got nearly three bob. I can now buy me mam the Morney soap and bath cube set from the chemist next door and still 'ave a tanner left over. Me mam'll be over the moon. She loves her smellies, but can't afford ter buy 'em 'erself. D'yer think Miss Benson'll give us a Christmas box, Kacie? Then I could get some extra treats for me brothers and sisters as well?'

Kacie doubted it but nevertheless said, 'Christmas is a time for miracles, Rita, so we can live in hope.'

Just then the shop doorbell jangled, and a tired-looking young woman, balancing several loaded brown carrier bags and pushing a cumbersome pushchair with two shabby-looking children inside, came in.

Madge, who just happened to be checking the contents of her

till, scanned the woman over and, sticking her sharp nose superiorly in the air, asked, 'What can I do for you?'

The woman eyed her hesitantly. 'Well, I wondered how much a trim and set'd cost? Yer see, me 'usband is due home from sea tonight and I ain't seen 'im for nearly four months. 'E's in the merchant navy. I've got three shilling left after doing me Christmas shopping. Is that enough?'

Madge eyed her dispassionately. 'A trim, shampoo and set costs four and six.'

Her pretty face fell, dismayed. 'Oh!' She eyed Madge hopefully. 'Yer wouldn't consider just giving me three shillings worth, would yer? Only I want to look nice for me old man, being's it's Christmas and all.'

Madge glared at her indignantly. 'This is not a charity organisation, nor is it the market where you get produce at knock-down prices at closing time. If you can't pay in full then I suggest you get yourself and your grubby children out of my establishment.'

Kacie gasped, mortified at Madge's callous treatment of the woman. As the proprietor she had the right to refuse if the woman couldn't pay in full for the offered services but there was no need for her rudeness.

Even Rita was horrified. 'Miserable old scrooge,' she whispered. 'Wouldn't 'ave 'urt 'er to give the woman three bobs worth, being's it's Christmas.'

Kacie made no comment, but rushed over to the door and pulled it open. 'Let me help you out,' she offered.

The young woman smiled gratefully at her.

Outside on the pavement Kacie looked at her apologetically. 'I'm sorry for the way my boss spoke to you. It's . . . just that we've had a long day and we're tired, that's all. She didn't mean to be so rude.'

'Oh, that's OK. I was just passing and I saw yer weren't busy and I just got the urge ter get me 'air done, that's all. I should have known I couldn't afford the price. I suppose I could've cut back on what I got the kids for Christmas but, well, yer don't think of yerself at special times like this, do yer?' She smiled fondly at her two offspring sitting contentedly in the pushchair. 'That's what it's all about, in'it, happy kids, warm, and with a fully belly? It's just that I suddenly wanted ter make an extra special effort for me 'usband too. But it's no matter, I know my Pete will still love me whether I've a posh 'airdo or not.' She smiled tiredly at Kacie. 'Thanks fer helping me out of the door. I'd best get me kids home.'

'Have you far to go?' Kacie asked.

'No, thank God. Just around the corner on Wilberforce Road.'

'What number?'

'Eh? Twenty-six. Why?'

'Oh, just asking. Have a good Christmas.'

'And you.'

'I don't appreciate my staff fraternising with riffraff like that outside my salon. You'll be giving my establishment a bad reputation,' Madge said stonily as Kacie returned inside. 'Please don't let anything like that happen again. Now,' she said, looking at both her employees, 'here's your pay.' She thrust their wage packets at them. 'And as a special treat for Christmas I've decided you can go home early. There's no need to thank me.'

With that she turned and headed through the back.

'No Christmas box then,' said a disappointed Rita as she studied the contents in her pay packet. 'And the miserable miser 'as deducted ninepence for that comb I accidentally broke. Still, I suppose she is lettin' us go nearly an hour early.'

'Be thankful for small mercies,' said Kacie. She pulled a small package wrapped in gaily coloured paper from her overall pocket. 'Just a token, Rita, but merry Christmas.'

'For me?' The girl took the proffered gift, delighted. She looked at Kacie worriedly. 'I ain't got you ote.'

Kacie smiled. 'I didn't give to receive. You have a lovely time, Rita, and I'll see you on the twenty-eighth bright and early.'

'And you, Kacie, and you.'

Dressed for outdoors Kacie paused by the office door to say her good nights before she departed for home. Madge was sitting behind her desk, staring down into a mug clasped between her hands which Kacie knew held a measure of vodka. It immediately struck Kacie what a lonely figure Madge cut and a feeling of great pity for the woman rose within her. A thought struck her. Maybe Madge's attitude towards life and people wasn't entirely her own fault. As a result of being a virtual prisoner for all those years, her jailer being her mother, Madge Benson just did not know how to make friends and had no idea how to treat people to gain their respect.

Sensing Kacie's presence, Madge lifted her head to look blankly at her. 'Oh, I thought you'd gone.' Her tone was brusque.

Kacie felt her hackles rise at her offensive manner. 'Just off,' she replied lightly, determined not to let her employer's attitude rattle her. 'I stopped by to say my goodbyes.'

A twist of indifference curled Madge's thin lips. 'Well, goodbye. Switch the salon lights off on your way out.'

'I will.' She made to leave, then stopped, feeling she couldn't go before at least wishing her boss glad tidings. 'I hope you have a good Christmas, Miss Benson. Have you anything planned?' she asked for no other reason but out of politeness.

The woman's face contorted with contempt. 'Planned? Such as what? Oh, are you referring to festive cheer and all that nonsense? All it means to me is that this salon is shut for two days and I lose money.' She put her mug to her lips and gulped back the contents. Then, unearthing a bottle from a drawer in her desk, she poured a measure into the mug and drank that back too. 'It's all a farce if you ask me, for one day a year people being charitable to one another. Well, let me tell you I was charitable to my mother and sister for years and years and where did it get me at the end of the day? Nowhere. No one came forward and showed me charity in recognition of what I'd done. Offered me their help, friendship. The only thing I have to show for my years of charity is this place, and I wouldn't have this if my sister hadn't died.' She tapped the side of her mug. 'This is all the friend I need. It helps me forget the life I could have had if I hadn't been given no other choice than to be charitable to others – family or not,' she added icily. She eyed Kacie hard. 'I hope you weren't going to offer to be charitable to me by asking me to join you for Christmas dinner. If you were, you're wasting your time. I don't envy you your family or friends. It's my opinion that you're better off without them. Now, as I said before, switch the lights off on your way out.'

As Kacie left the salon she sincerely hoped she never allowed what had happened to herself to embitter her the way it had done Madge Benson.

The woman who opened the door to Kacie half an hour later looked shocked to see her. 'You're the lady from the 'airdresser's, ain't yer?'

Kacie smiled. 'I'm glad you remembered me. Can I come in?' she asked.

The woman looked taken aback, and even more startled to see Kacie had with her a dismantled stand hair dryer and loaded carrier bag. 'Are yer sure you've got the right address?'

She nodded. 'You are the lady who wants to look nice for her husband's homecoming, aren't you?'

'I am, yeah.'

'Then I've the right address.'

'But . . . but I 'aven't enough ter pay yer.'

'I don't charge as much as the salon. In fact, I think you'll find my rates very reasonable. Now can I come in, 'cos if I stay out here much longer I'll risk catching pneumonia.'

Paula Wendall cried out in delight when she saw her reflection in the mirror a while later. 'Oh, oh, it's wonderful, Kacie.' She turned to face her children, playing happily on the peg rug by a sad-looking Christmas tree which had been covered with homemade decorations. 'What d'yer both think of yer mam, eh? Ain't she beautiful? Your daddy's gonna think he's got 'imself a new wife.' She looked at Kacie ecstatically. 'I don't know how ter thank yer.'

'You've more than done that,' Kacie answered, a feeling of great satisfaction filling her. All her efforts had been well rewarded by the happy look on Paula's face. Kacie just hoped Madge didn't find out what she'd done, knowing without doubt what her reaction would be.

Paula grabbed up her purse. 'A'yer sure three bob's enough?' she asked worriedly.

'Far too much.'

'Eh?'

'Your hairdo is courtesy of Florentina's salon. After you'd gone Miss Benson was really upset at how she'd treated you and asked me to come round and give you a free hairdo as an apology.'

'Really!' Paula said, astounded. 'Oh? She didn't look the type to make apologies. She looked ter me like a right old tartar and I felt sorry for you having ter work fer 'er. I was wrong about 'er. Please tell 'er, 'er apology was very gratefully received.'

Kacie nodded. 'I will. Now I'll leave you to get ready for your husband's return.'

'Oh, yes,' Paula said, looking at the tin clock ticking away on the mantel. 'Bloody 'ell, 'e'll be 'ere soon. Come on, kids.' She rushed over to gather them to her. 'Bath and ready for bed for when yer daddy comes home.' Cuddling her children she looked at Kacie gratefully. 'You'll be wanting to get home and get yerself ready for your own Christmas, won't yer? I 'ope yer 'ave a good one and yer get all yer wish for.'

Kacie doubted her particular wishes would ever be granted.

Chapter Twenty-two

Richard was looking out for Kacie, and as soon as he saw her turn at the gate he dived out of his room to meet her. 'I was worried about you, Kacie. You're really late. Let me give you a hand with that,' he said, taking the dismantled hair dryer from her. He looked at her, concerned. 'I don't mean you to think I'm checking up on you. I was genuinely worried, that's all, and I wanted to catch you before I left to spend Christmas Day with my father.'

She smiled tiredly at him. It was nice to know someone cared. 'I didn't think that at all. I'm late because I was doing a last-minute hair job for a very grateful woman.'

'I bet the money has come in handy,' he said as he turned to shut the front door. He jumped, taken aback to see a young woman charging up the path. She was brandishing a handbag.

'I've bin tryin' ter catch up with yer. Yer forget this, Kacie,' Paula Wendall panted breathlessly, thrusting the bag in her direction. 'This your husband?' she said, looking at Richard. 'Your wife 'as just given me a free 'airdo courtesy of 'er boss. That were nice of 'er boss, wannit, and smashing of Kacie, considering it was after hours and it being Christmas Eve an' all when she must have been wanting to get home to you. Well, I must dash. I've left me kids with a neighbour. Thanks again, Kacie.'

'It was my pleasure, and thanks for bringing my bag. I hadn't realised I'd left it behind.'

'Free hairdo courtesy of your boss?' queried Richard as they made their way into his room. 'From what you've told me about Madge Benson that doesn't sound like something she'd offer. I smell a rat, Kacie.'

'Well, sniff somewhere else,' she said, chuckling as she took off her coat. 'What Paula told you is the truth as she knows it and that's all you need to know too. I hope you've the kettle on, I'm parched.'

'So what time is your train tonight? Kacie asked as they sat supping their tea ten minutes later.

'The last one is at eight, so I'd better make a move very shortly.'

'Don't look so maudlin, Richard. You'll enjoy yourself, I'm sure you will.'

He gave a wry smile. 'I'll do my best to make the most of it but it'll be hard going, due to the friends I know my father will have invited. They're such bores, Kacie. What they talk about is of no interest to me in the slightest. And, of course, they think I'm a complete imbecile for choosing to live like this.'

'Let them think what they like, Richard. You're happy with yourself, and that's the main thing. Where is it you said your father lives?'

'Great Dalby. It's a village near Melton Mowbray. It's very pretty but quite remote. I shall have to get a taxi once the train drops me in Melton.'

'Melton Mowbray – is that where they make the pies?'

He nodded. 'Yes, it is and very delicious they are too.' He eyed her quizzically. Kacie had told him she had been invited to spend Christmas Day with people. What people, she hadn't elaborated, had changed the subject when he had enquired further, and he had a gut instinct Kacie wasn't telling him the truth. 'You'll be having a pork pie yourself, I expect, tomorrow with your tea, they being traditional,' he probed. 'So, er . . . who'll be at this gathering you said you'd been invited to? Is it family, Kacie, or just friends?'

She averted her gaze, not happy about the lie she had told Richard, but the last thing she wanted was for him to know she was spending Christmas by herself. 'A mixture,' she said evasively. From behind her back she pulled out a Christmas-paper-wrapped package. 'As I won't see you tomorrow you'd better have this now. It's not much, Richard, just a token.'

He looked at the gift in surprise. 'Oh, Kacie, you shouldn't have.'

'Yes I should. We're friends, aren't we? Don't open it until tomorrow.' He would probably guess it was a box of handkerchiefs by the shape and feel of the package, but nevertheless she wanted him to open it tomorrow when it should traditionally be done.

He accepted it and, leaning over, kissed her cheek affectionately. 'Thank you.'

'I also want to give you this,' she said, digging in her handbag for her purse. She extracted a pound note and offered it to him. 'I'm sorry it's taking me so long to pay you back but at least this is a start.'

'Kacie, there's no need, really.'

'Oh, yes there is. I must pay my debts. Please take it, Richard.'

He sighed resignedly, not happy about accepting the money, knowing that on the wage she must be getting, saving this up must have been a very hard thing to do. He put the note in his pocket, then smiled at her. 'Now I must give you your gift.'

'You've one for me?' she exclaimed.

'Naturally. We're friends, aren't we?' Then he grinned. 'Santa dropped it off early. Close your eyes.'

Intrigued, she obeyed. She heard him moving around and the sounds of rustling. After a minute or so, he said, 'You can open them now.' She looked at him. He was standing by the table and her eyes then automatically looked to what was sitting on it. She gasped. It was a record player.

'I hope you like it, Kacie.'

She was stunned, speechless. 'But . . . but you've already bought me the radio,' she said, finally finding her voice.

'Yes, I know. But you can't play records on a radio, can you, and I suspect you have been too polite to ask to borrow mine? I know how much you love music, Kacie, so now you can get yourself some records and play them to your heart's content. I hope you don't mind but I took the liberty of treating you to the number-one hit single too.' And as he leaned over, manoeuvring the arm on to a record that was already sitting on the turntable, he said, 'It's by the Leicester group that all the women at work are raving about at the moment. Vernon and the . . . er . . . oh, yes, Vipers. The song is called "Lover's Rock".'

Kacie froze rigid as the needle crackled as it hit the first groove on the record and a drum beat sounded, then guitars twanged into life, followed by Dennis's voice bursting out the words, 'Take your lover in your arms and dance to the Lover's Rock.'

Richard looked across at Kacie, expecting to see her beaming in delight at his surprise gift, and was shocked to his core to see her face crumpled in devastation, tears streaming down her face.

'What on earth is the matter, Kacie? What have I done wrong?' he cried, distressed.

'Nothing,' she chokingly sobbed. 'It's a lovely gift, really it is. I'm sorry,' she blubbered. 'Please forgive me . . .' She snatched up her coat and bag and dashed from the room.

225

Dazed, Richard stared after her, totally confused at her reaction. He raced after her and pounded on her door. 'Kacie, tell me what the matter is. If I've done something wrong I'm so sorry. Kacie, please, open the door,' he begged, pounding on it again. He put his ear to the door and listened, and after several long moments heard the Yale lock turning.

She stood before him, seeming composed now, but her face was ashen and held a frozen look. 'Richard, I'm so sorry for acting so stupidly. I never expected such a gift from you. It shocked me, that's all.'

He knew she was lying to him. His gift might have come as a total surprise but she was far too upset for that to have been the cause. 'Kacie, please—'

She held up a warning hand. 'You'd better hurry and catch your train,' she said lightly as she leaned up and briefly pecked his cheek. 'Enjoy yourself and I'll see you when you get back on Boxing Day.' With that she shut the door.

After she had heard Richard's feet pound across the landing and on down the stairs, Kacie walked back to her bed and sank down. Fresh tears of misery spilled down her face and, clutching her arms around her middle, she rocked backwards and forwards, a low moan, like an animal in distress, issuing from her.

Of all the presents Richard could have chosen for her it had to be something associated with music, and of all the records he could have picked, it had to be the one she was so desperate to avoid. It was like the devil was playing with her, extracting his macabre fun at her expense.

She lifted her face and looked heavenwards. 'Oh God, please help me. Help me to get over Dennis. Let me live my life without this pain. Please, I beg you, because I can't take much more.'

She had no recollection of falling asleep but she suddenly woke, shivering with cold and stiff from the awkward position she had lain in, her clothes all crumpled. Gathering her bedding around her she struggled to sit upright. Her eyes sought the clock on the floor by the electric fire and in the gloom she just managed to make out the time. It was nine thirty. She had slept for over twelve hours. Regardless, though, she felt far from refreshed.

It suddenly struck her it was Christmas morning and a great wave of loneliness washed over her. It was a day for togetherness, and because of her self-imposed exile she had no one to share hers with.

226

Without warning a vision of Dennis flashed before her. He had his arms around Abigail and was kissing her passionately. They were standing by a heavily decorated Christmas tree, underneath which was stacked a pile of presents. Had Dennis bought a special present for Abigail, agonising over his choice, wanting it to be perfect, like he had used to do for Kacie? But she must not think of Dennis. He was gone from her now, just a painful memory associated with her past. She must stop torturing herself like this. Somehow she had to find another way to lay his ghost to rest because she knew that until she did she'd never move forward, and innocent happenings such as last night's would continue to traumatise her.

Then out of the blue it came to her. Could it be she had tackled her situation wrongly? That her exile was not the way to face facts? How could she possibly accept Dennis's loss while she still held memories of him back in the streets of Evington, inside their flat. She needed to see for herself that he had gone for good, and maybe then she'd begin to rebuild her life properly. She had to do it now before she lost her nerve.

Taking several deep breaths she undraped herself of her bedding and got herself ready.

Fearing she would lose her determination, all during the two-mile walk across town she fought not to notice the evidence of Christmas carrying on around her, but to concentrate her thoughts entirely on her task in hand. It wasn't until she arrived across the road from the flat that her resolve lost its grip and she questioned herself whether she could do this. But she knew she must. In order to quell her jangling nerves and restrengthen her determination, she stepped inside a shop doorway for a moment to compose herself, and automatically looked up at the flat.

She was most surprised to see gaily coloured crêpe decorations strung across the top half of the living-room sash window, Christmas cards lining the inside sill. Then Kacie caught her breath as Caroline appeared. She looked out, glancing up and down the street. Kacie then witnessed her face breaking into a broad smile of welcome and she gave a cheery wave. Kacie saw her mouth moving, obviously addressing someone behind her, whom Kacie couldn't see.

For an instant Kacie's heart thumped wildly, she thinking Caroline was waving at her. She wasn't ready to face her sister yet, needed just a few more minutes to prepare herself for this

227

momentous ordeal. She then realised Caroline's wave had not been directed at her but towards two people who had now arrived at the street door below. Her heart raced. It was their parents. Both were laden down with bags, obviously holding presents, as she could see parcels covered in Christmas paper sticking out of the top. Her father also carried a large metal oven dish and from the shape of what was inside it, Kacie was in no doubt it held a turkey.

It was a touching family scene, one that was being played by millions of others up and down the country, across the world. Family and friends all gathering together to share this special day.

A tremendous urge to run over to her parents, throw her arms around them both and beg their forgiveness for being the cause of their estrangement and then her unforgivable disappearance without word overwhelmed her, but then as quickly a great guilt for what she was about to do overrode all. Despite her sister's reassurances, Kacie felt positive that if she hadn't have been so wrapped up in her own life when they were young then she would have been Caroline's ally, helped her stand up for her rights like sisters were meant to, and had she done, then there was a good possibility that Caroline would never have settled upon a job she detested nor have married the despicable Malcolm, and her life would have been far happier all round.

It was obvious Caroline had made up with her parents and they had become close, judging by what was happening before her, and Kacie's sudden appearance would no doubt upset her family's new-found stability.

She suddenly felt an intruder, outsider, through her own doing no longer part of the gathering taking place inside walls that had used to be her home. Her whole body sagged, shoulders slumped in shocked realisation that those walls were Caroline's now, her home, a place to invite her family and friends. She knew then that she had been wrong to alienate herself from those that she loved and who loved her. Despite their differences, Kacie realised, they would have helped her through her trauma over her loss of Dennis. Now she had not only lost Dennis but her family too. She had left her return too late. By now those she cared most for would have come to terms with her disappearance and rebuilt their lives without her. What she had witnessed moments ago proved that. She had made her decision to walk away and she must now suffer the consequences, let her family get on with their lives as she must do hers.

With a heavy heart Kacie retraced her steps.

Back at her bedsitter she purposely busied herself tidying around, although the room didn't need it. By the time she finally put her cleaning materials away, the windows gleamed, the shabby furniture shone, the good parts of the worn lino sparkled and night had fallen. She suddenly realised she was hungry and was just about to prepare herself something when she thought she heard the front door shut, then feet pound the stairs and a knock at her own door. She frowned, hesitant about opening it, wondering who it could be. It was Christmas Day, after all. Richard was the only caller at her bedsitter, and he was miles away, enjoying the day with his father. Well, she sincerely hoped he was.

Then she heard Richard's voice shouting her: 'Kacie, it's me. I know you're in.'

Perplexed by his unexpected early return she shot to the door and opened it.

He looked so relieved to see her. 'You're all right then?' he said.

'Of course I am,' she fibbed. 'Why?'

He exhaled loudly, running his fingers through his hair. 'After last night I was worried about you, Kacie. I couldn't get you out of my mind. As soon as dinner was over I asked my father to run me home. I told him I had a friend who was in need of me and he gladly complied. I had a feeling you hadn't gone to spend the day with other people. I was right, wasn't I?'

She looked at him. She had absolutely no doubt this man cared about her, really cared, and she realised that as the trusted friend he had become he didn't deserve her cover-up lies any more. She suddenly knew she was ready to unburden herself and knew her feelings would be safe in Richard's hands. 'Come in,' she offered.

Richard had from the moment they had met been intrigued to learn more about Kacie and what had brought her to 17 Danehill Road. He knew she was now ready, and he felt it would do her good to talk to someone she trusted, who wouldn't judge her for whatever had happened. He inwardly warmed, feeling very privileged that trusted person was indeed himself. 'No, you come down to mine, Kacie. No disrespect, but we'll be more comfortable there. I've brought some food back with me that Mrs Henshaw packed up. I have a notion you haven't eaten.'

She smiled wanly. How well this man was getting to know her. 'You're right, I haven't. Who's Mrs Henshaw?'

'Father's housekeeper.'

'A housekeeper, and a car, if he ran you home. Oh, Richard!' she exclaimed. 'No wonder people who know your background think you're nuts giving what you have up. I'm beginning to think that too,' she said, looking at him, a twinkle of amusement sparking her otherwise sad eyes.

'As a hatter,' he replied. 'But I've no regrets. If I'd stayed put I wouldn't now have you for a friend and I wouldn't have missed meeting you for the world. As I've told you before, you've changed my life and I've much to thank you for.'

'And where would I have been without you to look out for me?' she said, smiling.

'Precisely,' he said seriously. 'Now come on down and get some food inside you. Let me at least do that much for you.'

The spread Richard set before her was indeed a feast, and Kacie felt honoured to be sharing it with him. There were turkey and ham sandwiches, pork pies, mince pies and slices of iced rich fruit cake. Kacie tucked in with relish and it all tasted delicious.

'Mrs Henshaw is a good cook,' she said, as she put down her empty plate. 'That pork pie was home-made if I'm not mistaken.'

'It was, and I'll tell her you enjoyed it the next time I see her. Help yourself to more, Kacie.'

She rubbed her stomach and blew out her cheeks. 'I couldn't eat another crumb. I'm stuffed, Richard. I will have another cuppa, though,' she said, helping herself. She also topped up his cup, then sat back and eyed him fondly. 'I'm sorry if my behaviour yesterday worried you. I hope your father wasn't too upset about you leaving so early?'

'As I said before, once I explained my reason he was happy to bring me here. We got on really well, Kacie. He seems to be mellowing and not once did he mention a word about me going back. He was very keen to hear how I was getting on with my job; seemed really interested to hear the intricate details of what I did for a living.' Richard laughed. 'He even complimented me on my new style of clothes.'

'He did?'

He nodded. 'I was surprised he had noticed.' His face filled with a beam of delight. 'He even stuck up for me when one of the guests started berating me for the life I've chosen to live. "My son," he said, "is his own master, and it's his right to choose how he lives his life." I was speechless, believe me. For the first time that I can ever remember my father gave me the impression that he was proud that I was his son.'

'He'd be a fool not to be, Richard. He's more than likely always been proud, just probably didn't know how to show it before, and now he's learning to. I'm so happy for you.' Her eyes glazed distantly. 'I wish my parents were proud of me,' she uttered.

'What makes you think they're not, Kacie?'

She gave a shrug. 'I just know. I've never done anything they expected of me – the opposite, in fact – and they never gave up letting me know how disappointed they were in me. It wasn't just to me: they were the same with my sister but she's not as strong-minded as I am and she did what they wanted to the letter. Until recently that was. I thought what she did might cause bad feeling between them but after what I saw today, I'm glad to say it doesn't seem to have.'

'You've seen your family today?' Richard asked carefully.

She nodded. 'Only from a distance. They didn't know I was there. I needed to bury some ghosts, Richard. But when it came to it I found I couldn't. It wouldn't have been fair.'

He eyed her quizzically. 'What wouldn't have been fair?'

She took a sup of her tea. 'To walk back unannounced into a life I'd walked away from.'

'I see.' He looked at her for a moment before asking, 'Was your life that bad then that you felt you had no alternative but to leave it behind?'

'Bad? Oh, no, Richard, I thought I had a wonderful life. I was so happy. Despite our differences I do love my parents. I had a good job which I loved; plenty of friends; I'd just become close to my sister after being practically strangers from birth; I had the kind of mother-in-law women dream of having and . . .' her voice lowered to hardly a whisper, 'a husband I loved more than anything in the world.'

'So what went wrong, Kacie?'

She took a deep breath, lowering her head to study her hands. 'My husband fell in love with someone else and my world fell apart. She's beautiful, Richard, could easily pass for a film star. In a way I don't blame Dennis for falling for her. They didn't know but I saw them together, heard them discussing his plan to tell me he was leaving me. I can't describe to you how I felt. It's like someone had cut my heart out without an anaesthetic. I know that sounds dramatic but that's how it felt. I wanted to die. I felt my life had come to an end. I didn't care what happened to me.'

'I can imagine,' he said softly.

She lifted her head and the pain she was suffering in reliving this awful time was very apparent. 'I couldn't face Dennis, knowing he was going to tell me he didn't love me any more. I couldn't face anyone I knew, family or friends, and have to suffer their pity once they found out he'd left me for another woman. My parents were dead against me marrying Dennis in the first place so I dreaded their reaction. So I bolted. It was cowardly of me, I know.'

'You handled your situation the only way you could at the time, Kacie.'

'Yes, I did. It was all I could think of doing – getting away. If I'd had more money I probably would have left Leicester altogether, started fresh somewhere else.'

'I'm glad you didn't.'

She smiled briefly. 'So am I.' She took a deep breath. 'That record you put on yesterday, Richard, that upset me so much. Well, the group that was playing on it, the lead singer, is my husband. He's Vernon.'

He gawped in shock. 'Oh, Kacie,' he uttered, 'I'm so sorry.'

'You weren't to know.'

He eyed her tenderly. 'The man's a fool to leave you, Kacie.'

'Obviously Dennis doesn't think so. Anyway, I have to accept my marriage is over. I have to put it all behind me and move forward, which is easier said than done but I'm working hard at it.'

'I'll help you all I can, Kacie.'

She smiled at him. 'You already are doing. I think you must be my guardian angel, if there is such a thing.'

'That's such a compliment. I'm honoured, Kacie.' He eyed her searchingly. 'What about your family? They'll be worried about you. Are you going to go and see them, put their minds at rest that you're all right?'

She gave a heavy sigh. 'I know I should but after what I saw today, I can't bring myself to at the moment. Anyway, they seemed happy enough. Let's be honest, if they were that worried could they have been celebrating Christmas like they hadn't a care in the world? Because that's what it looked like they were doing to me.'

He stared at her thoughtfully. 'I suppose not,' he said softly. 'After my mother died my father didn't celebrate Christmas for years, not properly. What he did he felt obliged to do because I was so young. But are you sure what you saw today was what it looked like?'

'I'm positive,' she said with conviction. 'My old flat, that my sister is now living in, was all decorated and I watched my parents arrive. They were loaded with presents and my father was carrying a turkey. And there were other people there too. Caroline was talking to someone, though I couldn't see who it was – maybe a new boyfriend. I hope so. She deserves some happiness after the way her husband treated her. Anyway, to me the way they were all acting is not the carryings-on of people who are worried about a missing family member.'

Richard frowned thoughtfully. 'No, I suppose it's not.'

'I know I have to go back some time, Richard, if for nothing else to collect the rest of my belongings, and I'll have to contact Dennis so we can sort out . . . well, getting our marriage dissolved so he can marry again, but not yet, when I'm ready.'

She took a deep breath, her unburdening of herself had pained her deeply and drained her completely but in its way she felt it had also done her much good. 'Thank you for listening to me, Richard. I feel I'm beginning to accept what's happened now. I still love Dennis, I always will, but I want him to be happy. I do wish that for him.'

'Not many women in your position would say that, Kacie. They'd want to wring his neck.'

'Oh, I do want to do that too,' she said firmly. 'Believe me, I want to string him up by his unmentionables and have him flogged for the pain he's caused me. But then you see if I got the opportunity I wouldn't harm a hair on his head, despite what he's done. Now I'm thinking clearer, I don't think he purposely set out to find someone else. I know Dennis well and I guess it just kind of happened. These things do, don't they?' She suddenly looked at him hard, raised her chin in the air and announced, 'Enough of this, Richard. For goodness' sake, let's have a bit of life in this place. It is Christmas Day, after all. Put one of those awful long players on you bought. Winifred Atwell will do. She's lively. Have you anything to drink? And I don't mean tea or coffee.'

He grinned at her. 'I've whisky or vodka. Oh, and some of that port left you bought.'

'That'll do. We'll have ourselves a party.'

Chapter Twenty-three

Kacie stared out of the salon window. It was bitter outside, bleak. Winter had come with a vengeance in early January, the temperatures plummeting below freezing, and eight weeks later had still not lifted above zero. The people of Leicester were fed up with dealing with the severe elements. There was a shortage of coal, merchants being unable to keep up with demand, and power cuts had become an accepted regular occurrence. Prices for all commodities had shot up dramatically and now, near the end of February, people were having trouble coping with the above-normal strains on their finances for this time of year. As a consequence trade at Florentina's had dwindled alarmingly, customers' money needing to be spent on far more important things than hairdos.

Florentina's was a salon that was not hugely patronised in the best of weathers, despite word spreading that it now employed a first-class stylist in the guise of Kacie, and Kacie herself had realised not long after she had started her employment nearly four months ago that Madge, through lack of any business acumen, operated on a haphazard week-to-week basis. What money came in one week was the controlling factor of the salon's running expenditure for the following week, plus Madge's living requirements. It was a knife-edge existence, one that could not cope for long with a detrimental change of circumstance the severe weather conditions had brought about.

Sighing heavily, Kacie turned back to the counter and glanced down the appointment book – a futile exercise as she already knew what information it held. Two shampoo and sets for later that morning and one trim in the afternoon. Not for the first time did Kacie wonder how much longer Madge could keep the business running if the situation did not improve imminently.

Rita came out to join her. "'Ere yer are,' she said, handing Kacie a mug of tea. She shuddered. 'It's bloody freezing in 'ere. I asked

235

'er if I could turn the paraffin heater up and she said not until the customers come in, that if I wa' that cold I should have put more clothes on. She's in a right mood, Kacie. Got a face on 'er like a mouldy apple.'

'Mmm,' Kacie mouthed, knowing the reason why.

'Kacie, did yer know we've hardly any stock left? Madge ain't bin ter the wholesaler's for nearly three weeks ter my knowledge.'

Kacie sighed heavily. She was very aware of that fact. If a sudden demand for perms happened then they wouldn't be able to oblige as they hadn't any perming products left.

'Things are bad, ain't they, Kacie?'

Kacie looked at her, thinking they really must be if the slow-witted Rita had noticed. Face grave, she nodded. 'Yes, I think they are.' Bad enough she felt that she should be considering looking for other work before she was given her notice. Problem was that she still hadn't addressed the reason why she had been reduced to working for Madge in the first place. Unless Verna had taken them down, her certificates were still adorning a wall in her salon. If things at Florentina's did worsen and she was forced to seek work elsewhere she would have to collect them. Finding vacancies in other salons as matters stood – as she felt sure they were bound to be feeling the pinch too – was going to be hard without being able to prove she was qualified.

Just then the bell on the door jangled, and Kacie and Rita spun round, both automatically fixing smiles on their faces, hoping to welcome in a much-needed customer. Both their faces fell to see a man had entered carrying a box.

'Florentina's?' he asked.

They both nodded.

'Sign here for this delivery.'

Kacie obliged and he went on his way.

Madge, on hearing the bell, had jumped up from her desk, hopeful of custom. Her face portrayed her acute disappointment on seeing there was none. 'I heard the doorbell. Who was it?'

'A delivery man,' said Kacie.

'Delivering what?' she barked.

'This box,' Kacie said, pointing to it.

'What's in it?'

Kacie shrugged. 'I don't know.'

'I haven't ordered anything. Who's it from?'

'I don't know.'

'Did you sign for it?'

Kacie nodded.

Madge eyed her contemptuously. 'Then if it's anything that needs paying for the onus is on you, being's you signed for it. Well, let's not be kept in suspense. You'd better open it then, hadn't you?'

Fighting to hold her tongue Kacie complied. 'It's perming lotions from Schwarzkopf.'

'But I haven't ordered any.'

Kacie unfolded a piece of paper that was tucked down the side of the box. 'Oh!' she proclaimed. 'They've been sent free of charge. They're a promotional offer.'

'Free? Did you say free?' Madge demanded.

'That's what this paper says.'

'Oh? Give me that,' Madge said, snatching it from her. She read it. 'Oh, you're right, they are free. Oh!'

Kacie stared at Madge. She could see her mind ticking over and she could guess what she was thinking. In her desperate hour of need Madge had been sent a way of reversing her fortunes. She would use the free perming lotions to make herself money, Kacie was in no doubt, and she would milk it for all it was worth.

'I want you in my office now,' she ordered Kacie.

'Those manufacturers have more money than sense,' Madge commented as Kacie went in. 'But then who am I to turn down such an offer? If I play my cards right I can make a killing from this. I want you to make two big signs up for display in the window: "Special Offer. First eighteen customers get our best perm at half price." Put the "best" in capital letters. "Providing they book a shampoo and set for a fortnight later." Or words to that effect. That should bring them in. My most expensive wave is the Helmet wave at four pounds four shillings, so I'll charge two pounds two shillings. I've not known a woman yet who's not driven by a bargain.'

'Eighteen customers?' queried Kacie. 'But you've only been given twelve free perms.'

'Did I ask for your input? I want them posters up within the next half an hour. Hopefully this time tomorrow we'll be that busy you won't have time to question things I ask you to do. Off you go,' she said dismissively. 'Oh, and tell Rita to bring those bottles in to me.'

So you can thin them out to make eighteen from twelve, Kacie thought as she made her way back into the salon. She had won her own bet. Madge was certainly going to make the most of this situation and in a way Kacie couldn't blame her, although she totally disagreed with Madge's practice of thinning down whatever products she could, learning her principle from Verna: that that amounted to no less than theft from the unsuspecting customer.

'Are you ready for this?' Kacie asked Rita first thing the next morning. 'I know we shouldn't be complaining considering we both thought we'd be looking for jobs soon until those free perms arrived and appear to have given us a reprieve, but five perms all together is going to take some doing.'

'It's *'er* that's ter blame for bookin' 'em all in at the same time,' Rita said scathingly. 'She's a greedy old cus and it's all right for 'er, she just sits on her arse in the office and it's us that's got to do the donkey work. I'll do me best for yer, Kacie. I've already sorted the perm rollers into sizes and we've just about enough to go around five heads all at once, and I've laid the clean towels out ready, and the capes.'

'Good girl. Now, I've worked out a method for us to do this. I hope it works.'

''Ave yer?' Rita said, eyeing Kacie in awe.

'Well, I hope I have. It kept me awake most of the night trying to fathom it out. What I thought is, if I roller all the heads first, then you could help me soak the perming solution in. The hard part is the rollering up. You have to make sure all your ends aren't kinked. Soaking in the perming lotion is the easy bit. You just soak a wad of cotton wool with the perming solution and dab it in well all over, making sure it's soaked right through.'

'Yeah, I think I could do that,' Rita replied eagerly. 'It'll be like I'm proper 'airdressing, won't it?'

Kacie smiled. 'Good girl. After three-quarters of an hour we rinse the perming solution off and then we do the same with the neutraliser. We then leave that for half an hour to do its business, then we rinse and shampoo, and all that leaves me then is to set and style.' And hopefully the perms take hold, she thought, hoping Madge hadn't gone over the top in her greed and weakened them too much, meaning they might have to be done all over again. 'We've only got three dryers, so hopefully by the time I get to the fourth the first one will be dry. If not, well, we'll face that situation when we come to it. We couldn't have done this at all a few years ago.'

'Couldn't we? Why not?'

'Because perming was a nightmare. It was done using a huge metal contraption that hung down from the ceiling with metal rollers attached to it. The contraption heated the rollers up and used to take for ever to do one perm. Hairdressers were always burning themselves. And there was always the risk of singeing hair or overperming. You can overperm now but it's not so easy, done with these cold waves. A hairdresser's blessing, we call them.' Kacie's eyes flashed across to the door as she heard a muffled commotion building from outside. 'Looks like a couple have arrived, if not them all. Right, Rita, you'd better get the door blind up and open for business.'

An hour and a half later, Kacie had wound all the heads. All the time she had been labouring, Rita, as her right hand, passing her the end papers and perming rollers, the women had been chattering happily away, as Madge had prophesied, all thrilled to be getting such a bargain.

'This ain't like Madge Benson to give ote away, Kacie. So what's the catch?' Flo Hewitt asked as Kacie finished rollering her hair up.

'No, it bloody ain't,' agreed Nell Hardcastle. 'A right tight-arse she is, if ever I've met one. So what is the catch?'

'None, as far as I know,' Kacie said cagily. 'Miss Benson just felt that as we're all feeling the pinch right now that it would be nice to give you all a treat, being's you've been such good customers.'

'I ain't bin 'ere before,' said Daisy Dakers. 'It were Nell that told me about this bargain and I ain't one to miss a bargain.'

'Well, let's hope you're that pleased with your new perm that you come again,' Kacie said, smiling at her.

'I might,' she said noncommittally. 'I'll see what kinda job yer do first.'

Kacie pulled Rita aside, handed her a bowl filled with perming solution and a wad of cotton wool. 'Now you've remembered what I've told you. Put plenty on but be very careful about splashing any on to the ladies' faces or neck. If you do, wash it off immediately with cold water. All right?'

'Yes, Kacie.'

Kacie had seated the women in a long row. 'Right, you start that end, and I'll start this, and we'll meet in the middle. OK?'

'Yes, Kacie.'

'Good girl. Do this properly and no mishaps, and I'll treat you to the biggest cream cake the bakery has in their window.'

'Oh, yer on, Kacie.'

As the women continued to chatter, Kacie and Rita laboured away. As Kacie gave her final dab she allowed a sigh of relief and a broad smile to Rita. 'Well, that went without mishap. Well done.'

Rita beamed proudly at her. 'I really done well?' she asked.

'You did. Right, while we wait for the perming solution to do its job I think me and you deserve a cuppa and I'll make it. Ask the ladies if they'd like one while I wash out the perming bowls,' she said, taking Rita's from her.

'Righto, K . . .' Rita's voice trailed off as a wail erupted from the first woman Kacie had applied the perming solution to.

'Me scalp, me scalp,' she screamed. 'It's burning, it's burning.'

Kacie and Rita looked at her in utter shock but before they could respond the first woman Rita had tackled started screaming also.

'Me 'ead, oh, me effing head. It's on fire.'

Then one after the other they all followed suit until they were all hollering blue murder, hysterically running around the salon, trying their best to wrench out their rollers.

Madge shot through. 'What on earth is going on?' she demanded, eyes darting all ways.

Kacie ignored her. She couldn't answer her; all she knew was something dreadful was happening to the women she had just attended to. 'Quick,' she cried to Rita. 'Help me get them under the taps. We have to rinse that perming solution off. Something is wrong with it. Quick Rita, QUICK.'

Chapter Twenty-four

It was well after six that evening before Kacie walked into the office and looked at Madge Benson, fighting hard not to show her own anger and distaste for what her boss was responsible for. Madge was sitting hunched across her desk, cradling a mug. Kacie knew what it contained.

Madge raised her head and eyed Kacie blankly. 'How bad is it?' she demanded matter-of-factly.

'Bad enough,' Kacie replied gravely. 'Whatever chemicals were in those perms burned all their scalps, and they've all lost huge chunks of hair where it's broken off. Mrs Dobbs is the worse. Her hair was very fine in the first place and she's practically bald at the moment. The doctor isn't sure whether hers will grow back or not, but he's hopeful all the others will make a full recovery. It's going to take time, though. At the moment they're all in a lot of pain but they've been discharged. I, er . . . should warn you, I think you'll be getting visits from angry husbands or relatives.'

Madge's face rapidly paled to near parchment white as she listened to what Kacie told her. She gave a groan of despair. 'I'm ruined. Finished. No one will come near the salon after this.'

Kacie wanted to say, Do you blame them? Madge Benson had brought this state of affairs all on herself. If she hadn't been so greedy in the first place this catastrophe would never have happened. 'What will you do about the women?'

She eyed Kacie incredulously. 'Such as what? What can I do? What's done is done. It should never have happened, though. I can't understand it. I've always thinned down perming solutions to eke them out using the same concoction of acid and water from the formula I paid handsomely for from another hairdresser across town when I first inherited this salon, and never has anything remotely like this happened before.'

'If you don't mind me saying, you had had a good bit to drink when you tampered with the products. Do you think you made an error of judgement with the amount of acid of ammonia you added?'

'I do mind you saying,' Madge hissed, incensed. 'And no, I never made a mistake.' She leaned down and opened a drawer, yanking out a full bottle of vodka, which she slammed down hard on the desk top. She then eyed Kacie darkly. 'Just go home, will you? I want to be left in peace.'

Kacie gnawed her bottom lip anxiously. 'Look, Miss Benson, I don't think—'

'You don't think what?' she demanded harshly.

Kacie was going to say that she didn't think it a very good idea that Madge stayed here on her own and drank herself into oblivion, which is what Kacie feared she was about to do. But Madge wasn't the kind of woman to take advice kindly so Kacie was wasting her time offering it. She took a deep breath. 'Nothing. Are you sure you're all right?'

'Never felt better,' she said, issuing a mocking laugh. 'This is the best day of my life. Look, just go, will you? Get out of my sight. Turn the salon lights off on your way out.'

Sighing resignedly, Kacie turned and walked out.

'It was awful, Richard. Those poor women are in agony. If only me and Rita hadn't swabbed the perming lotion on so fast maybe this would have shown itself in time and not all of them would have been hurt.'

'You can't blame yourself for any of this, Kacie.'

'I know, but it still doesn't stop me from feeling I should have sussed something was wrong. I'm a qualified hairdresser, for God's sake. But everything looked fine to me. I knew the solution had been thinned down but it was impossible to tell just by looking at it that it contained far more acid or ammonia than it should have done.' She exhaled sharply. 'I can't get over Madge Benson. She just stood there, like she was made of stone while the women were charging around the salon screaming their heads off. She never made any effort to help me and Rita rinse the stuff off. There's only three sinks in the salon, so you can imagine what it was like. Then it seemed to take ages for the ambulance to come. When it finally arrived and we all piled in she was still standing in the doorway at the back of the salon, her face . . . well . . . it was . . . no expression on it. Like she was wearing a death mask.'

242

Kacie shuddered. 'She was really nasty with me tonight. Like it was all my fault and nothing to do with her. She didn't seem sorry at all for what she'd done, just worried what was going to happen to her business.' She paused and eyed Richard worriedly. 'But I still shouldn't have left her, you know. Madge, I mean. In the salon by herself. She had a full bottle of vodka and I know exactly what she's going to do with it. It doesn't do any good, though, does it, drinking yourself stupid? It might make you forget for a while but you still have to face up to things in the morning. And suffer a raging hangover.'

In an effort to lift the mood of the conversation Richard smiled and said, 'You talk from experience, I take it, Kacie?'

'I've had one or two hangovers in my time, yes, and suffered the consequences. But I doubt I've ever had one as bad as I suspect Madge will have in the morning. I should go and check on her.'

'I doubt she'll make you very welcome, Kacie, but if you want to go I'll come with you to make sure you're safe. It's very dark outside. By now she might be at home, passed out in bed. Anyway, you look dead on your feet, Kacie. That's some ordeal you've had today.'

'I am tired. Knackered is more the word. I just want to curl up in bed with my hot-water bottle and sleep for a week. I hope Rita is all right.'

'I'm sure her family are looking after her. So what happens now, Kacie?'

She shrugged. 'To be honest I don't know. I suppose I should turn up for work as normal and see what the situation is. I suspect Madge was right when she said we'd have no more customers in the salon. What happened today will've spread all around the area by now. I suspect myself and Rita will get our notice and I doubt we'll have to serve it, so it'll be job-hunting for me.'

'You don't look very happy about that. I thought you'd be glad to be looking for something else, as you didn't really like that job, did you, Kacie?'

'No, I didn't. I hated it.'

'Then why did you stay?'

She took a deep breath and looked hard at him. 'Remember when I told you I walked away from my past life.'

He eyed her quizzically. 'Yes.'

'Well, I left my qualification certificates at the salon where I used to work. That's why I ended up working for Madge Benson, as I doubted anyone else would take me on without me proving I was qualified.'

'Oh, I see, and you still can't face collecting them?'

She shook her head. 'I'm not quite ready, Richard. I'm much better in myself but not enough to face all that yet.'

He smiled kindly at her. 'There's no rush, Kacie. Only when you're a hundred per cent ready and not before. So what will you do now, then?'

'Hope someone like Madge will take me on. But someone a bit more pleasant this time.'

'I'm sure they will.'

'I hope you're right. If not, then I will have to go and collect my certificates whether I want to or not, because I have to work.'

Chapter Twenty-five

Kacie was the first to arrive for work the next morning and immediately noticed Madge hadn't pulled the door blind down when she had left the previous night, which was something she always insisted was done so as not to invite burglars.

Just then Rita joined her.

'Mornin', Kacie.' She stamped her feet on the icy ground. 'Bloody freezing in'it. I 'ope Miss Benson hurries up and gets 'ere before we catch our deaths. You all right?'

'Morning, Rita. I'm OK. Didn't get much sleep worrying about those poor ladies. I bet they didn't sleep much either. What about you?'

'After one of me mam's cups of cocoa with a dollop of rum in it I slept like a log. Er . . . wadda yer thinks gonna 'appen to us, Kacie?'

Kacie patted the girl's arm reassuringly. 'Best we don't make guesses but wait and see.' As she glanced around she peered through the door glass into the salon, then looked a little closer. 'Rita, the door at the other end of the salon is pulled to but is it my imagination or is there a light shining through from the back?'

Rita pressed her nose to the glass in the door. 'There is. Miss Benson must 'ave left her light on in 'er office when she went last night. And she moans to us about the cost of 'lectricity. She wa' probably too drunk to see to it when she left, that's why she forgot,' she added scathingly.

'Rita!'

'It's true. She drinks like a fish. I ain't that daft I've not noticed how much she gets through a day. I wish she'd bloody 'urry up. I'm beginning to turn into an icicle.' She looked at Kacie thoughtfully. 'Eh up, if Miss Benson were that sozzled when she left that she forgot to put the light off, d'yer think she might have forgot to lock the door too, Kacie?'

Kacie looked at her surprised. That possibility hadn't occurred to her. 'Let's find out,' she said, grasping the handle and turning it. It opened, the bell above jangling, announcing their presence.

'Silly old bugger could've bin burgled,' Rita said as she gratefully walked inside. 'Bloody 'ell, it's as cold in 'ere as it is outside. I'll light the heater, Kacie.'

'And turn it up to full,' Kacie said, rubbing her hands together. 'I'll go and put the kettle on.' She walked through to the back.

As she made her way down the short red-tiled passageway, a door off it leading into Madge's office, a door further down leading out into the back yard, she stopped, looking down, her face masked, confused. Directly outside the office there was a puddle on the floor, a thick trail of it leading inside the office. The light from the office made the contents of the puddle appear as red as the tiles. Then horrifyingly it struck her. It was red because it was blood. A lot of it.

She stared at it, her mind racing frantically. Why was there a pool of blood outside Madge's office? Had she cut herself badly before she had left? If so it would have to be a very large wound to cause that amount of blood. Gingerly she stepped astride the puddle and peered inside. The sight that met her stunned her senseless, and she issued a gasp of shock. Madge was lying awkwardly on the floor beside the desk. The smashed remains of the bottle of vodka lay all around. The stream of blood, which ran to puddle outside the office had come from a huge gash on Madge's neck. Her pallor was of a ghostly white. She was dead, there was no doubt about it.

Bile rising up from her stomach, Kacie spun on her heels and ran back to the salon. 'Rita?' she cried.

Rita was kneeling on the floor holding a box of matches in her hand. The front of the paraffin heater had been pulled off to expose the wick and Rita's head was almost inside the heater in her effort to light it. 'I can't get this bleddy 'eater lit, Kacie. The wick's damp or summat. I hope that kettle's boiled for a cuppa. I need summut to warm me.'

'Never mind that now, Rita. I need you to go and fetch the police,' Kacie said, far more calmly than she felt.

Rita stopped what she was doing, sat back on her haunches and looked at Kacie, stupefied. 'Did yer just tell me ter fetch the bobbies or was I 'earing things, Kacie?'

'You weren't hearing things. I did ask you to do that. Can you hurry, please? There's a police box on the corner of Upperton Road. Use that. Tell them to come quick.'

Rita stood up, frowning at Kacie in bewilderment. 'But why d'yer want me to fetch 'em?' she asked.

'Oh, I'm sorry, Rita. I've had the most awful shock, please forgive me for not making much sense. There's . . . there's been a terrible accident.'

'Accident? What sort of accident? What's going on, Kacie?'

'Just fetch the police, please, Rita,' Kacie cried urgently.

At her tone Rita jumped. 'OK, OK. I'm goin', I'm goin'.'

'Nasty business. Very nasty business.' The stocky policeman, with a large protruding stomach, but very kindly ruddy face, eyed Kacie gravely. 'It's obvious Miss Benson had had a lot to drink. It looks to us like she stumbled as she was leaving, dropped the bottle she was carrying, it smashed and she slipped on the spilled vodka and fell on to the glass. A large chunk lodged in her neck, severing an artery. She bled to death. There'll have to be an inquest but I think you'll find that's what it'll show up. We don't suspect foul play.'

Kacie shuddered, wishing the constable hadn't been so graphic with his interpretation of events.

'You all right, Mrs Cooper?' He took her arm. 'You look faint, you'd better sit down,' he said, guiding her over to one of the salon chairs.

She sat down and he sat in the chair next to her.

'Do you think she suffered much, Constable?' Kacie asked him, her ashen face grave.

'I shouldn't have thought she knew much about it, me duck. I think she was pretty inebriated meself. Me sergeant thinks so too.'

Kacie sighed relieved. She hadn't liked Madge much at all but didn't like the thought of her suffering an agonising death. An ironic thought struck Kacie. She had died like she had lived. Alone. The knowledge brought tears of great sadness to her eyes and formed a lump of distress in her throat.

'You'd best get off home. There's n'ote you can do here,' said the constable, looking at her, concerned.

She took a deep breath, then sighed heavily. 'I can't do that, Constable. I don't mean this to sound terrible, considering what's happened to my boss. But with her gone, I've just lost my job and in the circumstances there's no chance of getting the pay I'm due, so I have to go and look for work.'

247

'Oh, I see. Well, I suggest before you do that you get yourself a cuppa in the café across the road and something to eat, if you can manage. You've had a awful shock and it ain't really sunk in yet. When it does it could hit you like a ton of bricks.'

She smiled wanly at him. 'Thanks, Constable. I'll bear that in mind. I ought to go and see Rita, check she's all right.'

'She seemed it. She's quite a tough little nut, I'd say. When my colleague took her home he said her mam was fussing over her, so I shouldn't worry too much. You concentrate on yourself. Leave seeing Rita until tomorrow.'

'Should I do something though, Constable? Inform somebody of what's happened?'

'Like who? Miss Benson hadn't any relatives, you told us.'

'She hasn't. I meant the landlord of this place. He'll need to know, won't he?'

He patted her arm reassuringly. 'My dear, if the landlord lives in this area then I'm sure he knows all ready. You know how quick gossip travels. Probably already re-let these premises.' He eyed her remorsefully. 'I'm sorry, I shouldn't joke at a time like this.'

His joke, though, had a ring of truth in it. Kacie wouldn't be surprised at all if the landlord knew what had happened. As soon as the police had arrived a crowd had quickly gathered outside. 'You're right, Constable, he probably has. The same will happen with the house she lived in. I understand that was rented too.'

He nodded.

'So there's nothing more for me to do here, is there, except collect my belongings?'

He looked at her kindly. 'I'm afraid there's not.'

Despite her very worrying financial position, when it came to it, Kacie couldn't face going off to seek work. Regardless of how upset she was, doing that so soon after Madge's accidental demise seemed disrespectful. And the kindly constable was right. Halfway home she felt her legs give way and, supporting her weight on a garden gate, without warning she burst into great floods of tears. Sobbing hysterically, she managed to get home and once inside her room, collapsed on her bed, weeping uncontrollably until utterly drained. Then she fell asleep, not waking until the next morning.

Richard showed great sympathy towards Kacie when he found out what had happened to her, fussing over her like a mother hen, insisting she rested until she fully recovered from her terrible

248

ordeal. He also instilled in her that she wasn't to worry about her lack of finance, and promptly handed her a five-pound note, offering her more if she needed it, and telling her that she wasn't to worry about paying him back. He also made her promise to give herself at least until after Madge Benson's funeral before she tackled looking for work.

To Kacie, it wasn't the debt of money she was worried about returning to Richard, it was her debt of gratitude. More than ever she felt she was just so very glad and lucky she had him as her friend.

Only herself and Rita were present at the funeral, which had been arranged by the officials on the Leicester Council. Madge had made no provision for her burial, and leaving no ready cash or having anything of real value that could have been sold to raise some money, Madge was given a pauper's send-off, and it was the saddest occasion Kacie felt she would ever attend.

The weather was bleak, the vicar conducting the service, grim. Obviously he had something more important to do, as he rushed through the short service before making a hurried getaway.

Once it was over, Kacie took Rita for a cup of tea and, depressed by the event they had just attended, neither felt like jovial chatter, so they mostly sat in silence. Kacie did learn, though, that Rita had already secured herself work at another small hairdressing salon, a very similar business to Florentina's, on the Fosse Road North. Mrs Downend, the owner, was a nice woman and, Rita enthused, she'd be very happy working there. Her securing of the job was all thanks to Kacie and her patience in teaching Rita all she knew, for which Rita profusely thanked her. As they gave each other a hug as they prepared to go their separate ways, they agreed to keep in touch, but both knowing it was most unlikely that they would, as it was doubtful their paths would ever cross again.

Chapter Twenty-six

The following Monday, having slowly recovered from Madge Benson's death thanks to Richard and his mothering, Kacie made her way down Churchgate to the labour exchange.

The weather had improved drastically. After week upon week of snow, frost, high winds and lashing rains, the sun had decided to come out of hibernation, and the day was bright and warm. For the long-suffering people of Leicester, spring was finally on its way and the majority were showing their delight by the smiles upon their faces and the bounce in their steps.

Churchgate was a long, narrow street running from the crossroads at the clock tower in the town centre down about a quarter of a mile to the St Margaret's bus station. Its buildings were mainly Victorian and were, in the majority of cases, four storeys high. From the second floor upwards, an assortment of firms ran their businesses from these large old buildings, but in most cases the ground floors and basements were occupied by shop retailers. As she meandered by them Kacie was enjoying herself gazing in the windows at the variety of goods on display, which ranged from hardware to millinery, when she happened upon premises that were in the process of being renovated. As she wasn't in a particular hurry, she stopped for a moment to watch the carryings-on inside and trying to work out for herself what sort of establishment it was being turned into. It was obviously going to be quite a large concern as it appeared to encompass what would normally have been three smaller shops.

Out of one of the doorways a middle-aged, weather-beaten workman appeared. He took a long look at the very attractive woman nearby and issued a wolf whistle at her.

Instead of being indignant at his unprovoked attentions, Kacie grinned good-humouredly. 'Well, thank you, kind sir,' she said, laughing.

At her unexpected response he looked surprised, then laughed too. 'I'll pinch yer bum if yer like,' he said cockily.

'Cheeky beggar,' she responded. 'Er . . . what is this shop being turned into?' she asked in curiosity.

He shrugged his muscly shoulders. 'I'm just a plasterer, me duck, and we don't get told n'ote. But I understand when it's finished it'll be some sort of new-fangled record shop and coffee bar. It's aimed at you youngsters, I do know that. Oh, I did 'ear someone mention an 'airdresser's as well, but that's about all I know.' He noticed the look on Kacie's face and frowned quizzically at her. ''Ave I said summat wrong, gel?'

'Pardon? Oh, no, no. Thanks for telling me,' she said. She watched in deep thought as he went on his way. A combined record shop and coffee bar and possibly a hairdresser's too. That had been her idea, her dream. How peculiar that someone else had thought of it too, but, more than that, was actually in the process of putting her idea into practice. She gave a despondent sigh. Her dream had been something she had longed to do with Dennis, and because of what had transpired between them, it had no hope of ever coming to fruition, if indeed it had ever had a chance in the first place. But she felt deeply bereft, as though some faceless person had stolen her dream from her.

'Kacie. My God, it is you, isn't it?'

Startled out of her thoughts, she swung round and her face lit up. 'Unless I've turned into someone else overnight,' she replied, grinning. 'Oh, Myrna, it's great to see you.' She leaped on her and gave her a hug. Seeing a friendly face was just the tonic Kacie needed right now.

'You mean that?' she asked, looking at Kacie worriedly. 'You do know I had nothing to do with that stuff I gave you being messed about with?'

'I know, Myrna, stop worrying. We came to see you at your shop and it was all closed up. We heard what had happened to you on your first day of opening. One of your customers gave us her version of events. She wasn't a happy girl at all. We put two and two together on the rest.'

Myrna sighed with relief. 'I'm so glad about that. I was frantic you thought I was responsible. I went to the salon where you used to work on St Saviours Road. The woman who I imagine is your replacement wasn't very helpful but said the young girl might know but that she was off out somewhere on an errand for her boss and

didn't know how long she'd be. I intended going back but, well . . .
you know how it is, and I was so down at the time.'

Kacie nodded in understanding.

'I was so upset knowing you were ruined like I was,' Myrna
continued, 'but there was nothing I could do.'

'Did you ever find out who sent you that box of products,
Myrna?'

She shook her head. 'No. It's most peculiar. But someone had it
in for me, that's for sure.'

Kacie's lips tightened. 'Yes, it's obvious.'

Myrna eyed her, bothered. 'You said *we* came to the shop? Was
that you and the police?' she asked.

'No. I came with my friend Richard.'

'Oh. I wouldn't have blamed you if you'd got the police
involved. I'd have done the same in your position. Not that
anything about this could be proved in any way, shape or form. I
have no idea where that box of stuff came from or who sent it or
why.' She eyed Kacie, relieved. 'It's fate, us bumping into each
other like this. It's put my mind at rest, knowing you know it
wasn't anything to do with me, and I can leave Leicester in a
happier frame of mind now.'

Kacie gawped at her. 'You're leaving Leicester?'

Myrna nodded. 'I'm off back to London. After what happened I
can't settle here. I tried hard but it's no good. I tell you, Kacie, if I
ever find out who sabotaged me I'll be banged up for murder. I just
wish I knew what they had to gain by it all. Maybe I'd make sense
of it then.' She gave a deep sigh. 'My mum is sorry to see me go but
she knows I'll never be happy again here. My auntie says she'll be
glad to have me back, so I've somewhere to go.' She gave a sad sigh.
'Oh, Kacie, I keep picturing my salon. It distresses me so much to
think about all the hard work I put into getting it right and using
every last penny I had to do it. I would have been a great success, I
know I would. I get so upset, knowing that the person who bought
it from me is benefiting from it now.'

'Someone bought the business from you?'

She nodded. 'I was made an offer several days later. I was really
low, Kacie. I'd had no customers and the locals were treating me
really nastily, throwing bad eggs at the salon windows, jeering at
me, that sort of thing. Out of the blue I was offered fifty pounds
for the whole caboodle. The offer was a joke; considering how
much it had cost me, but as things stood it wasn't likely I'd get

253

another buyer easily – probably would have had to wait for weeks and I couldn't afford to – so I had no alternative but to accept it. I was desperate for cash. It was like a godsend to me.'

'Fifty pounds *is* a joke,' Kacie agreed. 'But, as you say, at the time you were desperate.'

'Believe me, I was. I went to see the shop yesterday. I know it sounds daft but I needed to say my goodbyes, impress in my brain that it was no longer my shop but belonged to someone else. It's still got all my original fittings but it's been renamed Modern Miss. It's a bit too formal-sounding a name for my liking, I preferred Cut and Curls. Still, from where I was standing across the road it looked to me like it was going to prove a great success, judging by how busy it was.'

'Maybe you'll have another shop one day, Myrna.'

'Oh, I don't think so, Kacie. I couldn't risk going through all that heartache again.'

Kacie sighed. 'I can understand that. So what have you been doing since you lost the shop?'

'I've been working for a small salon on Belgrave Road. Ever such a nice bloke I worked for, and although he's really sad to lose me he was so understanding when I told him my reasons for leaving. That's where I've just come from. I was saying my goodbyes and collecting my cards and pay I was due. All I've got to do now is collect my bags from left luggage at the railway station and it's goodbye Leicester. Anyway, enough about me. What's been happening to you since I last saw you?'

'Oh, not much,' Kacie said evasively. 'I've been working for a salon on Narborough Road for the last three months or so but unfortunately the owner . . . well, she's just passed away. I'm off now to the labour exchange to see what's going.'

Myrna frowned. 'That's a bit of a rum way to lose a job, the owner dying. But why the labour exchange, Kacie? I know things are a bit slow in the hairdressing trade after the awful winter we've just had, but business is picking up now and someone like you, with your qualifications, could walk into any salon and they'd snap you up.'

Kacie took a deep breath, loath to lie to Myrna but feeling she had no choice unless she divulged her past, which she didn't want to, and especially not in the middle of the street. 'Well, that's the problem, you see. I can't exactly prove I'm qualified.'

Myrna eyed Kacie incredulously. 'Why ever not? Eh, don't tell me you're not properly qualified and have been passing yourself off as though you are?'

'Of course I haven't.' Kacie tutted in disgust that Myrna could even think she would do such a thing. 'I've . . . well, I've lost my certificates, that's all.'

'Lost them! How on earth did you manage that?'

'If I knew that then I'd know where to find them, wouldn't I? I got the job with Madge Benson because she didn't ask to see them.'

'She was probably just too glad that someone with your talents was knocking on her door to be bothered about asking for qualifications.' She eyed Kacie thoughtfully. 'My old job is being advertised in the paper tomorrow night – why don't you apply for it? Tell Bill, he's the owner of the Belgrave Salon, that I sent you. Be honest with him and I'm sure you'll get it, Kacie, certificates or not. It's worth a try.'

Kacie scratched her chin thoughtfully. 'I suppose it is. The worst he can do is show me the door. Anything is better than having to face Cedric Brindle down at the labour exchange. I will, Myrna, I'll go now. Thanks for telling me.'

'I wish you luck, Kacie.'

Kacie eyed her fondly. 'You too.'

Kacie started to continue on her way when she heard Myrna call, and turned to see her racing back to her. 'Just a thought, if things don't work out for you maybe you'd consider joining me in London? My auntie's got lots of spare room and she'd love to have you. I'd love you to come too. I'd soon help you get work and we could have a ball. Anyway, think about it. Here's my auntie's address,' she said, thrusting a piece of paper in Kacie's hand. 'Ta-ra again.' She headed off.

'Yes, Ta-ra, Myrna. Hey, and thanks,' Kacie called after her.

William Aberson eyed Kacie keenly. He was a tall man, boyishly handsome with a thatch of thick light brown hair which was perfectly groomed in a modern cut. He had readily agreed to interview Kacie once Kacie had told him Myrna had sent her.

'I was sorry to lose Myrna,' he said, seated across his desk from Kacie. 'She's an excellent stylist and I know that if she's recommended you then you must be in her calibre too. So, Mrs Cooper . . . or . . . may I call you Kathryn?'

'You may call me Kacie,' she said, smiling.

'Kacie? How unusual, but it suits you,' he said, his electric-blue eyes twinkling in interest at her. 'So, Kacie, you want to apply for Myrna's old job as my second in command, so to speak?'

'Yes, please, I do. I've got a lot of experience, but . . .' her voice trailed off and she eyed him anxiously.

'But?' he prompted.

She took a deep breath. Well, here goes, she thought. 'Well, I can't prove I'm qualified, you see, as I've lost my certificates. Stupid of me, I know, but, well, I have. I was hoping you would take me at my word.'

He smiled at her. 'I admire your honesty and at least you have some certificates to lose.'

'I beg your pardon?' she said quizzically, wondering what he meant.

He leaned over his desk, his voice lowering. 'I'll let you into a secret if you promise not to tell anyone. I know everything there is to know about hairdressing. I learned off my father, who was a very talented man where hair was concerned. But paper qualifications he hadn't got and neither have I. My grandmother was a hairdresser and my father learned from her and I learned from him. It was my father's opinion that anyone could wave a piece of paper at you proclaiming excellent skills but it's what's produced in practice that's of importance and I agree entirely with him. I've had some people in here that have reckoned they're the bee's knees in the hairdressing trade and, believe me, after witnessing their so-called talents I wouldn't let them touch a client of mine if they were the last hairdresser on earth.' He eyed her searchingly. 'Are you good at what you do, Kacie?'

'I'm very good,' she said with conviction.

'Then prove it to me. There's a customer due in any minute and she's booked in for a number three perm and a root tint. That will be your test.'

'I can't do that,' she said, eyeing him, bothered.

He frowned. 'You can't? Why?'

'Because you never perm and colour hair at the same time. It's asking for trouble. I'm surprised you've booked her in for both, considering you know so much about hairdressing.' She stood up. 'If that's the sort of carry-on you do here then this is not the salon for me. Thank you for your time.'

'Sit down, Kacie,' he said, smiling at her winningly. 'Your answer was the one I was hoping to get. The customer has actually been booked in for just a perm. We would never do both together. As you say, it's asking for trouble. I run a quality establishment here and only use the best products and expect a first-rate job and loyalty from my staff, which I pay well for.'

Just then a young girl popped her head around the door. 'Mrs Arbuthnot is here,' she said, smiling at Bill.

Bill looked at Kacie. 'Off you go then. Janice will show you where everything is.'

Three hours later William Aberson offered Kacie the job.

'Has anyone ever told you you're in a minority and possess real talent, Kacie? Mrs Arbuthnot was singing your glories and I'll now tell you that she is just about our most difficult customer. If she can find something to complain about she will do, believe me. She's the bane of our lives and we all dread her coming in. She's married to a judge and has connections in very high places and never lets us forget that. She thinks I should be honoured that she chooses to patronise us instead one of the more salubrious salons in the centre of town. You pleased her and if you can satisfy her then you'll satisfy anyone. She's demanded you attend to her in future and I can't oblige her unless I offer you a job, can I?'

He was looking at her very intently, and it would be obvious to any onlooker he was smitten by the good-looking woman who had applied for a position in his salon, but Kacie was completely oblivious to his admiration. She had come to seek work and all her thoughts were centred on that aim. 'And I'll be delighted to accept,' she said, smiling happily at him.

Richard was thrilled with Kacie's news. 'I'm so pleased for you,' he enthused.

'So am I,' she beamed. 'Bill, the owner, is really nice and the salon is bright and cheery. It's got a lovely friendly atmosphere. The apprentice, Janice her name is, is really bubbly and she's got a brain in her head. I shall enjoy working there, I know I will. I've bought a bottle of wine and I'm going to cook you bubble and squeak to celebrate.'

'Oh!'

'What's the matter, Richard?' she asked, worried by the look on his face.

'I'd love to celebrate with you but . . .'

'But what?'

'Well, it's just that I can't.'

'Why can't you? Are you ill or something?'

'Oh, no, far from it. I . . . I have a date, Kacie.'

Her mouth fell open. 'A date! A proper date with a woman?'

He proudly nodded. 'I want to ask your opinion on what I should wear.'

She stared at him, stunned, for several long moments. 'More important things first. Who is she? What's she like? How did you meet her, Richard?'

He laughed. 'I knew I was going to get the Spanish Inquisition once I told you. I had an appointment at the dentist this morning and I met her there. Her name is Cassie and she's just started as the receptionist. I was early and we got talking. She likes the same sort of music as I do. Reads a lot. I don't know, Kacie, it just seemed we have so much in common. I couldn't believe it when I found myself asking her if she'd like to go for a meal tonight, and I nearly fell off my chair when she accepted. So there you are. I have a date.'

'Oh, Richard, I'm so pleased for you,' she cried, clapping her hands in delight.

He eyed her worriedly. 'But now I'm feeling very nervous and beginning to regret asking her. I shall make a fool of myself, Kacie, I know I will.'

'You will not. Just relax, be yourself,' she ordered. 'You got on well with her at the dentist so why not across the dinner table? Anyway, she'll probably be as nervous as you are.'

He took a deep breath. 'Do you think so?'

'I'll eat my hat if she's not. Well, if I had a hat, that is. I remember my first date with Dennis.' A flood of sadness came over her which she hurriedly thrust aside. 'I was that het up I put my blouse on inside out. Dennis never said a word and I never noticed until I got home. I felt such a fool but we had a good laugh about it afterwards. We all make idiots of ourselves, especially at times like this. I know what you should wear. Your light trousers and cream shirt with your brown jacket. You'll look very smart in that, but casual. No, on second thoughts, not your jacket, that nice green jumper with the cable stitching down the front. You don't want to look too much like you're trying hard to impress her. Where are you taking her for this meal?'

'I thought the Grand Hotel.'

She shook her head. 'Oh, definitely not. A very special occasion, maybe, but not for a first date. Unless she's a titled lady or something and would expect that kind of thing?'

He shook his head. 'No, she's just a nice, ordinary woman but definitely one I'd like to get to know better.'

'Then take her to somewhere like Molly's Kitchen on the High Street. I've passed by it and it looks a nice place.'

'I'll do that,' he said. 'Should I buy her flowers?'

She eyed him thoughtfully. 'Dennis never bought me flowers but then he couldn't afford to. I would have liked that, so yes, but just a small bunch, nothing elaborate.'

'And a box of chocolates, do you think?'

'Just the flowers – you don't want to go over the top. Oh, this is so exciting, Richard. I shall be thinking of you all night and hoping it goes well. I'd better leave you to get ready.'

He eyed her fondly. 'I'm sorry I can't celebrate with you, Kacie.'

'We can do that another night. You have a date, Richard, and that's far more exciting than celebrating my job. Now hurry and get yourself ready. You don't want to keep her waiting.'

As soon as Kacie heard Richard return she bolted down the stairs to quiz him. 'How did it go then?' she asked, following him into his room.

'Cocoa or tea?' he asked, putting on the kettle.

'Richard!' she scolded.

He grinned at her. 'It was a wonderful evening, Kacie,' he said ecstatically.

She sighed with relief. 'Oh, Richard, I'm so glad. And you're seeing her again?'

'Next Saturday. We're going to the pictures.'

'Saturday is days away. Not before?'

'No. Slow and steady. I don't want to frighten her off.'

She looked at him seriously. 'I'd better start saving in earnest.'

'What for?' he asked puzzled.

She looked at him incredulously. 'My bridesmaid's dress, silly.'

'Oh, Kacie, stop it,' he scolded. 'It's one date and you have me married already.'

'But it was a promising date, yes?'

He nodded. 'Very promising. And before you ask, you'll meet her when I feel she's ready. She's very . . . well, shy and proper.'

Just your type, she thought. 'I'll have to be patient then, won't I?'

'You will.' He looked at her tenderly. 'I've you to thank for all this, Kacie. If you hadn't given me faith in myself I never would have asked Cassie out. I just wish . . .'

'Wish what?' she asked.

259

'That you could be happy, Kacie. You still pine for him, don't you?'

She looked hard at him and nodded. 'Yes. I still miss Dennis. I try not to. I keep telling myself that he belongs to someone else but I can't let go.' She felt tears prick her eyes. 'I'm a stupid woman, Richard.'

He leaped across to her and gathered her in his arms, giving her a protective hug. 'No, you're not. Don't ever say that. You'll let go one day, Kacie, when you're ready to – maybe when you meet someone else.'

'But he won't be Dennis,' she uttered.

'No. But then you might learn to love whoever it is just as much if you gave them a chance. You never know, by doing that you'll be able to let go of Dennis once and for all and get on with your life.'

She pulled away and looked up at him. 'You're very wise, aren't you?'

He smiled at her. 'I have my moments. Now, cocoa or tea?'

It took Kacie no time at all to settle down at Belgrave Salon and within days she felt she had been there for years. Bill was a lovely man to work for. His expectations of his staff were high, but in return he endeavoured to make sure they were happy and worked in a relaxed and friendly atmosphere. He allowed Kacie to express herself and never interfered unless she requested him to. Janice Preston, the apprentice, was a very able, lively girl, with an out-going personality and readily took direction from Kacie, willing to learn as much as she could off the capable new member of staff. She wanted to become a good hairdresser and was enthusiastic to do anything to ensure she would.

Unlike Florentina's, where the clientele had consisted mainly of middle-aged-to-elderly women with very set ideas on what they wanted, the Belgrave Salon boasted an assortment of age ranges from the very young to the very old, bringing with them a desire for a diversity of hairstyles which enabled the staff to show off their creative skills.

For the first time since she had left Verna's, Kacie felt at home and content in her workplace. Now all she needed to do was concentrate her efforts on repairing her emotional wounds and then she would be completely whole again.

Chapter Twenty-seven

Kacie walked into Bill's office just as he was finishing off a conversation on the telephone, and by the look on his face as he put the receiver down she could tell he'd had bad news.

'Are you all right?' she asked him.

'Er . . . I am yes, but I've just had some awful news. That was a call from a friend of mine who's got a salon on Woodgate. She was ringing me to ask if I'd heard about June Gibbons. June worked for my father years ago. Lovely lady, she is. She was left a bit of money by her grandmother when she died and decided to use it to open her own salon. She found a nice little place well situated at the bottom of Uppingham Road and my father helped her plan out the refit. There was only herself and a youngster but she did very well, worked all hours God sends to build her reputation. She's had the place over fifteen years but it seems she's gone out of business and the shock has landed her in the Towers Mental Institution.'

'That's terrible,' Kacie said. 'But you don't just go out of business, so what happened?'

Bill gave a shrug. 'I don't know the ins and outs but it was something to do with a bad accident to one of her clients who was having a perm. What had happened spread like wildfire around the area and the clients stopped coming.' He shook his head ruefully. 'When something like that happens people have short memories and you're very quickly branded. I don't need to tell you, Kacie, that businesses like ours can't survive for long without customers and it's not many who've the resources to ride out a storm so she very quickly went under.'

As Bill was telling her the story a niggle of something was playing at the back of Kacie's mind. 'Are you all right, Kacie?' he asked. 'You didn't know June, did you?'

She shook her head. 'No. But it's strange that something similar happened involving permed solutions at the last salon where I worked, but it must be just a coincidence. I'm sorry to hear about your father's old employee.'

'Yes, so am I.' Bill put his feet on his desk and leaned back in his chair. 'Am I glad today's over, Kacie. I know I shouldn't complain about being busy but it gets a bit much when we're nonstop. How are you?'

She gave a yawn. 'Bushed. I can't wait to get home and put my feet up. I'm just going to help Janice finish clearing up the salon, then I'll be off.' She put a piece of paper on the desk. 'I've made a list of items we need from the wholesaler's.'

'Oh, thanks, Kacie, that's much appreciated.'

Folding his arms around the back of his head, he looked at her searchingly. There was something about Kacie, something different, she had a presence about her that had drawn him like a magnet to her the moment he had set eyes on her standing in his salon. As the time had passed that attraction had grown, and Bill now realised that his feelings for this woman were very strong and he was finding it hard to keep them to himself.

Kacie closely guarded her private life and Bill knew hardly anything about her background. She had the title of Mrs but as far as he could find out she didn't live with her husband, she never talked about him and didn't wear a wedding ring, was probably divorced, and it was Bill's opinion, despite not knowing what had caused the breakdown, that her husband was a fool for letting someone like her go. But her ex-husband's loss was his own gain, he hoped. Problem was, there was a shield around Kacie, an invisible barrier, that told him to tread carefully. He intended to. She was special, was Kacie. He wanted desperately to find out how special.

'I can't believe you've only been here for a month. It seems you've always been here,' he said. 'You do like working here, don't you?'

She grinned wickedly at him. 'I think you'd know if I didn't.'

He grinned back. 'Yes, I believe I would. You're not backwards in coming forwards, are you, Kacie? That's what I like about you.' And unable to stop himself, he added, 'Well, one of the many things I like about you. Er . . . I was thinking of going for a drink just to wash the day out of my throat. Fancy coming?'

She shook her head. 'No, thanks. As I said, I'm tired and just want to get home.'

He tried not to show his dismay at her refusal, but then neither was he prepared to give up without a fight. 'Oh, come on, it'll do you good, Kacie. Just a quick drink, that's all. I don't like drinking on my own and I'd be grateful for your company.'

She made to refuse again but suddenly remembered the words of wisdom Richard had told her: that if she didn't start living again, she risked never moving on. She had to do this; make a step towards the final closing of her emotional wounds. What better way to move in the right direction than to go for a drink in the company of another man, even though that man was her boss who had requested her company sooner than drink alone. 'All right, just a quick one.' Then added to save the risk of upsetting her still delicate state of emotions: 'But on one condition.'

'Anything for you, Kacie,' he said, too delighted at her acceptance to be too concerned what the stipulation was.

'That we go somewhere that hasn't got a juke box. I've a headache, you see,' she hurriedly added. 'Not a bad one, but I don't want to risk it getting worse.'

He grinned at her. 'I know just the place. Old-timers go there. It's still got sawdust on the floor and the odd spittoon but definitely no juke box.'

She laughed. 'It sounds ideal.'

Bill was good company to be with and Kacie was surprised how much she was enjoying herself. It was an age since she had been out to a pub for a social drink and she realised how much she had missed doing so. They passed congenial chitchat over their drinks until Kacie felt it was time to go.

'Oh, but it's only eight o'clock,' Bill said, dismayed when she said she was leaving. 'Stay for just another,' he urged. 'I've already told you I don't like drinking on my own.'

She shook her head. 'I'll pass, thank you.' Then she laughed, inclining her head towards a female at the bar. 'I don't think you'll be stuck for company.'

Bill looked across at the woman Kacie was referring to. She was around his age and very attractive, and normally he'd have welcomed her attentions but Kacie was the woman he wanted to be with, wanted to get closer to. But then it was obvious Kacie was a woman who had her own mind and wasn't going to be easily seduced. He quickly realised that if he didn't want to scare her off he'd need to take things slowly.

263

'We'll do this again, Kacie?' he asked her.

'Yes, if you like,' she replied matter-of-factly.

His heart raced. She'd agreed to go for a drink with him again and that to him was a start, maybe, of better things to come.

Chapter Twenty-eight

Several days later Richard was looking bothered at Kacie over the dinner table. He knew immediately she had come into his room about an hour ago that she was doing her utmost to appear her happy self, but she was far from all right. He now knew her well and saw without doubt she had something on her mind that was deeply upsetting her.

He decided to take the bull by the horns. 'Come on, out with it. A problem shared and all that.'

She had been toying with her food and lifted her head to look at him distractedly. 'Out with what?'

'Don't play games with me, Kacie. I'm your friend, remember. What is it that's upset you? It's nothing to do with your job, is it? They are treating you well?'

'Oh, yes, I like it here, like it as much as I'd like any job.'

'So if it's nothing to do with work, what it is then?'

She gave him a wry smile. 'You can read me like a book, can't you? If you must know, Janice was going on today about a concert she was going to. She's so excited about getting the tickets, as apparently they've been snapped up. Her and her friend queued all Friday night to get them. I wanted to shout at her to shut up going on about it. I tried to ignore her, but it was hard. I didn't want to appear rude or ignorant so I had to force myself to show an interest.'

'And why did her getting tickets for a concert upset you?'

'Because the group she's going to see is Vernon and the Vipers. They're doing a tour around the country promoting their new single. You know how much I avoid reading newspapers, magazines and such like, and I'd no idea they were doing so well. Part of me is so pleased Dennis and the boys are riding high but the other part doesn't want to know.'

Richard felt he might have guessed Kacie's state had something to do with Dennis. 'I can understand that, Kacie. But this sort of thing will happen now and again. You can avoid reading matter as much as you like but because the band is so popular and in the limelight like it is, hearing gossip about them is unavoidable.'

'Yes, I know. Thankfully it's not often, but when I do it always catches me off guard.' She forced a smile on her face. 'Anyway, I'll be all right after I've slept on it, so don't worry.' And to change the subject she asked, 'So my liver was to your liking, was it, sir?'

He smiled appreciatively. 'It certainly was. Better than Mrs Henshaw's and that's saying something. Who taught you to cook it so well? Your mother?' He could have bitten his tongue off for asking that, but it was too late for retraction.

Her answer was slow in coming. 'No, my sister actually.'

He eyed her remorsefully. 'Oh, I'm sorry, Kacie, I didn't mean to remind you of things you're trying to forget. You've had enough of that today as it is.' He eyed her searchingly. 'But I have to say I know you miss her dreadfully, don't you? Why don't you go and see her? In fact, make it up with all your family. After all, it's been nearly nine months now since you last saw them.'

She gave a forlorn sigh. 'I made a bad mistake when I walked away after what happened with Dennis but I feel it's best to leave well alone. I still keep picturing what I saw at Christmas and, yes, it does hurt me so much to think they're all getting on happily without me around. But I haven't changed my mind: I still think that to go back could upset that. I daren't risk it; it wouldn't be fair.' Her eyes filled with sadness. 'I can't understand why it's taking me so long to get over Dennis, Richard. It's like for some reason I can't let go. I still love him so much, I still miss him dreadfully. I know he's with someone else but even now I can't picture the rest of my life without him.' She gave a deep sigh. 'I need more time. I live in hope one morning I'll wake up and Dennis won't be on my mind, that I get through the day without thinking of him at least a hundred times and I go to sleep at night without dreaming about him.'

Kacie had said she needed more time. She needed for ever, it seemed to Richard. 'What about Bill?' he asked.

She eyed him puzzled. 'What about him? He's my boss. Well, a little more than that, admittedly. He's a friend.' She smiled warmly at Richard. 'But not such a close friend as you are.'

He eyed her, concerned. Outwardly no one she came into contact with would think she had a care in the world by the way she went around with a happy smile planted on her attractive face. Apart from the friendly, as she seemed to think it was, drink with Bill after work, she never went out, still didn't listen to popular music or went anywhere that would bring her into contact with anything associated within the industry her estranged husband was connected with.

Richard worried that a young, attractive woman like Kacie should be out enjoying herself, not wasting her life, shutting herself away. He had tried everything he could to coax her out of herself but she flatly refused any suggestion he made.

'Are you sure Bill sees it that way, Kacie?' he casually asked.

'Oh, yes,' she said positively. 'Bill has no more interest in me than a boss has for an employee. He's a lovely man, though. I'm surprised no one has snapped him up before now.'

'Probably just hasn't met the right woman,' Richard commented. And thought to himself, did Kacie not realise that Bill maybe thought that he had found what he was looking for in her but she was too blind to realise because she was so still wrapped up in her errant husband?

'Probably,' she replied. She eyed Richard thoughtfully. 'He told me an awful story the other day which I've got to say has quite bothered me ever since. I kept meaning to tell you about it.'

Richard looked at her keenly. 'Go on then, I'm all ears.'

'I'm probably being stupid but Bill told me about a woman who used to work for his father and left to open her own salon. Apparently she was doing very well when this awful accident happened, and it severely damaged her reputation and she went out of business.'

Richard looked at her baffled as he picked up his glass of wine and took a sip from it. 'And why does that bother you?'

'The accident was caused by perming lotion.'

'So?'

'Well, what happened at Florentina's was caused by perming lotion.'

'Yes, but didn't Madge bring that about herself by making a bad error of judgement when she thinned the lotions down?'

'Yes, she did.' She eyed him thoughtfully. 'I'm bothering unnecessarily, it's just a coincidence. But regardless, two salons in Leicester to my knowledge have gone out of business because of something to do with perming lotions. Strange, isn't it?'

'Mmm, I agree it is.'

A thought suddenly struck Kacie and her mouth dropped open. 'Oh! You don't think . . .'

Richard eyed her sharply. 'Think what, Kacie?'

'That this perming lotion business is in any way connected to what happened to Myrna and, because of the products she generously gave me, to me too? I mean, all of it involves solutions that've been messed about with.'

He grimaced, shaking his head at her. 'This is beginning to sound like a subplot from a bad detective novel, Kacie, and you and I are the amateur sleuths that after turning themselves inside out, find out there was nothing to investigate in the first place.'

She sighed. 'Yes, I expect you're right.' She stared distantly into space. 'I liked Myrna. I think if that terrible thing hadn't happened, me and her would have become very good friends. The three of us would have.' She tilted her head and looked at Richard blankly. 'As it is I'll have to make do with just you, won't I?'

He gave a laugh. 'You could do worse, Kacie. More wine?'

'Just a drop, please. So, how's it going with Cassie? How many times have you seen her now? Three, isn't it?'

'Yes.'

She smiled at him. 'You are taking it really slow, Richard.'

'I told you before, I don't want to risk ruining things by rushing her. I have learned a bit about her. She has a couple of rooms on Forest Road, which she's very proud of, and has told me how she likes to scour the second-hand shops in search of decent furniture. She likes to walk, visit museums and art galleries, that kind of thing.'

'What about her family?'

'We haven't gotten around to that yet. She doesn't know that much about my background yet either. She knows I live here and where I work but nothing yet of my father and his stance in life. I shall be careful to pick my moment when I divulge all that. I, er . . . do know she's been married before, she was quite open about that. I know she was worried about telling me, thought it would put me off. But I told her it wasn't important to me, her past is her own business, it's the future that concerns me. I do think she's been badly hurt too.'

'Oh? But she's over that, is she? No hang-ups?'

'She doesn't seem to have.'

'So what else do you talk about?'

'All sorts. Our jobs, music we like, books we read.'

'Have you told her about me? Does she know how good friends we are?'

He looked sheepishly at her. 'No.'

She pulled a face. 'Charming, I must say.'

'Oh, don't take offence, Kacie. You're very important to me and when the time is right I'll tell her about you but when you first meet someone it's not easy to explain a close relationship with someone of the opposite sex to them without them thinking there's more to it than there is. I've waited so long for someone like Cassie to come along – to be honest I never dared dream it would happen. I daren't risk spoiling our relationship by telling her things that might be misconstrued. You can see my point, can't you?'

She smiled at him affectionately. Despite his outward change, inside Richard was still the gentleman he had been raised to be, still approached matters in an old-fashioned way, and he wouldn't change. It was obviously those qualities in him that had attracted Cassie to him in the first place, qualities that no woman had allowed herself to see in him before. Richard was wise to allow their relationship to develop slowly; make sure he got it right. 'Yes, I do,' she answered, smiling affectionately at him.

Chapter Twenty-nine

April had brought with it blustery showers, and folks were concerned the spell of warm spring weather had come to an end, and they would have to dig out their winter attire again. Fortunately their fears were unfounded and it was a lovely sunny day that invited Kacie out of the salon, she having volunteered to collect the cobs for lunch and afford herself a blow of fresh air. She was just about to step out of the doorway and into the street when she collided with a person about to enter.

'Oh, I'm sorry,' she said, rubbing her shoulders where the pair had bumped each other. Then she gawped at the other person, shocked. 'Rita!' she exclaimed. 'What a nice surprise. Come for a hairdo at a proper salon, have you?' she said laughing.

The young girl frowned, perplexed. 'Wadda yer mean?'

'It was a joke, Rita. You work at a very good salon and wouldn't need to get your hair done anywhere else. I was just— Oh, never mind. Why are you here?'

'Looking for work.'

'What on earth for?'

''Cos I've lost me job.'

'Oh, Rita, how? You didn't fall back into your old ways, did you?'

'No. It weren't nothin' to do with me. It weren't my fault it happened.'

'What wasn't?'

'The accident. I didn't touch the perming lotion. I swore I never but she wouldn't believe me. All I did was pour it out from the bottle into a bowl like I was told ter do. Mrs Downend said I must 'ave put summat in it 'cos nobody else could've. But I didn't, honest, Kacie.'

Kacie's heart was pounding rapidly. 'What happened to the client, Rita?'

271

'She ended up wi' badly singed 'air and wa' really angry 'cos it'll tek an age ter grow back. She said she'd never use the salon again.'

Kacie was staring at her worriedly. 'Do you know where your boss got the perming lotions from originally, Rita?'

She nodded. 'I were there when they came. They were brought by a delivery man. Mrs Downend wa' all hot and bothered when they arrived 'cos she hadn't ordered anything, but then it turns out to be a prummy summat from one of the top product makers.'

'A prummy summat? Oh, a promotion offer?'

'Yeah, that's it.'

Alarm bells started to ring – not just ring, they were clanging loudly – and Kacie's thoughts were racing wildly. That was three salons that she knew of now that had suffered accidents through perming lotions. The other two were now out of business. 'Is the salon you worked for still open for business?' she asked Rita.

'Yeah, I think so. Why?'

'Ah, that one didn't work out then.' She issued a loud exhale. 'I'm beginning to see now.'

'See what, Kacie?'

'Just how the jigsaw fits together. Go home, Rita.'

'What?'

'Look, I can't promise anything but I'm going to try and persuade Mrs Downend to give you your job back. But don't build your hopes up.'

The young girl's face filled with expectation. 'Oh, Kacie, will yer? I'd be ever so grateful. I really liked working there.'

'As I said, I can't promise but I'll try.'

What was going through Kacie's mind didn't bear thinking about, as it involved someone having a very devious mind and absolutely no regard for anyone's safety, that faceless person being purely driven by a need to achieve their aims. Though who could possibly be so callous was beyond Kacie to comprehend. And another thought struck her. What had they to gain by what they were doing? Regardless, though, something awful was taking place, of that she was almost positive, but to further confirm her suspicions she needed to visit Rita's last place of work.

So consumed was she, she completely forgot her own job and raced off in the direction of Fosse Road North where the salon was situated.

Mrs Downend was very reluctant to speak to her, even though

Kacie assured her she wasn't anything to do with any authoritative body.

'Look, Mrs Downend, I know you think it was Rita who put something in the perming lotion that caused your client to suffer the damage to her hair, but why would she do that?'

The proprietor shrugged her shoulders. 'I don't know. She seemed such a willing girl but there was no one else who could have done it, so I had no alternative but to blame her.'

'Don't you think the bottle might already have contained whatever it was that caused the trouble before Rita handled it?'

'Of course not. They were from L'Oreal, a most respectable firm. I've been using their products for years and had not one bit of bother.'

'But what if those promotional bottles didn't come from L'Oreal?'

Mrs Downend eyed Kacie as though she was mad. 'Well, of course they did. The name is on the bottles and I've no reason to suspect they've come from anywhere else. L'Oreal often give promotional stuff away, same as other firms do. How else do we hairdressers get to know about new products and give them a try? Look, what are you getting at?'

'Have you used any of the other free bottles you received?'

'No. I'm waiting for the L'Oreal rep to come in just in case I got a completely bad batch and I shall await their findings and, hopefully, replacements. Luckily for me, the lady it happened to wasn't one of my regulars and I managed to hush it up and didn't suffer any other consequences. That doesn't compensate for the embarrassment of what happened to that poor lady's hair, though.'

'No, it doesn't. But it's my guess all those bottles have been tampered with, but L'Oreal won't find out who did it because what's inside is not of their manufacturing.'

'You're not making sense, young lady.'

'I'm sorry, I'll try to. What has happened to you also happened at a salon where I was working, only on a larger scale, but the owner was in the habit of thinning down her products so it was automatically assumed that she had made the mistake herself.'

'Thinning down, eh? I'm dead against that practice – wouldn't entertain the idea. I wouldn't dream of duping my customers. I value them too much. It's obvious then that she was responsible and it's nothing to do with what happened here.'

273

'I don't agree with you. I think someone is deliberately trying to put salons out of business.'

'Why? Whoever is doing this, what have they to gain by it?'

Kacie looked at her stupefied as she realised the puzzle she had thought fitted together still had a big piece missing. She shuffled on her feet uncomfortably. 'I don't know.'

Mrs Downend gave an irritated sigh. 'You've just wasted ten minutes of my time. Now if you don't mind I have customers to see to.'

'Look, Mrs Downend, I know you think I'm crazy—'

'You're right there, I do.'

'Well, I'm not. I know something is going on. Think me as doolally as you like but please be convinced that Rita wasn't to blame. If you really think about it, why would she tamper with that perming solution – that's if she knew how to in the first place. By doing so she'd got nothing to gain but the risk of losing her job, and she loves working here. Please consider giving Rita her job back. She's not to blame for what happened to your customer, believe me she isn't.'

Mrs Downend stared at her. 'Maybe I was hasty in my judgement. Maybe it *was* just a bad bottle. I must admit, Rita has been missed around here. I'll consider it.'

Kacie sighed with relief. If nothing else, with luck she had got Rita's job back for her.

Distractedly, she slowly made her way back towards her own workplace and was surprised when she entered the salon to find the place deserted, the lights dimmed.

At the sound of the bell on the door, Bill leaped up from his office chair and bounded through. His relief to see Kacie was most apparent.

'Oh, Kacie, thank God. I've been worried sick. Where have you been?'

His distress at her absence shocked her greatly. 'I'm sorry, I had to do an errand.'

'But you've been gone hours.'

'Have I? I hadn't realised.'

'I thought you'd had a bad accident or something. Kacie, I was so worried.'

'Were you? Oh . . . I'm sorry I left you in the lurch like that. Did you manage to cope without me?'

'Yes, we weren't that busy. But having to cope without you is not what's upset me. I was worried about *you*, Kacie?'

'Well, there was no need to be because I'm all right. As I said, I suddenly had an errand to do.'

'What was so important that you had to rush off like that without telling anyone?'

She exhaled loudly and her shoulders sagged. 'I'm so mixed up I don't know what to think. Any chance of a cuppa, Bill, and I'll try to explain?'

The tea was made in a flash and seated across his desk from him she took a sip, then fixed her eyes in his. 'When I left to get the cobs for lunch I bumped into a girl I used to work with. She's been working in a salon on Fosse Road North. She said she was looking for work, which I couldn't understand because as far as I was aware she had a perfectly good job. It turns out she'd lost it because of an accident involving perming lotions. A customer's hair was badly singed.'

Bill looked at her nonplussed. 'And?'

'Bill, that's three incidents like this to my knowledge. Don't you think that's unusual?'

'I suppose. But some salons aren't so competent as others.'

'I know accidents happen, Bill, in any business, but three to do with perming lotions happening so close together is very unusual, don't you think? Two of those salons are now out of business and it worries me how many more there are we don't know about.'

'You're making too much of this, Kacie. It's just a coincidence.'

'No, it can't be. Someone is doing this, Bill. Someone is tampering with bottles of perming lotions and having them delivered to salons under the guise of promotional offers, and they don't seem to care that innocent people are being maimed in the process.'

'OK, say they are. But why?'

'I think the aim is to put salons out of business.'

He eyed her dubiously. 'But why? What's to be gained by going to all that trouble?'

'I keep asking myself that question. I don't know, Bill.' Then a terrible thought struck her. 'Oh hell. It's the same person, it's got to be. It's also happened to a friend of mine. Myrna was opening her own salon and out of the blue received a box full of products from a well-wisher. But what was labelled on the bottles and containers wasn't what was inside, only we didn't find out until it was too late. Myrna ended up out of business. It happened to me too because she innocently gave me some of the stuff.'

275

Bill was looking at her, astounded. 'Oh, Kacie, now you really are—'

'What?' she erupted. 'Being melodramatic? Is that what you were going to say? Well, I'm not. I know I'm right. We have to put a stop to this before they strike again and more people get hurt.'

'But how, Kacie?'

She shook her head. 'I don't know.'

Suddenly the strain was too much for her and she started to cry. 'The police would laugh at me if I went to them with this,' she blubbered. 'But we have to let people know, somehow. Warn them.'

Bill shot up from his desk and rushed around to her, gathering her in his arms. 'There, there, Kacie,' he said soothingly, kissing her forehead. 'Please don't upset yourself like this. I hear what you're saying but I still think—'

Her head shot back and she looked up at him. 'That I'm stupid?'

'No. I'd never think that, Kacie.' He looked at her tenderly. She looked so vulnerable and felt so good in his arms, and an overwhelming desire to kiss her filled his being. He bent his head and placed his lips on hers. His kiss was urgent, full of passion.

His action took her completely by surprise and she struggled against him, fighting to free herself. 'What are you doing?' she cried.

'Kissing you, Kacie.'

'I didn't invite you to do that.'

'I know, but you like me, don't you?'

'Yes, as a friend, no more than that.'

His face fell, deeply hurt. 'But I thought—'

'You thought what?'

'That it was more than that between us.'

'How? I've never led you on, Bill. I couldn't. I'm sorry, but I still love my husband.'

'But you're no longer together.'

'I know, but that doesn't mean I'm over him.'

'But is it not time to let go, Kacie, give someone else a chance?'

Her face clouded in pain and she issued a deep sigh. 'I want to, Bill, I want to start living again, but I can't. Just because someone you care for doesn't love you any more doesn't mean that you can switch off your feelings for them like magic. I wish I could – you don't know how much. But until that happens I can't consider anyone else. I feel I'm being disloyal. Think me a fool, idiot, whatever you like, but that's how it is.'

276

'He's the fool to let you go, Kacie, not you.'

'You know nothing about him,' she snapped defensively. 'You've no right to speak of my husband like that.'

'But he's not your husband, Kacie. He gave up that right when he stopped loving you, and I presume left you. Feeling what I do for you gives me that right to say what I did, Kacie. I'm in love with you,' he whispered. 'You must know that?'

His words shocked her rigid. 'I didn't realise, I'm so sorry. I can't return your feelings, Bill. I wish I could, you're a lovely man. I've already told you, I'm not over Dennis and the way it seems to be going I never will be. I'd better go. I . . . don't think it wise I work here any more.'

His face fell, astounded. 'Don't say that, Kacie, please. You're just upset over this perming lotion business. Look, I didn't mean to force myself on you, it just happened. I wanted you so much, you see. I'll wait for you. I won't pressure you, I promise, and when you're ready you can let me know.'

She shook her head. 'I can't let you live in hope like that, Bill. It wouldn't be fair on you. I can't say: give me a week, month, year. I don't know when I'll wake up one morning and know I'm over him. And I can't live with that pressure. It's best I go. You'll soon find someone to replace me in the salon.'

Before he had time to respond she had picked up her bag and, with tears pricking her eyes, she smiled wanly at him. 'Goodbye, Bill.'

With that she hastily left.

Chapter Thirty

The warm day had turned into a chilly evening and the near-deserted streets were dark and uninviting. Shoulders slumped, head bowed, Kacie wandered slowly towards home. She felt bewildered and confused. Had she just made the biggest mistake of her life turning Bill down like that? Bill was a good man who possessed many excellent qualities and he would have treated her well – she may even have grown fond of him in time – but to pursue a serious relationship with him would have been futile. Bill wasn't Dennis. She had been cruel to Bill and she felt guilty for that, but she had acted only out of fairness to him.

When Bill had kissed her, it had reawakened a need that she knew could only be satisfied by Dennis. How she longed just once again to feel his arms around her, his tender lips on hers, his naked body pressed close. These raging emotions proved to her that Dennis was the only man she could ever love, ever want to be with. He was her soulmate, her destiny. Destiny, though, had played her a cruel hand and parted them. Dennis had replaced her with another. But she could never replace him. There was no one that could ever fill the space Dennis had left vacant, she now knew that. She must learn to live with this knowledge, just be happy by herself.

She lifted her head and blindly stared upwards. 'Dear God,' she prayed. 'Please help me? Please show me the way forward.'

As she slowly lowered her head a vision of Myrna suddenly flashed before her. She was saying her farewell, leaving Leicester to begin a new life. Kacie realised that maybe she should have accepted her offer and gone with her. She had her address in her bag. Myrna would be delighted to see her, help her get a job, away from the hairdressing trade this time. Most importantly, away from Leicester and all her memories.

What was there left to hold her here? She was jobless again. She had mindlessly turned her back on her family, and she doubted their welcome of her back into the fold would be a warm one.

There was Richard. He was the only person that would miss her. His need of her friendship now, though, was not so great; he could well manage without her. She smiled distantly as she thought of him. Such a good friend he had been to her, her saviour, and without him she would never have survived such a difficult period in her life. She had repaid her monetary debt to him in full but her debt of gratitude she could never repay. He would miss her dreadfully, that much she knew. But her own help in his outward transformation had brought Cassie into his life. He had someone else to care for now, and unlike herself, Cassie could offer Richard much more than friendship. Hopefully she would grow to love him as a man should be loved. Cassie had invited him to her rooms for dinner tonight, Richard was there now, so the relationship did indeed appear to be very promising. If not, he was stronger now, more confident in himself, and if matters did not work out between him and Cassie, he possessed the self-assurance to seek another. Kacie had served her purpose with Richard.

She owed no rent to Mrs Slattery – in fact, if she left tonight, Mrs Slattery would owe her if she let her room immediately. She hadn't much in her purse, but more than she'd arrived with, enough to see her settled with Myrna and until she found work, which she hoped to do quite quickly.

She made her decision. She was leaving Leicester for good and she was going tonight. She would slip a note under Richard's door, explaining what she was doing and maybe in the future, when she was completely healed in herself, she would let him know where she was.

She took a deep breath and looked around her. In her distracted state, she had missed her turning off the Narborough Road towards home and had walked so far along she was across the road from Florentina's.

Automatically she looked towards the salon and as she did so a great sadness engulfed her as she remembered the tragedy that had taken place inside those premises. The shop appeared to be occupied by another hairdresser and had been renamed Modern Miss, which was a good name, she thought, and sincerely hoped the new owner faired better than Madge Benson had.

Remembering her urgent need to get home and pack her belongings, she made to resume her journey when suddenly a memory struck and her eyes flashed back to the sign above the hairdressers.

Modern Miss. Where had she heard that name before? She stood in deep concentration for a moment. Then it came to her. Myrna had said that whoever had taken over her shop had renamed it Modern Miss. But then it wasn't very likely that there would be two hairdressers in Leicester operating under the same name, so she must be mistaken. But she knew she wasn't. Myrna had definitely said whoever had bought her shop had renamed it Modern Miss. Oh, of course, Kacie thought, the salons were both named the same because they were obviously owned by the same person.

Then she gasped, hand flying up to cover her mouth in shock as it all made sense. She *had* been right; all her instincts screamed at her that she was.

There had been an end gain for the person responsible for sending anonymously those doctored products. It had been purely to acquire hairdressing businesses as cheaply as possible. And how much cheaper could they have been bought when whoever was after them had ensured they were all but bankrupt before they had named their price, the owner in the circumstances snatching their hand off, only too grateful to be receiving any offer at all. How clever.

But what could she do with this knowledge?

Go to the police? She had no proof whatsoever. No name of a culprit. She'd be laughed at, thought crazy.

She could write letters to all the hairdressers in the city, warning them. But they would likely think her letter a hoax and ignore it.

And what if she was wrong? That all this was just her imagination running riot? Bill had thought so; Mrs Downend too.

Her shoulders sagged. There was nothing she could do but hope that whoever was behind it was satisfied now with what they had already achieved.

She had to forget all this. She had her own future to think about. She had a case to pack, a train to catch and she needed to hurry if she was to leave town tonight.

She made to resume her way home then she was stopped short. There was one person Kacie had forgotten about who ought to be enlightened on what she had uncovered. Due to past loyalties, and the possibility that her salon could become a target, Verna deserved to be made aware of what may happen.

In doing so, Kacie would have to travel down roads in Evington near where she had used to live; face Verna's wrath for the way she had abruptly left her employment; risk Verna thinking she had lost her mind to come to her with such an elaborate tale. But, regardless, Kacie knew she had no choice but to inform Verna of what she suspected if she was to leave Leicester with a clear conscience.

It didn't take her long to pack her belongings into Caroline's case. She decided to take Richard's gift of the radio with her. It easily fitted inside her case and it would be a welcome reminder of his friendship. The rest of the bits she had acquired since she had moved into 17 Danehill Road she would leave for the next occupant. Except, that was, for her other gift from Richard, the unused record player. That she left outside his door, along with a letter shoved under the door, explaining what she was doing, and asking for his forgiveness and understanding.

When she closed the front door behind her and walked purposely down the weed-encrusted path, she didn't look back.

Chapter Thirty-one

It was approaching eight o'clock when the taxi deposited Kacie and her case on the corner of the street where Verna lived with her husband, Jan.

Verna lived in a two-storey palisade terrace, in a tree-lined street in a nice part of Evington, the residents taking great pride in their properties. Brass door knockers gleamed and snow-white-lace-curtained windows shone, doorsteps were swept and polished at least once a week.

When Kacie arrived at the house the front was in darkness and for a moment she was worried no one was at home and she'd had a wasted journey. Then she remembered Verna telling her she spent her evenings in her sitting room at the back. Her husband, depending on his health, was in the habit of retiring early to bed.

Depositing her suitcase at the end of the front path by the house wall, she made her way round the back of the house. The light in the back room was on but Kacie could detect no presence inside. She knocked on the back door and waited. No response. She knocked again. Still no response. So she opened the door and poked her head inside.

'Mrs Koz,' she called softly, conscious of waking the woman's sleeping husband. Then she listened. Nothing. She stepped inside and called again, a little louder this time. No answer. It was then she noticed a half-opened door down the hallway. Verna, for whatever reason, was obviously down in the cellar. She hesitated for a moment, unsure whether to wait for Verna's return or go after her. She was very conscious time wasn't on her side, so she decided to go into the cellar and announce her presence.

The age-worn steps were steep, curving midway down, and as she gingerly descended a musty dank smell assailed her nostrils. 'Mrs Koz,' she called, wrinkling her nose. 'Are you there?'

283

There was still no answer.

She reached the bottom and in the dim light, she hesitantly looked around. The light didn't reach as far as the corners and they were dark, eerie, and Kacie shuddered. The low brick roof was covered in cobwebs. Stacked by the walls were numerous long-discarded items: an old mangle; lawn mower; base of a lampstand; old paint pots; rusting tools; the remains of a rotting push bike. Numerous overflowing boxes containing old clothes, curtains, bedding; chipped pots and pans were stacked higgledy-piggledy.

Then she saw that a space had been cleared in the middle of the cellar to make way for a large table, over which hung a length of cable attached to which was a light socket and bulb. This was the only source of light. The top of the table was littered with bottles and what appeared to be glass measuring equipment, plus a hand-operated labelling machine, rolls of blank labels stacked by it. On the stone slabs by the table, several boxes lay strewn. There were also large plastic containers stacked to one side. It was not apparent what was in them. Kacie's immediate thought was that Verna was now using her cellar as a storage place for the salon's stock. It was also painfully obviously Verna had started to mix her own solutions, judging by her possession of the empty bottles and equipment to print labels. Kacie then worried that her ex-employer's reasons for doing this were because the salon was suffering hard times and she wanted to save money. If this was the case, Kacie was saddened, as she knew Verna worked very hard to keep her business afloat.

Guessing Verna must have popped away for a minute, probably to check on her husband upstairs, she decided to wait for Verna's return, hoping she'd be quick. The deafening silence and the spooky atmosphere were making her feel edgy and Kacie moved across to the side of the table where the light was strongest.

Leaning her weight against the table, she idly scanned the items littering the top. It struck her as very odd that Verna should possess all the chemicals to make her own perming solutions, an arduous task she had vehemently avoided since the availability of manufactured products. Business must really be bad, Kacie thought sadly. Then she spotted a stack of leaflets half hidden behind bottles and inquisitively she leaned across and picked one up. What she read shook her rigid.

284

PROMOTIONAL OFFER
PLEASE ACCEPT TWELVE OF OUR NEW RANGE OF
PERMING SOLUTIONS WITH COMPLIMENTS OF
L'OREAL

Kacie's mind whirled frantically, a sickening bile rising up from the pit of her stomach. She picked up the rest of the leaflets and flicked through them. They were all the same except that every so often the name of the manufacturer was different but all were top suppliers to the hairdressing trade.

She stared at them blindly, having terrible difficulty accepting what this represented. She prayed she was wrong, but the evidence before her was far too damning. To Kacie, Verna Kozlowski had epitomised everything that was honest; she was the very last person Kacie would have suspected of carrying out such devious acts.

What was she going to do? Fetch the police and let them sort out this terrible situation? Or, out of past loyalty to Verna, lock it all away in the back of her mind and walk away?

Suddenly her thoughts were interrupted by heavy footfalls descending the cellar steps. She jumped, dropping the leaflets back on the table, heart banging painfully against her chest. Kacie struggled to make out who was coming but the light was too poor.

A great fear of being trapped in such a dreadful situation raced through her, and she watched, hardly daring to breath, as a ghostly figure lumbered slowly in her direction. For a fleeting moment, a vision of Frankenstein, portrayed in the black-and-white horror films she had seen at the cinema with Dennis, rose before her. Suddenly the figure halted, sensing her presence.

'What the hell . . . Oh! Kacie? It is you, isn't it?'

She gulped. 'Yes . . .' She gulped again. 'Yes, it is me, Mr Kozlowski. I . . . I was looking for Mrs Koz. I saw the cellar door open and thought she was down here.'

The silence that invaded the damp, dank cellar for several long moments was deafening.

Finally, Jan Kozlowski spoke, his accent markedly showing his Polish origins. 'Well, as you can see, she's not here. She's out at the moment, at a Hairdresser's Guild meeting, won't be back for another hour or so. I was in the bathroom and didn't hear you come in.' His eyes narrowed and he looked at her hard. 'Mrs Kozlowski was of the opinion you had gone for good. You upset her going off without a word. It was wrong of you, Kacie, leaving her stranded like that, considering all my wife has done for you.'

She took a deep breath. 'Yes . . . yes. I'm very sorry about that but, at the time, I felt I had no other choice.'

'Huh, well, your apology has come a bit late and it's to Mrs Kozlowski you need to be saying it to, not me. I suggest you call again at a more fitting time. Now, I'll ask you to excuse me as I am busy at the moment.'

His tone was brusque, dismissive. She had caught Jan Kozlowski in an awkward situation and he wanted her out of here. All her instincts told her to go now, leave Leicester as she had planned, turn her back on it all to start a new life, but she suddenly remembered all the suffering and damage that had been caused by what was going on in this cellar and, before she could stop herself, she blurted, 'Yes, I can see you are.'

His face darkened. 'What do you mean by that?'

She flashed a glance across the table, then rearing back her head, fixed her eyes defiantly into his. 'I might be some things, Mr Kozlowski, but I'm not stupid. I came here tonight to warn Mrs Kozlowski of some terrible things that are happening in the hairdressing trade, but it's silly of me to be warning her about something she must be fully aware of as it's going on under her own roof.'

'What am I fully aware of? What's going on, Jan? Kacie, what are you doing here?'

They both spun to face Verna, dressed in her outdoor clothing, as she advanced towards them, her face wreathed in confusion. She stopped in front of the table then brought her eyes to rest on her husband. 'Jan, I asked what is going on here? You know I don't like being in this cellar, it gives me the creeps, but I heard raised voices.' She pointed at the table. 'What are you doing with all these things?'

He was staring at his wife nervously. 'You're . . . you're back early?'

'The meeting was cancelled. Several of the members are ill with this flu that's going around. Jan, you haven't answered my question. What's going on?'

'She doesn't know, does she, Mr Kozlowski?' Kacie gasped not knowing, as yet, whether to be relieved or not about this fact.

'For God's sake,' Verna demanded. 'What don't I know, Jan?'

'If you won't tell her, I will,' Kacie cried. 'Your husband—'

'Don't listen to her,' Jan erupted. 'She's accusing me of all sorts of things and they're damned lies, damned lies I tell you.' He began pacing the small space between himself and the table, his arms flaying. 'I'm . . . I'm trying to formulate some new perming solutions so you don't have to buy manufactured stock. I . . . I thought if I was successful I could raise your profile in the trade by using your own branded products and also save you money. I . . . I didn't want you to know about it in case I didn't succeed.'

'He's lying, Mrs Koz, your husband was doing no such thing. He's contaminating already made-up perming solution bought from wholesalers, re-bottling it and forging labels of proper manufacturers by using that printing machine,' she said pointing at it. 'Then sending them out to salons as promotional offers in the hope it will damage the customers' hair.'

Verna stared at her husband astounded. 'What? But why? And what do you mean by contaminating? I don't understand?'

'He did it so he could bankrupt the salons then he could buy them up cheaply. Go on deny it, Mr Koz?'

Verna's face paled. 'Please don't tell me this is true, Jan? Please, please, I couldn't bear it,' she implored.

He stopped his pacing and stood before his wife. 'Of course it's not true. I told you not to listen to her, Verna,' he cried. 'She barged down here making all these accusations and they're all lies, all of them. Now you get out of here,' he shouted furiously at Kacie. 'Go on, before I . . . I . . . fetch the police and have you arrested for trespassing.'

He made a lunge for Kacie but she was too quick for him and stepped out of his reach. She grabbed up one of the leaflets and waved it at Verna. 'If I'm not telling the truth, what are these?'

Verna snatched the leaflet from Kacie and as she read it her face turned grey. She looked at her husband. 'Answer her, Jan?' she uttered.

He was staring at his wife, his mouth opening and closing fish-like. His game was up and there was no way out for him. 'I . . . I did it for you, Verna,' he implored. 'You have to believe me. You were so worried by that new salon opening, so bothered it would affect your trade. I lay listening to you tossing and turning at night, not able to sleep. It was making you ill.'

'But that salon was no real threat, Jan. I knew I was worrying needlessly.'

'Knowing that didn't stop you though, did it? Worrying how we'd manage in our old age if the business didn't make enough for us to retire. But it was Kacie leaving your employment that drove

287

me to despair. You lost custom over her departure, don't deny it, Verna, and if that new salon had taken some of your customers away then the threat of going under would've been serious. I had to do something to try to stop it. You'd worked too hard all these years just to have your business whipped from under your feet through no fault of your own. But what could I do, that was my problem. Then, like a miracle, it came to me, and I have you to thank Kacie.'

'Me,' she issued, shocked.

He nodded. 'You remember, my dear,' he addressed his wife, 'you were mulling over how much you could cut your prices by if it came down to it and you then repeated a conversation you'd had with Kacie while you were checking the stock shortly after you'd heard the other salon was definitely going ahead. You,' he said, looking at Kacie, 'said it was a pity something drastic couldn't happen on opening day and the shop would be forced to shut before it had had a chance to steal my wife's customers away. Verna said that she didn't wish the new owner any ill fortune but if something like that happened then her worry would be over. You then added,' he said turning his attention back to his wife, 'that if you didn't know better you'd have thought that whoever sabotaged Kacie at the competition had heard that particular conversation and that's how they'd got the idea to get her out of the way before the judging. That's when it hit me. That's what I had to do, Verna. Get rid of your threat before it became a reality.'

He raked his hands through his thinning hair and began pacing again. 'I thought, what if I could tamper with *Cut and Curls'* products like the saboteur at the competition had done. But then I couldn't work out how to interfere with them. It wasn't like I could breeze into their stock room. So I thought I'd supply the products once I'd fiddled with them and just hope that the hairdresser didn't twig they were fakes before they were used.' He stopped pacing and faced his wife. 'If it stopped you worrying, Verna, and kept your salon in business then to me it was worth a try.

'I decided it best you knew nothing, my dear. Ignorance is bliss, the English say, don't they? I knew I was safe using the cellar because you never come down here, the place frightens you, doesn't it? And I had so much time on my hands while you were at work. Making up all the concoctions was no problem. I just mixed up flour with bad eggs and water, using food colourings to make the concoction look realistic inside the empty bottles I'd bought from

288

the plastics factory across town. The hardest part was copying the labels off top manufacturers' bottles. When I'd made up a large enough amount of stock, and was happy with the labels, I had them delivered anonymously by a man I'd found out about who had a van, and for a few shillings, was willing to pose as a delivery man. I just had to wait then to see if my plan had worked. It was nerve-racking. I had such a job pretending I knew nothing when you told me of the salon's failure, Verna, but the relief on your face and you being able to sleep again was worth it.'

'Worth it,' Verna cried astounded. 'You put that poor woman out of business, Jan, and you encouraged me to use our savings to buy the shop, you did the negotiating, were very proud of how cheaply you'd got it. Oh, God, no, no, please tell me I'm not hearing this.' A terrible thought struck her and she gawped at him. 'We have *five* shops, Jan.' She cast her eyes across the table before bringing them back to rest on him. 'Please tell me this is not how we have procured all of them, by harming their customers, forcing them into bankruptcy so they would accept what little you offered them?'

He gave a helpless shrug. 'The first plan worked so easily, Verna. With the success of that I saw a way of achieving your dream of owning your own string of salons. I saw a chance to secure our future and make sure you never worried over lack of money again. You can't blame me for that, Verna, surely you can't. Doing what I did to *Cut and Curls* was so chancy and I couldn't possibly expect it to work with an already successful concern. Coming up with the plan of doctoring the perming solutions was child's play. You've told me of mistakes by hairdressers who've added too much of a chemical when making up your own. I know how delighted you always are when you receive free promotional products from manufacturers and how readily you try them out. I couldn't see my plan failing and I was very careful to make sure there was no chance anything could be traced back to us. My plan was fool proof. Well almost,' he added, glaring at Kacie. He turned to his wife who was staring at him blindly. 'Kacie can't prove anything. If she fetched the police now, by the time she's convinced them to pay us a visit we'd have this cellar cleared out of all the evidence. The salons were bought fair and square at an agreed price by the owner. So it's all right, Verna, we're safe.'

'Have you no conscience,' demanded Kacie. 'None of those salons was bought fair and square. In truth, you stole them, Mr

Kozlowski, and have you any idea of what pain and suffering you've caused in the process? What you did maimed innocent people. It also put hard-working people out of business. A woman I was working for accidentally killed herself after those perms you sent her badly burned the scalps five of her customers and another salon owner I heard of went demented and she landed up in the mental home.'

Verna's face filled with horror. 'Oh, my God, Jan, what have you done?' She spun to face Kacie. 'I had no idea, Kacie, you have to believe me. If I'd have had an inkling I'd have put a stop to this.' She then leaped over to her husband and grabbed his arms. 'I have always prided myself on honesty, Jan,' she said shaking him hard. 'I was under the mistaken impression that we had acquired those salons by scrupulous means. I was so proud of our growing business. I walked down the road with my head held high. Now . . . now I'm so ashamed. What you took *must* be given back. I don't care how we do it, those salons will be given back to their rightful owners. And those poor innocent people who were harmed . . . I don't know how, but we have to compensate them in some way. We will do this, Jan, or I will report you to the authorities myself and our marriage will be over.'

He looked at her astounded. 'You don't mean that?'

'Oh, but I do. I've never meant anything so much in all my life. I never, ever thought you capable of anything like this, Jan. I thought you were a kind, gentle man, as honest as I am.'

He looked at her shamefully. 'My honesty was put aside when I saw the chance to make you smile again, Verna. I did this for you, as my way of thanking you for loving me, marrying me. You stood by me, Verna, when ignorant people have spat at me in the street and called me names because of my birth place. You don't know what it's been like for me, year after year, watching you graft so hard for not much reward, and me not able to contribute in any way. This was my way of giving something. Yes, it was wrong. But is it wrong to want the best for my wife?' He wrung his hands distraughtly. 'I never thought that people would be so badly harmed. I must have got my measurements wrong, and I thought I'd been so careful.' His face filled with remorse. 'I'm so sorry for that.'

'Then prove you're sorry, Jan, by putting what's wrong right.'

He eyed her disbelievingly. 'You really want to hand it all back? You'll be back where you started, Verna, worrying about money again. Couldn't we just keep what we have. I promise I won't do it again. We could pay Kacie to keep quiet—'

'Pay me! How dare you, Mr Kozlowski,' Kacie cried, deeply insulted. 'If Mrs Koz asked me to, then out of loyalty for her I would, but take payment, *never*.'

'Jan, how could you suggest that,' Verna scolded furiously. 'I would never put Kacie in such a position, never. I don't care if I'm left with nothing, I'd sooner live in dire poverty than with this knowledge on my conscience.'

His body slumped defeatedly and he stared at Verna for several long moments, then his face flooded with humiliation. 'I've been a foolish man, haven't I, Verna?'

She nodded. 'Very.' She rushed towards him and put her hands on his arms, looking up into his face with great tenderness. 'But I accept your reasons for doing what you did, Jan, even though it was terribly misguided of you.'

'Please forgive me,' he implored her. 'I'll do anything you want rather than lose you.'

Verna patted his arm affectionately then turned to Kacie. 'It's up to you if you want to go to the police. Whatever you decide to do, I fully appreciate it has to be what you think is right, my dear.'

Kacie smiled warmly at her. 'I know *you* will do what's right, Mrs Koz. I have no doubt in my mind. I won't be going to the police.'

She sighed in relief. 'Thank you, Kacie. We must talk, but not tonight, maybe tomorrow when I've fully digested all this. I need to come to terms with it all and start to make a plan as to how we can sort this out. I just hope I'll be in a position to offer you a job when this is over. I can only promise that I will do my best but then I don't know what I'll be left with, if anything.'

'Surely you'll manage to hang on to your own salon, Mrs Koz?'

She gave a weak smile. 'I hope so.' She looked tenderly at Kacie. 'I'm so sorry we meet again under these circumstances, but it is so good to see you and to know that you're back safe and sound after whatever it was that caused you to go away like that. Your family must be so relieved. Dennis—'

Kacie held up her hand in a warning gesture at the mention of his name. 'I must go, Mrs Koz. I won't be needing a job but thank you for offering. You see I'm leaving Leicester for good. I'm catching a train tonight. I'm going to start a new life with a friend in London.'

'Kathryn Cooper, you're bloody well not going anywhere till you tell me what's going on.'

At the sound of a voice that was so recognisable to her, Kacie jumped, shocked, swinging round, eyes bulging, mouth gaping. 'Dennis!' she gasped, stupefied.

He leaped across to her, grabbed her arm, shaking her hard. 'You have a lot of explaining to do, Kacie,' he snapped, glaring at her angrily.

Chapter Thirty-two

In silence, Dennis hurriedly dragged Kacie all the way back to the flat and, once there, shoved her inside. He stood before her in the living room.

'Just tell me, Kacie, why you left me,' he shouted at her, arms flailing wildly. 'We'd had a row, a stupid row, but that's not enough to leave me. I shouldn't have gone to Butlin's without you but I had no choice, you know that. I know I'd been unreasonable with you over Caroline staying with us but you know I didn't mean it really. So I spent too much time with the band, but you didn't seem to mind that much. And I was mad at the time by what Brenda said, but I never believed a word. It just made me madder that you weren't here when I came home and I was so excited with what was happening, and you above all people I wanted to tell, and I was stupid to storm off like that but I couldn't help it at the time. I never telephoned from London because it was so difficult. We never seemed to have a minute to ourselves. Besides, I couldn't tell you what I was going to on the telephone but I travelled back as soon as I could on the Saturday morning so I was only gone five days. But none of these reasons are bad enough to do what you did to me. So why? For God's sake, tell me why you left me. I need to know, Kacie. Then you can go, if you want to, and I won't stand in your way.'

Still reeling over her shock at finding out that Verna's husband was the devious brain behind all the salon business, Kacie was absolutely stunned senseless, couldn't take it in that she was actually standing in front of the one man she loved so desperately and never expected to see again. She couldn't understand why he was shouting so angrily at her, seemed so distressed. Why was he accusing her of leaving him when it was the other way round?

She finally found her voice. 'Me leave you? What are you talking about? It was *you* that was leaving *me*?'

His face contorted in his confusion. 'Eh?'

'I heard you, Dennis, you and that woman, Abigail, discussing what you were going to do. I heard her suggest she came with you to break the news to me about you two. I was outside the hotel in London. I'd come to see you, Dennis. I was hoping we'd patch up our silly squabble. You got out of a taxi with her. Then you stood talking. You didn't know I was there. I heard you both planning to tell me you were leaving me for her. You kissed her, Dennis. You acted so . . . so . . . like you were in love with her.'

He slapped his hand to his forehead. 'It was a grateful kiss I gave her, Kacie, nothing more, despite what you think it was.' He looked at her incredulously. 'Oh, Kacie, you stupid woman. You stupid, stupid, woman. I wasn't planning to leave *you*. It was the *band* I was planning to leave, and Abigail was helping me to do it without damaging the future for the rest of them.'

She froze in utter shock. 'What?' she uttered. 'It really wasn't *me* you were leaving, but the *band*?'

His shoulders sagged despairingly. 'Why would I leave you, Kacie? I love you, for Christ's sake.'

She felt her life blood drain from her. 'Oh, Dennis, what have I done?' she whispered.

'Sent me demented with worry, that's what you've done, Kacie.' He scraped both his hands over his head, looked at her hard then, without warning, threw his arms around her, yanking her to him and kissing her so fiercely she thought she'd choke through lack of air. 'Oh, Kacie, Kacie,' he uttered. 'I pledged my soul to the devil for one more chance to hold you in my arms but I'd got to the stage I thought it'd never happen. Where have you been all this time, Kacie?'

She pulled away from him and looked at him shamefully. 'Across town, living in an awful bedsitter. My saving grace was that I made a wonderful friend without whom I know I'd have had trouble getting through this. Apart from work I hardly ever went out, and never to places that would remind me of you. And every second of the day and night I was missing you like hell.' She hung her head, wringing her hands distraughtly. 'After what I thought I'd heard I couldn't face coming back to the flat to wait for you to come in to tell me you were leaving me. I couldn't bear to hear you say you didn't love me any more. I couldn't face anyone, Dennis. I didn't want their pity, to hear whispering behind my back. But worst of all, having to still live here, everything around me reminding me of you. So I decided it best not to come back at all – run away, if you like. Oh, Dennis,' she cried, tears gushing down her face. 'What a fool I've been. I should have known you'd never betray me.'

'I could never betray you because no other woman would come close to you, Kacie. Never, ever. Oh, Kacie,' he cried in despair, 'what a bloody mess. Why couldn't you talk to me about this instead of jumping to the wrong conclusions? We're man and wife, for Christ's sake. If we can't talk to each other who can we talk to?'

'Oh, Dennis, I'm so sorry,' she wailed. 'But it did look to me like there was something going on between you and Abigail, and when I heard what you said, well, any woman would have thought like I did.'

'Abigail just happened to be assigned as the band's assistant. We could have got a bloke. She's a nice woman and we hit it off straight away but only as friends, Kacie, nothing more. When I realised that being a pop star wasn't for me after all, I needed someone to talk to and Abigail was the obvious choice. She was such a help, Kacie, but there was nothing more to it than that. Didn't you read in the newspapers that Abigail and Brian, the chap they brought in as my replacement, started seeing each other not long after he took over? They tried to keep it quiet but it leaked out somehow to the press and they had a field day. It was splashed all over the front covers because the band had had a number-one hit by then.'

She solemnly shook her head. 'I purposely didn't read anything that might carry articles on you and the band. It was all too painful for me, Dennis. I couldn't bear the possibility of reading anything about you.'

'Oh, Kacie, of all the bad decisions you made that has to be the worst – not to read the papers. If only you had you would have known months ago that Abigail was nothing to do with me, and this stupid situation between us would have been over.'

He slumped down into a chair and cradled his head in his hands. 'Can you imagine what I felt like when I came back from London, all psyched up to tell you I was leaving the band? On the one hand I thought you'd think I'd gone barmy, giving up my chance of stardom and of earning huge amounts of money; on the other hand I thought you'd be relieved, glad I'd finally come to my senses and we could live a normal life. I paced up and down the street for ages before I got the courage to face you, and I was absolutely shattered to find you not here. Caroline told me you'd gone to

London, to the hotel where I was staying so I immediately raced back to London again. There was no sign of you so I questioned the porter at the hotel. He remembered you and told me that he wouldn't believe that you were my wife, thought you were just a fan trying it on and he'd sent you packing. I won't tell you what I said to him but I assumed you'd returned to Leicester. Thankfully it seemed that the record company was giving us a day off, so I was able to catch the next train back.

'When I got back to the flat and Caroline told me you still hadn't returned, I didn't know what to think. She was worried sick by that time too. I had to go back to London to break the news to the record company that I was leaving the band. As it turned out, I stayed for a few weeks but while I was still down there every time I was able, I searched every possible place I could think you might be and I was constantly in touch with Caroline to find out if you'd returned home. I couldn't find a trace of you. London is a huge place and when I'd done what I'd agreed with the record company I knew to stay on would be stupid as I could never search all that place in a hundred years. I was frantic, Kacie, beside myself. I didn't know whether to think you'd been kidnapped, murdered, lost your memory even. I was constantly in touch with the police and the hospitals.

'We lived in the hope that you had come back to Leicester, and me and Caroline went around everywhere we knew, checked with friends, everyone who knew you, in fact, to see if they had seen you or knew where you were, and we didn't care whether they got sick and tired of us calling around or not. But nothing, not a sign. It was like you'd disappeared off the face of the earth. After a couple of weeks we knew we had to tell your parents, and my mother too – you know how much she loves you, Kacie. We couldn't keep it to ourselves any longer. When we told my mother, she went crazy because I hadn't told her sooner, called me all sorts, but, bless her, she said she'd help us look for you all she could and she has. I was dreading telling your folks, knew they'd blame me, but they had to know. It was only fair.'

She rushed across to him, sat down beside him and took his hands in hers. 'Were they really awful to you, Dennis?'

He shook his head. 'No, just the opposite, in fact. I was so shocked by their reaction and so was Caroline. They just stood and listened, not saying a word, and when we'd explained what had gone on your mother sat and cried, blamed herself and your father, said it was all their fault that you'd gone away because you couldn't stand the way they'd treated you over me and it was even worse when Caroline broke the news about herself and Malcolm. Your mother really did break down then. I've never seen a woman cry like she did.'

She gawped at him, stunned. 'My mother cried, Dennis? I've never seen my mother cry.'

'I have, Kacie.' He ran his hand gently down the side of her face, and eyed her tenderly. 'Your mother does love you, I have no doubt of that now, and you mustn't be afraid to see her. You'll be very happy with the change in her, I know you will. Up until a couple of months ago most afternoons she was still working her way through all the types of hairdressing shops that we thought you'd work in that we hadn't already tried in the hope that you'd taken a job with one of them. It was a big task but she was adamant about helping.'

'Oh, Dennis,' she cried. 'I saw her! She seemed to be looking for something. So that's what she was doing.'

'Yes, she was looking for you.'

'I hid from her, Dennis,' she uttered regretfully.

'Oh, Kacie, that's such a pity,' he said sadly. 'This would have been over sooner if you hadn't. But there's no point in dwelling on that. Eventually your mother had covered several times all the salons this side of town and in the town centre. She was going to start asking around the West End area but the worry of you had taken its toll and she took ill with the flu and was off her feet for a while. I made a trip up that side of Leicester myself one day, visited one or two salons that looked the type where you'd work. There was one I came across which looked so dismal from the outside I never even bothered going in. Florrie's or something, I remember it was called.'

Kacie remained silent. She hadn't the heart to tell Dennis that the salon he thought was too awful for her to work in was the one salon he should have tried.

'About four months after you'd left we all agree that this pavement slogging wasn't doing any good. After all, we weren't even sure if you were in Leicester. We all made a pact that we would get on with our daily lives as best we could but still keep our ears and eyes open for any sign of you, and just hope that one day you'd turn up out of the blue.' He looked at her searchingly. 'That decision didn't stop me standing at the window night after night, praying I'd see you walking down the street, though, Kacie.

'I was dreading Christmas. None of us were looking forward to it. It was my mother, though, who thought that if there was any good time that you might come back, Christmas-time would be it. Your mother suggested that in case you should, that we should all be here to welcome you home. We trimmed the place up, cooked a big dinner and sat and waited. As the day wore on and you never showed up . . . it was awful, Kacie.'

'But I did come, Dennis,' she uttered remorsefully. 'I stood across the road. I was going to come in and make my peace, honestly I was. But I saw Caroline wave to Mam and Dad, them arriving with presents and a turkey. I thought . . . oh, Dennis, I thought that you were still in London with your new woman and that Caroline and my parents had made up their differences and were celebrating Christmas like close families do. I knew there was someone else in the flat as I saw Caroline talking to them. I had no idea who it could be but I never thought for a minute it was you, or that your mother was there, either. I thought everyone in their own way was getting on so well without me around and I thought it best I stayed away, let you get on with your lives without me, as you all seemed to be doing. I've been such a fool, haven't I? How could I have been so stupid as to think my family would just forget me like that, just get on with their lives as though I never existed?'

He grabbed her in his arms again and hugged her tightly, seeming afraid to let her go. 'We'd have all gone on mourning your loss until the day we all died, Kacie,' he whispered chokingly. He pulled slightly away from her and eyed her searchingly. 'There's still so much I want to know, so much for us to talk about, and I know it's getting late but I must go and see your parents and my mam and tell them you're back. Caroline too should be told as soon as possible.'

'I should come with you. I'm desperate to see them all.'

'They'll be desperate to see you too, Kacie – but after you've had a good night's sleep, as I can see you're exhausted. I know they'll all sleep soundly tonight when they hear this wonderful news. I know it sounds selfish as your family are so important but I can't bear the thought of sharing you with anyone at this moment. I would like to have you to myself tonight, get used to the idea that you're finally back with me where you belong.'

She said, looking at him in complete understanding, 'I feel like that too. Tell them all I love them, won't you, Dennis, and that I'm looking forward to seeing them after I've had a good night's sleep.'

She looked up at him adoringly. 'I haven't slept properly since the last time I was with you, Dennis. I'll sleep so well tonight in your arms.' Then a thought struck her. 'Oh, I've left my suitcase by the front of Mrs Koz's house. When you dragged me back like you did I was so confused with what was happening I forget about it.'

'Don't worry, I'll pick it up on the way to your folks.'

She looked at him. 'It seems strange, hearing you say that – that *you're* going round to *my* folks.'

'It took me some getting used to. At first I wondered if it was a flash in the pan but they have changed, Kacie, especially your mother.'

Talking of Verna Kozlowski reminded Kacie of something. 'Dennis, how did you know I was at Mrs Koz's tonight?'

'I didn't.'

'Then why were you there?'

'I just got this terrible urge to go round and see if she'd had any news of you through customers that came into the shop. I thought I'd be wasting my time, like all the other times I'd been to see her. Mrs Koz had already promised me that the slightest bit of news she heard about you she'd let me know as soon as she could, but I still decided to go. It was an excuse to get out of the flat. Tonight, for some reason, I couldn't settle. I could see you everywhere I looked and it was driving me crazy.'

'Oh, Dennis, I'm so glad. If you hadn't come when you did . . . well, I might never have seen you again.' She smiled at him tenderly. 'I prayed to God for help and He answered me, didn't He, by sending you?'

'He finally answered my prayers too.'

Kacie gave a deep sigh. 'I still can't believe what Mr Koz did, Dennis.'

Dennis, who had overheard enough of the conversation to realise what Mr Koz had done, grimaced thoughtfully. 'People are driven to desperate measures when they feel their backs are against the wall. Some have done far worse, Kacie, far far worse than Mr Koz.'

'Yes, I know. I'm sure he never set out to hurt people, Dennis, and I'm sure Mrs Koz will put it all right. I'll help her if I can.'

He smiled at her. 'I know you will.' He looked at her searchingly. 'I don't want to leave you but I'd really better go and tell the family our good news.'

She leaned up and kissed his cheek. 'Yes, I know, but another minute or so won't hurt, will it, Dennis?' She snuggled close to him

299

and together they sat in silence for several long moments. It was Kacie who spoke first.

'Dennis, why did you decide to leave the band?'

'Because of you.'

'Me?'

'I quickly realised it wasn't the life for a married man, not when that man loved his wife so much. I couldn't bear the thought of you spending most of your time alone while I was recording in a studio, or the weeks apart from you while the band went on tour. You would have had to stay in the background, Kacie. Fans aren't keen on married idols. They like single pop stars to fantasise over. The boss at the record company made that very clear right from the start. Our marriage would've have to been kept secret. I didn't marry you to keep you a secret. The money and the glamour didn't seem so important when it came to it. My marriage to you is.'

She felt so humble that her beloved husband had given up his chance of stardom and riches all because of his love for her. Then a thought struck and she eyed him, puzzled. 'If you left the group so soon how come I heard you singing on your first record, Dennis?'

'Because everything in that business moves so quick, Kacie. It was go from the minute we arrived. We were given a pep talk first from the boss of the record company, telling us what we were in for if they decided to take us on, and before any of it had time to sink in we were herded into a studio to cut a demo record. As soon as the powers that be heard it they said they felt positive we were the next chart-toppers. All hell seemed to break loose then and we never seemed to get a minute to ourselves.

'While songwriters were instructed to get busy on new material so a choice could be made which was best for our first single, we were rushed off to a department so a new image could be decided for us. Then it was off to shop for clothes and get our hairs restyled. A fortune was spent on us. It was all so exciting, Kacie, but at the same time it just didn't feel comfortable because you weren't with me. But if I was to do this, that's how it would be all the time. I didn't like that thought, Kacie, and I knew I couldn't go on with it.

'Abigail had been assigned to us to take care of all we needed, make sure we got where we were going on time and show us around, that sort of thing, so automatically I chose her to talk to. She's a nice woman, Kacie; she understood. She did try her best to talk me out of leaving but when she realised I was serious she did her best to help me smooth the bosses over. The last thing I wanted was to ruin it for Jed and the boys. When they asked me to front the first single while they found a suitable replacement for me I agreed; it seemed only right. They soon came up with Brian. He sounds like me, even looks like me too. By the time the record came out, although it was my voice that was on it, it was Brian who mimed to it on the television shows and got all the glory. So everyone was happy in the end.'

'No regrets though, Dennis?'

'None at all.'

She looked at him tenderly as she ran her fingers gently through his hair. 'I love your new style. It suits you. I couldn't have done better myself.'

He grinned mischievously. 'Fancy me, do you?'

'Oh, Dennis, need you ask? I fancied you rotten with your old style too.' She took a deep breath, looking hard at him, drinking him in. 'Oh, I'm still having trouble taking this all in. I keep worrying I'll wake up in a minute and realise I've been dreaming.'

He pinched her hard.

'Ouch!'

'Now you know you're not,' he said, laughing. 'I have to admit I feel like that too, so you can pinch me if you like.'

She did, as hard as he had her, and when he cried out, she said giggling, 'Serves you right.' Just then a momentous thought struck her and she leaped up to grab her handbag, delved inside it to pull out her purse.

'What are you doing?' Dennis asked her.

'Putting this back where it belongs,' she said, slipping her wedding ring back on her finger, to hold her hand out and stare at it tenderly.

He joined her, putting his arms around her, holding her tight. 'You'll never take that off again,' he said.

'Never,' she replied.

Just then there was a knock at the door.

'Are you expecting anyone?' Kacie asked.

'Your parents have never called this late, Caroline neither, and my mam is usually tucked in bed at this time of night so when I go round and tell her the good news I'll have to knock her up, so no, I'm not expecting anyone. Stay where you are, Kacie. I'll get rid of them and be back in a minute.'

She heard him open the door and short murmur of conversation, and the next thing she knew, Caroline was flying over to her. 'Oh, Kacie, you're home!' she cried ecstatically, throwing herself on Kacie, hugging her so tightly she was taking her breath away. 'I can't believe it, I really can't. When *he* told me tonight *he* had a friend and then started to talk about her I was confused because the person *he* was telling me about sounded so much like you. Then when *he* said your name—'

'Caroline,' Kacie cut in, 'it's wonderful to see you too but you keep saying *he*. Before you go any further, who are you talking about?'

'Me, Kacie.'

Kacie's eyes shot over to the doorway and she stared in stunned surprise. 'Richard?' she gasped, rising up. She flashed a look back to Caroline, who had stood up to join her, then back to Richard, who was advancing over to them. 'Caroline is Cassie?'

Caroline giggled. 'Kacie works for you, so I thought, why not Cassie for me?'

'It suits you. I like it,' Kacie said. She eyed Caroline, bewildered, then looked from her to Richard. 'You two—'

'Yes, we're courting,' cut in Caroline.

Kacie eyed her, stupefied. 'This doesn't make sense to me. Richard told me the woman he'd met worked for a dentist. You work in a newsagent's, Caroline . . . Cassie.'

She laughed. '*Did* work for a newsagent. It turned out the owner was expecting me to mind his children as well as do my duties in the shop. That wasn't on my agenda, Kacie, so I got myself the job as a receptionist, and left.'

'I should have known, shouldn't I, Kacie, that the woman I was falling in love with was related to you?' Richard said, putting his arm round Caroline and pulling her close.

'You love me?' said Caroline, looking at Richard astounded.

'Yes, he does,' erupted Kacie. 'He adores you, Caroline, and judging how you are with him, you do Richard.' She clapped her hands in delight. 'Oh, this is wonderful. I'm so excited. I couldn't have picked better for each of you. When you get married we'll be related, Richard. Not only my best friend but my brother-in-law too. Oh, I can't take this all in, so much has happened tonight. We've so much we have to talk about but I don't know whether I can stand any more right now. But, Richard, I must introduce you to my husband. You'll really get on well together. Where is he?' she said, looking around for him.

'He's in the kitchen wi' the rest of 'em, but I couldn't wait no longer to come through and tell yer 'ow glad I am ter see yer back. Dun't looked so shocked ter see me, Kacie ducky, it was yer sister what fetched me on 'er way 'ere.'

'Oh, Mrs C!' Kacie exclaimed, launching herself at her mother-in-law. 'It's so lovely to see you.' She threw her arms around her and gave her a hug.

'And me you, ducky. You 'ad us all worried sick. I've 'eard of folks teking long holidays before but nine months is pushing it a bit, don't yer reckon, Kacie lovey?' she said, her eyes twinkling wickedly at Kacie. 'Anyway, there's lots I want ter know but there's time fer questions later. I just wanted ter give yer a quick hug and let yer know I'm glad ter see yer back at last. Now there's someone else that needs ter speak to yer, Kacie. Come on, you two,' she ordered Caroline and Richard. 'Let Kacie's mam have five minutes.'

'My mam?' Kacie mouthed, confused. 'She's here too?'

'Yes I am, Kathryn.' Freda Carter smiled warmly at Dotty Cooper, Richard and Caroline, as arm in arm they left the room to join the others in the kitchen. She then turned back to face her daughter. 'When Caroline found out through Richard tonight where you were, she immediately fetched us all in a taxi and we came here to collect Dennis, and then we were all coming to see you, convince you to come home. You can imagine our delight when Dennis opened the door and told us that we had reached journey's end.' She paused for a moment and took a deep breath. 'I have something to say to you, Kathryn, and I would ask you not to interrupt until I have finished.'

Kacie was astounded to see tears in her mother's eyes.

'First, I have to beg your forgiveness for the way me and your father have treated you all these years – Caroline too. We have failed you both as parents. We were adamant we knew what was best for you both. You have to believe me we thought at the time we were doing our best by being so strict with you. Your father and myself had very humble backgrounds, both seen what poverty can bring, and we were resolute that neither of us wanted either of our children to suffer the hardships that we both had and the struggles we faced to improve ourselves.

'We thought by insisting you went to college it would give you the skills to enable you both to make good livings which in turn would introduce you to the sort of men we felt would make you suitable husbands, who could provide well for you and you'd not go short. We never considered your happiness.

'Caroline was afraid to stand up to us and did exactly what we expected of her and as a result she suffered a miserable life. We're both so sorry for what we put her through. I'm so gratified to see she took matters in her own hands and, with help from you, she's now so happy. I'm glad to say you had spirit, Kathryn, although neither myself nor your father thought that a good trait in you at the time. The reason we were so incensed when you wouldn't go to college was that we were convinced you'd end up doing a menial job for a pittance of a wage. We didn't want that for you. We're glad now you stuck out to be a hairdresser, Kathryn, and we realise those skills are as rewarding in their way as any you'd have gained by becoming a secretary. And we now realise with what happened to Caroline, when we made her do a job that she didn't want to, that you would have hated it too. Being stuck in an office all day would have driven you mad, wouldn't it, Kathryn?

'As you know, we strongly disapproved of your choice of husband. Very remiss of us, but we never gave the lad a chance. We judged him by where he came from. We worried sick that you'd end up beaten and starved like many women who come from those parts. Like I might have done if I hadn't been lucky to meet a man like your father.

'Your leaving, Kathryn, was what brought us to our senses. I speak for myself but I know your father feels the same – that as I stood and listened to Dennis telling us that you'd disappeared and I saw how broken he was it shook me rigid to see how badly I had misjudged him. He is a good man, of good character and of how much he loves you I was left in no doubt. When I discovered just what he had given up by leaving the band so as not to risk destroying his marriage to you, I felt so terrible. Then it struck me that if I had been so wrong about him, what else had I been so wrong about? When Caroline told me of her failed marriage, how badly Malcolm had treated her and how unhappy she had always been, I realised then that what your father and myself thought was the right way to make sure your futures were good had really had the opposite effect.

'We've learned the hard way that it's a parent's job to make sure their children are well informed about the outside world, then allow them to live it the way they choose and make their own mistakes. We were trying to shield you both from making those mistakes by forcing you into living as we dictated.

'I can't begin to tell you how sorry I am, Kathryn. I've learned my lesson and so has your father. I want to ask you if you'd be willing for us to start again. I want you to feel able to throw your arms around me and give me a hug like you did to Dennis's mother just now. I want to see your eyes light up when I come to visit you. I want you and Dennis to visit me and your father because you want to and not because you have to. Will you please let us try?'

The tears rolled then, cascading down Kacie's face to splash on her clothes. She held out her arms and welcomed her mother inside them. 'Oh, Mam,' she wailed, 'of course I will. I love you.'

Caroline and her father came in then and the four cried and hugged together.

A while later, when they had all gone back to their respective homes, Dennis took Kacie in his arms. 'Happy?' he asked her.

'Can't you tell?' she said, smiling up at him.

'Mmm. I know I am. I can't remember the last time I felt this good, Kacie. It's been an eventful night, hasn't it?'

She leaned against him and laid her head on his chest. 'I can't believe that only a few hours ago I'd my suitcase packed and was ready to leave Leicester for good. Now look at me. I'm back where I belong, surrounded by my family – and what a family they are now. The transformation in my parents almost makes it seem worth all the pain we went through while we were parted, Dennis. Now all I need to do is make amends with Brenda and I'll be all hunky dory.'

'I've no doubt you will. Tired?' he asked.

'Mmm, but not too tired for you to make love to me,' she said, looking up at him seductively.

He grinned down at her. 'I'm sure I can manage that. But first, I've something to show you but to do so we need to go out.'

She pulled away from him and looked at him sharply. 'Out? I'm in no mood to go out, Dennis. It's nearly midnight. Can't it wait? I've had a hell of a day already.'

'I suppose it could wait, but I can't. I'm desperate to show you. Anyway, it's my guess you'll be very busy tomorrow and I want to show you why. Come on, Kacie, just get your coat. It won't take long – just a quick run in the car.'

'Car? Whose car?'

'Our car?' He looked at her mischievously. 'You remember I said I fronted the band's first record.'

'Yes.'

'Well, I got paid for it.'

'Did you?'

He nodded. 'A few quid. It did reach number one in the charts, after all, and is still selling and being played on the radio. I still get royalties, in fact.'

She eyed him suspiciously. 'You got more than a few quid if you bought a car.'

'Maybe a few more,' he said cagily. ''Cos I bought something else too.'

'What?'

'That's what I want to show you. So get your coat.'

'Blimey, Dennis, this is a spanking new Mini Minor. These are all the rage at the moment. I'll be the envy of everyone. I can't wait to learn to drive,' she said, not noticing the look Dennis gave her as she settled in her seat. She turned and looked at him as a thought struck her. 'You've bought us a house, haven't you? You have, haven't you, Dennis?' Her eyes sparkled excitedly. 'What's it like? Is it far from here?'

'Wait and see,' he said, revving up the engine.

A house, she thought, their very first house, and whilst they drove along her mind was fully occupied with the happy life they would both have living inside it.

She was surprised when they pulled up halfway down Churchgate, just off the town centre.

'This is a funny place to buy a house, Dennis,' she said dismayed. 'I didn't know there was housing down here, just shops and business premises. Has it got a garden?'

Without saying a word he got out of the car, ran round and opened her door. She got out and looked around, bewildered. 'Where is this house then?'

He smiled at her. 'I never said I'd bought us a house.'

'So what have you bought us then?'

'This,' he said, pointing towards a large shop front.

He grabbed her hand and led her towards the shop door, and in a flash had unlocked it, flicked on a light switch and walked her inside.

Kacie couldn't believe it. It was the shop she had stopped by several weeks previously when it was in the process of being

306

renovated. Three-quarters of that renovation had now taken place, and the equipment and the stock for it was in place all ready for operation – though there was a large area to the side that was completely empty and she wondered what it was going to be used for.

'It's your dream, Kacie,' he said, putting his arm around her and pulling her close. 'What you've always wanted. A combined record shop for me to run, a coffee bar which I thought we could talk Caroline into running, and that space over there is for your hairdressing salon. It's been left so you can plan exactly how you want it yourself.'

She was staring around in amazement. 'This is all ours, Dennis?' she uttered.

'Every last piece of dust, my sweet. When I agreed to sing on the band's record, I vowed that every penny I earned, except what I had to use for my living expenses, would go towards bringing your dream alive for you. While I was so taken up in my search for you the money just sat in the bank. After we'd exhausted our search and agreed to wait and just hope you came back out of the blue one day, I knew I needed something to keep myself from going crazy in the meantime, so I decided to go ahead with this and hope you wouldn't mind I'd done so much of it without you. After all, it was your baby originally.

'I was going to give it a year, Kacie, and if by then you hadn't come back I was going to sell up and buy something else with the money. After all, the idea was that it was for both of us, and a year was all the time I could just about manage the thought of running it without you. Of course, if when I officially opened the shop you still hadn't returned, I would've just boarded up the side that was intended for your salon. As it is now I don't have to, do I? Now you'll be busy, won't you, getting the salon equipped and you'll need a couple of staff to help you. I hope you'll get down to it straight away because I intend to open for business as soon as possible. If we're going to buy that house, Kacie, we need money coming in.' He looked at her concernedly. 'You are pleased, aren't you?'

She was speechless so she just nodded.

He turned her towards him and pulled her close, a happy sparkle twinkling his eyes. 'You said being a pop star would never make us rich. Well, it might not, my darling, but it's certainly brought in enough to help us on our way.' He then added, 'I do hope I've just made you the happiest woman in the world, Kacie?'

She looked up at him and, with a happy twinkle sparkling her eyes, a contented smile twitching her lips, she said, 'Take me home to bed, and afterwards I'll let you know.'